Frank Coates was born in Melbourne and, after graduating as a professional engineer, worked for many years as a telecommunications specialist in Australia and overseas. In 1989 he was appointed as a UN technical specialist in Nairobi, Kenya, and travelled extensively throughout the eastern and southern parts of Africa over the next four years. During this time Frank developed a passion for the history and culture of East Africa, which inspired his first novel, *Tears of the Maasai*. He followed with *Beyond Mombasa, In Search of Africa* and *Roar of the Lion. The Last Maasai Warrior* is his fifth novel.

Also by Frank Coates

Tears of the Maasai
Beyond Mombasa
In Search of Africa
Roar of the Lion

FRANK COATES

The Last Maasai Warrior

HarperCollins*Publishers*

HarperCollins*Publishers*

First published in Australia in 2008
by HarperCollins*Publishers* Australia Pty Limited
ABN 36 009 913 517
www.harpercollins.com.au

HarperCollins*Publishers*
25 Ryde Road, Pymble, Sydney, NSW 2073, Australia
31 View Road, Glenfield, Auckland 10, New Zealand
1–A, Hamilton House, Connaught Place, New Delhi – 110 001, India
77–85 Fulham Palace Road, London, W6 8JB, United Kingdom
2 Bloor Street East, 20th floor, Toronto, Ontario M4W 1A8, Canada
10 East 53rd Street, New York NY 10022, USA

National Library of Australia Cataloguing-in-Publication data:

Coates, Frank
   Last Maasai warrior / author, Frank Coates.
   Pymble, N.S.W. : HarperCollins Publishers, 2008.
   ISBN: 978 0 7322 8647 7 (pbk.)
   Masai (African people) – Kenya – Fiction.
A823.4

Cover design by Nada Backovic Designs
Cover images: Necklace image © Wolfgang Kaehler/Alamy; Warrior image © Michael
Melford/National Geographic Image Collection
Author photograph by Belinda Mason
Maps by Laurie Whiddon, Map Illustrations
Typeset in Sabon 11/14 by Kirby Jones
Printed and bound in Australia by Griffin Press
70gsm Bulky Book Ivory used by HarperCollins*Publishers* is a natural, recyclable product
made from wood grown in sustainable forests. The manufacturing processes conform to the
environmental regulations in the country of origin, Finland.

5 4 3 2 1   08 09 10 11

To Demitri, Maddison, Eleni, Ashleigh and Jack.
Cousins.

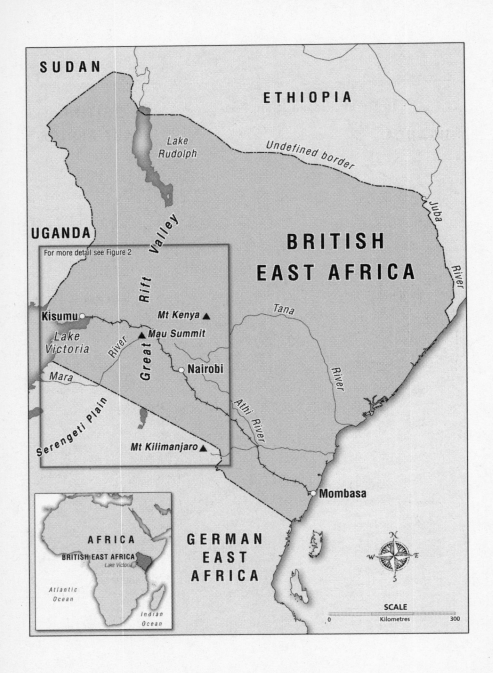

SUDAN

ETHIOPIA

Lake
Rudolph

Undefined border

UGANDA

For more detail see Figure 2

Rift Valley

Great

BRITISH
EAST AFRICA

Juba River

Kisumu

Mt Kenya ▲

Lake
Victoria

River

▲ Mau Summit

Nairobi ○

Tana River

Mara

Serengeti Plain

Athi River

Mt Kilimanjaro ▲

Mombasa ○

AFRICA

BRITISH EAST AFRICA
Lake Victoria

GERMAN
EAST
AFRICA

Atlantic
Ocean

Indian
Ocean

N
W   E
S

SCALE
0   Kilometres   300

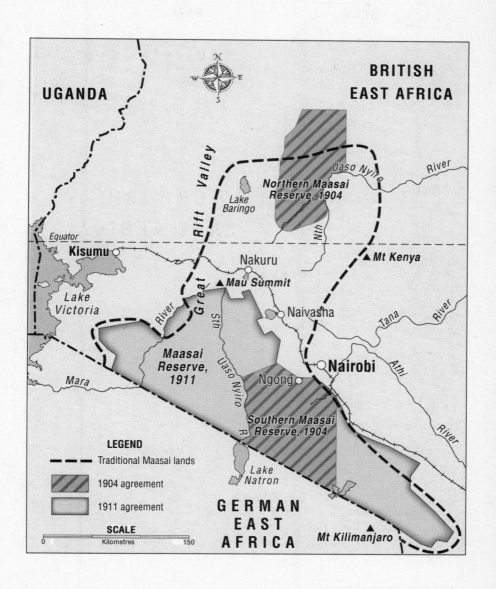

UGANDA

BRITISH EAST AFRICA

Rift Valley

Lake Baringo

Northern Maasai Reserve, 1904

Uaso Nyiro River

Nth

Equator

Kisumu

Nakuru

▲ Mt Kenya

▲ Mau Summit

Great River

Lake Victoria

Naivasha

Tana River

Sth

Maasai Reserve, 1911

Uaso Nyiro R.

Nairobi

Ngong

Mara

Southern Maasai Reserve, 1904

Athi

River

LEGEND

Lake Natron

---- Traditional Maasai lands

▨ 1904 agreement

▧ 1911 agreement

GERMAN EAST AFRICA

▲ Mt Kilimanjaro

SCALE

0   Kilometres   150

ACKNOWLEDGEMENTS

While this is a work of fiction, my starting point, as always, is with the historical and cultural facts surrounding the people and times within which I set my story. In this regard I found no better reference than *Moving the Maasai: A Colonial Misadventure*, by Dr Lotte Hughes (Palgrave Macmillan, 2006). Nor did I receive more generous encouragement than from Lotte herself. Her guidance during the time I spent researching the novel at Oxford University in 2007 and her remarks during the writing of my story are very gratefully acknowledged.

For updates on the current situation in Kenya and her down-to-earth comments, I thank Dr Deborah Nightingale. When not up-country studying her baboons, or involved in her projects in one of many exotic locations, Debbie has been unstinting with her time and feedback. Many thanks, Debbie; may I one day find a niche in Kenya as exciting as yours appears to be.

I am indebted to Lotte and Deborah, but I take full responsibility for *The Last Maasai Warrior*. I trust they will forgive the liberties I've taken while slightly 'bending' history to add the drama needed for my story.

As I become increasingly enthralled by the history and culture of East Africa I find myself drawn more to the facts than to any fiction I might create. For keeping me on the path of popular fiction I thank my editors at HarperCollins and Nicola O'Shea, who continue to make solid contributions to my writing, and my agent, Selwa Anthony, whose instinct for fiction is uncanny.

Again I must thank Rosalind Williams and James Hudson — my focus group — for the encouragement and feedback they provide on my early drafts. Our 'workshop' at James and Sally's delightful hideaway in the foothills behind Byron Bay has become an established and invaluable part of my creative process.

PROLOGUE

1875

Sianoi tugged at the halter around the Laikipiak woman's neck. The woman was slow because her belly was large, but the child she carried was the reason he had claimed her. Now that the Purko had destroyed the Laikipiak, he could use a boy child to tend his share of the Laikipiak cattle he had taken in the raid.

He looked to the north, where a huge dust cloud indicated the progress of their captured herd, and smiled. After the cattle were shared amongst his brother Purko, they would take them back to graze on the succulent grass of the Laikipia Plateau, now theirs.

The crushing victory was sweet vengeance for the disrespectful arrogance the Laikipiak had shown the Purko over recent years. Sianoi had taken part in several minor raids over that time — all of them unsatisfactorily indecisive — but now there would be no more disputing it: the Purko were the dominant section of the Maasai.

If the Laikipiak had fled, they might have survived to fight another day. It was well known that the Purko were an indomitable power and anyone foolish enough to confront them in open combat would be annihilated. However, the Laikipiak were Maasai brothers and stubborn fighters, reluctant to withdraw from a battle once joined. It was a mistake. Now the entire Laikipiak section was either dead or had been chased into the forests, where they would live a miserable existence, compelled to eat the unclean meat of wild game and to forage like baboons for titbits. There would be no more Laikipiak in the years ahead. They had even lost their women to the blade or to a more worthy Purko *morani*.

The halter jerked abruptly. Sianoi turned to see the woman doubled over, holding her belly, her face contorted in pain. He was inclined to bring his *orinka* down on her useless head because these disruptions were becoming more frequent, but the beating would only make his task of getting her back to his camp the more difficult. He waited a moment before giving the halter a vicious tug, forcing the woman to stumble forward, but she lost her footing and fell sprawling in the dust at his feet. She whimpered in pain and water gushed from between her legs, darkening the dusty red earth.

He was appalled. Was there no end to this disgrace?

The Uaso Ngiro was a short distance away. She could clean herself there, or do whatever she must. He tugged on the halter and had to raise his *orinka* threateningly to get her moving, but they were soon at the stony edge of the river, where he let her slump into the shallows.

The woman tried to stifle her agonised cries, writhing in the lapping waters and clutching her swollen abdomen.

It was enough that he had to observe her shameful intolerance to pain. Surely Purko women in childbirth conducted themselves with more dignity than this Laikipiak whore. In any case, a *morani* was not meant to witness such undignified behaviour. Sianoi turned his back on her.

The screams ended and he heard a squawk and a muffled cry. He turned back to see the woman reach between her legs and pull the baby from the bloodied river.

Sianoi staggered backwards in horror. He fell, sending his shield and spear clattering onto the rocks.

Recalled from somewhere among childhood memories came a story about a child born holding a stone in its palm. His mind reeled as he tried to recall the allegory's ominous warnings, for before him, lying on the river bank, this newborn child held a stone in not one but each of his tiny fists.

PART 1

MAASAILAND

CHAPTER 1

1885

'Laikipiak!'

The cry hung in the still savannah air like a hovering martial eagle. The young Maasai boy froze. Above him, five figures were etched against the sky — each hand holding his herding stick aloft.

'Laikipiak! Laikipiak!'

The cry leapt from one Purko boy to the next, running like a grass fire across the hillside until all five were shouting excitedly.

A cold knife of fear plunged into Parsaloi Ole Sadera's heart. Like a startled gazelle, he darted towards the river, his tormentors whooping as they plunged down the hill in hot pursuit.

Parsaloi dashed through the scrawny savannah scrub and into the heavier riverside foliage. Thornbush whipped his flesh and vines grabbed at his legs. He fell, tumbling headlong into a carpet of slimy plants prostrated by the recent flooding. He was on his feet again immediately, barely breaking stride, but the leading boy was gaining on him.

The boys ran in silence to conceal their position from him, but Parsaloi could hear their laboured breathing and the pounding of their feet. They made the foliage whistle and snap behind him. He knew he had only moments to find a hiding place or they would be upon him like a pack of hunting dogs.

There were many holes along the steep river bank, cut and shaped by the recent wet season floodwaters. His only chance was to quickly find one to hide in. He would just have to hope that he didn't stumble on one of the river's huge crocodiles as he made his search.

In desperation, he dropped into the first crevice he found and huddled there as the leading boy galloped over him. He waited until he had heard all the runners pass, and then made a swift retreat back along the river to find a more secure hole.

The only one he could see was too close to the water to be safe. Crocodiles eyed him from the distant bank as he dashed about trying to find something more suitable, but nothing presented itself before he heard the boys returning. He scrambled into the hollow, which turned out to be smaller than it appeared. His bottom was hard against the rear wall and his nose an arm's length from the opening, which was only a couple of paces from the water's edge. As he listened to the boys scouring the river bank in search of their quarry, two of the large reptiles slithered into the muddy water and disappeared from sight.

The Purko boys gradually moved away from the vicinity of his hiding place and the crocodiles became bolder, lifting their heads from the shallows a few feet from him to stare with cold topaz eyes, seeing all, acknowledging nothing.

Parsaloi knew that the boys would soon be compelled to return to their herding duties, at which time he could escape. To move too soon would be to risk being caught; too late and the crocodiles would be at his hideout blocking his departure.

His leg muscles complained at their cramped confinement, but at last he heard the boys shouting threats, intended for his ears, about the punishment they would inflict should they find the Laikipiak pig fouling their grazing grounds again.

He waited a little longer to be sure they were gone, checked the water for any sign of the crocodiles, then crawled out of his hole, stiff and sore.

Out of the corner of his eye, he saw the surface of the river lift. An enormous shape surged in a muddy wave towards him. The crocodile swung its huge head at Parsaloi, making a thunderous thud as its jaws snapped shut inches from his legs. He fell backwards, pushed himself away on his bottom, feet slipping and sliding on the river bank now rushing with water from the crocodile's lunge. The jaws opened again, revealing the exquisite detail of teeth and tongue in the instant before they slammed shut with another thud.

The steep bank blocked Parsaloi's scramble for safety. He needed to turn his back on the crocodile to climb away from the water, but was afraid to take his eyes from the creature. The saurian monster coiled its tail in readiness for another strike. Parsaloi spun around and reached over the edge of the bank. He felt a tuft of grass, grasped it, and strained every fibre of his small frame to pull himself up the steep slope before the crocodile made a last effort to snare its scrawny prey.

Parsaloi pulled his legs clear of the edge and turned in time to see the crocodile's head slide out of sight. Only an angry vortex in the swirling river indicated its departure.

The boy rolled onto his back and took a slow, deep breath. The sky filled him, wrapping him in a blanket of blue more intense than he'd ever seen it. He lay there savouring it, letting it fill his consciousness until his thumping heart returned to normality.

Parsaloi lay on the river bank longer than he'd intended. The uppermost reaches of the fever trees were throwing long shadows over the river when he realised he needed to make his way home. It would be dark in an hour, but he was in no hurry to return to Sianoi's hut. The beating he had fled following his failure to complete some minor task to Sianoi's satisfaction would still be awaiting him. He smiled at the irony. He had escaped two beatings in the one day, but he knew that both victories would be short-lived.

Misery had been his constant companion in recent months. It had started soon after his mother died, worn out by work and ill health, leaving him the only Laikipiak in his village and a constant reminder — at least to the older Purko boys — of the fratricidal wars that had raged between their sections for many years. By her hard work, his mother had won the admiration of

7

the village, if not her husband, who had never shown anything but proprietary interest in her. But as soon as she died, all the ill feelings about the Laikipiak returned. The night owls of hate now roosted squarely on Parsaloi's small head.

The man he would not call father had never shown any compassion for him. But without the calming influence of his mother, the leather cord, the fist, the smarting open hand were a constant reminder that Sianoi's sympathies were unaffected by her death.

Parsaloi trudged along the river bank lost in his personal misery. Suddenly some instinct made the hair on his neck and arms prickle and his heart thump in his chest. He scanned his surroundings, but could see nothing remarkable. He sensed it had been a sound rather than a sight that had alerted him to danger.

His first thought was that he had subconsciously picked up the sound of the Purko boys returning, but upon reflection he dismissed this. The alarm had stirred from somewhere deeper — something almost primordial. As he struggled to reconstruct its exact form, it came again, briefly and indistinctly, but with sufficient clarity for him to know exactly what it was. The sound that every Maasai boy learned to recognise almost as soon as he knew his mother's voice. From somewhere in the tall grass came the soft, deep grunt of an agitated lion.

His immediate instinct was to flee, but with a wall of grass ahead of him and only the crocodile-infested river at his back, Parsaloi knew that to move without establishing exactly where the sound originated could mean his death. He held his breath until his ears rang, and just before he took a quick shallow breath he heard it again.

It was quite close, ahead of him on his left quarter. Parsaloi suspected that by some miracle the lion was not yet aware of his presence. When he scampered up the nearest tree, he discovered the reason. The lion's attention was on another tree, a small acacia, which it repeatedly circled, making occasional attempts to leap into its lower branches. A boy, a little older than Parsaloi, clung for dear life to the tree's slender trunk.

At first, he thought it was one of the herd boys who had been chasing him and he felt the heady euphoria of justice swiftly and sweetly delivered on his behalf. It would be quite easy to make his escape, leaving the treed boy to occupy the lion. On closer examination, however, he realised the boy was a stranger.

Their eyes met, but instead of looking pleased that someone could go for help, the older boy's face fell. Parsaloi suspected that he didn't want his disgrace shared among all the boys in the village. He knew what it was to feel the scorn of his peers and decided to do what he could to help the boy.

He carefully climbed from his tree and selected three smooth stones from the river bank. They had to be heavy enough to inflict a painful blow on the lion, but not so heavy that he could not throw them accurately over the distance. He then found a dead tree branch and, slipping out of his clothing, arranged the pieces on the splayed branches to form two fluttering red flags.

The boy seemed to understand Parsaloi's plan for he made a gesture to indicate that he thought he was taking a great risk. That thought hadn't escaped Parsaloi either, but he had committed himself to the challenge now and could not afford to show cowardly second thoughts.

Taking the best of the stones, he gave it a little heft to gauge its weight before hurling it full force at the lion. It clouted the beast behind the ear, causing it to spin around and give a startled grunt. It raised its tail in an aggressive stance, wrinkled its nose and shook its magnificent mane in a show of supremacy. Parsaloi flung the second stone, which made a soft thud as it struck the lion on the right eyebrow, instantly drawing blood. In the same moment, he lifted his standard and waved it above his head and emitted a frantic screeching bellow at the top of his lungs. The boy in the tree joined in, and after a moment's ignominious confusion the lion dropped its tail and trotted off with a dismissive snarl.

Parsaloi puffed out his chest in victory. There were few occasions when he bettered his adversaries and they were not times to defer to modesty. He sauntered over to the tree and looked up at the older boy.

'I saw the herd boys chasing you,' the boy said. 'What is it you have done?'

'Nothing,' Parsaloi replied.

'Then why do you run?'

'Because they chase me.'

A moment of silence followed.

'How did you learn to shoot stones so well?'

'I keep to myself. There is time to practise.'

'You throw stones well for one so young,' the boy said, nodding his approval. 'But you look foolish fighting a lion naked.'

Parsaloi peered up at him. 'You speak of foolishness, but who is the one sitting in a tree?'

The boy scowled, and then burst into laughter.

As they walked to the *enkang* together, he told him his name was Nkapilil Ole Mantira and he had come to Parsaloi's village with his family to attend his sister's wedding. He would be staying with his sister and her husband for some time to help them with the herding.

Parsaloi had seen the group arrive, but had kept his distance. He had enough trouble with the children in his own *enkang* without further tempting providence by making himself known to a new boy. Even allowing for the age difference of a few years, the boy was quite tall and broad of chest. In comparison, Parsaloi felt like a child with his slight frame and bony arms and legs.

Nkapilil asked again about his skills in stone throwing.

'While the others play hunting games together, I practise with the stones,' Parsaloi said. 'I can kill a duiker with a single throw.'

'I believe you.'

The sun had disappeared by the time they reached the thornbush gate to the village.

'I failed to thank you for driving off the lion,' Nkapilil said.

'There is no need. Why wouldn't I help a brother Maasai?'

'You speak of brothers. Your age mates could use a reminder about that.'

Parsaloi smiled grimly. 'They don't see me as their brother.'

'Why not?'

'I am . . . different.'

'How so?'

Parsaloi paused, unsure if he should reveal his heritage to the newcomer. They had shared an adventure and laughed together. Surely these were the elements of friendship. Perhaps this new boy might agree to be a companion, if not a friend, for the few days he would spend in their village. He might be someone with whom Parsaloi could share his time and thoughts. They could hunt together. He could show Nkapilil the leopard's den and cubs he'd found, and the best place to observe the *moran* playing love games with their girlfriends in the evenings. But he hesitated to reveal his terrible truth. It might jeopardise everything.

'Why do you say you are different?' Nkapilil said, pressing the issue. 'I know you have the skinniest legs I have ever seen, and a willy to match, but what else is there to know?'

'I am Laikipiak,' Parsaloi answered, setting his jaw pugnaciously.

'Hmm,' Nkapilil replied. 'Is that all?'

The bland response was deflating. Parsaloi had prepared himself for the usual ill-concealed contempt and the inevitable fight that would follow. He let his shoulders relax. 'Yes,' he mumbled. 'That is all.'

'Well, I knew that. It's not important, but this is important.' He drew Parsaloi into a conspiratorial huddle. 'Do you want to know how to win the other boys' respect?'

Parsaloi experienced a moment of fleeting defiance when he was tempted to deny he cared what the others thought. Then he almost laughed at Nkapilil's confidence. Had he not seen the hatred in the boys' eyes? But there was something about the newcomer that seemed to place him apart. Parsaloi decided to trust him, and nodded his assent.

'Then this is my plan. There is no need for you to let anyone know that I was caught in a tree by a lion.'

Nkapilil waited for Parsaloi's agreement to this. Parsaloi had no intention of informing his tormentors of anything. He nodded.

'Good. Now, this is what you must do. First, you will not run away when the boys chase you.'

'Not run? Am I mad? The boys will beat me.'

'Maybe. But they are like the jackal with a badger. They chase him because he runs. When the badger stops running and is ready to fight, the jackal finds better things to do.'

Parsaloi considered the wisdom of Nkapilil's words, and slowly nodded again.

'And when they want to fight you, make that same face as you did just now when you said you were different. It makes you look twice your size.'

Parsaloi didn't try to hide his scepticism.

'And if that fails and they do decide to beat you,' Nkapilil finished, 'it will be two of us that they must fight from now on.'

CHAPTER 2

Mbatiani Ole Supeet knew he was dying. He had seen many die in his eighty years as the healer, or *laibon,* as the Maasai called such men. This realisation did not shake him. He knew it was his time.

He lay in his hut, the low cooking fire the only light in the darkened space. His first wife, who was old and slow, attended him. She was the only one he could abide. The younger ones were too eager to help and didn't understand the pain that an old body could suffer merely by lying on a bed platform.

Mbatiani knew his old wife had difficulty bending her ancient knees, and she used her stick to struggle to her feet after feeding him his warm blood and milk mixture. He wanted to tell her to lie down with him as the days and nights were flying and he was afraid; to lie down with him so he could tell her again of the old days when he was one of the glorious *moran,* the brave, handsome, strong and formidable warriors. Maybe he would make love to her one more time, for was he not still a man?

But as she stood in the doorway, her withered hand on the hide covering, all he said was, 'Old mother, you are going where now?'

His breath came in short puffs, like a gazelle spent from its dash from danger. It made his voice abrasive, but his use of the pet name told her it was not intended to be so.

'Is your belly not satisfied, husband?' the old woman asked with a sigh, playing with words for she too remembered their nights together.

The firelight twinkled in his eyes. 'For now, yes. But you would do this old man a blessing. Call the elders for me. Bring them here.'

A moment's silence. A heartbeat. His wife's steps came shuffling towards him again. His words had frightened her, for calling the elders together was a signal that he had accepted what was coming, and now she must too.

He stopped her with harsh words, born of his own fear. 'Are you so foolish to think I can simply lie here while there are important matters to attend to? Am I so old and useless that I cannot still do my duty?' He softened again. 'Just go,' he added in a whisper.

He couldn't see her, but he knew she stood motionless in the blurred darkness.

'I will bring them,' she said finally, and was at the entrance, pushing open the hide covering, letting the light of day flood into the hut and strike at his milky grey eyes.

Nine distinguished elders, their gangly arms hanging like thin leather thongs, silently entered Mbatiani's hut where they squatted, legs curled effortlessly beneath them, their elbows on their knees.

Mbatiani was propped up on his bed platform. Someone had opened the small roof hatch, allowing a shaft of brilliant light to pierce the hazy interior.

Mbatiani took a deep, wheezy breath. 'I am about to die,' he said. 'And you must carry on without me. But I give you my final words. Listen carefully, for I see disaster coming. I say to you, you must not leave your land.'

The advice surprised the elders. There was never a Maasai who would willingly leave his land. How could they conduct their lives without cattle and the land needed to feed them? They exchanged glances, wondering if the Great Laibon had already lost his senses.

But Mbatiani saw none of this. He continued. 'I see pink

men. They are riding a black rhino. It comes from the east like a long black snake. Its head is west of the Nandi Hills and its tail beyond the forests at Kinangop.' He paused and inclined his head, as if straining his cloudy eyes to see into the darkness. 'I see death and disaster. You must not leave your land, for if you do your cattle will perish, your children will die of a terrible disease and you will face a powerful enemy.' He paused again. 'And you will be defeated.'

The elders fidgeted at such a terrible thought. Their *laibon*, the Great Laibon, was a healer without peer, but was also renowned for his predictions. The portent of these words was too horrible to imagine, however. Could it be possible that he had lost his powers? Perhaps this was the ranting of a man unable to face his own death.

One among them found the courage to speak. 'These are very bad words you give us, Mbatiani.'

The *laibon* tilted his head to one side. 'Heed them.' He struggled to draw breath, as though there wasn't enough air in the hut for him.

'Who will succeed you as *laibon* when you are gone?' asked another, perhaps thinking that the new *laibon* might find a more acceptable future for them.

'I will give the insignia of office to the son who will be my successor.'

'But which son?'

'You will know him by the sacred iron rod I will give him.'

They all nodded, and when Mbatiani's head began to dip with exhaustion they departed.

A warm night. The breeze — barely enough to stir the brittle grass — wafted in from the savannah carrying the vague scent of leleshwa. A three-quarter moon threw pale moon shadows as it sailed among hazy clouds hanging in the ink-blue sky. There was really too much light to make it a good night to creep to the elders' campfire and lie in the darkness listening to their conversations, but Parsaloi had convinced his new friend, Nkapilil Ole Mantira, to join him for the fun of it.

The old men's voices carried easily to where they lay, flat on their bellies, peeping through the grass. Even the night insects seemed breathless and strangely quiet. The old men sat with their cowls over their shaved heads, staring into the fire. The firelight made hollows of their eye sockets and cheeks. Their toothless mouths were wrinkled caverns.

Usually the old men engaged in polite debate, or gossiped and exchanged stories until late. But tonight something was wrong. Instead of the usual quiet discourse, the old men were babbling in a most unruly manner.

'Silence!' the old one called Lekuta demanded. 'Are we to squabble and chatter like women in a market? Let the holder of the olive rod speak, and the others . . . Well, do I need to remind you how to behave?'

All eyes turned to one of the elders, who seemed startled to find himself the centre of attention until he realised he held the olive rod.

'I have heard that the *laibon* is near death,' he said. 'I also hear that his two sons are preparing for battle to decide the succession.'

Several hands were thrust into the firelight. The olive rod passed to the nearest.

'Mbatiani is near death, that much is true. But I heard that he called for Sendeyu, the oldest son of his first wife, and intended to give him the sacred iron rod. Lenana had his loyal *moran* confine his half-brother to his hut and tricked his father into giving him the succession.'

The olive rod passed again.

'Ai, ai. What is all this nonsense I am hearing? Does anyone believe that the Great Laibon could make such a foolish error? Is Mbatiani not the most powerful *laibon* ever to have lived? Did he not give us the medicine to cure the falling-down sickness? Did he not predict the terrible drought and its ending three seasons past? To say that he has erred is disrespectful to his name. The truth is that he chose Lenana, who is not the son of his *first* wife but the oldest son of his *favourite* wife.'

There was a muted note of accord around the circle.

The rod passed again.

'The Great Laibon was indeed our saviour on many occasions. Not only by his ministrations during times of famine and sickness, but for his wise counsel during times of unrest among our people. How many times was he the voice of reason when the hotheads among the *moran* would see the great valley aflame with war?'

Another took the olive rod. He had only joined the elders' ranks in recent years, but had been a well-respected senior *morani* before that time.

'Yes, it is hard to believe that Mbatiani could make an error in such an important matter as the succession. But how many of you have seen him in recent times?' There was silence around the campfire. 'Well, let me tell you, I went to visit my sister whose husband is of the same Ilaiser clan as Mbatiani, and while there I went to pay my respects to the Great Laibon. I can say that he is very old and frail.' His dark eyes moved around the circle of elders. 'Very old and frail. I have seen it with my own eyes. And let me tell you this. I heard from my brother-in-law that the old *laibon* did indeed make an error.'

He paused to allow the clamour to fade.

'Lenana overheard Mbatiani telling Sendeyu that he should come to his hut at first light on the following morning. Lenana crept out in the darkness before the dawn, knowing the Great Laibon could no longer see, and tricked him into believing it was dawn and that he was Sendeyu. Thus the iron rod was passed to Lenana by this deception, and therefore a great error was committed.'

Arguments erupted and the elders' meeting fell into disarray. When order was restored, the junior elder continued.

'Mbatiani was indeed a great *laibon*. He has worked wonders for our people in the past. But now he is failing and has made a serious error. I can only agree with the earlier speaker.'

The elders exchanged glances, unsure of his meaning.

Seeing this, he added, 'There will be war.'

Parsaloi had been walking for four days. Four days when he should have been tending Sianoi's goats, for which neglect he would no doubt be punished. Four days during which time he had been threatened by hyenas, almost charged down by an irate rhino mother defending her calf, and had gone without food and often been in dire need of water. Parsaloi had walked for those four days to reach the village where the Great Laibon was dying.

When he found Mbatiani's village, he discovered he was not alone in his desire to see the Great Laibon before it was too late. There were many visitors to Mbatiani's *enkang*, drawn there as Parsaloi had been, but these were distinguished people — elders and leaders of the various Maasai warrior age sets. There were also representatives from other tribes who had come to pay their respects. The curious Ilkunono were there — the workers of iron who smelted and forged Maasai spears and other weaponry; and the mysterious forest dwellers, the Ndorobo.

No one paid much attention to the young Maasai boy who, when he was not hovering outside the Great Laibon's hut awaiting his chance to slip inside, hung around the cooking fires accepting scraps when offered them.

If anyone had asked Parsaloi why he was there, or why he wanted to see the Great Laibon, he would have been unable to answer them. A powerful urge had driven him to risk his life to cross the great valley, but it was a journey of the heart, not the head. He knew that punishment awaited him on his return to Sianoi's hut, but such concerns were unworthy of the higher calling he felt he was heeding in making his trek. When he reached the village, however, he found he could not gain entry to the great man's hut. The elders guarded its door, scrutinising everyone who sought an audience.

On the sixth day, all the Maasai assembled outside the *boma* where they began to sway to a slow rhythmic song led by the women and accompanied by the deeper male voices. It was Parsaloi's first real chance to enter Mbatiani's hut, but he hesitated at the calfskin door covering. He wondered whether he would be breaking some profound taboo by bursting into the Great Laibon's hut uninvited. After a final furtive glance around the *enkang* to ensure no one was watching, he lifted the door covering and slipped into the hut.

When the calfskin fell closed behind him, he was plunged into darkness. He breathed in the familiar musty, smoky air and felt a pressure on his bare skin as if he had walked into a flimsy spider's web. He ran a hand down his arm but found nothing there.

His eyes slowly became accustomed to the interior darkness and he made out the remains of a cooking fire. Daylight found its way through tiny chinks in the cow-dung walls and fell in slender, silvered shafts to the compacted dirt floor.

He searched the silent gloom and felt a sudden cold clutch at his heart as his eyes met those of the old man. The Great Laibon was staring at him from his bed platform. From the stories around the elders' campfire Parsaloi had believed that Mbatiani was blind, or nearly so, but these eyes were ablaze in the dim firelight, and firmly fixed on Parsaloi's. More than fixed, they pierced him.

'So you have come,' the Great Laibon said in a strained and breathy voice that appeared to come from a long distance.

Parsaloi moved a step closer. 'Yes, my . . . I am sorry; I do not know how to address you.'

'As you will, my boy. It is of no consequence.' The Great Laibon waved a surprisingly expressive hand in the darkness. It fluttered in the firelight, indicating a butterfly perhaps, or something light and unimportant. 'You have come, but do you know why you have come?'

'I . . . I am not sure, my father.'

He wondered again why he had made his journey. Perhaps it was to know a little of what the Great Laibon knew before he died, taking his immense knowledge with him. He was afraid that the elder would consider such thoughts foolish and wasteful of his time, so he kept them to himself.

'Then I will tell you,' Mbatiani said. 'You have come because you are afraid. No, do not be ashamed. Only a fool knows no fear. A fool has not the wit to see what threatens him. And you are right to be afraid. There is a war coming, a war between brothers. Just as an earlier war destroyed your section, the Laikipiak, another will soon see many more die.

'The Maasai have conquered all, but we are in danger of losing all unless we again become united. To do that we need leaders. Strong leaders who will draw the Maasai together.

'You will one day be an important leader, my son. Yes, you will be the *olaiguenani* of the age set that will be called the Il Tuati. It will be difficult for you, but you must continue to show your bravery and do what must be done for your people. Not just your age set, not just for the Laikipiak or the Purko sections, but for *all* the Maasai. Do you understand me, my son?'

Parsaloi nodded, unable to trust his voice.

Mbatiani began to chant the litany of his forebears. It was as if he were reciting a prayer, a prayer that he wanted Parsaloi to remember.

'I am the son of the *laibon* named Supeet, who was the son of the *laibon* named Kipepete, who was the son of the *laibon* named Parinyombi . . .'

The wavering voice filled Parsaloi's head and continued until Mbatiani had taken Parsaloi back to Maasinta, the first Maasai man who was blessed by Enkai and given all the world's cattle for his safekeeping.

The droning chant made Parsaloi's eyes heavy but suddenly he awoke as if from a long sleep. The hut was now very still and he noticed that the slight pressure he had felt against his skin since arriving was gone.

He looked to the bed platform where Mbatiani lay. The Great Laibon was still. His eyes were cloudy and vacant. The hand that had flittered like a butterfly in the darkness appeared leaden. Parsaloi reached out, hesitated a moment, and then touched it. It was cold. As cold as if it belonged to a man who had been dead for many hours. Even since early morning. Perhaps it was a body that had been dead even before the whole *enkang* had filed out of the *boma* gate to sing their mournful dirge.

CHAPTER 3

1890

'Look at you,' Mantira said, shaking his head and wearing a grin as wide as the river that ran past their camp. 'I remember when you were a little drop of donkey's piss. Now — ai, ai! You have come a long way since the days when you were throwing stones at lions.'

Ole Sadera was smearing red ochre over his legs in preparation for the four days of dancing that would soon begin. All the young men in his age group were about to enter the first part of the process that would ultimately see them become warriors. He straightened up and returned the grin.

'And it is also good to know, my friend, that you have learned to keep your arse out of thorn trees.'

They laughed together. Neither had ever again mentioned the day Ole Sadera had fled the herd boys for the last time and a lion had treed Mantira. Ole Sadera was delighted that his friend was the one to bring it to mind, especially on this special day — the day Ole Sadera would receive his greatest honour. It somehow put a seal on the already strong bond of friendship between them — a friendship that had endured five difficult years.

When Ole Sadera returned from Mbatiani's burial years before, he had passed through a countryside decimated by the first wave of internecine war. Villages were in ashes and the remains of the dead could be seen strewn across the valleys and hillsides. The stench of death carried on the wind and the skies were thick with circling vultures.

Sendeyu's loyal warriors from the south had initiated the killings in a pre-emptive strike intended to force Lenana and his supporters to return the iron rod of the *laibon* to its rightful owner. Ole Sadera knew the northern Maasai would not sit idly by in the face of such an atrocity. As the elders around the campfire had predicted the night he and Mantira had spied upon them, there was war.

When Ole Sadera reached his own *enkang* he found a similar scene of carnage to that he had witnessed in the villages he had passed. There were bodies strewn over a wide area, providing a fortuitous feast for hyena, jackal and vultures. He chased them away with sticks and stones as he made his grisly search. By the time he found the body he was looking for, the scavengers had devoured the genitals and commenced on the intestines. Ole Sadera's stomach churned, but he made himself study his stepfather's features objectively, without the fear that had always dominated while in his presence.

The brutal nose was so unlike the long elegant nose typical of the Maasai that, until Ole Sadera found out it had once been broken, he had privately wondered about Sianoi's pedigree. Now he saw there could be no doubt. The earlobes — stretched to impressive proportions — and the high cheekbones declared the face distinctly Maasai. The mean, narrowed eyes had widened in the final strictures of agony, but otherwise this was the cruel-faced individual he remembered. Ole Sadera felt no remorse for his satisfaction at seeing that the man who had worked his mother to her death, and mercilessly beaten a child, had not died well. It appeared as if the scavengers had begun disembowelling him before he was dead.

He had found Mantira in the forest with his mother and a few of the other villagers. His father had died defending the *enkang* from the raiders. Mantira seethed with frustrated rage. He was old enough and strong enough to handle a spear and *simi*, the short Maasai sword, but was not yet initiated into the ranks of the *moran* and so could do nothing. It was the worst possible situation to be in: trapped between age sets; a boy-man unable to inflict vengeance on those who had shattered their lives.

This had left an indelible impression on Mantira over the following years. By the time he had graduated to warriorhood, the war had been won, the sections had been reunited under Lenana and peace was restored. Mantira had felt cheated by fate.

On the other hand, the raid had been the liberation of Ole Sadera. His new status as an orphan brought hardship, but also the freedom to be what he wanted to be. He chose to travel between the many Purko communities, offering his services as a herd boy to any who were willing to feed and house him. When he needed a more permanent home, he returned to the community of survivors from his *enkang*, and in particular to Mantira and his family. There he was treated as a lost brother and son. Even after Mantira graduated as a *morani* — a time when, traditionally, the newly promoted warriors made life hell for their younger, uninitiated brethren — he and Ole Sadera remained friends.

Now it was Ole Sadera's time to become a member of the standing army of warriors, but there were a number of ceremonies that would precede it; the first being the *emorata* or circumcision ceremony. The occasion was one of great importance to the families of the new initiates who helped the young men prepare for the occasion. Mantira was the nearest person to family that Ole Sadera had, and this wasn't the first time he had come to Ole Sadera's assistance. Without him, he might not have qualified for circumcision at all, which reminded him that he needed to acknowledge his friend's contribution to the day.

He wiped the ochre from his hands on a piece of calf hide and placed one palm on Mantira's shoulder. 'I have not thanked you, my brother,' he said.

'What is this now? Thank me for what?'

'I have not thanked you for helping me to be here.'

'That much is true. I swear, if I wasn't at your back steering you like a herd boy steers a stupid goat, you would never have found your way here.'

'No, Nkapilil. You know my meaning. Without you I would not have qualified.'

The test of whether a boy was old enough to be circumcised was his ability to carry home a newborn calf on his shoulders. Mantira knew that Ole Sadera, smaller than most of the boys his age, would have great difficulty with the test, so he searched out the smallest heifer in the district and quietly arranged to have her moved near the *enkang* before she calved. Even then, it was only Ole Sadera's determination that got him and the calf to the *enkang*'s enclosure. That night the boy who would be a warrior and the warrior who had made it possible had drunk honey beer until dawn.

Seeing that Ole Sadera would not allow the matter to be laughed off, Mantira dropped his attempt to do so. 'If anyone owes me thanks it is your age mates for they will have a worthy *olaiguenani* in you.'

Ole Sadera had learned only that morning that he was to be made the leader of his age set, their *olaiguenani,* which meant he would speak for the whole age set in important tribal meetings and even lead them into war when necessary. It was a great honour for an initiate younger and smaller than the rest.

'I will not disgrace you,' he said.

'There is no question of disgrace. It was not I but wiser heads who chose you for the position.'

'But as an *olaiguenani* yourself, your word would have carried much weight. Without you, I would not be here. There would be no circumcision for me for many years, and I would certainly not be the *olaiguenani*.'

Mantira took the calf hide from him, wiped his hands and then threw the skin aside. 'Look at me, Parsaloi,' he said, glaring at him. 'That is the last time I will hear you speak ill of yourself. It is a childish thing. A habit unworthy of your position. There is no room for false modesty in a leader. To be *olaiguenani* you must lead. You must do what is right for your brother *moran*. And to be truthful, I had nothing to do with your selection. Even though you are younger and not as strong as many others, you have skills that many admire; characteristics of strength and determination that others can only envy. You are what you are by your own power. You have earned respect. That is something that mere size can never demand.'

'I . . . I thank you for the advice, my friend. As usual, it is well received.'

'Good! Then now you must keep your mouth shut, and rest. You have two full days of the white dances and two of the red ahead of you. You will need all the strength in your legs for the dance and, if you are lucky, all the strength of your soon-to-be-circumcised cattle prod for what may follow.'

Lenana stood under the sacred fig tree and watched as Ole Sadera came up the slope. He moved like a cat, placing his feet between the grassy tufts on the meandering path up the hill — a path that only the eye of a herder could see. The long muscles of his taut, compact body shone with sweat and rippled as he used the haft of his spear to help his climb. He threaded his way between the stunted thornbush and rounded grey boulders that guarded the gnarled fig tree like fat sentinels.

Even before he was initiated as a *morani*, Ole Sadera had been thrust into Lenana's attention. He had been nominated as the *olaiguenani* of what was to become the Il Tuati age set. The younger of the two age sets comprising the warriors' ranks were always the most troublesome and it was the *olaiguenani*'s responsibility to see that their enthusiasm was channelled into useful pursuits. Lenana had initially had difficulty understanding why the young Ole Sadera had been nominated by his peers. He was slim, even for a Maasai, and not as tall as most of his fellow initiates. However, Lenana had found that he met all the important criteria of an *olaiguenani* and could not object.

He was very well versed in the traditions and the history of the Maasai. It was as if he had spent all his time at the feet of the elders, absorbing their endless stories from the past. Also, he was a very good orator. Lenana had heard that in the period after the war, he had spent much of his time wandering between the Purko clans herding cattle for anyone who would feed him. It had obviously taught him the skill of disarming people with his tongue.

He had a strong character — of that there was no doubt. It had obviously been forged during some trial, possibly a difficult childhood. Ole Sadera's stepfather, it was said, had been afraid of the boy and had beaten him often to keep him subdued. Many of the older Purko told of Ole Sadera's birth in the waters of the Uaso Ngiro, how, when his mother pulled him from the waters, he was found to be holding a stone in each hand. Lenana was sceptical. It was a story a Laikipiak mother might spread among her new husband's Purko relatives to ensure her son, born into a hostile world, survived. In the teachings of the elders, it was said that a child born clutching a stone would inherit certain indefinable powers. They might be the ability to see the future, or to inflict pain on a distant enemy. They might give the insight of a wise man or the skills of a great lover. Whatever powers one stone gave, two stones were unimaginable. Lenana thought it could not be possible, but then he remembered the boy at the time of their first meeting — so intense. It was as if he had inside him a terrible power that could not be contained by his small frame.

In spite of his stature — or perhaps because of it — the boy had been strong; not so much in the physical sense, but spiritually, with enough resilience to surmount the many difficulties that his life had put before him. As the Maasai saying went: he was like a hyena's sinew — tougher than most. It was this discipline and strength of character that the members of his Il Tuati age set had recognised when they nominated him their *olaiguenani,* and why, after an initial hesitation, Lenana had appointed him.

It was the reason, as his age set's spokesperson, that he was now climbing the hill to sit under the sacred fig tree with his *laibon* to tell him of the war he and his *moran* were about to wage.

'*Sopa,*' Lenana said in greeting.

'*Hepa,*' Ole Sadera replied. 'I trust your cows are well?'

'They are. As are yours, I pray.'

'Thank you. They are.'

Lenana took a seat on a flat rock, indicating it was now appropriate to commence discussing the real reason for

Ole Sadera's visit. He indicated that the younger man should sit, and waited while Ole Sadera found a suitable rock.

'I have heard of the coming of the Swahili caravan,' Lenana said.

'It is an outrage.'

'So it is time,' the *laibon* said after a moment's silence.

'Yes.'

'And the *moran* — they are ready for this raid?'

'They are.'

'And what says Mantira?' Lenana asked.

Mantira was the *olaiguenani* of the senior age set — the men who had been warriors for almost thirteen years. By choice and tradition, Ole Sadera listened to his older friend when it came to important matters like war.

'He agrees it is time for the Il Tuati to blood our spears.'

'And your decision to strike the caravan?'

'He agrees it is time, but he says we should not attack this caravan. He says it is too strong and has many rifles.'

'Sound advice.'

'But my *moran* are ready. Their impatience grows with my delays.'

'Such is the lust of the young. I was once young.' The old man's leathery face creased into a thin smile that quickly faded. 'So why do you delay? You have doubts?'

'No. There is no doubt that we must strike.' Ole Sadera put one hand inside the other and clenched it tightly. 'The Swahili and Wakikuyu must be taught a lesson.' He stared at his knotted fingers for some time, but said no more.

'What then?'

'Our warriors can brush aside the Swahili like flies on a cow's back, but I am thinking . . . about your father's prediction.'

'About the pink men riding a black rhino — I know. It troubles me also.'

'And the disasters he foretold. Our scouts say the whites are gathering in camps at the edge of Maasailand. Will they stop there, and be content to pass through with their accursed snake? Will they leave the Maasai and our cattle in peace?'

'The Wakamba say they are many and their weapons are fierce,' the old man said.

'The more reason we should be joining the sections together in preparation for war with the whites, rather than go on killing each other as we have these last many seasons.'

'It is done. We cannot undo the past.'

'No.'

'And there is no stopping what must be.'

'Are you speaking now of the whites or the caravan?'

Lenana paused. 'Both.'

They sat in silence then, each with his own thoughts.

Finally Ole Sadera stood. 'I will call the *moran* to prepare for the raid.'

'Go swiftly. If you are to strike, you must catch the caravan before they reach the forest.' Lenana stood too. 'First, let me give you my blessing, and I will follow you down to bless the *moran* before you go.'

He lifted his sacred iron club over Ole Sadera's head, circled the *morani* and spattered him with light spittle in the Maasai traditional blessing. When it was done, Ole Sadera stood as if reluctant to leave, and stared into the *laibon*'s eyes for a long moment, causing Lenana to wonder again at the intensity of this young man.

On the eastern escarpment, two thousand feet above the Great Rift Valley, the land fell away in leaps and bounds to the flat yellow plain where the Kedong River — from that height no more than a verdant ribbon — meandered at the foot of the slopes.

Ole Sadera came to the escarpment's edge, planted his spear in the ground and watched another ribbon below. A mottled assortment of colours and shapes, it moved like a snake: this way to avoid a pile of boulders, that way to skirt a patch of thornbush. In its wake was a plume of vaporous dust that hung in the air over Maasai land. It was a Swahili trading caravan, fourteen hundred strong. Among them were men who had, just days before, taken and defiled two Maasai women.

Four hundred Maasai *moran* stood with him at the escarpment edge, bodies gleaming with sweat, the sun catching the many colours of their war shields and glinting from the edges of their long iron spears. They were the Il Tuati, with the closely shaved heads of the newly initiated.

Ole Sadera's heart thumped against his ribs. It was as much from anticipation of the battle ahead as it was from the ten miles the raiding party had run to reach the caravan. He glanced along the rows of warriors to his left and right, and felt the air grow taut with tension. It was a sensation similar to a hot day on the savannah, when the rumbling thunderclouds gathered above and the air crackled with power.

In their *manyatta*, the *laibon* had read them the signs. There were favourable omens for a swift and deadly revenge. The warriors had painted their bodies and, wearing only the white and red ochre and their short red *shukas*, had gathered for a celebratory dance. They whooped and sang as each took his turn to spring into the circle and leap to the sky to display his vigour and preparedness for battle. As their *olaiguenani*, Ole Sadera had waited until last, and with the adrenaline surging through his body had reached heights he'd never before achieved. His age mates had whooped the more.

The women of the *enkang* had lined their path, ululating and singing songs of glory as their younger army jogged out.

Now, perched above their quarry, excitement rippled through the assembled *moran* like a wildfire. Yabbering and jostling, whooping and chattering — they were keen to be away. A chant began to sound among them. *Hhuunh-huh! Hhuunh-huh! Hhuunh-huh!* It grew in strength as its power seeped into each tightly muscled body.

When Ole Sadera climbed onto a rock preparatory to speaking, his four hundred warriors immediately fell silent and closed together into a tight formation. Not a murmur passed between the red shaved heads as their leader issued his orders, allocating *moran* as flank attackers, advance guards and reserves. When it was done, Ole Sadera raised his war shield and a collective sigh came from his warriors. The war party was ready.

The four hundred poured down a fold in the escarpment like the molten lava of nearby Mount Longonot, leaping boulders like gazelle, sending small stones flying from beneath their feet.

The natural shape of the slope kept them hidden from the enemy as they descended. Ole Sadera led his Il Tuati proudly. Today would be their day — the blooding of their spears.

On the flat ground at the escarpment's base, they gathered into fighting formation and moved quickly towards the point where they would engage the invaders. They took up positions behind a small rise on the valley floor that was without thornbush or trees and where the attacking phalanx could manoeuvre freely.

Ole Sadera knew that the women and elders would sing of this day for years to come. It would be a glorious revenge.

CHAPTER 4

Andrew Dick put down the grubby sheet of paper containing his list of supplies, took from his pocket a filthy handkerchief and wiped it under his full black beard, around the back of his neck and then screwed a corner of it into an ear. In the morning, he would lead his caravan from Fort Smith to Lake Rudolph. Today he was making his most important purchase — ammunition for his men. It would not do to be caught in Turkana country with twenty empty Sniders.

A shout went up from the guards who opened the fort's gates to a dozen battered and bloody Swahili men. The officer in charge, Commander Gilkisson, sent orderlies running for water and ushered the injured to the veranda of his office building. Dick joined the crowd that quickly gathered to hear their story.

In a mixture of Swahili and broken English, the porters told a confused and garbled account of a terrible and bloody attack by over a thousand Maasai warriors on their peaceful caravan. Hundreds had been speared or hacked to pieces. The few survivors had fled in all directions to escape their murderers. It had been a completely unprovoked attack.

Gilkisson heard them out, then called for volunteers to mount a mission to bring the wounded to the fort. He turned to Andrew Dick.

'Will you stand guard here at the fort while I'm gone? I could use your extra guns in case those bloodthirsty scoundrels make a run on the fort.'

'I'll be damned if I'll sit here as nursemaid while those black buggers get clear away,' Dick replied. 'I say let's go after them before they get their cowardly arses back to the devil where they belong. What about it, men? Who'll join me?'

He could see the hundreds of Maasai cattle there in the valley ready for the taking. They didn't call him Trader for naught.

'I'll have none of that nonsense from you, Mr Dick,' Gilkisson said. 'Citizen reprisal raids are strictly forbidden — you should know that, being a trader.'

'I do indeed, Commander, but I also know that I haven't been here for more than eight years without learnin' a thing or two about these black bastards.' His beard jutted pugnaciously. 'Go on with your rescue, Commander. I say we strike 'em and strike 'em hard. Else you'll not see the end of this bloody tomfoolery on caravans.' He turned back to the crowd. 'I say again, who'll join me?'

The crowd started to melt away and Dick saw his chances of annexing the Maasai cattle — the best of all trade goods in the Turkana country — vanishing with them.

'You! Frenchy!' he called to the three Frenchmen he'd spoken to the previous night. They had a number of armed men in their party. 'Call yourselves hunters? What good is a sharp eye and steady hand without a worthy target? Come with me and you'll see sport of the kind you'll never find on those Kilimanjaro slopes. Come on, I say.'

The Frenchmen exchanged glances.

'Are you going to let a single Englishman take the place of all three of you?'

There was a hurried conversation among them before they strode over to join him.

'That's the spirit!' Dick crowed. 'Now what about you, young Irish? Will you not come along for a bit of a laugh?'

Much to Gilkisson's disgust, Trader Dick had soon gathered a small private army around him.

*   *   *

Dust rose lazily behind the herd, catching the long rays of the sun and turning them from gold to red. Andrew Dick, riding behind the cattle, allowed himself a small smile of satisfaction. It had been an easy day's work. His twenty *askaris* and a dozen or more heavily armed volunteers had swept along the base of the escarpment first, finding nothing. But when they wheeled to the west, they came across what Dick had hoped for — the Maasai herd.

A few old men and boys guarded the cattle. It took Dick's troop no time to dispatch them. Then they waited for the onslaught from the warriors. It didn't come.

Dick had contended that the *moran* had fled beyond the escarpment in fear of reprisal following their attack on the Swahili caravan. There was therefore no need for haste.

As he rode along, Trader Dick estimated the return on his small investment. It would be very profitable, even allowing for the share of cattle he'd give to the white members of his little army. Most of them were hunters, however, and would be glad to accept something in exchange for the cattle. Perhaps a box of ammunition, or even a fistful of rupees. He would make a fuss about the price, of course, but would keep the cattle regardless. The Turkana loved cattle almost as much as the Maasai and would pay a high price for the herd in fine Somali ponies. Horses were in demand among the new settlers who were starting to arrive. There was hardly a broken-down nag to be had in Nairobi.

Yes, the investment of a few bullets would return a handsome dividend, he thought smugly.

Ole Sadera and his warriors lay in wait in the ravine. It was no more than a gathering of two folds in the red earth at the edge of the valley, but it would serve his purpose. The cattle were approaching, and when they reached the cutting in the valley floor they would fill it, blocking the northern end. The thieving herders would have nowhere to run but to the south — and onto the spears of his Il Tuati.

It needn't have been like this. Ole Sadera understood the whites' need to retaliate. A warrior may honourably seek revenge. And if the white men had merely engaged him in battle, then he and his Il Tuati would have retreated; not because Ole Sadera was afraid of a fight or thought his cause was unjust, but because older and wiser men had warned that if he continued to make war with the whites, others would come in great numbers to destroy their *enkangs*. But a peaceful retreat became impossible when the whites stole their cattle.

Even then, Ole Sadera had agonised over his choices. He didn't willingly ignore the elders' counsel, for he well knew that the Maasai's strength had waned in recent years. The wars between the various sections, the dreaded smallpox, the terrible toll that the rinderpest had taken on their cattle and the resulting starvation — all these had reduced their standing armies to a shadow of their former power. But how much could any man tolerate before he was forced to fight? If the *moran* didn't show their determination to protect their people, their land and their cattle, what would become of them?

The herd began to move past the place where he and his warriors lay concealed. The hiding place was too small to confine all his Il Tuati, but surprise was essential so he'd chosen just half of his *moran* for the mission. The bush wasn't so thick that he couldn't identify his own brand on some of the cattle in the stolen herd. They moved steadily along, but not without a good deal of lowing in protest.

Now the thieves — the whites and the Swahili *askaris* — came into view. Ole Sadera let them pass, then raised his shield. When he let it drop his warriors sprang from their hide and charged the horsemen, whooping in savage fury. Ole Sadera saw about ten whites fall to their first torrent of spears, but the white men wheeled to defend themselves and fire leapt from the barrels of their rifles.

As the *olaiguenani*, Ole Sadera was the commanding general. Following ironclad tradition, he was bound to keep himself apart, forbidden to engage in the battle. He must direct its operations from a safe distance. His four bodyguards were similarly removed from the encounter and stood close by their leader.

His frontal attack fell back, and the enemy followed, as planned. A gap opened between the riders and the cattle, allowing Ole Sadera's flankers to sweep in with slashing *simis* at close quarters. The air was thick with dust and the pungent odour of cordite. Horses reared and men fell, skewered on the heavy blades of Maasai spears.

But Maasai casualties were heavy too. Ole Sadera watched his men fall in increasing numbers. Helpless to stop or change the course of the battle, he clenched his fists in anguish and frustration, cursing his inability to become directly involved. The whites and their *askaris* were few but their firepower was great.

In spite of its ferocity, the battle was suddenly over. The cattle had stampeded off through the valley — to be collected by the remaining body of the *moran* — and the surviving cattle thieves had bolted after them.

Only one of the whites remained. He was a big man with a thick, black beard. He had lost or fallen from his horse and was shooting any *morani* who approached while he made a retreat along the hillside. The *moran* would mount an assault, but then fall back when the bearded one turned and brandished his weapon. In this way, he had made good progress and it appeared he would make his escape into the bush before long.

Although Ole Sadera was not familiar with white men's weaponry, he realised, as the pursuing *moran* obviously had not, that the white man had fired no shots for some time. Somehow, the gun had lost its power.

Ole Sadera grabbed his spear and, to the absolute horror of his bodyguard, charged up the slope to cut off the white leader's escape.

The man pointed his weapon threateningly at Ole Sadera as he rushed forward, spear raised, but it did not speak.

In the moment before he plunged his spear through his enemy's body, Ole Sadera was gratified to see the man's eyes widen in horror.

From the women's circle came the ululating songs of tribute to the *moran* — the sons, the brothers and the lovers — who had returned from the battlefield. It had been a glorious victory over the white men who had dared to offend two of their number.

The sweet words came winging through the air like soaring night birds to where the *moran* were gathered to feast and to dance in celebration. There were scores of warriors in full regalia of beads and red-ochred bodies. Many wore the lion's mane headdress while others wore an alternative *olewaru* of black ostrich feathers. In either case, the effect was to make the tall warriors even more impressive.

Into the middle of the circle would break a young man who leapt into the night sky — as high and as straight as a gleaming black arrow. His companions kept up a relentless, breathy chant, which seemed to drive the lone dancer to ever-greater heights. Each leap brought forth whoops of delight and encouragement. Driven on in a trancelike state, the dancer became streaked with sweat and reached the brink of collapse before his place at the hub was taken by another.

Eventually, the warriors retired to drink and feast. Large chunks of half-cooked meat were hacked from the bullock's carcass and passed among the *moran*. There was laughter and joking, congratulations and recollections of brave deeds done during battle. The most remarkable dancers of the evening were showered with praise.

Soon the noise and chatter around the *moran*'s campfires dwindled, and the women's voices, carried from far away in the village, could be heard once more. One song, which seemed to have been composed for the occasion, brought the warriors to silence. Even the surrounding bush was quiet of night calls, both predators and prey appearing to pause to listen.

It was sung by a single, strong female voice:

Others may dance while I sit alone
With the songs of my age mates unheard
They wonder why I am so forlorn
But I am sending a prayer to Enkai's home

The woman's song was of thanks to their god for granting victory to the *moran* and entreaties to find a place of glory for those who had fallen. As the song unfolded, it became clear that the singer was the mother of a dead warrior.

The clouds that cross my eyes are cruel
I will not see what now is true
Remembering the days when he was mine
Clouds wash my cheeks and the nights are unkind

The song ended, and there was a period of awkward silence among the *moran*.

Ole Sadera stared into the fire, which burned hot on his eyes. In the flames danced the faces of the dead; brothers he had not allowed himself to see until then. Again, he pondered the questions that followed every battle. Could he have conducted the raid any better? Could he have avoided some of those deaths? The answer was unknowable, but it didn't stop the question echoing through his mind, torturing him.

After a short time another song began, and grew in strength as voices were progressively added. It lifted the solemn mood from thoughts of death to promises of glory. Soon the mood in the *manyatta* had returned to something approaching its previous buoyancy; and a song or two later, the young women — the *entito* — sent a love song into the night, pledging untold pleasures to unnamed lovers and asking for permission to visit the *moran*'s camp for it was taboo for women to see the *moran* eating meat.

As the women sang words of love, the warriors' thoughts turned from the celebration of a battle well fought to the promise of a night of passion.

Although Ole Sadera held a position of importance within his age set, to his great disappointment his status of *olaiguenani* had won him few girlfriends.

Of the three formal boyfriends a Maasai girl may have, he had never been selected *asanja* — the sweetheart, a girl's first choice as a sexual partner — by anyone. Should her first sweetheart be unavailable, a girl might choose the second boyfriend, the *oljipet*. Ole Sadera had not been chosen as anyone's *oljipet* either.

If neither first nor second boyfriends were available, the *entito* could choose her *olkeloki* — meaning 'the one who crosses over'. A girl might name a boy as her *olkeloki* for sentimental reasons or because of a kindness shown to her by the boy. Many an *olkeloki* was in recognition of a childhood friendship.

Ole Sadera had been chosen as *olkeloki* by two girls, which was no disgrace considering most *entitos* favoured the older *moran* for their official boyfriend choices. But neither girl had found the need to ask him to cross over.

Ole Sadera and his Il Tuati brothers had earlier that day marched in triumph through the ranks of the women who were even then singing their praises. The *moran* had passed by aloofly for it was not becoming for a warrior to show interest in girls. It was for the girls to make their intentions known first. However, he had been unable to prevent his eyes wandering more than once to one particular girl, Nashilo. He tried to read into her expression the interest that he felt for her, but after giving her too many more sideways glances than was proper he decided he couldn't be sure. Experience told him it was unlikely he would be chosen when the moment arrived. He was not handsome like many of his brother *moran*.

The sound of girlish giggling came from the darkness beyond the throw of the campfire light. Soon the flash of white teeth and the flare of many-coloured beadwork could be seen. Ole Sadera searched among the approaching young women for the pretty face of Nashilo. With a leap in his heart, he found her. Her small pointed breasts poked through a many-stranded beaded necklace. Her earrings were dangling white circles. Across her forehead was a beaded band with tiny silver disks hanging on a string of red beads. A feather fluttered above the front of her closely cropped hair as she walked. Her short red skirt revealed long shapely legs and metal anklets.

He had promised himself that he would not gawk like a pubescent herd boy, but as she drew closer the very sight of her aroused him so that he had trouble sitting comfortably with his legs crossed and his rising manhood threatened to disgrace him.

Suddenly she was standing before him. He could think of nothing acerbic to say as his more sophisticated brothers might, but sat dumbstruck in her presence, waiting for her to speak. Perhaps she intended to ask him the whereabouts of Keriko or

Moirori or one of the many other eligible young warriors she might be interested in; any of whom, he thought dismally, would have handled the situation more adroitly than he. But she simply stood in front of him with a shy smile revealing her beautiful teeth.

He sat like a fool, with leaden legs and a stupefied look on his face, waiting. Then realisation dawned and he leapt to his feet, causing the gentle Nashilo to step back in surprise.

He attempted a smile and hesitantly touched her arm to reassure her.

Her smile returned and she touched her hand to his.

Ole Sadera led her to his hut, his heart thumping in his chest.

CHAPTER 5

The scout came loping into camp with the setting sun at his back, and immediately went to where Ole Sadera was meeting with his lieutenants.

'What news from the great valley?' the *olaiguenani* asked.

The scout wiped the sweat from his brow. 'Men on horseback are crossing the valley towards us.'

'How many?'

'Six wearing the scarlet tarboosh and khaki tunic. Two in dark jackets — one of them has something on his eye that flashes when it catches the sun.'

'Where are they now?'

'They have made camp in the great valley. By noon they will be here.'

Ole Sadera knew this could not be the reprisal raid he had expected. Even the whites with their formidable weapons would not be so foolish as to confront the amassed Maasai army with so few. It was also odd that they came from the west whereas most of their soldiers were in camps to the east.

'What do you make of this?' he asked his men.

'Some days ago I saw the one with the sun flashing from his face,' a *morani* replied. 'He went west from Fort Smith. Perhaps he is visiting soldiers nearby.'

Another said that there were no soldiers within the distance that a *morani* could run in a day and a half.

Since the whites had first come from the east, their customs and in particular their military strength had been a matter of keen interest to the Maasai. Knowledge was freely passed from one section to another until quite a deal was known of the whites and their ways. Shortly after the Great Laibon died and the savannah had flowed with Maasai blood, the whites had made it known that they would not tolerate such a disruption to the peace. They had made a forceful demonstration of their strength with explosive devices that caused the very earth to shake and convulse, and iron weapons that could fell a gazelle at great distances.

'Maybe they are returning to Fort Smith,' one of the warriors suggested.

'But for what?' asked another.

Ole Sadera was in no doubt. The Maasai raid on the caravan and the subsequent battle with the trader and his band of hunters would be discussed at the fort. What he would not admit to his men was that he had no idea what the whites would do about it.

'Here is more trouble because I listen to a dunghead like you,' Mantira said, concentrating on the blade of grass he was idly stripping with his thumbnail.

'Who is the dunghead if you are here of your own free will?' Ole Sadera responded.

The two men were sitting under a leleshwa bush at the side of the road that the whites had cleared so their wagons could cross the great valley. They were waiting for the small party of whites to pass by on their way to the fort.

'Then, yes, I am a dunghead,' Mantira said, 'and you are a baboon's arse for attacking the caravan in the first place.'

'A fine pair,' Ole Sadera said, nodding in agreement. 'A baboon's arse and a dunghead — waiting to be taken to a white man's prison.'

He began to chuckle and after a moment Mantira joined him. 'I don't even know why I am here,' he said. 'I should be in the north with my brothers.'

'Then why aren't you?'

'Because I feel guilty. I should have been with you on the raid. At least I could then feel I deserved the punishment.'

'Yes, you should have been there. The Il Talala are approaching the age when you can look forward to drinking honey beer with all the other old farts and wondering where your warrior days have gone.'

The teasing was part of the usual friendly rivalry between the two age sets, but Mantira didn't rise to it. He returned to shredding his blade of grass.

'Whatever comes of this,' he said after some reflection, 'you must never regret defending the honour of our people.'

'Thank you, Mantira. And thank you for sitting with me. I have no regrets for revenging the wrongs, but I worry now about the consequences. Have I brought big trouble to the Purko?'

'You did what had to be done. When the white soldier with the sun's light in his eye passes this way, we will tell him the truth: that it was a matter of honour.'

'But I worry that our words will not help; true or otherwise,' Ole Sadera said. 'I fear he will not believe us. If these white men are as many and as powerful as we have been told, why would they bother with the truth? They could crush us no matter how truthful we were or how bravely we fought.'

'I know, Parsaloi. We can only do what we must. If they fine us many cattle, then we must give them. If they chase us from our land, we must go. And if they fight us, then . . . perhaps we must die.'

'Surely they will not make us leave the great valley?'

'No. I do not think so. But who knows these people? We can only listen, and try to understand.'

Ole Sadera sat silently. The situation revived an idea that had been on his mind for some time. He decided to voice it to his friend.

'Mantira, I have been thinking about these white people and how difficult it would be to defeat them in battle.'

Mantira smiled. 'You are not alone, my friend. All of Maasailand shares such thoughts.'

'But I have been thinking about how we can beat them.'

'Oh-ho, now you sound like a herd boy, penis in hand, itching for a great battle. There is great bravery in ignorance.'

'You think they are unbeatable?'

'I know only Mbatiani's words, as you do. He prophesied that the black rhino would come with pink men riding on its back. He said that those who stand against those pink men will be wiped out.'

'There are more ways to win than with weapons. What if we made allies of these Britishers? What if we were to share *en-kiyieu* with them?'

'Share the brisket?' Mantira said, his brow lifting in surprise. 'With a white man? We have never —'

'Never mind that it has not been done before. There could be no better time to make brothers of the blood than with a possible enemy.'

'But *en-kiyieu* is . . . It is such a bond. I wonder what the British would make of it. They are not educated in such matters, and from what I have heard there appears no hope that they could understand. I fear they are too dim-witted.'

'Without doubt, but we could explain that it is the most important bond we have and make sure they understand. If we share the brisket, we can be confident that our lands will be respected and our cattle protected.'

'I am not sure about this,' Mantira said, scratching his head. 'It may be a good plan, but it worries me. It is a matter for the *laibon*. Lenana will know what is the right thinking.'

'I do not believe that Lenana is like his father, Mbatiani. The Great Laibon was one who could see the future. He knew what was best for all of the Maasai. I am not sure if Lenana is such a person. Many say he stole the position from the legitimate successor — his older brother. If this is true, surely it must be a cloud over his appointment. It must affect his judgements.'

'Maasailand has more rumours than cattle. Nobody knows if that story is true, so how can we allow it to destroy our respect for him?'

'Wasn't it you who told me a man must earn respect rather than expect it because of his position?'

'They come,' Mantira said, as a group of white men rode into view.

The two *moran* stood, gathering their *shukas* about them to be presentable for the white men.

'Which one do you think is their *olaiguenani*?' Mantira asked.

'I cannot see them clearly enough,' Ole Sadera replied, straining his eyes through the heat haze. 'Maybe it is the one with the flashing light in his eye.'

He stooped to gather a handful of grass — a sign of peace he felt sure was universal. Mantira did likewise. They stepped onto the road and into the path of the advancing horsemen.

Ole Sadera knew he was right about the leader as soon as the white man came into full view. He wore a circle of glass in a gold ring fitted into his eye socket. A string connected it to a silver button on his jacket. He rode easily in the saddle, but held his head straight and looked directly at Ole Sadera with strangely pale eyes. He had a great drooping moustache that covered his mouth, and when he removed his hat to wipe a sleeve across his brow, he revealed a thin covering of lank hair, severely parted on one side.

Despite the man's slender frame and soft, fair skin, Ole Sadera somehow knew he had seen much of the land he now rode through. He would understand the importance of cattle and land. He would know that a man must fight for what was rightfully his, and must defend his women. But Ole Sadera wondered how he could make the man know what had truly happened so he could make his judgement.

'Good afternoon,' said the man with the flashing glass at his eye. 'I'm Fred Jackson.'

The mess hall at Fort Smith had been built to double as a defensive command post should the fort ever come under sustained attack. It was a narrow rectangular building constructed from cedar logs with limed wattle and daub interior walls. The ceiling was almost as high as the room was wide and, together with the tall, narrow window openings, gave the impression of an English country church. Commander Gilkisson had hung a portrait of Queen

Victoria in the room for the duration of the court hearing. She glared across the several officers sitting in the front row of seats to where Ole Sadera and Mantira sat together on a bench along the opposite wall.

Behind the officers were arranged a motley collection of chairs and benches, occupied by the witnesses and spectators. At the front of the room Mr Frederick Jackson sat at a large table. A Union Jack was pinned to the wall behind him.

Neither Ole Sadera nor Mantira understood what was happening during the morning session, but during the lunch break — when they were given jerky beef and a flask of water — the court interpreter, a Keekonyokie Maasai from Magadi, explained the proceedings. Jackson had heard from the witnesses that the Maasai had killed four hundred and eighty-six men in the Swahili caravan; and that Trader Dick had led a punitive mission against the Maasai, but himself had been killed along with many of his band.

'Did he ask why the Maasai did this? Does he know that we were avenging two of our women?' Ole Sadera asked.

'No. The British are slow in making their decisions. They go creeping, creeping. They speak so many words and say nothing. Even I can not understand them and I have been interpreter at many of these trials.'

'What happens if they find we were wrong to kill these people?' Mantira asked.

'Ah, in that case the British are swift. You will be shot. Tomorrow.'

'Ask Mr Ole Sadera why he took his warriors into the Kedong Valley on 26 November,' Jackson told the Keekonyokie interpreter during the afternoon session. 'Tell him that we have heard that two Maasai women were taken unwillingly and quite possibly detained against their will. What I want to know is, why did he feel that slaughtering hundreds of the men of the caravan was necessary to retrieve the situation.'

When the interpreter had finished his question, Ole Sadera looked at Jackson for a long moment, trying to read his mind. In the stillness of the courtroom, Jackson had lost none of the qualities that had been apparent when they had met on the edge of the Great Rift Valley. Ole Sadera also saw in his expression a genuine interest to know and understand.

He made his reply, with the interpreter periodically interrupting to translate.

'First let me say that our women cannot be treated like cattle. They cannot be taken from their village and used by men who think it is their right because they are many in number. The elders of the village made this known to the men of the caravan, but they beat the old men and showed no respect. Because they were of the Kikuyu tribe, our great enemies, they dishonoured the elders by such treatment.

'When we heard of this atrocity and came to the village, the elders begged us to show restraint. But that is not what you have asked. You have asked me why we must kill so many to save so few. I believe by your appearance that you are a soldier, Mr Jackson. If not, you have the look about you of a man who knows the way of battle. I sent forward as many men as I could gather in the vicinity of the caravan yet we were still a thousand fewer than them. To send a smaller force would almost certainly have been to send them to their death, and for what gain? It would only embolden our enemy and reveal our tactics, making the end battle even more bloody and prolonged.

'If the *askaris* in the caravan had retreated and sent back our women, they might have avoided what followed; but they didn't. As a commander of men in battle, you would know that once it is joined in earnest, nothing but a decisive victory will end it.

'We killed a great number of Swahilis and Kikuyu, that is true, but we did heed our elders' advice for restraint. If we had not, all one thousand four hundred would now be lying dead in the Kedong Valley.'

Ole Sadera and Mantira were led to the gates of Fort Smith, given their *simis* and spears, and told by the *askaris* that they could leave. For a moment they did not move, uncertain if they had correctly understood the *askaris*' gestures. When the gate was closed behind them, they realised they were free.

When he and Mantira reached the rise that would take Fort Smith from their sight, Ole Sadera turned back for one last look, trying to fathom the outcome of the trial under the British justice system.

'I think you are right, Mantira. I am truly a dunghead. I understood nothing of what happened there. Did you?'

'Nothing,' Mantira replied with a shrug.

Ole Sadera shook his head at the wonder of it all. Here was a government so profoundly powerful that it could afford generosity. Not the generosity of gift-giving so that a favour might be won, but the generosity of spirit that dispensed justice equally between its friends and its enemies.

He admired them for it, but in the back of his mind he began to idly search for strategies that might defeat such a power.

*   *   *

Memorandum
From: Frederick Jackson
Officer-in-Charge
Eldama Ravine Station
For the attention of:
Secretary of State for Foreign and Imperial Affairs
Lord Salisbury
22 January 1896
Sir,
Further to my correspondence to you on 2 January 1896 regarding the events of 26 November 1895 in the Kedong Valley, and subsequent events near Mt Margaret two days thereafter, I wish to report the following.

After conferring with my colleague Mr Ainsworth, who shares my views, I can say that there can be no possible doubt that the behaviour of the caravan as a whole was abominable and that the Maasai received the greatest provocation.

Furthermore, Mr Andrew Dick acted precipitously and foolishly in conducting his punitive raid. Consequently, the

Maasai were forced to meet force with force in defence of their property.

I therefore had no cause to take action against the Maasai. However, recognising the severity of the Maasai attack on Mr Dick's reprisal raid, I indicated our expectations for restraint in future by confiscating the herd excised by Mr Dick and distributing it among the dependants of the deceased Wakikuyu porters.

What I would now like to draw to Your Lordship's attention is that in the course of my journey to Fort Smith I came upon two moran who came bravely forward offering signs of peace. They were members of the local Purko section, normally in residence around Naivasha but, depending upon seasonal conditions, they may wander as far as the Laikipia Plateau. The men were Mantira, leader of the Il Talala age set, and Parsaloi Ole Sadera, leader of the junior Il Tuati age set.

Sadera admitted to the attack on the caravan as well as on Dick's abortive reprisal mission. Although I have now had the opportunity to question many about the incidents, Sadera was the first to explain to me the circumstances leading to both attacks. I must say that he is not typical of his race. He is not as tall as some, wiry of limb with quite a long, forlorn face, although when the mood takes him he can display a quite engaging smile. For all his physical dissimilarities, he obviously shares his tribe's sense of self-esteem; what some may call arrogance. I would even go further to say that he struck me as a man of undeniable strength of character. Unlike many natives, who appear to be evasive, even timid in the presence of authority, Sadera showed none of that. I was immediately of the impression that here was a natural leader; one we would be wise to cultivate as a leader of supporting resources in operations against such an intractable people as the Nandi.

Yours sincerely,
Frederick Jackson
Officer-in-Charge
Eldama Ravine Station

CHAPTER 6

1903

Wadley leaned over the large map of British East Africa spread out over Sir Charles Eliot's conference table and deftly ruled a few pencilled lines to enclose a portion of the yellow area labelled *Great Rift Valley*. 'This is the area allocated to the South Africans,' he said.

Eliot, the Commissioner of British East Africa, approved of Wadley's meticulous attention to detail. Whether it was in his correspondence, his manner or even his personal dress, the man was thoroughly proper. Eliot had no doubt that the area the Assistant Deputy Commissioner had marked on the map was exactly the size and position that Eliot had promised to his South African land agent. Fifty square miles, or thirty-two thousand acres, of which ten thousand would be made freehold after five years at a cost of eight pence an acre. The agent had lost no time in selling lots on the Johannesburg exchange. There had already been a flood of applications from well-heeled British South Africans keen to settle in the protectorate.

Eliot nodded. 'And show me again, if you would be so kind, the route we will use to remove the Maasai from that area.'

Wadley took a crayon and drew a broad line from the leasehold land in the Great Rift Valley northward to the Laikipia Plateau — a large area far removed from the valley, and another to an area to the south on the German East Africa border.

'The proposed northern reserve is almost unoccupied except for a few dozen miserable Boer families trying to scratch out a living from smallholdings. The southern area is already occupied by a few Maasai tribes. Lord knows why. It's mostly barren. I shouldn't imagine it would interest even the most desperate white farmer.'

Eliot nodded again. The plan was good but not without its challenges. There was a Foreign Office policy that freehold offers of more than a thousand acres had to be approved by London. However, given the precedent set by Sir Clement Hill, who had leased ten times that amount to his nephew, Eliot felt no qualms about cutting red tape to get things moving. The real issue was finding the resources to move the Maasai. Eliot would need men to supervise the move, and supplies for the few months it would take. There was also transport for both men and supplies — horses, wagons and oxen — and he had no budget for any of it.

Whatever the shortcomings of the Foreign Office in creative endeavour or empathy for those labouring in the far-flung corners of the empire, they were absolute wizards at reading financial reports. Every task of administration or development had to be approved at budget time, and every penny spent had to be costed against a line item in that budget. Begrudging approval was generally given to make small adjustments to budget for unforeseen events, but these generated far too much attention in the Foreign Office.

Eliot asked the ever-efficient Wadley if he had found a way around this problem too.

'We have approved funding to compensate natives forced from their land for white-owned farms,' Wadley said in reply.

'Of course we do. A hundred acres here or there. But how does that help us find the extra three thousand pounds needed to move all the damned Maasai?'

'So far, we've only used that line item to pay the Kikuyu for land outside Nairobi, sir. The Maasai have not been involved in that process to date. Using the old adage that what the heart doesn't know, the head cannot ponder, may I suggest, Sir Charles, that we use that compensation allocation a little more imaginatively?'

Eliot smiled. It would not be an acquisition as such, and therefore the Foreign Office would not be aware of how the Rift Valley land had become available for large land grants — the type that wealthy prospective settlers would find attractive.

He was tickled by the plan: there was a certain irony in having the Maasai pay for their own banishment.

Sir Charles Eliot scrutinised the man sitting opposite him. He couldn't understand how a British peer could allow his appearance to degenerate to the level Lord Delamere had. He understood that Delamere was the outdoors type, as they were so quaintly described, but there was really no excuse for the stained shirt, the frayed trouser cuffs and the ridiculous hat — twice the size any respectable Englishman would wear. And the hair — wild, uncombed, probably unwashed, and sticking out in long reddish wispy tufts.

Eliot was a scholar and a gentleman. He had won most of the awards for academic achievement contested at Oxford before taking up a post in the diplomatic service. He was fluent in a score of foreign languages and a world expert on the sea slug. His appointment as commissioner in British East Africa had surprised many, including — some were bold enough to suggest — Eliot himself. It was now his unfortunate duty to deal with such colonial types as Lord Delamere.

Delamere had been harassing him about his request for a land lease at Njoro in the Great Rift Valley. The valley, and all the country to the west of it to Lake Victoria, had been excised from Uganda and added to the territory of British East Africa the previous year. As commissioner, Eliot had the power to grant leases and small freehold grants, and there were quite a few interested parties. He had already decided to grant Delamere 100,000 acres, and his neighbour — Gilbert Colchester — a large lease of land, but he didn't want it to appear too easy. He decided to probe a little more into what Delamere had in mind for the land.

He interrupted his visitor's droning monologue. 'Did you say something about a permanent native reserve, Lord Delamere?'

'I did. It doesn't make sense to build a five million pound railway line and have nothing use it until it reaches Uganda. The Maasai will never repay that investment — they wouldn't sell a cow to save their souls. They should be granted a suitable reserve and let get on with their simple way of life. We need settlers along the railway line — people who know how to work the land and are prepared to put in a solid day's work to make it productive.'

'Certainly, I agree with you there, Lord Delamere. East Africa is not an ordinary colony. It's practically an estate belonging to His Majesty's government. I also agree that the highlands around the Rift Valley are pre-eminently a white man's country. But surely there will be trouble with the Maasai?'

'The Maasai are a spent force, Commissioner. They were already reduced by their internal wars before the smallpox took more than half of them. I employ a few dozen of them on my present holdings. Incomparable cattlemen. Pity about their thieving ways. The days when any section of them could raise a standing army of a thousand warriors are long gone.'

'Not according to the reports from my predecessor. What about that beastly business in the Kedong Valley back in '95? What was it — four, five hundred murdered? There are hundreds of skeletons still scattered all over the valley.'

'There was extreme provocation there, Commissioner. It was a Swahili and Kikuyu caravan, poorly led, and the porters ran amok, taking liberties with the Maasai women.'

'Never mind the blacks. There was an English chap who got speared.'

'That was Trader Dick, a hothead who charged in to take reprisal without stopping to ask for the facts. Some say he had his eye on the Maasai cattle rather than on justice.'

'Hmm, I see. Well, getting back to the matter at hand — your application for a lease. You've been nothing if not persistent.'

'That's correct. I've been applying for a grant of land since I arrived, but with no luck.'

'Because of the issue of Maasai land rights?'

'Exactly. Maasai *bloody* land rights. I'm sick of hearing about them. What about the rights of the people who want to see the country progress? Those of us who would extend Mother England's influence into the wilderness?'

'There is no need to distress yourself, Lord Delamere. I am offering you a lease of one hundred thousand acres.'

* * *

Memorandum
   From: Frederick Jackson
              Officer-in-Charge
              Eldama Ravine Station
  For the attention of:
     Secretary of State for Foreign and Imperial Affairs
     Lord Lansdowne
  22 February 1904
  Sir,

This is in response to your request for my assessment of the Maasai situation in British East Africa as it continues to unfold. When you made your request during my home leave, you asked that I speak frankly, and I hasten to state that these are indeed my personal thoughts about matters that I believe may be at odds with views held by others here in the Protectorate.

The issue that concerns me is the present policy of granting long-term leases to settlers in the Great Rift Valley. There are influential people here and elsewhere that would have Your Lordship believe that there are limitless expanses of unoccupied land available for settlements. In fact, the truth is that the land is already occupied by the Maasai albeit in a semi-nomadic manner. The Maasai move about their territory depending on seasonal variations. They also manage endemic stock diseases by vacating fouled land until it becomes free of the disease. Therefore under this sensible husbandry, the Rift Valley is presently fully utilised by the Maasai.

The Maasai will never give us serious trouble so long as we treat them fairly and do not deprive them of their best grazing grounds. Up to the time I left Mombasa on leave,

*the large grazing areas applied for in the Naivasha district
were 320,000 acres by the East Africa Syndicate, 100,000
acres by Lord Delamere and 32,000 acres each by Messrs
Chamberlain and Flemmer. I pointed out to Sir Charles
Eliot that these areas not only incorporated the most
favoured grazing grounds of the Maasai between Lakes
Nakuru and Naivasha, but also embraced both banks of
the only four rivers in the vicinity.*

*Apart from the just cause for complaint that removal
from the Rift Valley would give the Maasai, it would be a
great mistake to push them to one side and away from the
close vicinity and control of the government stations.*

*I predict there may be trouble in future years should this
policy proceed to the extent that some would have it.*

*I trust Your Lordship will see value in my suggestion
that the Foreign Office intervene in these matters.*

Yours sincerely,
Frederick Jackson
Deputy Commissioner

'Insubordinate ingrate,' Commissioner Eliot muttered,
throwing the letter onto his desk in disgust. 'Such utter
disloyalty.'

The memorandum had been copied to him by a well-meaning
friend at the Foreign Office with the intention of keeping him
informed and therefore prepared for eventualities. However, it
fed Eliot's growing paranoia that there was a plot afoot by a
few men — officials and others who should know better — to
undermine his vision for East Africa.

Of all those voicing concerns about Eliot's recent and most
ambitious plans, Fred Jackson would be heard above all others.
He was greatly respected by many in power in England. He had
served the protectorate well since its inception, and before that
had worked for Mackinnon in the Imperial British East Africa
Company.

Eliot wasn't surprised by Jackson's attitude. Like many of the
old-timers, Jackson had a sentimental view of the natives and
their place in the life of the protectorate. What did surprise him

was that Jackson had felt sufficiently motivated to write to their political master about it.

It was also disturbing to learn that Lansdowne had solicited Jackson's view. Was there no end to the duplicity of politicians? Lansdowne had not shown any indication that he was less than enthusiastic about his commissioner's broad objectives. Eliot could only imagine there was some skulduggery taking place in the corridors of power, causing cabinet ministers to lower their colours.

'Damned cowards.'

Eliot's jawline was taut with pent-up tension. He ran a hand to the back of his neck and kneaded the aching muscles there, reminding himself that he must remain focused if he was to achieve his objectives.

Since becoming commissioner in 1900, he had been determined to avoid the kind of woes that had befallen Britain's emerging and most promising new colonies. In South Africa, it was the illiterate and ignorant Boers who had driven the country to war twice in the last quarter of a century. In Australia, where the utter dregs of society had been sent under the British penal system, there had been nothing but trouble, beginning with a miners' rebellion in the gold fields.

Eliot was determined to avoid similar errors in British East Africa by populating it with a better class of immigrant — men who could bring expertise to the land, or at least capital, which would be needed in considerable amounts if they were to tame it. Such men would rightfully expect a decent land grant and the usual government services. Most importantly, they would expect the government to keep the natives at a distance other than as a supply of labour.

He picked up the offending letter, crushed it in his hands and threw it at the wall. Whatever else happened, he was determined to press ahead.

CHAPTER 7

'That's a nasty cough you've got there, laddie.'

George Coll wiped his mouth and streaming eyes with his kerchief, stuffed it back in his pocket and, as the tears cleared, regarded the man standing beside him at the ship's rail. He was grey-haired and wore a well-cut suit and waistcoat. Coll's own suit was in need of a stitch or, better yet, a new pair of trousers, but there had been no money for that in Cape Town.

'It's this blasted sea air, sir. Gets into my chest.' He gave the ribs on his narrow chest a gentle thump.

'Norman Lewis.' The gentleman extended his hand. Coll guessed he was about twenty years senior to him, perhaps fifty years of age, but he looked the type who would always appear fit.

'How do you do? I'm George Coll. I saw you get on at Chinde.'

'That's right. Been there since '01. Time to move on. Two years in a rat hole is enough for anyone.'

Coll followed Lewis's eyes to the Portuguese East Africa coastline. 'You didn't like Chinde?'

'Oh, it's not so bad. When you've worked in the Glasgow slums you'd be tossed to find worse.'

'Glasgow, eh? I haven't seen much of Chinde — just what a man can learn in a half-day tied up at the wharf — but from what I know of Glasgow, I'd have to agree.'

'Then you've seen Glasgow?'

'I was a student there around ten or so years ago.'

Lewis turned to him. 'So was I. Well, it was more than ten years ago. Glasgow University. The medical college.'

'I attended the veterinary school.'

'We're in the same field then, just different patients,' Lewis said.

Coll smiled. 'I didn't finish my course. I had to leave Glasgow. The weather damn near killed me.'

'Aye, it's bitter.' Lewis shook his head sadly. 'How some of those poor buggers in the slums survive winter I'll never know. Of course, hundreds never make it to spring.' He was silent for a while, studying the retreating coast. 'The government could be doing more for those poor wretches in the slums, but what do those good Tory gentlemen with their fancy London addresses and Scottish country estates care? In my experience, there's a direct link between poverty and ill health. The evidence is overwhelming.' He turned back to Coll. 'Sorry, I'm getting on my high horse again.'

'No need to be sorry. I imagine you're quite right about that.'

Coll remembered his own time in Glasgow; lumping coal on the black-ice roads between university classes. His grandfather had said the hard work might strengthen his chest, but after a year or so young Coll had felt that if the bitter cold didn't kill him, the coal dust would. He'd been advised to quit the damp cold of the British Isles and head to the more benign climate of Africa or Australia.

'Aye,' Lewis continued, seeming encouraged by Coll's comment, 'there's movement afoot to change all that. Plenty are now saying it's time to share the wealth around. And not just for the poor at home. What about in these parts?' He gestured towards the African coast. 'If the empire can buy the raw materials of trade, they can pay a little to improve health conditions. And education.'

Coll was not of any particular political persuasion, and while he shared Lewis's sympathy for the underprivileged, the man's harsh words against the British government made him feel uncomfortable. He changed the subject.

'So you're a doctor?' he said.

'Aye. Off to Mombasa to take up a position with the government there.'

'So am I. There was a chap from East Africa down in Cape Town, spruiking the great opportunities to be had on the land.' Coll had been interested, but found Commissioner Eliot's requirement that applicants for land grants had to hold assets of at least three hundred pounds well beyond his capability. 'I'm no farmer, but I reckoned where there were farmers there'd be farm animals. I have been promised a job as a stock inspector.'

'It sounds very interesting,' Lewis replied. 'Where will you be stationed?'

'I'm not sure. Apparently, the natives have huge herds but no idea how to treat stock diseases. The authority doesn't want the new settlers' stock to inherit whatever beasties the native cattle carry. So I'm to tour an area making inspections. The agent in Cape Town called it Maasailand.'

George Coll removed the kettle from the fire and poured its boiling water into the teapot. Then he added the tea, waited until he counted to thirty and gave the pot a sharp tap with a spoon. He took his steaming enamelled mug to where he had spread his groundsheet beside a boulder. He could feel the rock's residual warmth through his shirt as he leaned against it, contentedly sipped his tea and gazed out over the darkened landscape.

The moon had poked its face above the Kikuyu Escarpment and sent shimmering silver ribbons across the distant surface of Lake Naivasha where, away in the darkness, a bull hippo bellowed its territorial claims.

For a long time he had agonised over his decision to apply for the job in East Africa. It was so far from home. What would he do if he changed his mind and wanted to go back? He had spent his last penny on the fare over. But after four months, he'd settled in well, and the pain of separation from the familiar surroundings of home were receding.

There was so much to do as the stock inspector in Maasailand, but he felt he was making progress. His regular reports to Commissioner Eliot in Nairobi seemed to be well received. Not only that, they were followed up by actions, including approval for him to commence his disease control program. In the morning he would continue along the Great Rift Valley to Nakuru, where he would supervise the first stock dip.

Coll was a believer in the new theory that cattle ticks were the carriers of many of the diseases affecting livestock. It would take time to convince the Maasai of the benefits of the dip, which was one of the reasons he was learning Maa — the Maasai language. By explaining the theory in their own language, and countering their reservations about it, he was confident he would eventually win them over to the modern techniques.

The moon glided behind a thick cloud — one of the few guarding the star-studded sky. The hippo bellowed again, this time receiving a belligerent reply from a nearby rival.

Coll sipped his tea and stared into the fire. Although he had yet to become acclimatised to the heat, he knew it was good for his medical condition. The warm dry air of the valley seemed to be helping him throw off his persistent cough. Overall, he felt at home and at peace with himself. More so than at any other time of his life.

'What do you mean, they won't drive their cattle in?' Coll spluttered.

'Just like I said. They don't trust the dip,' the assistant district commissioner replied.

The ADC was a wiry old ex-poacher who had made some money in the ivory business before the Belgians had clamped down on the chaotic situation in the Lado Enclave north of Uganda.

'But it's perfectly safe.'

The ADC merely smiled and took a pull on a wad of tobacco.

His attitude was infuriating. Coll would not be fobbed off so casually. 'The district commissioner said you would arrange for the Maasai to get their cattle dipped,' he persisted.

'He said I was to get the Maasai and their cattle *to* the dip.' Nodding towards the dozen or so old Maasai men and boys, he added, 'There they are. Reckon there's more'n a hundred cows there for you to make a start on.' He released a stream of tobacco juice.

'Very well,' Coll said, marching towards the nearest of the herders. 'Now, you men, I want you to drive your cattle through that gate.'

The elders' eyes followed his extended hand then returned to stare sullenly at him.

'Drive your cattle,' he said, pointing emphatically at the herd, 'over there, to the gate.'

They again followed his hand, and again remained unmoved.

Coll thought his rudimentary Maa was not ready for a trial under such circumstances, but desperate times called for desperate actions.

'*In kishu*,' he said, again pointing at the cattle. '*Emugur*,' indicating the dip.

Spontaneous laughter erupted.

Coll, flustered, searched his limited vocabulary. He was confident he'd said 'cattle' and 'water hole'. Perhaps it was the pronunciation.

One of the elders, trying to control his mirth, rattled off a series of remarks that set Coll's head spinning. He detected a few familiar words and phrases. 'Unhealthy' was one, and words literally meaning to remove a covering. They were telling him they thought his dirty water would skin the hide from their cows.

The ADC, leaning against one of the dip's fenceposts, wore an irritating grin. Coll ignored him.

'No, no,' he said, returning to the speaker, 'the water is very good, very healthful.'

More laughter.

Coll was floundering with his Maa syntax and thought perhaps he might have said, 'Your water' — the man's urine — 'is very healthy for cows.'

In desperation, he said, 'I will show you,' and marched to the dip. He swung the gate aside and waded into the foul-smelling water. It was deeper than he had expected and he almost immediately disappeared from sight.

When he surfaced, the Maasai were in stitches. Coll could barely see the funny side but kept a grim smile on his face as he dragged himself from the dip.

He waited until he had the elders' attention again and insisted they examine his flesh for any signs of damage. This they did soberly, as much to humour him, he imagined, as out of genuine interest.

'Healthful,' he said again in Maa.

This elicited a nod and a wry smile from some of the elders. There followed what appeared to be an earnest debate among the Maasai, which lasted for some twenty minutes. They then dispersed. Coll expected that they'd had enough of his tomfoolery and had decided to attend to more important matters.

The ADC strolled up to him, a knowing smile on his smug face.

But before he could make any comment, the Maasai returned with their cattle and drove them through the gates and into the dip.

Elephants had broken into the bottom acres of maize the previous night and in the morning the cattle had discovered the hole in the fence and made matters worse. One of her Kikuyu farm workers had been cut by a strand of fencing wire when he tried to chase the elephant away. Permanganate of potash and a clean bandage would see him right, but the morning had gone by the time she had rounded up the cattle and moved them to the southern pasture.

Katherine Wallace pressed her hands into her lower back and stretched. Around her the Kikuyu women's colourful bandanas bobbed among the maize as they tried to encourage the many bent and broken stalks to stand again.

She sighed. Again. It had become a frequent habit. If it wasn't the difficulties of growing a crop or raising stock, it was keeping Africa — be it ruminant or predator — on the other side of the fence. Thereafter, she was at the mercy of the markets before she knew if all her work had been worthwhile.

Katherine looked up at the sun. There was the fence to mend before dark, which meant she would have to leave taking the eggs to the local Limuru market until the following day.

Where was Bill when she needed him?

Katherine took a deep breath and let her shoulders relax as she watched the sun slip slowly behind the purple hills that sat above the boundary of the farm. She rested her hands on the lacquered buffet under the window, letting the events of the day recede with its passing. She was tired, but strangely at peace.

She resisted the call of old memories. It was not good to reflect upon the past too often. She recalled that she had come to the buffet to pour herself a well-earned sherry. As her hand went to the cut-glass decanter, the dying rays of sun caught the plain gold band on her finger. She searched for reassurance in the mirror above the buffet that her face was not as lined as her hands appeared in that unkind light. But what could be expected when a couple tried to coax a living from the unsympathetic soil of Africa?

The mirror revealed the delicate sculpture of her cheekbones, the bright, intelligent, flint-blue eyes. If there was any grey in her abundant, almost shoulder-length fair hair it had yet to reveal itself. She tentatively pressed her fingers into her cheek. The skin was soft and the flesh firm but yielding to the touch.

A woman is not finished at forty, she recalled her mother saying. During her teens, she'd found it hard to believe.

She lit the paraffin lantern, poured a sherry, and took it to the cupboard that held the shellac gramophone records. She drew out one of their favourites from its brown-paper sleeve and placed it on the player, which stood on its very own purpose-built cedarwood table. She gave the player a few cranks and carefully lowered the needle to the record. The slightly scratchy sounds of the stringed introduction began as she took her sherry to the best piece of furniture in the house — the horsehair-padded two-seater sofa that she and Bill had shared in their rare idle moments. It was one of their prized possessions. They had bought it in Whitechapel Road and had it shipped to British East Africa as soon as they had settled. She lowered her weary body into it and leaned her head back, allowing the voice of Harry Lauder to soothe her.

> *In summer when the sun is bright,*
> *When frost and snow have taken flight,*
> *It is MacKay's and my delight*
> *Like travellers in a story,*
> *To go exploring here and there*
> *In search of pleasure and fresh air;*
> *So last year for our holidays we went to Tobermory.*

The song was one of Bill's favourites, and might well have described their married life together. It had been Bill's delight 'to go exploring here and there' too. In his case, it was to find a place where they could settle and make a good living, rather than Lauder's search for 'pleasure and fresh air'. That was how Bill had described it, at least, although there were times when Katherine had wondered how anyone could find a place to settle in some of the lands he had taken them to. Australia and South Africa were reasonable choices, and in both Bill had tried his hand at gold-mining, with modest success; but she'd had her doubts about Paraguay and Venezuela from the outset. She couldn't remember what Bill had said would be their bonanza in South America, but he wouldn't be Bill unless he had three or four schemes up his sleeve.

The Turkana country in the semi-desert two hundred and fifty miles north of Nairobi was another of his unlikely choices. It had been almost unknown territory when they'd filled a bullock wagon with all their possessions and set off with little more than a sketch map to find their land.

Turkana was a harsh, savagely beautiful country and nothing like what they had expected. It wasn't good for much else but trading store-bought goods with the Turkana and Pokot in exchange for skins and ivory. Bill tried his hand at hunting when there was game nearby, but he drew the line at leaving Katherine alone for more than two or three weeks at a time, although Katherine insisted she could manage. When he returned from his hunting trips, dusty and smelling of sweat and the musty odour of animal hides, their lovemaking was as wild and untamed as the land.

Turkana was the most isolated place imaginable, but Katherine had found this the very essence of its strange magnetic appeal. She discovered there a great ability to live comfortably with only herself for company, although she almost always drew a small crowd of mystified natives whenever she brought out her gramophone and let Harry Lauder's Scottish brogue drift across the desert. The tall, elegant Turkana would stand in utter silence for as long as Katherine was content to crank the gramophone's mechanism and place one disc after another on its spinning table. Word spread, and soon the short, naked Pokots began appearing from nowhere to marvel at the voices and the skirl of the pipes. She and Bill had persevered for more than a year in Turkana with scant rewards.

Katherine didn't really blame Bill for trying and failing in so many places. During the first fifteen years of their married life she learned to live with it because she knew Bill was searching for something, and was realistic enough to understand that if she tried to stop him he might have gone off anyway. She didn't want to harness his adventurous spirit, and hoped her motivation was love rather than the plain fear of being left alone if she tried.

Looking back on those days, there had been a great many difficulties but great excitement too. She could berate or thank Bill for them, depending upon her mood. Their only real regret, and one they seldom mentioned even to each other, was the loss of their only child, Billy. The boy was conceived in Australia, born in Paraguay and laid to rest just six years later in Venezuela. Katherine hated Venezuela for the black water fever that had claimed her son, but she couldn't bear to leave South America, and Billy, behind. Eventually Bill had convinced her they must move on, so they had sailed to Africa to make a new start and to try to forget.

Oh! My! You ought to have seen MacKay
And me, for we were fairly in our glory,
For we roamed about together

Among the bonnie blooming heather,
With the bonnie lassies up in Tobermory.

After so many years roaming in search of an elusive wee patch to call their own, Limuru had come as a blessing. The work was hard, especially when they were obliged by their lease conditions to clear so much land each year and to make capital improvements to the satisfaction of the government, but soon the rich red soil of the Kikuyu hills began to yield its rewards. They managed to achieve two good years in their first three, which was better than they'd ever done. They had also begun to raise sheep and cattle, with promising results.

It wasn't until they had arrived at their farm there in Limuru that Bill finally decided he'd had enough of wandering and felt it time to settle. Not that he'd ever expressed that much to Katherine. She doubted Bill knew himself he'd made the decision, but she knew it. Bill had found peace and, knowing her man had finally found his home, Katherine found peace too.

Their future was looking secure, but Katherine sensed that Bill needed something more than the daily ritual of hard work occasionally punctuated by the small community's demure social events. She did something that she had never done in all their time together: she told him he needed to take some interest in himself, to find friends and activities more compatible with the adventurous side of his spirit.

And when the time for parting came,
The tears ran down Mack's cheeks like rain,
Yon night we be remembered by the lassie in Tobermory.

Katherine both loved and hated evenings like this, when the day had been particularly trying and the soul demanded a sherry and the sepia-coloured memories of the past. But those memories also brought the bittersweet pain of loss.

After Bill's death, Katherine's married sister in Scotland had insisted that she come home. But she hadn't the heart for Scotland any more. Bill had shown her the world and a life so far removed from the heather and the hoarfrost, she thought it would be difficult to return.

But the real reason she was determined to stay was that having buried one loved one in a distant land and greatly regretting it later, she would not leave another to lie buried and alone so far from those who loved him.

CHAPTER 8

As a *morani*, Ole Sadera could not afford to show too much interest in the wedding ceremony in the *enkang*, but as it occurred while he was visiting a friend, it was permissible to pay a passing interest.

The bride was hidden from his view by the many women attendants surrounding her, a flurry of finery. A brief opening allowed him to catch sight of her beautiful tanned sheepskin garment studded with coloured beads, and the beaded bridal collar with coloured strings that reached to her knees, but he could not see her face.

She was lost to him again as the women swirled about her, fussing to arrange her accessories as they ushered her towards the gate. She was about to leave her mother's *enkang* and join her groom, an elder from the next village. Ole Sadera had hoped for a final glimpse of her but the crowd was all about her, tying tufts of green grass to the tails of her cloak for luck.

'Don't look back,' he'd warned her the last time they'd met. 'The old women say it will turn you to stone.'

'I don't want to go.'

'You must. Your family have accepted all the dowry gifts since you were a child.'

'Then I *will* turn back. I would rather be with you in stone than in his village without you.'

Ole Sadera had said nothing. He later regretted his silence, but until that moment he hadn't realised the depth of her emotions. He should have told her how glad he was to hear her words, and how much their time together meant to him. Now it was too late.

He watched the women swarm through the gate, leading Nashilo away while singing the bawdy songs people sang at weddings. She turned, and his breath caught in his chest as her eyes met his. Her silver earrings and the finely studded collar framed her beautiful face. In the brief moment before the women realised she had turned back, she stood in the gate opening, embracing him with her gaze.

Then, with a great deal of caterwauling, the women reclaimed her and whisked her away, praying now to Enkai not to punish her young foolishness.

He watched the procession disappear from sight over the rolling hills towards her new husband's *enkang*. Then he too walked out the gate, to return to the *moran's manyatta*.

Katherine noticed the young African girl as she was weeding the coffee plantation with the Kikuyu women. She was quite noticeably different from the other children. For a start, she didn't look like a Kikuyu. She was long-limbed and a little gawky as a result of it. Her clothes were in tatters. She didn't play with the other children, although she was of an age — probably around eight or nine — when an occasional childish game, rather than weeding, was tolerated. And she looked sad. There was something in her manner that set her apart; as if she inhabited a small space that she had determinedly made her own to the exclusion of all others. Katherine recognised in the girl something of her own inclination to avoid dealing with other people.

After a couple of weeks, she asked one of the women who understood a little English whom the tall child belonged to.

'This strange one, *memsabu*?' the woman said, pointing at the child. 'She nobody's, *memsabu*.'

'Nobody's? But how can that be?'

'She belong some Maasai place, *memsabu*. Now she nobody.'

Katherine was intrigued by the situation and prised the girl's story from the Kikuyu woman piece by laborious piece.

There had been a Kikuyu reprisal raid, some years ago, on a Maasai village. The girl was captured, along with a number of cattle and goats. Eventually the administration came in and settled the ongoing repercussions. Property was returned where practicable, and compensation paid where appropriate, but somehow the girl had been overlooked. She was, after all, a minor trophy, destined to be offered to some aging Kikuyu man in need of a young wife to tend his vegetable garden and warm his bed.

Katherine guessed that her concern about the displaced Maasai girl stemmed from her own present state of mind, but she couldn't stop thinking about her. It took several more visits to the coffee plantation before she finally approached the girl.

'Hello,' she said, startling the child, who had apparently been lost within her own world as she weeded.

The girl stared into Katherine's eyes for a moment before dropping her gaze to her feet.

'I have something for you,' Katherine said encouragingly. 'Do you speak English?'

After a long silent moment she answered her own question. 'It doesn't appear so.'

She crouched beside the girl so that she was in her line of sight. 'Look. For you.'

The girl looked first at Katherine and then at the orange, staring at it as a pup might stare at a bone.

Katherine offered it to her, but it took time for the girl to comprehend. Her small thin hand went to it hesitantly at first, then with conviction. She held the orange before her, looking from it to Katherine.

Katherine said her name, pointing to herself. 'And you?' she asked, pointing at the child. It took several attempts to convey the meaning. Finally the girl said 'Katherine', in response to the pointing finger, and then, reluctantly, 'Kira', when it was pointed in her direction.

'Hello,' Katherine said. 'You may not know it, Kira, but we are alike, you and I. We have both lost all we have. I can't think of a better reason to become friends, can you?'

After further gesturing from Katherine, Kira bit into the orange, including the peel. Juice trickled down her chest, but her wide dark eyes remained fixed on the white woman.

It took Kira only a day or so to realise that Katherine intended her no harm. It took a few more to know that the small bed in the kitchen annexe, warm and safe, would be her new home, but more than a week to learn her duties in the running of the house and *shamba* — the small garden Katherine kept to supply the household with vegetables. She quickly understood the *shamba* work — it was no different to that done with the Kikuyu women on a larger scale — but the inside workings of a white person's house were an odd concoction of procedures that remained incomprehensible for many weeks. Even after she understood the routines, the reasons remained elusive.

Kira could not understand why Katherine needed more than one pot to prepare her meals. There were also many metal instruments used to prepare the food and others to consume it. These had to be placed in precise positions on the table, surrounded by cloth napkins, and the spicy additives that white people added to their meals.

Removing the dust from the small fragile items that were seldom, if ever, used, seemed a pointless exercise. When Kira dropped a small figurine soon after Katherine explained how she should clean them, it exposed their truly delicate nature. The item fractured into a score of jagged shards on the bare floor boards. Katherine's expression of shock then sadness concealed behind a brave smile revealed to Kira that while useless, the items were cherished. She learnt to be more careful after that.

She trembled in fear when dusting the four frames that captured the images of people behind a window of glass. In one of them was a girl about her own age, seated on a large padded chair. She was dressed in a dark tunic and her fair hair was cut to a sharp line sitting just above her white lace collar. Clutched stiffly under an arm, clearly lifeless, was a small woolly animal with shining bead-like eyes. The girl looked remarkably like a younger version of Katherine, which did nothing to settle Kira's anxiety while going about her chores.

The box that squarked when Katherine cranked a handle also frightened her at first. Then the strange and beautiful sounds became familiar and when alone she would mimic the way Katherine moved in time with its unchanging tempo while humming in tune with its peculiar intonations.

Soon Kira was able to accept the changes to her life that had been thrust upon her. Although living with Katherine was much more comfortable than life with the Kikuyu, it was much further removed from the life she had left in the Great Rift Valley.

After she had recovered from the crushing grief of being taken from her family, Kira had adapted to life in the Kikuyu village quite quickly. There were many similarities between Maasai and Kikuyu society. The women of both tribes were entirely responsible for house building and maintenance, tending to the poultry and livestock, keeping the family fed and clothed, educating the children and tending to the sick. The men intervened only when matters were not to their liking. Kira understood these arrangements and needed only a small adjustment to conform to her new situation. This was not the case for life with Katherine.

Katherine let her know that when she had completed her chores she could occupy her time as she may. This was unheard of in a village, either Kikuyu or Maasai, where women were rarely allowed the luxury of leisure time. Kira soon learned that she need not have worried about how to occupy herself. Katherine made it clear that she expected her new housemaid to not only clean and attend to all the paraphernalia of a white's world, she had to know how to use them. More than that, she insisted she learn the indecipherable babble that they spoke.

The murram road to Limuru stretched ahead of Coll like a roll of rust-red ribbon that had spilled to the ground. It ran through the verdant green valleys before disappearing among the hills, winding past plantations of maize, bananas and coffee. Although the sun was yet to climb above the trees, the humidity was surprisingly low. He imagined it was the reason he'd slept so well, relatively free from the congestion in his chest that usually awoke him several times a night whenever he was at home in Nairobi.

Coll let the mare set her own pace between the buggy's spars. His trip to the Rift Valley was a routine one and, for once, free of any urgent business. He had decided to use the opportunity to make an inspection of one of the new farms along the way. Early in his appointment as stock inspector, he had developed a program of visits that would enable regular checks on all stock holdings. One of his most important tasks was to detect and arrest any contagious stock diseases before they spread to other herds and flocks. But there were too many new farms sprouting up, particularly in the hills above Nairobi, and too many extraneous duties like tending to the governor's need to know what the Maasai were doing in the valley. It became a matter of catch as catch can.

He turned the mare off the road through the open gate marked 'Tobermory' and, in smaller print, 'Wallace'. At the end of a rudimentary track was a typical farmhouse: a boxlike building with a veranda stuck on the front. There was a kitchen annexe, a barn and a small outhouse. Hens scattered as he drove towards a woman at the water tank filling a kettle.

'Good morning,' he called as he pulled the buggy to a halt.

'Morning to you,' she said, putting a hand to her back as she straightened.

He supposed she was a little more than middle-aged, perhaps forty, but he had never been good at judging a woman's age, particularly in Africa where the harsh climate and hard work usually added years.

'I'm George Coll, stock inspector for the Nairobi district,' he said, climbing down from the buggy. 'Just here on routine matters. Is your husband around?'

'No, but if it's about the animals, you could talk with me, I suppose.'

She put the kettle on the top step of the veranda and pushed an invisible strand of her golden hair into place among the others captured by a clasp at the back.

She had a fine Scottish accent, Coll noted, but, like many women on the land, she was very business-like, which didn't fit with the charming brogue. He was, in any case, uncomfortable around women and much preferred to deal with the men.

'Thank you,' he said. 'But I can come back at a more convenient time, if you'd prefer.'

'You can suit yourself. Won't do any good, though. It'll still be me you'd be talking to.'

'Oh.'

He liked the smile lines around her eyes, but wasn't sure if she was offended or concealing amusement at his discomfort.

She must have pitied his embarrassment, for she added, 'I'm a widow, if you must know.'

'I'm sorry, ma'am. It's just that —'

'Just that it's unusual to find a woman working a farm alone,' she said, guessing his thoughts. 'And for good reason.'

She didn't elaborate, nor did she need to. Coll had never heard of a woman single-handedly managing a farm. He didn't doubt it could be done, but from his observations, the task was often beyond experienced men.

The woman seemed to be studying him. 'I can't quite place your accent,' she said, wrinkling her brow. 'Are you a Scot or not?'

'Born in Liverpool, but raised by my grandfather in Lanarkshire, not far from bonny Glasgow.' He pronounced it *Glasgee* as the Glaswegians did.

'Well, aren't you the lucky one,' she said with a smile. 'You'd better come in the now. I was just putting the kettle on for a cuppa.'

He followed her up the steps into a room that on first sight appeared to be a sitting room, although an old cast-iron stove filled a large fireplace and a number of cooking utensils hung from the heavy mantel. A young black girl was idly pushing a broom around the floor.

'That'll do for now, Kira. I'll call you when I need you.'

The girl, wearing a straight white skirt and blue checked apron, nodded to Katherine and gave Coll a shy glance before leaving for the kitchen annexe.

The sitting room had a well-padded floral sofa — the only feminine touch in the room — four of the locally made rattan chairs standing at a large rectangular table, and a tall cupboard with lead-glazed doors that dominated one wall. Its feet stood in small water-filled vessels to stop the ants. Beside it was a gleaming gramophone player on a small wooden table. A number of what Coll assumed were family portraits hung on the walls.

The woman slid the iron cover from one hole in the stove. Flames licked at the kettle as she placed it over the hole.

'I always keep a fire going in here,' she said. 'It keeps away the chill of the evening. Won't you take a chair, Mr Coll.'

'George. Please.'

'George it is then. And I'm Katherine. Katherine Wallace.' She smiled.

They chatted about the unusually clement weather and farming trivia while the kettle boiled. Katherine told him that her lease covered one hundred and fifty acres, on which she had a few acres of the superior American maize, some wheat that had not done well, and potatoes that had. She had given up on sim sim, which appeared to be more palatable to elephants than to humans. The coffee bushes that she and her husband had planted soon after arriving were now bearing good berries, and she had plans to plant more next season. Her fifteen cattle and thirty sheep were doing well, but she was having trouble with a leopard at the moment.

The kettle whistled, and Katherine poured the tea.

Coll nodded to a photograph of a man with his foot on a big cat and a rifle hanging casually under an arm. 'That's not a leopard, is it?'

Katherine said no, it was a jaguar.

'The chap looks like a capable sort. Is he your husband?'

'He was,' she said. 'That was taken just outside Caracas. Bill was a good shot.'

'So how long have you been managing single-handed?'

'Bill passed away more than a year and a half ago,' she said.

'I'm sorry to hear that, Katherine. I suppose it was malaria or one of those other terrible things we all face out here.'

She shook her head and glanced up at the photograph again. 'It was a lion,' she said, showing no emotion other than a sad smile. 'As I said, Bill was a hunter, although he hadn't been able to spend much time hunting after we started the farm.'

Katherine described how the American, Paul Rainey, had introduced the sport of lion hunting with imported hounds.

Two dogs would be released to find the scent of a lion, and the remainder of the pack would be let loose to bail it up until the mounted hunters arrived to shoot it.

'I've heard of it, of course,' Coll said. 'They say it's the best way to be rid of a lion, but I understand it can be quite dangerous.'

'Yes,' Katherine said. 'It's one of the reasons Bill invited Rainey and the hunting club to our farm. A big black-maned male had been troubling our cattle for months. And you're right, it can be dangerous. If the lion goes to ground, as they often do, the hunter has to be very careful.'

Coll regretted his intrusion into such a personal matter. 'I shouldn't have asked,' he said. 'Perhaps we should talk about something else. It must be very distressing.'

'No, it's all right. Funny enough, this is the first time I've been able to speak about it to anyone. All our . . . all my friends tend to keep quiet about it and I'm not so sure that's a good idea.'

Coll fought the urge to fiddle with his cup. This sharing of acutely personal stories seemed particularly common in remote locations. It made him feel uncomfortable and helpless, but he always did his best to listen sympathetically. In this case, discussing personal matters with a woman — an attractive one at that, and alone — was something else. However, Katherine's frank manner and the control she seemed to have on her emotions made the situation less difficult and he soon became caught up in the story.

She told him that, typically, Bill had made his invitation to the hunting club conditional on him having first crack at the lion. After they'd found the pack of hounds, Bill had circled the thicket trying to spot the lion. On the far side of the circle — away from the other hunters — a couple of cowardly dogs had bolted. In their wake came the charging lion. It had knocked Bill down before he could level his rifle at it.

Katherine paused, looking down at her fingers as they played with her thin gold wedding band.

'Bill didn't die there,' she said. 'He received a terrible mauling but I really thought he might have survived. He had such . . . such a lot of *go* in him. But complications set in . . .'

For a horrid moment Coll thought she might break down, but she sniffed and cleared her throat before continuing.

'The doctor explained how a lion's claws have tiny grooves in them, which capture particles of the putrid flesh the lion feeds on.' She sounded almost clinical now, and searched Coll's eyes to see if he understood what she was trying to describe. 'It causes serious infections.'

Coll nodded.

'Bill finally gave up after fighting death for two weeks,' she said flatly.

Coll felt useless. 'I'm so sorry,' he said.

'Bill was a good man,' Katherine continued. 'He dragged me around the world for years, trying to satisfy whatever craving he had in his heart, and when he finally stopped, here in Africa, I thought we were settled. But then, as if to make up for all that running around, he worked and worked. He had no time for anything else; none of the fun he had enjoyed all his life. In the end I became worried about him and told him he had to do something with himself other than working from day to night, day in, day out.'

She looked up at the photograph. 'It wasn't the kind of sport I had in mind, but it suited Bill's nature. The thing was, Bill had got over his interest in hunting. He only joined the blessed club because I asked him to. If I hadn't pushed him to do something for himself, he might not have ended up in the path of that black-maned lion. He might still be alive.'

CHAPTER 9

Coll slapped the flanks of his mare with the reins and she responded by breaking into a brisk trot. He used the department buggy whenever he could as riding on horseback irritated his chest and usually brought on a coughing spell. But today he was hastening to Naivasha following a summons from Commissioner Eliot to join him at a meeting with Lenana, the Maasai *laibon*. Coll was usually informed of any visit that the commissioner intended to make to Maasailand, but this one had come as a surprise.

There were rumours that the government planned to push the Maasai away from the railway line. Why would the government, the rumour went, give preference to a bunch of ignorant savages when white settlers were craving good land for grazing? At least the settlers would trade their cattle rather than horde them like the Maasai did, and they would use the railway to do so, thereby helping to repay its enormous cost.

Coll had originally thought the rumour preposterous, emanating from a few avaricious ranchers and more than a little self-serving. But when he considered it alongside the unscheduled meeting and some recent matters he had discussed with the commissioner about the Maasai, he changed his view.

He was concerned that he had given Commissioner Eliot the wrong impression on Eliot's recent visit to Nairobi, which had prompted the meeting. Eliot had asked Coll his opinion on the existing situation where natives and white settlers intermingled throughout the protectorate. This mingling was not a policy, but had come about because there were not enough government land surveyors available to process the many land grant applications. As a result, settlers simply went out into the bush, made a sketch map of the land they wanted and submitted it to Eliot's office. Coll had said that intermingling might work with native farmers like the Kikuyu and Kamba, but that pastoralists, like the Maasai, had for centuries, if not millennia, enjoyed the unchallenged right to wander throughout the Great Rift Valley with their herds. As a result, they had developed an insatiable appetite for land.

Shortly after that discussion, he'd read a copy of the commissioner's memorandum which stated that wandering tribes had no right to keep other and superior races off large tracts of land merely because they had acquired the habit of straggling over a far greater area than they could utilise.

The other matter that might have got out of hand was his report of a small outbreak of rinderpest among the Maasai herds south of Naivasha. On that occasion he had suggested that the Maasai should be allowed to follow their customs and drive their herds north to avoid the fouled land until the disease had passed.

But nothing that he'd said was intended to imply that he thought the Maasai should be removed from the Great Rift Valley.

He flicked the reins again. He must speak to Commissioner Eliot to clarify these matters before the meeting with Lenana commenced.

When Coll arrived in Naivasha he found it bustling with activity, which worsened his fears that something important was afoot. A large number of Maasai elders had gathered on the outskirts of the town. They stood about in clusters like so many marabou storks, with hunched shoulders and their shaved heads poking out of long dark cloaks.

Eliot's train pulled in shortly after Coll arrived. The commissioner stepped down from his carriage straight-backed and stiff. He removed his sun helmet and wiped his brow with a white kerchief — there was not a hair out of place. His dark moustache, a thick straight line under his nose, might have been chiselled from ebony. He spotted Coll and gestured him over.

'Morning, Coll,' he said in his usual abrupt manner, not pausing in his march up the hill to where the Maasai were gathered. 'I want you to sit in on this chitchat with Lenana and his council of elders. He speaks passable English, but the others don't. He has an interpreter for them, but I want you there to make sure nothing is misinterpreted, because I'm going to address some important land issues. Some of which you will be familiar with. Wadley here,' he indicated his assistant trotting at his side, 'will take notes. You will translate as necessary, and nothing more. If you hear anything out of the ordinary, you are to tell me.' He came to an abrupt halt and his bright blue eyes drilled into Coll. 'Is that clear?'

Coll said it was. Before he could launch into his prepared speech, Eliot had headed off to where the *laibon* and a group of elders were seated under a tree.

'Sir!' Coll spluttered as he hurried to catch up.

Eliot turned with a scowl on his face. 'What is it now?'

'Commissioner Eliot, I'm worried that you may be about to make a mistake. It was not my intention in my recent reports on the Maasai to —'

'What are you blathering about, Coll? Mistake? Mistaken about what, exactly?'

'About my suggestion that the Maasai should move out of the Rift Valley. It was not my intention to —'

'Have you lost your senses, man?' His smile was incredulous. 'Do you think I rely on the advice of a mere stock inspector for my administrative decisions? I suggest you confine your involvement with these people to the search for ticks and other such vermin. I shall handle policy.'

Coll's mouth opened, but before he could muster a reply in his defence, Eliot said, 'Now, come along.'

The meeting began with the usual pleasantries. The Maasai elders, ever courteous, individually paid their respects to the

79

commissioner, which Eliot patiently reciprocated. Coll was impressed with Eliot's attention to Maasai protocol. However, when the preliminaries were completed, he immediately turned the discussion to the matter of Maasai land and stunned Coll with his audacity.

'Now, Lenana,' Eliot said, 'I am at the end of my patience. I am here to tell you that there will be no further discussion. I have decided that the Maasai will move out of the Rift Valley.'

Coll spluttered and cleared his throat to speak. Eliot shot him a glance that cut him dead, and continued with his demands, the Maasai translator struggling to keep pace with him.

'We will establish a large reserve for the Maasai in the Laikipia region and another in the south near the border with German East Africa. The amount of land we offer is very generous — larger than what you presently hold in the Great Rift Valley.'

Lenana's face became stern, and the elders muttered and exchanged glances.

Eliot ploughed on, quoting map references and reciting ordinances that he had put in place to facilitate the reserves. 'You will lead your people to the new reserves with the assistance of some of my soldiers and *askaris*. I foresee no need for concern. We should be able to resettle you in the new reserves well before the next wet season.'

'Commissioner Eliot,' Lenana said, 'the land that you speak of is already known to us.' He pointed out that the Maasai moved through their range in a manner defined by the seasons, including the lands to the north and south of the Rift Valley that Eliot had so graciously granted them as reserves. There had never been a time that anyone could remember when it wasn't so.

'That arrangement will cease,' Eliot responded abruptly. 'The Maasai will confine themselves to reserves as many others do. The British Government has built a railroad across the Rift Valley, and it is our intention to make use of it by settling the area with farmers and graziers who will make use of the railway in the manner that we intended.'

Lenana launched another protest but was interrupted.

'That is the end of it,' Eliot said. 'We have talked enough about this. Now we will draw up the papers for signature by you and your council.'

When this was related to the Maasai elders, there was a clamour of irate voices.

Eliot told Lenana that he needed to speak to him alone, and that he wanted everyone else to leave.

Lenana rose with his advisors and accompanied them a short way off where they exchanged hushed words.

Coll was now apoplectic with indignation. He decided to have no part of the sham agreement and stood to leave with the elders.

'Sit down, Coll. I want you to stay.'

'Sir Charles, I must protest. This is hardly fair dealings with these people. I cannot sit idly by while the Maasai are bullied so unfairly.'

'Utter balderdash, Coll. These people can give as good as they get. Anyway, I have no intention of forcing an agreement on Lenana. That was just my opening gambit. I know Lenana well enough. He'll come round to my point of view, never fear.'

Lenana returned to his seat under the fig tree.

'Now sit down,' Eliot hissed to Coll.

Coll stood there like a chastised schoolboy, hating his indecision. Had he acted rashly in assuming his superior would cheat his subjects? The commissioner had made a plausible explanation. Should he not take him at his word and remain to see that Lenana did indeed agree to the resettlement willingly?

Eliot glanced at him. 'Mr Coll, if you please.' His tone was conciliatory.

Coll paused a moment more, then sat as requested.

Eliot began to chat to Lenana about the wonderful system of government that the British had refined over the years. He talked about law and order, and the superb legal structure supported by what he called a whole tribe of lawmakers. Coll thought the commissioner was rambling, but then, quite subtly, he started to weave in the consequences of breaking any of Britain's many laws. His voice became menacing.

He made reference to an earlier discussion, where he had obviously told Lenana that Britain's retribution against those who chose to defy its rules could be brutal. He mentioned a case he said he was personally involved with in Nigeria, where a recalcitrant chief had been flogged, then banished from his land. He had been sent to a small island to spend the rest of his days alone and lonely in that faraway place.

Where earlier, in the company of his advisors, Lenana had appeared stern and defiant to Eliot's bombastic approach, he now seemed to shrink into his cassock of calfskins. His face was grey. Coll could almost feel his fear.

'On the matter of your position,' Eliot finished cheerily, 'I have set up a government salary for you. That will commence immediately you sign the agreement.'

He extended his hand to his assistant. 'Wadley, the papers, if you please.'

George Coll paced about like a penned lion. He might have made it home before dark, but had set up camp on the sloping ground above Naivasha in the late afternoon, needing time to think, and to resolve the sickening feeling that he'd been part of a massive injustice.

He wasn't a religious man, but he had grown up under his grandfather's deeply moralistic influence, and what he'd heard during Eliot's meeting with Lenana under the fig tree had greatly disturbed him.

The Great Rift Valley was Maasailand. Coll was standing in the very heart of it, here above Lake Naivasha. Further up in the hills was Kinangop, the sacred site where the Maasai performed their rites of passage to become men and warriors. The Maasai and this Great Rift Valley surely could not be separated.

He was outraged by the idea, but to his shame had been too afraid to speak when the commissioner's scare tactics had resulted in Lenana signing the agreement to move out of the valley.

He could imagine what his grandfather, a Presbyterian minister, would have said. He would have thundered about humanity, and rights, and the need for compassion by the conquerors over the conquered. He would have spouted fire and brimstone.

Coll had said nothing.

He stopped his pacing, and was surprised to find the valley already darkening. Unlike the lingering twilights at home, here in Africa the sun fell quickly, allowing darkness to claim the savannah in an unguarded moment. But the beauty of the evening, and the haunting call of an eagle owl, did nothing to calm his heart.

It was wrong. It was just plain wrong!

He looked down at his hands with their long pale fingers and knobbly knuckles, which his dear mother had thought would one day be those of a pianist. They were shaking in anger and shame at his abject failure.

He clenched them into fists to make them stop.

Ole Sadera was alone in the valley with his cattle. He stood perched on one leg, his other foot braced into the side of his knee, as he watched the day slip away. It was nearly time to drive the cattle back to the *boma*, but he was reluctant to leave. His mind was in turmoil, torn between obeying tradition and doing what he felt he should to prevent his people from losing their most precious possessions.

He believed that their way of life would be unutterably altered, in fact lost, if the British moved them from Maasailand. Ole Sadera already knew Lenana would agree to it, but that would not normally be the end to it. Others would have their say, other choices would be discussed, and a consensus would be found. But there was talk that the British were planning to appoint Lenana to a position where he would speak for all the Maasai. Not only the people of the *enkangs* — the women, children and elders — but even for the *moran*. It was against all their traditions.

The *moran* answered to no one but themselves. Their primary duty was to protect the tribe, the section and the village. They had foregone all ties with family, with childhood acquaintances. Their single bond was with their age set brothers

— the men who would stand with them, and die for them if necessary. In such a world, there was no place for a chief or single leader. The Maasai world was in fact three: child, which included younger women; warrior and elder. The leadership of those three worlds was a complicated matrix of duties, of formal and informal roles, of mentors, administrators and judges. There were also positions such as his, the *olaiguenani,* an elected representative of his age group. His friend, Mantira, represented the older age set. Between them, their voices could influence large numbers of the warrior group.

His mind simply couldn't cope with all the possible consequences and potential disasters that a change such as the British were contemplating might inflict upon his people. Over the past few weeks it had made him sick with worry. It was why he had chosen to tend personally to his cattle that day. He needed time to think.

Above his valley, where the crest stood dark and strong against the red sky, came a lone silhouette. He knew it was a woman by the way she moved — a swaying, ambling gait too soft to be the pace of a man. But the fact that the figure was alone made him sure it was not one of his fellow warriors. A *moran* must always travel with an age-mate.

He lost her for a moment with the sun's glow behind the rise, which threw the void below the ridge line into a gloom. Then she was there again, emerging from the thin copse of cedars. She seemed to know where she was going, and with something of a surprise he realised she was coming towards him.

She was now clear of the shadows and he let his hope take wing. He had not dared imagine it was she until her features became clear. It had been many months since he'd even caught a glimpse of her, and years since they had made love. There had been many nights when they had shared the joy of their coupling, but it was the memory of that night of utter passion when they had celebrated his Il Tuati's victory in the Kedong Valley that now reminded him of how much he wanted her.

The light was quickly fading, but he could clearly see she was now very much a woman. As she neared, he noted the same perfect small white teeth of her smile and her quick, short steps.

He briefly wondered about her wealthy husband who, he heard, had recently taken another wife — his fourth.

Her ornaments were beautiful, as usual. A vision flashed back to him. She had been a young girl in the first budding of womanhood when he'd met her — forbidden even then. He had slowly and carefully removed the red skirt, the necklace, the headdress and the armlets from the sleek body that glowed in the light of the guttering oil lamp.

'Your cattle are late to their *boma*,' she said now, by way of greeting.

'They keep me company.'

She smiled. 'It is not good to be often alone. Can you not find better company than your cows?'

'Is that why you are here?'

She paused, dropping her eyes for a moment. When she lifted her head to meet his gaze, she said, 'I have been to the village. You shouldn't carry this problem alone.'

He said, 'No,' but wondered if she was referring to the land or his loneliness.

'You need someone.'

'I need you. I always need you.'

She stepped closer to him, raising her hand to brush his shoulder. She ran her finger down his arm. His flesh tingled under her touch.

The feeling was not only erotic but liberating. He was able to enjoy the delicious extravagance of doing what his body desired; released from the compelling need for continuous vigilance; to be always in control; to be disciplined.

He crept a hand towards her small pointed breast with its dark erect nipple. He caressed it and she moved closer, untying his *shuka*. It slipped to the ground between them. She reached for him, and he felt his firm shaft grow to fill her palm.

On the hard ground they made love.

His climax came rushing from him like a river of relief and his moan was a sweet but painful mixture of ecstasy and torment.

CHAPTER 10

Despite the age disparity and their different social standing, Dr Norman Lewis found that he and George Coll shared many interests. They met regularly and continued to build on the friendship that had begun on the ship to Mombasa.

As the government's chief medical officer, Lewis needed to make regular visits to the new and decidedly unhealthy township of Nairobi. Set on flat grassland at the base of the Kikuyu forest, Nairobi became a swamp in the wet season. Poor drainage converted the rock-hard earth into a black-cotton ooze, sewage pooled in foul cesspits, and the Indian bazaar became a breeding ground for bubonic plague. Preparatory to these brief visits, Lewis would send a telegram to Coll and, if he were in Nairobi, they would meet to share a meal.

This evening, Lewis and Coll were sitting on the veranda off Lewis's room in the Victoria Hotel, which everyone in Nairobi simply referred to as Wood's after its flamboyant owner. Lewis preferred Wood's to its more pretentious rival, the Norfolk, where disenchanted peers of the realm gathered for sundowners and, more often than not, created mayhem by smashing glasses and overturning furniture to break the boredom of life in the colonies. What had brought Lewis to Nairobi this time, well ahead of his scheduled visit, was a telegram from Coll saying there were important developments that they must discuss.

When they had met in the lobby, Coll had seemed more than usually anxious. Lewis had imagined it was because the information Coll was to confide in him was confidential and the stock inspector was in fear of being exposed. It might also have been that disclosing government secrets did not sit well with what Lewis was discovering to be Coll's strong moral code. To ease his friend's distress, Lewis had suggested they take their drinks to his private veranda.

Lewis had a whisky and ice sitting on the railing. Coll, a teetotaller, was sipping at his cup of tea like a nervous bird. Lewis was pondering the details Coll had hastily whispered to him in the lobby.

'About the meeting between Eliot and Lenana,' he began. 'Are you saying it wasn't the first time they'd discussed moving the Maasai onto a reserve?'

'Indeed. Eliot gave me the impression he had already discussed a number of things with Lenana, including a government salary.'

'Do you think Lenana is interested in money?'

'It's hard to know what the old man was thinking. Mind you, my Maa is still pretty infantile so there may have been nuances I missed, but Eliot certainly found his weakness.' And he described Lenana's terror following Eliot's vivid portrayal of British justice and the consequences of breaking British law.

'So he signed,' Lewis said.

'Yes.' Coll set his cup on the table with a rattle. 'And I sat there like a coward, without a word of protest,' he finished miserably.

Lewis told Coll that he was being too hard on himself. There was nothing he could have done to prevent the commissioner taking such action. 'There are other ways to protest against this kind of behaviour. People are beginning to call it imperialism. And many are now fighting it, all over the world.'

Coll looked worried. 'Don't get me wrong, Norman. I'm not against the government. I'm actually a great admirer of the British Empire and all it's done for people in many parts of the world. I'm just against this thing with the Maasai.'

Lewis sipped his whisky, watching a pair of black rickshaw boys hauling a mountain of luggage from the station up Government Road towards the Norfolk. He seldom missed an opportunity to lecture friends on his liberal view of the world, but Coll was feeling wretched. There would be another time to tackle politics.

'You've really become close to the Maasai in this job of yours, George,' he said, changing the subject.

'I suppose I have. When you understand a man's mother tongue, you learn a lot about him. Things you might never imagine, no matter how much you talk to him in English. In a way, you get inside his head.' He twisted his thin hands together, causing his whitened knuckles to crack.

Lewis could see that Coll was becoming distressed — a situation that often brought on a coughing fit that seemed to tear at his already weakened chest and lungs.

'You mustn't take this too much to heart,' he said. 'We English might be arrogant, ruthless bastards at times, but by and large this kind of thing gets sorted before it goes too far. The system of checks and balances sees to it.'

'But out here in the wilderness?' Coll said. 'Who will ever know? How will they ever hear of such things in parliament; in Downing Street?'

'Because policy is made in London, George. And the official policy is to respect and preserve native rights. The Eliots of the colonial system are mere facilitators of government policy from home.'

Coll looked sceptical. 'That's not answering my question. How will they know?'

'Reports. The Foreign Office is bureaucratic to the back teeth. Every senior official has to prepare reports to head office. Even me.'

'What if Eliot and his assistants don't choose to report any of their little chats with the natives?'

'Then it comes down to budgets. You can't do a thing without a bloody line item in a budget.'

Coll shook his head, unconvinced.

'Look,' Lewis went on, 'I don't think this thing will go ahead. From what you've told me about Lenana, he won't accept the money and there'll be no movement of the Maasai, with or without duress from Eliot.'

'But how can you be so sure?'

'This is the twentieth century, George. The age of enlightenment. I have some friends at home who would take a great deal of interest in something like this if it went ahead. Remember, Eliot doesn't act alone in these matters; he'll seek counsel from others on his staff. Why, he might even ask my opinion.' He gave Coll a broad, reassuring smile. 'And you can be sure I'll have a thing or two to say about it.'

'Wouldn't that go against you in your career?'

'Nonsense,' Lewis replied. 'There are no worries about that.' He patted Coll on the back. 'Now finish your tea and I'll stand you a meal downstairs.'

In truth, Lewis knew there was no chance he could influence a colonial commissioner who had his heart set on a particular course of action. These men were kings in their own little domains. And it would be a foolish person who openly stood against the likes of Eliot. Instead, Lewis would follow the course he had always taken in such matters. He would compile a dossier on the commissioner and keep his contacts in London and Edinburgh informed. It might only be a matter of time before another tyrant fell to the power of the people.

Norman Lewis opened his office door and looked out into the larger, darkening outer area. As he had hoped, he could see no sign of James, his assistant. He closed the door, sat at his desk and put a match to the paraffin lamp. From the bottom drawer, he removed a pad of plain paper and an envelope. Dipping his pen carefully into the ink well, he wrote: *Dear Gilbert . . .*

He studied the two words, wondering how to continue. He had no tangible evidence to support his claims, but he had to write the letter or he felt his anger and frustration would consume him. He was not confident that his friends in London could do anything to help, but he felt compelled to share his suspicions with them.

It seemed to him that he had struggled against the inequities of the British system of administration and government all his life. In his early days in the Glasgow slums, tending the sick with not a penny's worth of medicines to work with, he'd had to battle against heartless bureaucrats more intent on keeping their shiny arses secure in their office chairs than doing what they were paid to do.

Now he was witness to another great injustice. When Sir Charles Eliot had been recalled to Britain for reasons not entirely clear to members of his administration, he and Coll had believed that his plans to relocate the Maasai into reserves would go with him. But his replacement, Commissioner Stewart, was obviously a man of similar mind. Within a month of arriving, he had decided to force through the land resettlement agreement.

There was no doubt in Lewis's mind that the Maasai had been coerced into moving. According to George Coll, Eliot had all but put a gun to Lenana's head, but the copy of Stewart's covering memo to the secretary of state that Lewis had seen in the official correspondence file made no reference to earlier discussions by Eliot. No doubt the Foreign Office would have looked more carefully at Stewart's proposal had it been known that Eliot's influence was still at work.

He had tried to bury his concerns after Coll had first informed him of what he had heard said between Eliot and Lenana. In the interests of his friend's peace of mind, he had reassured him that the agreement would not proceed. For a time it had appeared it would not, and he had shamelessly allowed Coll to believe he had something to do with its repeal, accepting his praise and admiration. Now he felt he had to take action, otherwise the impersonal machinery of government would again roll relentlessly over the unfortunates caught in its path. He dipped the nib in the ink again.

When I last wrote it was with a feeling of relief that the issue of creating a reserve for the Maasai had been put to rest. Alas, I was mistaken. Commissioner Stewart has picked up where Eliot left off. It is a most brutal misuse of power and an absolute disgrace for the empire to be witness to it.

He stared at the glistening pen strokes. Why did he feel compelled to write this letter? As a young doctor in Glasgow, he had made similar attempts to bring fairness to the treatment of those unable to speak for themselves, but all it had done was to harden the bureaucrats' resolve against him and, in the end, made life more difficult for those he wanted to help. In this case, if he were discovered it would surely mean his dismissal or at least banishment from British East Africa.

He screwed up the page and threw it in the wastebasket. In an instant he realised the discarded letter might be found and he would be exposed. He thrust his hand into the receptacle and rummaged around among the discarded papers. The door swung open. James stood there, looking quizzically at his boss.

'Is there something I can help you with, Dr Lewis?' he asked.

'Wh-what? No! No, thank you, James, I just dropped my ... I'm looking for some blotting paper.'

'No need to use the old sheets, Dr Lewis. I'll get you a new pad.'

'Oh, would you? So kind.'

James stepped back into the outer office. Lewis found the discarded letter and stuffed it in his pocket. 'I thought you'd gone home,' he called through the open door.

James came back with a thin pad of absorbent paper. 'I had, but I realised I had forgotten my umbrella. You never know when we might get a decent downpour.'

'No, you don't,' Lewis agreed.

There was a moment's silence until James said, 'Oh, well, I'm off again. Goodnight, sir.'

'Goodnight, James.'

Lewis felt a rush of relief. He went to the door and this time locked it. He was about to return to his desk, but pulled a whisky bottle from the cupboard under his bookshelf and poured himself a shot.

With the whisky burning a line down his throat, he struggled to resolve the conflict raging within him. His rising indignation at the injustice of the situation decided the matter. He pulled another sheet from the pad in his desk drawer and tried to compose himself before again starting the letter to Gilbert Murray.

Murray had been a student with him at medical school, and was now an influential scholar and advisor to the British Labour Party. He was one of those rare individuals who, when finding a wrong, made every effort to right it. Lewis felt sure he could trust Murray to keep his name confidential. He picked up the pen and jabbed it in the ink well.

Dear Gilbert,

When I last wrote, I was hopeful that the proposed government reserve for the Maasai had been forgotten following Commissioner Eliot's resignation. Unfortunately, I was badly mistaken. Commissioner Stewart has revived the whole terrible mess, and has already put in motion the resettlement. I fear the situation is now almost beyond anyone's control, and the Maasai will soon be told to vacate the land of their birth.

I am distraught and ashamed to be a part of a government with such callous disregard for the rights of the less fortunate.

Stewart claims he has the full support of the laibon. *My confidants assure me that this support comes under duress. Alas, I am also informed that no age set leaders will stand against Lenana to say he is misguided, nor will they otherwise accuse the government of acting against their best interests. As you may well understand, such actions are alien to them. The Maasai would happily go to war on a whim, but faced with divisions within their ranks, they believe they have no option but to concede to the government's request.*

The saving grace in this litany of unkind happenstance is that, unlike any other of the so-called agreements that I am aware of, the Maasai have been assured they will not be further inconvenienced, and that the reserves will remain in their hands in perpetuity. This will be scant consolation to a people who have been proudly independent since the days of creation.

The documents have been sent to the Secretary of State for Foreign and Imperial Affairs for ratification. I fear Lord Lansdowne will be guided by his colonial representative, Commissioner Stewart, and therefore sign them.

I know not what use can be made of this information, nor whether your contacts in the Labour Party will be interested in taking up the cause of the Maasai, but I am otherwise at a loss to know what to do about it.

I would be grateful if you would inform Mr J H Oldham and our other friends at the Anti-slavery Society of this sad state of affairs.

Yours faithfully,
Norman

CHAPTER 11

1904

Commissioner Sir Donald Stewart sat in his first-class carriage as the train snaked its way down the face of the Kikuyu Escarpment. Below him, the Great Rift Valley spread from south to north like a vast carpet of grassland. It justified his decision to come so soon after arriving in Mombasa to take up his appointment. Without seeing this part of the country, in such stark contrast to the verdant jungle running the length of the coastline, he would have been unable to appreciate its significance, nor understand why there had been such a fuss between his predecessor and the Foreign Office over its use.

He now knew what was at stake. Below him, the land bounded and leapt down to the valley floor, where a settler could run thousands of cattle on those sparse but succulent grasses. Parts of it might even be favourably disposed towards agriculture, with permanent water available in the lakes and streams that he could see from his lofty height on the railway line.

Stewart was very clear about his mission to the Great Rift Valley that day. He would go through the motions of inspecting the land in question and then finally settle the matter. He had no intention of repeating the previous commissioner's mistakes. Sir Charles Eliot had issued land grants in the Great Rift Valley to a number of prospective settlers, including one hundred and fifty from South Africa. The Foreign Office learned of these grants and deemed them unacceptable because there was no agreement in place to move the traditional owners — the Maasai — which breached guidelines.

Eliot had been incensed by London's interference. It made his promises to the settlers impossible to fulfil. As a gentleman, he had found resignation the only honourable course.

The South African land speculator continued to make loud noises about his unfulfilled grant and the shoddy state of British justice. Stewart had to concede that the man had every right to be upset. On the strength of his handshake with Eliot, he had sold a considerable amount of his leasehold to British South Africans — the very essence of Eliot's 'right type'. When the Foreign Office disallowed the land grant, he used the South African press to mercilessly lambast the Foreign Secretary of State and had threatened to carry the fight to the House if necessary.

How the Foreign Office had learned of the land grants was a matter for some speculation. Assistant Commissioner Charles Wadley, sitting opposite him in the carriage, was of the view that someone from within the protectorate's administration must have informed London. Stewart had already quietly begun to investigate who that might be. As an old soldier, he would not tolerate disloyalty in the ranks, regardless of the perceived justification.

Wadley had been acting commissioner following Sir Charles Eliot's departure and had drawn up a draft agreement to be signed by Lenana that would settle the Maasai in two reserves. The Foreign Office had seen this draft but had made no formal response. It was clear to Stewart that Wadley's plan would allow a settlement to be reached with all those demanding land. The Secretary of State, Lord Lansdowne, was adamant that if there was any dispute over ownership, or if the Maasai were unhappy about the suggested relocation, they should not be forced to accept it. However, Stewart was well aware that there was an election in the offing and the minister wanted nothing from the backblocks to distract the electorate over the next few months.

'Tell me again, Wadley,' Stewart said, 'this Lenana fellow, he was agreeable to move from this area?' He again let his gaze run into the grassy distance.

'As agreeable as any man can be, given few choices.'

'Are you saying he was coerced?' Stewart asked.

'I would more say, *induced*,' Wadley said cautiously. 'Commissioner Eliot effectively made him a member of the administration with a handy annual stipend and the prestige it attracts. He officiates at several minor events. For example, he was a cattle judge at the last annual agricultural show.'

'Is prestige so important to this fellow? I understand he's getting on in years. I should have thought he would be seeking a quiet life.'

'Prestige, but also perceived power, Commissioner. And the perception is all-important to Lenana. Years ago, his brother, Sendeyu, viciously fought him for the position of *laibon*. I don't wonder that he holds it dearly as a result.'

'But the other leaders, the elders and such, they know nothing of your plan and Lenana's support for it?'

'No. I didn't want it to go that far without your involvement, Sir Donald.'

Stewart nodded his approval.

The train was approaching Naivasha where he could see a small gathering on the station. Invariably they were the more well-to-do members of the settler community. The real men of the land were too busy to waste their time welcoming him to their neighbourhood. He had little patience with the idle chatter of spoiled second sons of aristocrats, but he would go through the motions, smiling and pressing the flesh of every man-jack of them, then he would be gone and could get down to the real business of his trip.

Stewart was not disposed towards Eliot's philosophy of intermingling the Maasai and the settlers. There would always be the threat of conflict arising over boundaries and theft of stock. In any case, he felt that the idea of allowing roaming savages to occupy some of the best land in the country was preposterous. Unlike his predecessor, he would implement standard practice in such matters and establish native reserves outside the contested area for the traditional landowners.

Stewart was a man of action. As soon as he returned from this inspection tour, he would instruct Wadley to call the Maasai leaders together where he would inform them of his decision to move them. He would tell them where they were going and tolerate no further discussion or delays.

Ole Sadera stood to the fore among the hundreds of his fellow Maasai *moran* and elders, waiting for the new commissioner to speak. Scores of armed government *askaris*, their crimson tarbooshes sitting perkily on their heads, their bodies held rigidly to attention, ringed the large tree where Lenana and the white leaders sat behind a long wooden bench.

Commissioner Stewart stood and held up his hand although the Maasai had been standing silently for some time. Stewart was as straight and as narrow as a walking staff, with rimless spectacles that flashed in the Rift Valley's brilliant sunlight, turning his eyes into white stones. Even the closest members of the gathered Maasai could not read what was behind those flashing mirrors. Ole Sadera felt that anything could be going through Stewart's mind and nobody would know.

'We have called you here to this meeting,' Stewart said through his interpreter, 'to speak of important matters. There has been much trouble in the Rift Valley and the government is not pleased.'

Ole Sadera searched his mind for the trouble that the commissioner referred to and could find none; none since the attack on the Swahili caravan years before.

Stewart continued. 'We are here to tell you that we want all the Maasai to leave the Great Rift Valley. Not as you do now, for dry-season grazing, but for always and forever.'

Ole Sadera stared at the interpreter, for a moment believing it was he who had made this demand, then was even more shocked to realise they had been Stewart's words. He looked at Stewart — his stone eyes unreachable. The assistant commissioner, Mr Wadley, seemed to have no interest in what had been said. Only Lenana — shrunken inside his old army greatcoat —

expressed his feelings in the tilt of his head and the firm line of his mouth. This said to Ole Sadera that these were words the *laibon* had already heard at another time and so they brought him no pain. Ole Sadera was shaken.

'You will leave Naivasha and the valley,' Stewart continued, 'because the government has built a railway from the sea to the great lake. We will use this railway to bring many wonderful things to this land. Already we have brought our cattle, which have been bred from buffalo, and they will defeat and kill your cattle if they fight. We will bring sheep and goats that are unlike your stock and you will think them strange and think them wild animals and will want to kill them, but you must not, for you will be heavily fined. And pigs, like hippopotamus calves, which we keep as you keep cattle and which your warriors will want to spear, but again it is forbidden. For all these reasons, the Maasai must leave this place.'

The white men sat impassively at the table as the interpreter mouthed the words to the assembled Maasai. The silence among the warriors and elders deepened. Ole Sadera wondered if the others had heard. He himself found it difficult to believe what had been said.

Commissioner Stewart spoke again. 'You will vacate the Great Rift Valley and, in return, His Majesty's Government will grant you two very generous land reserves, one to the north and another in the south. 'The northern reserve will be in the country you call Entorror. It will have the following boundaries: on the west, by the Laikipia Escarpment; the south by the Lesuswa and Uaso Ngiro rivers; in the east by Kisima; and in the north by the Loroghi Mountains.'

Ole Sadera could see each boundary landmark as Stewart mentioned it for he had travelled to all parts of Entorror. The names alone brought back memories of his times there — good and bad. But of far more impact were the places that these boundaries excluded. Gone was the silver water of Naivasha, the curative minerals of Nakuru, the sweet cool grasses on the slopes of the Aberdares.

'In the south,' the commissioner went on, 'the Maasai sections who presently reside in that vicinity shall confine themselves to the area bounded by the Donyo Lamuyu mountain, the Kiserian stream, the Matapatu Mountains and the Donyo Narok, to the western extent of Sosian. We will reserve a road of one mile wide so that you may access water and the people of the two reserves can communicate with each other.

'European and other settlers shall not be allowed to take up land in the settlements,' he said. 'This land will never be taken from you. You will live in peace and prosperity there.'

Stewart had the satisfied expression of a man who had completed a difficult task, and had done well. But with his words, a great divide had opened, cleaving the Maasai in two.

The commissioner's spectacles flashed bolts of sunlight as he ran his gaze around the assembly. Ole Sadera turned also, seeking the expressions of surprise and outrage he felt must surely be found among the elders, but there was none. It appeared they had come only to hear what they had already heard. Only the younger *moran* — his brothers the Il Tuati, still to be accepted into the conventional circles of Maasai authority — showed any surprise. Even Mantira stood impassively, ignoring Ole Sadera's attempts to catch his eye.

'This is agreed by your leaders, and so now I ask that they come forward to sign these papers so the settlement becomes bound in British law.'

Mr Wadley stood and handed a roll of paper to the commissioner, which he unfurled and held flat. Lenana made his mark on the paper. Mantira followed, then Lemani and Mepaku and all the other *olaiguenani* and elders until it appeared that only he, Ole Sadera, had been unaware of this agreement.

When Ole Sadera reached the table, he felt Lenana's eyes on him, but when Ole Sadera faced him, the old man could not meet his piercing look and turned away.

CHAPTER 12

Nashilo spread her freshly washed tunic over a large flat stone by the stream to dry. The other women had finished their laundry, and had called to her to join them on their walk back to the village, but Nashilo waved them on. She wanted to be alone with her thoughts, and her time at the stream on washing day was a rare opportunity to do so.

When the departing women's voices faded, the weaverbirds returned, wheeling above the stream to steal a sip of water on the wing. They filled the silence with their twittering calls and brightened the morning with flashes of yellow.

Nashilo sat on a rock and began to pick around the edge of the water to find a small, round stone. She felt the smoothness and weight of each before discarding it to search for something more suitable. The task helped her to pick among her thoughts and sort them too.

It had been a troubling month, culminating in her monthly flow, which had angered her husband yet again. 'Sons,' he'd said harshly. 'I want sons, and you have failed again.' She had waited for the back of his hand, but it didn't come on that occasion. Perhaps he was losing hope in her.

He was often short-tempered with her, and she knew it was her fault. She felt nothing for the man. He had been chosen for her, or she for him, during family meetings while she was still a child. The bride price of ten cows that her husband had paid for her was a huge compliment, and the biggest deterrent to her leaving him — which she was free to do — as it meant her family would have to return all ten cows: a fortune. So she stayed where she felt she wasn't appreciated, with a man she couldn't respect.

She had in her hand a stone that had the smoothness she imagined she needed, and it was about the right size. She began to search for another.

Her love affair with Parsaloi was against Maasai custom. She was only permitted to lie with members of her husband's own age set, which was their privilege. Parsaloi was breaking the rule against *moran* making love to a married woman. They could be severely embarrassed if their affair was discovered. This would be worse for Parsaloi than it was for her because of his position as *olaiguenani*.

She now had a collection of small, round stones and began to sort through them to find a matching pair.

Why she and Parsaloi continued to play their dangerous game, she could not say. She was even incapable of describing what it was about him, with his deep brooding eyes and solemn demeanour, that attracted her; more than attracted her — he drew her to him as if he had the magic of the Great Laibon at his fingertips. He excited her and, at times, frightened her too.

Two round, white stones sat in the middle of her palm. She pushed them about, studying every aspect of them to assure herself they were almost identical. They were.

In her imagination, these were the stones that Parsaloi had grasped from the bottom of the river as he was born. They were beautifully formed, round, and now warmed by her hand. But they were still stones. Parsaloi's spell over her was something she couldn't unravel simply by studying stones. She would have to unravel that mystery by some other means.

Nashilo knew that old Ntooto was in a disapproving mood. She fussed around the cooking fire without accomplishing anything constructive, and when Nashilo asked if there was anything she could do to help, she received a cool *hhhumph* in reply.

Ntooto had been Nashilo's substitute mother ever since her birth mother had died in a Kikuyu raid when she was a child.

As Nashilo's father's second wife, Ntooto took the girl in as if she were her own. The bond was not that of mother and daughter, but in some ways was much closer. They could discuss topics that would be inappropriate between mother and daughter. It was the reason Nashilo was not concerned about Ntooto's present mood. She knew she would not be left wondering what had annoyed her for long.

'And you don't even care if it worries me to my sick bed,' Ntooto sniffed, as if she had read Nashilo's mind.

'I can't care if I don't know, Mama,' Nashilo said, smiling at the older woman's predictability.

'And don't think that because I've said nothing to your father he won't learn of it too. Not to mention your husband. May Enkai look elsewhere and not see your sin.'

Ntooto seldom invoked Enkai's name without good cause. Nashilo became serious at last. 'Now, enough of these games, Mama. What is in your mind that brings forth mention of God and my father? And my husband?'

Ntooto sighed and turned to face her adoptive daughter. The eyes that had been haughty and reproving softened. 'I know that you have troubles with your husband. He becomes impatient for a son, and his temper is often not good, but, Nashilo, take care. You know it is forbidden to lie with the young *morani*. It matters not that he is a respected *olaiguenani*. Your husband will be furious if he learns of it. And why won't he? Even this old woman who never stirs from the *enkang* has heard of it. Does the owl not have ears? In his anger your husband will beat you even more than he does now, and this time he will have every right to do so.'

Nashilo slumped to the stool beside the cooking fire. She closed her eyes and covered her face. 'I am sorry that this has come to your notice, Mother. It must be very embarrassing for you to have this known among the other wives.'

'It is, child, but that is not why I am sick with worry. What will become of you if your husband not only beats you but sends you away? What will happen to a woman who cannot bear children and has no family to turn to?'

Nashilo shrugged and made a gesture towards her old village.

'No,' the old woman said, 'don't give me those eyes. Your father will not have you back. It would be a disgrace if he did. I can't say what he might do. And don't think that the *olaiguenani* can come to your assistance,' she said, refusing to use his name. 'It would finish him in the eyes of his *moran*. And it would be a great scandal in his position.'

'What am I to do, Mama?' Nashilo wailed.

Ntooto could hold back no longer. She embraced Nashilo and brushed the tears from her cheeks. 'There is only one thing you can do, my daughter. You must stop seeing the *morani* who would bring ruin on our whole family.'

But Nashilo knew she could never willingly leave Parsaloi. Even the possibility of losing contact with him after they moved from the great valley filled her with a dread worse than death.

A dozen or so *moran*, in the full finery of their ochre-red braids, decorative beads and body markings, surrounded the small cluster of shrubs, excitedly jabbing and lunging at it as they kept up a constant cry of '*Yip! Yip! Yip!*'

Nkapilil Mantira and Parsaloi Ole Sadera stood some way off, idly watching Ole Sadera's age set brothers and discussing the impending move from the great valley.

'But what can we do, Parsaloi?' Mantira asked. 'We are few and the whites are many.'

'It is sometimes unnecessary to fight with men and spears. Sometimes the battle can be won with words.'

'Lenana has used many words on the British, but they are deaf like stones,' Mantira replied. 'How many times has he been to Nairobi? How many times have the British gone to Ngong? It is useless. We have no choice but to hear what they say.'

'And then?' asked the younger man.

'And then we must do what they ask.'

Ole Sadera clung to his argument. 'I say we surrendered too soon. We should have resisted them.'

Mantira looked at him incredulously. 'Are you mad? Don't you see that our time is finished? You are a young man, but your head is in the past. The times have changed.'

Ole Sadera was silent for a moment, watching the *moran* prance around the cluster of foliage. A savage snarl came from within the clump of bushes. The *Yip! Yip! Yip!* cries grew more excited.

'Yes, my head is in the past,' he said, 'but I think there is a place for the old ways, even today. We can find new strength from them. We must learn the whites' ways and defeat them with their own weapons.'

'Put aside these ideas. There is nothing that can be done. Let your good judgement be your guide. The Maasai have many problems these days. Lenana understands the British.'

'The problem is that the British believe he speaks for all,' Ole Sadera said. 'And they are hearing only what they want to hear. They do not hear the words of the *moran*.'

'What do you mean, the words of the *moran*? Lenana speaks for the Maasai. He is the *laibon*.'

'But we are the spokesmen for our age sets. And so far as the *laibon*'s words are concerned — they are from British mouths.'

'What are you saying, Parsaloi? Do you accuse the *laibon* of treachery?'

'If a hyena sings to the moon, does he sing alone?'

Both men looked over to the *moran* as a large male lion charged out of the bushes. It snarled at them in confusion and defiance. The warriors quickly formed a large circle with the lion at its centre.

'Lenana is trying to find a place where the Maasai can stand with the British,' Mantira said.

'Stand? Or kneel before them?'

The *moran* tightened their circle around the lion. Their cries of *Yip! Yip! Yip!* and the din from their spears beating on their shields was driving the beast into a fury of hatred and fear.

'We must take note of Lenana's advice,' the older man said.

'Why? The elders are few. It is our age sets that hold the power now.'

Mantira studied his friend a moment before speaking. 'After we met, I heard the story of your birth, how you clutched at stones when you were born. Two stones. One in each hand. I have kept that thought, and I have watched you for the ill omens it is said that such a child can bring, but there has been none. I have seen nothing but the characteristics that make a good leader: courage and inspiration. But when I hear words like these, Parsaloi, it makes me wonder if you will lead us all to ruin.'

'You think I bring an ill omen by standing up for what is right?'

'No. I think it an ill omen to deny the new world we live in.'

'I am not the one to deny change, but it was the old ways that made us great. And, yes, I do live in the past in many ways, because the past will guide us. But here is the difference. We *moran* are the protectors of the Maasai. Do you not remember the song the women and children sing? *Young are the warriors, and we feed you our best meat. Healthy, you will protect our herds from enemies and famine.*'

'I remember the song. It is for women and children to sing. It is what they do.'

'When the elders were the *moran* they fought many, many wars. How can they now tell us to meekly accept our place? Their case is as thin as the dry-season clouds. It is we *moran* who must take the greater responsibility now — your Il Talala age set and my Il Tuati. We are the power. Our people will listen to us.'

'What nonsense is this, Parsaloi? Are you suggesting we now fight with our elders?'

'No. I am suggesting that if we don't do the fighting, then at least we must do the talking.'

In a rage, the lion bounded towards one of the *moran*, avoiding the wall of spears, and knocked the warrior onto his back. His brothers quickly formed a cordon of spear tips around him before one, then another, and another, drove their spears at the lion.

Mantira turned from the kill. 'You would see us take the *laibon*'s role with the British?'

'If we must, then yes.'

There was silence. The two *olaiguenani* watched the *moran* lift the injured warrior to his feet. He hobbled away with the assistance of two of his age mates. Others set about removing the lion's mane as a trophy for their injured comrade.

'At least you are not insisting on the spear and sword,' Mantira sighed. 'But your call to take up the battle is too late, Parsaloi. We have signed, and to resist now would mean outright war.'

'A good warrior knows when to regroup.'

'There is no need to regroup. We have accepted the pittance that the British have offered.'

'It wounds me to hear this talk of defeat.'

'Hear me. These reserves are now ours. We will not be forced to move again; no more disagreements; we can avoid the risk of war.' Seeing that Ole Sadera was not convinced, he added, 'Here is what I propose. Let us work with the whites. Let us become their blood brothers as you once suggested. Let us learn their ways and their words so we can win any future battles. I can agree with you that we should find new ways to defeat the whites. You say it is with words, but what words? We don't know enough about their ways. To do battle before we are properly prepared will be to show our enemy our weapons before we have perfected their use. Then, if Lenana and the elders are unable to stand up to them, I agree with you: we will take their power from them.'

CHAPTER 13

Coll arrived at the Wallace farm — Katherine's farm — and found she was not at home. 'Where is she, Kira?' he asked her housemaid.

'The cattle, Mr Coll,' she said, pointing up over the hill to indicate the back pasture. 'She go to look. Too many hyena and leopard already.'

'I see. When will she come back?'

Kira shrugged and smiled, showing him her perfect white teeth. 'I not sure.'

He thanked her and walked outside to his horse, marvelling at how much the skinny Maasai girl had changed in the year or so since he'd first come riding down Katherine's road.

Instead of unhitching his horse, he decided to take a walk to the back pasture. His visits had become a fairly regular affair. Coll enjoyed Katherine's robust Scottish sense of humour, and the tea and homemade biscuits she offered him. And the conversation. There was some Celtic magic at work when they sat for a chat. It had become apparent on their first extraordinary meeting, when Katherine had revealed to him the tragedy of her husband's death, and had continued to flourish each time they met.

He liked Katherine very much; perhaps all the more because, at her age, ten or more years his senior, he felt she had no other expectations about their friendship. He wasn't sure about his own feelings though.

There had been times in Coll's life when he'd shared a woman's bed, and there was once — when he was at college in Glasgow — when he had fallen in love. Then he fell ill and the TB was confirmed. He had decided it would be unfair to Jennie to take their love any further. Sometimes, when he camped alone under the stars on the Laikipia Plateau or in the Great Rift Valley, Coll would let his mind wander back to the days of his unencumbered youth and thoughts of Jennie. He wondered where he would be now had he not contracted the tuberculosis. They might have married. Perhaps they'd have had children. He fondly thought it likely he would have completed his examinations and become a vet. Sometimes he became confused and it was Katherine's face that appeared in his imaginings. And he knew why.

If his visit to the farm happened on his homeward journey, he tried to arrive in the afternoon to join Katherine for one of her thick soups taken with creamy buttered jags of fresh bread. The talk often stretched into late afternoon, but Coll kept an eye on the sun. Leopards were not the only night-time hunters. It was not widely known, but the lions in the hills of Parklands and Limuru didn't keep public servants' hours, as could be confirmed by the disappearance of several tardy travellers. Katherine often mentioned the danger and told him to be careful. Coll both hoped for and dreaded a suggestion that he should stay the night, purely for safety's sake. But the offer never came.

It was the possibility of this invitation that inflamed his imagination in the cool nights on the savannah when the rustle of grass and muted grunts from outside his tent sharpened the mind. Much to his shame, he allowed his imagination to wander amid fantasies of Katherine entering his room on some pretext to be near him; to tempt him; to slide under his sheet with him where he would touch that firm body and compact breasts, caress her finely honed Celtic shoulders and run his fingers down her pale soft skin. Inevitably, such nonsense was followed by self-disgust at his weakness.

There was no doubt they enjoyed a meeting of minds, but any other interpretation of their relationship was daft. Katherine was recently widowed and still in mourning for her husband. Or maybe it was the other way. Maybe she had decided that her love for Bill could not be matched and therefore had turned her back on the whole matter of finding another partner. Otherwise, an attractive woman like Katherine would surely no longer be alone.

Coll reached the rise and paused there for breath, wheezing. He was beginning to doubt the wisdom of attempting such a long walk.

Under an aged African olive tree was a headstone with a border of pale river stones. He read the inscription:

> *Here lies William Alexander Wallace*
> *24 October 1854 — 4 March 1903*
> *Loving Husband of Katherine*
> *Father of Billy*
> *Taken by Lion*

Coll was surprised to realise how old Katherine's husband had been when he died. From her description, he'd imagined a much younger man; but of course he would have been close to Katherine's age — maybe a few years her senior.

He stared at the headstone trying to imagine achieving as much in his thirty years as William Alexander Wallace had in fifty. He found it impossible.

Katherine saw Coll walking down towards her from what she called Olive Tree Hill. His narrow frame and slightly stooped shoulders were unmistakeable. He walked with his head down, apparently far away in his thoughts, and didn't notice her until she gave him a shout.

'What are you doing way out here without a horse?' she asked as she reined in alongside him and dismounted.

'I thought I'd take a walk to find you,' he said, a little short of breath. 'But it's a lot further than I thought.'

'Well, you've found me. Come on, I'll walk with you.'

They started back towards the house.

'I had a feeling you might be around,' she said. 'I've made a big plate of drop scones.'

'Lovely. I thought I'd just pop in to say hello on my way to the Rift Valley.'

'What is it this time?' she asked. 'Cattle or people?'

He smiled at how she managed to distil his entire range of responsibilities into two simple categories.

'The Maasai,' he said. 'The government insists they have to leave the Great Rift Valley.'

'Another quarantine?'

'No. It's more than that this time. They've been dawdling about it, but the Maasai are being moved out of the Rift Valley into a native reserve.'

'Just like the Kikuyu?'

'In a way, although the effects on the Maasai are quite different. Being seasonal herders the Maasai have always occupied a large range. It overcomes any locally bad conditions, like drought or, indeed, cattle diseases. The Kikuyu, being predominantly agriculturalists, don't have the same needs. The move could be disastrous for the Maasai.'

'Doesn't the government understand that?'

'Apparently not. Or else they are unmoved by it.'

'Well, either the government knows more than we do or else they will soon learn about the problems and surely fix them.'

'I like your optimism, Katherine, but I have yet to see an instance where the commissioner has admitted he's made a mistake. In the meantime, think of all the sufferings imposed by his —' Coll stopped, wheezing, and put his hands on his knees, taking deep breaths.

It wasn't the first time Katherine had seen him struggle for breath like that. She put her hand on his back, giving him reassuring pats until the wheezing had eased.

'Please, Katherine, that's not necessary. I'm just a little out of condition.'

She retracted her hand, chastened by his abruptness. 'Sorry,' she said.

'As I was saying, in the meantime, think of all the sufferings imposed by Stewart's actions. What distresses me is that over the last year or so I've become quite familiar with their ways. They have a strong connection with the land. The care of their cattle and their grazing areas is almost a religious thing for them. Worst of all, they only have me and a couple of Maasai interpreters to explain what is being said to them. In most cases their leaders are being fed untruths that they are unable to see for themselves.'

'Why don't the leaders learn English?'

'What?'

She was surprised that such an obvious solution had never occurred to him. 'It seems only logical. Why not teach them English so they can speak for themselves and hear what's being said?'

'But . . . but who could teach them?'

'You could, George. You already know some of their language. I know nothing of the Maasai's language, yet Kira's English is coming along nicely.'

Coll appeared stunned at the thought. 'Why . . . yes . . . Why not indeed?'

'Who are the leaders? Who would best be able to speak up for the Maasai?'

'Well, Lenana is the *laibon*, but he doesn't represent the younger men, the *moran*. And anyway, I'm not at all sure he represents the best interests of the Maasai, although the government would like to think so.'

'Then who represents the others?'

'There's a position among the *moran* called the *olaiguenani*, a kind of spokesman for their age group.' He thought for a moment. 'You know, the more I consider it, the better I like it. You remember my mention of Dr Norman Lewis and his support for the Maasai cause? And his contact with people in London? Well, if we had an *olaiguenani* to be our access to the Maasai, we would find it a lot easier.'

'He certainly sounds like your man.'

Coll fell silent, going over the idea in his head. It was an aspect of his personality that intrigued her. George was certainly not a person to make rash decisions. In fact, she felt he could be infuriatingly cautious at times.

Eventually, the clouds of uncertainty cleared and he brightened, 'Katherine! You're a bloody marvel!' he said, and in a single motion swept her into his arms and gave her a forceful kiss on the cheek. It took her breath away, and she was at a loss to know what to say. *So much for being overly cautious*, she thought.

Coll became flustered and started to cough. When he had recovered, he gave her an abashed smile. 'I'm sorry, Katherine. That was quite —'

'No, it's really —'

'I mean, I got quite excited about —'

'Yes. I'm sure. But it was nothing. I mean, to me it was an obvious solution.'

'But that's you, Katherine. You have a way of looking at things in a simple way, while I bumble around . . . Here I am, wrestling with what I think is an impossible problem for weeks, and you give me the solution in a nutshell. You are quite an exceptional woman, aren't you?'

Katherine spluttered something unconvincing in reply. She was still reeling at her adolescent-like response to his emotional display. His friendly embrace had given her a rush of pleasure.

Norman Lewis's new accommodation on the hill above Nairobi was as good as he thought he could reasonably expect given his relatively low status within British East Africa's governing establishment. The chief medical officer's bungalow had four decent-sized rooms with three outhouses serving as kitchen, laundry and privy. It was high and dry — as had been tested by the recent downpour — and the large veranda with its bentwood chairs and table served his informal entertaining needs quite well. When friends came to visit — as George Coll had on that day — they could enjoy the air on the veranda while watching the bustle of life in the township below.

'Not tea again, George?' Lewis said, as his servant poured from the pot. 'In a land of hard drinkers, how do you remain teetotal?'

'I'm surprised a doctor need ask such a question, Norman.'

'I've not known a doctor who couldn't enjoy a wee dram now and then. Some say it can be therapeutic.'

'For some, perhaps. Not for me.' Coll brought his handkerchief from his pocket and coughed into it.

Lewis raised his whisky glass and took a sip. 'I've noticed that cough of yours isn't getting any better. Why don't you let me examine you?'

'There's no need.' Coll shot a glance at his friend then dropped his eyes to his teacup. 'But thank you.'

'I take it that you've had a diagnosis then and you know your condition?'

Coll nodded, studying his tea as if reading the leaves.

'It's tuberculosis, isn't it, George?' Lewis said softly.

Coll's silence confirmed it.

'No need to be embarrassed. You're not the only chap out here with it. Many come for the same reason — in search of a cure — and I've no reason to doubt it's possible. Some say the warm, dry air fixes it.'

Coll took a sip of tea. 'Norman, I'm not embarrassed by my condition, simply resigned to it. And, quite frankly, heartily sick of the whole topic. It's been ruling my life since I first became aware of it as a young man. I did all the doctors told me to, but I didn't recover. I was told I had to do more. They said the burden of study was too much for me, so I gave up college in Glasgow and in so doing lost my chance to do what I most wanted in life, which was to become a vet. At that point, I felt I had given all I could, but still my condition worsened. They said I should go to Africa. Walk away from all I had and everyone I knew. And I did it. But I made a promise to myself — that would be the last concession I'd make to it. Now I'd rather let the pieces fall where they may. I'm here to do or die, so to speak.' He smiled to soften the edge on his voice. 'Can we change the subject? I'd like to tell you about a wonderful idea someone gave me recently.'

'Yes, certainly,' Lewis said, then decided he was not prepared to give up on such an important matter so easily. 'But not until I say one more thing on the subject. Although Nairobi's wet is better than Scotland for you, and you have a good chance to throw off the TB here in Africa, you can only achieve it if you take care of yourself. Don't try to overdo it. By that I mean take your time when going about your business and make sure you get your rest. Every day. Most importantly, don't get caught out in the highlands during the wet. It's every bit as bad for the lungs as a Glasgow winter's night ever was. There, now ... another cup of tea?'

Coll nodded. 'And now, if I may continue?'

'You may, but not before our drinks arrive. Rahim!' Lewis called to his boy. 'Bring more whisky and the teapot!'

While Rahim refreshed their drinks, Lewis let his eyes wander down the lightly wooded slope, with its scattering of acacia trees and baobabs, to the rambling collection of shacks, tents and thatched huts that was the indescribable ugliness of Nairobi in the wet season. He then traced the road to Ngong — a long line of black ooze that ran arrow-straight from the railway station before making an inexplicable wiggle near Lewis's house. In the space made by the wiggle stood a formation of thriving Australian eucalypts, eighteen to twenty feet tall.

'Why do you suppose Ainsworth planted those trees?' Lewis asked.

'The gum trees? Who knows? The Maasai say they suck too much water from the ground.'

'Then that's probably it. They drain the swamp. Ainsworth was a clever fellow, wasn't he?'

'Norman, the other matter I mentioned?'

Lewis turned back to his friend. 'Sorry, I just find there's so much to know about this place. So many curious things. Plants, animals, people.'

Coll sighed in exasperation.

'But do tell me. Who is this fellow who's given you this wonderful idea? And what is it?'

'It's not a fellow, it's a farmer. I mean, a woman. I might have mentioned her previously,' Coll said.

'You mean one of the settlers' wives?'

'No, she's not married. Katherine Wallace. I'm sure I've mentioned her to you.'

'I don't recall. But she's obviously made an impression,' Lewis said, raising his eyebrows.

'No, no, it's not like that,' Coll said, becoming ill-at-ease at the inference. 'She's got a farm up in Limuru. A widow.'

'A woman farming on her own? Most unusual.'

'She decided to carry on with the farm after her husband died. Seems to be doing a fair job of it too, I'd say.'

'What did you say her name was?'

'Katherine. Katherine Wallace. She's got quite a lot on her plate up there, what with one thing and another. She runs a few head of cattle, but she's also trying out a number of different crops — experimenting, as it were.'

Lewis listened patiently while Coll rolled off a list of Katherine Wallace's fine traits. For a man who was not interested in her *like that*, Lewis thought, his friend seemed quite taken with the woman.

After Coll had talked himself to a standstill, Lewis asked, 'And what was this great idea she came up with?'

'What? Oh, yes, Katherine suggested I should give English lessons to one of the Maasai leaders. It would make it easier for them to know what was going on. Hear it straight from the horse's mouth so to speak.'

Lewis considered it and nodded. 'Quite right. I should think it would give the commissioner something to worry about if he learned that the Maasai were sending a spokesman to England to represent their case to members of parliament.'

'I hadn't gone that far with it, Norman. I am rather thinking it more useful for them to become aware of local issues. Perhaps one of the missions could start a school for the Maasai. They've done as much for the Kikuyu.'

'But the Maasai are essentially nomadic. How can anyone set up a school for a people perpetually on the move?'

Coll gave it some thought. 'You're probably right.'

'Who do you propose to coerce into your English college?'

'I've heard a lot said about a junior *morani* by the name of Ole Sadera. He's an age set leader, and the Maasai believe he was born under some kind of special sign. They seem to look up to him because of it.'

'What kind of sign?'

'I don't know. An omen of some kind. I get the impression that it means he has an unusual strength — something beyond the physical.'

'Good. He'll certainly *need* something special.'

'To learn English?' Coll asked, perplexed.

'That, dear boy, depends upon your teaching ability. I was more referring to the battles that lie ahead of him. You don't believe that the likes of the commissioner and the BEA system care a fig about special signs, do you?'

CHAPTER 14

It was a hot evening, even for London in August. Lord Lansdowne, an angular man with the bushy moustache fashionable since Victoria's early reign, spied his friend Roseford in one of the plush armchairs in a quiet corner of the club. They exchanged greetings in muted tones and Lansdowne ordered a whisky and soda from the head waiter.

'Beastly hot,' Roseford said, giving his open copy of *The Times* a shake.

'Rather,' Lansdowne replied, drumming his fingers on the padded arm of his chair.

Roseford was of a similar age to Lansdowne and had served as Secretary of State for Foreign and Imperial Affairs a few years before Lansdowne had acceded to the position. Roseford had been a rising star in the Conservative Party before his position became untenable due to internal bickering among party members. He had never regained favour, but Lansdowne considered him a useful sounding board and occasionally sought his opinion on contentious issues.

When Lansdowne's whisky and soda arrived, Roseford folded *The Times* and put it on the small table next to his chair. 'And how are things down at the Foreign Office?' he asked, reaching into his pocket to retrieve a pipe.

'Mmm . . . Much the same,' Lansdowne said. 'I received that blasted Maasai paper from East Africa today, you know.'

'You mean the one to resettle them somewhere?'

'Mmm, yes.' Lansdowne took a sip of his whisky. 'That young upstart Ramsay MacDonald has caught whiff of it.'

'Trouble-makers, the lot of them,' said Roseford. 'Call themselves Labour — *pah*! Jumped-up Liberals is all they are. My advice is to ignore all that nonsense. Just take note of your man on the ground out there. Your new fellow — what's his name? Stewart? He was quick off the mark. Got himself a move on, didn't he?'

'Quite. An unlucky bit of haste, I suspect,' Lansdowne said.

The head waiter appeared at Roseford's shoulder with a flame. He sucked it into his pipe, sending a cloud of blue-grey smoke towards the ceiling.

'You don't agree with his actions?'

'Well, I signed the bloody thing, but I wonder if he's really explored all the issues. I mean, it's essentially a treaty.'

'What sort of chap is he? Can't say I know him all that well, but his father was apparently the right type.'

'To give him his credit, he *has* conceded that he fully expects the settlers will eventually cast envious eyes on the northern reserve. That is, once they see how the Maasai cattle have improved the pasture.'

'Do you think he'll hold fast on that?'

'He'd damn well better. I've sent off a reply with the agreement to that effect. I made it quite clear that the definite acceptance of the policy of native reserves implies an absolute guarantee that the natives will, so long as they desire it, remain in undisputed and exclusive possession of what has been set aside for them.'

'There's always compensation, of course.'

'Roseford, old chap, it's too early to start talking about compromises and compensation. I've only just signed the bloody thing.' He took another sip of whisky. 'Mind you, Stewart was a soldier — and a damn good one — so I don't expect he'll have trouble holding the line when the settlers realise what they've let go.'

'And are the Maasai aware of this immutability?'

'I suspect so. Stewart's put it plainly enough in the agreement.

Something about it remaining so long as the Maasai exist as a people.'

'My word!' Roseford said around the stem of his pipe. 'Can't get plainer than that.'

He relit the pipe with a match of his own, waving the waiter away. Leaning forward in his chair, he said, 'Now tell me this, Henry. Has that nasty business with Eliot blown over?'

He was referring to the action taken by Sir Charles Eliot in retaliation over his recall to London. It was well known that the issue was the promises he had made about large land grants to settlers in the Great Rift Valley. Even after his resignation, the affair failed to go away.

'There are some issues surrounding that matter that I'm not at liberty to discuss at present,' Lansdowne said.

'Now, now, Henry. I know all about the grants to Clement Hill's nephew and others.'

'Then you'll also know there's a legal suit pending by another of the benefactors of Eliot's largesse, and it's *sub judice*.'

'Very well. All in good time.' Roseford puffed away for a moment, before adding, 'It's just that I'm a little concerned that moving the Maasai from the Great Rift Valley may create a precedent for moving them yet again, this time from the northern reserve. Then you'll have another round of fights with the Labourites.'

Lansdowne finished his whisky and placed the glass on his side table. 'Must dash. But you're not listening, my dear Roseford. When the Maasai move from the Great Rift Valley to the Laikipia Plateau they are there to stay.'

'Are you sure?' Roseford asked.

'Indubitably.' Lansdowne stood and straightened the wrinkles from his waistcoat. 'As I said, Roseford, as long as the Maasai shall exist as a people.'

Nashilo placed the broth beside Ntooto's stool and sat beside her, leaning her back, as Ntooto did, against the wall of the hut.

'Thank you, child,' the old woman said with a sigh. 'Of all of the young ones, you are the only thoughtful one.'

Nashilo smiled, not wishing to encourage the round of plaintive grievances that Ntooto was prone to recall whenever she thought of her many offspring who, in her opinion, neglected her. The 'young ones' to whom she referred were the many grandchildren of her four grown sons. The fact was that her sons had moved to their own *enkangs* and her grandchildren were far away. But that wasn't an excuse Ntooto would accept.

'If only my Lokatira were here,' she continued. 'She would do as you do, my child. I would not go without. She would respect her mother and care for her as a good child or grandchild should.'

Lokatira had been a small child when taken in the same Kikuyu raid that had brought the death of Nashilo's mother. Nashilo remembered her as a pretty little girl with large bright eyes and an inquisitive mind.

'Do you know, my child, I still see her, here.' Ntooto patted her breast. 'She was my only girl child. My only hope for a comfortable life in my old age. Except for you, my dear. You are this old woman's treasure. Without you I don't know what I would do.'

Nashilo was anxious that the discussion not deteriorate into another bitter diatribe against her family. '*Ai*, this heat, ah?' she said. 'The rains cannot be far away.'

Ntooto squinted into the sky. 'One more moon,' she said authoritatively. 'And then, of course, the young ones will have another reason to stay away.'

'I wonder how the herders are, with the land so dry. It must be difficult for the cows.'

But it wasn't the cattle that Nashilo was concerned for; it was Parsaloi Ole Sadera she thought of, whose absence somewhere on the savannah pained her. She wanted him back. Her husband was visiting his fourth wife in her *enkang* and there were already many precious days lost when she and Parsaloi could have been together.

She closed her eyes, shutting out the heat and the flies, and drifted into delicious memories of their last time together, locked in an urgent coupling on the damp sandy banks of the water hole. When they'd spent their passion, he knelt above her, his body gleaming with sweat and wet from her body. She looked into his eyes, and for a moment it was there — the slightest hint of vulnerability. It made her heart fly to him.

She knew that expression, brief as it was, and so rare. It was a treasure whenever she found it in him; a joy beyond that of feeling him fill her body. Was the look an expression of his regret that he had allowed himself such pleasure while everything else about him was so serious? Perhaps it spoke of sadness — a sadness, she hoped, because their lovemaking was finite; one day to end. It was an expression she had never found in any other man's eyes — the more surprising as it came from the man born of two stones; a man known to have mystery in his heart and a mind forever turned to matters of dire importance.

Ole Sadera stood under the old fig tree on the hill above the *moran's manyatta*. In the distance was the sparkling blue of Naivasha, with its green circle of lush reeds and water grasses, but he wasn't admiring the scenery. His heart was heavy as he watched the leader of the contingent of *askaris* searching from hut to hut in the *manyatta*.

For as long as Ole Sadera could remember, the Purko Maasai had come to the lake during the dry season. It had always been a place of solace, a period of rest from the ceaseless search for grasses elsewhere in their sprawling domain. They would stay near Naivasha until the rains came, and with them the new shoots that drew the Maasai and their stock out into the vast ocean of grass. With the rains came the countless millions of wild grazing animals that shared the season's bounty with the Maasai. The grazing animals were not competitors but collaborators in the process of sweetening the pasture by their constant cropping.

Ole Sadera knew the sergeant was searching for him. He and his Il Tuati were the last group remaining in the great valley. But he was in no mood to speak to yet another emissary from Commissioner Stewart. He was tired of talking; exhausted by the arguments about justice, by his efforts to remain in the valley until it was beyond all hope. He simply wanted to hold on to what was his — what was theirs — as long as possible.

Bad enough the *askaris* had come again to harass him and his people, but the crowning insult was that this was a contingent of Kikuyu — the enemy of the Maasai for as long as the old ones' stories crept back in time. The Kikuyu had been the Maasai's hated foe — and at times a formidable one — since the Maasai's first arrival in the great valley. Now they were here as the friends of the British; as their running dogs to badger and hound their old enemies from the valley that the Maasai had won from them with blood.

Ole Sadera had to admit that the Kikuyu's service to the British cause was no worse than what the Maasai themselves had done. What in fact he, Ole Sadera, had done to others such as the Nandi, when he and his brothers were paid in cattle to assist in a punitive raid against them years ago. Now his hands itched for the spear and *simi,* this time to strike at the haughty British. But he knew Maasai power was a thing of the past. Too many wars had been fought; too many *moran*'s lives had been lost to war, smallpox and the starvation that followed the death of their cattle to the rinderpest. One scourge after another had decimated their numbers. Now he and other leaders could only lament their powerlessness, and rue the day they had allowed the British to seduce them to take up arms against another tribe for the sake of the meagre spoils of war.

He contemplated what might have been. The Nandi had successfully resisted the invasion of their land by the white man for years — far longer than the Maasai had. They had inflicted great damage upon the railway and the men who would drive the lines through the Nandi Hills. At that time, the British forces were not so strong. He wondered what might have happened if the Maasai, rather than take up arms against the Nandi, had joined forces with them and any others with the will to fight the common enemy. If they had, traditional land might still be in the hands of its rightful owners.

Ole Sadera gritted his teeth. He was postponing the inevitable. He left the shade of the fig and walked reluctantly down the slope to speak to the sergeant, who would make strong words and wave his arms about. He would threaten and rave. Ole Sadera would listen, and this time agree to leave Naivasha. Forever.

As *olaiguenani*, he held a position of influence but not of authority, even over his own age set. The *laibon*, Lenana, held sway with all sections of the Maasai, and he had firmly stated his belief that the people must move into the two reserves. Ole Sadera knew his battle was lost. His heart was heavy with sadness. He felt he had failed, yet he knew there was nothing more he could do. To fight would take his people down the road to annihilation.

The Kikuyu *askaris* had spotted him and were excitedly clambering up the slope towards him. Their white sergeant stood at the *boma* gate, arms folded across his chest in triumph.

He was sad that he had failed, but more than his personal loss was the devastating feeling that the Maasai way of life was slipping away on a course to oblivion.

CHAPTER 15

It took Katherine some time to define what was different about George Coll that day. He had arrived in the early afternoon while she was organising the farm hands in curing the small tobacco crop. Tobacco was another of her experiments that had done well, but she reminded herself not to become too excited about the early results. From past experience, a trial might go very well, raising her hopes of commercial success, but then as soon as she took the next step some mystery blight would strike; or, in the case of her Angora goats, a hitherto unknown parasite would reduce the mohair clip to a diseased mess.

George had been a frequent visitor, perhaps once a week over the previous months, stopping by on his way to or from an inspection in the valley or in nearby Kikuyu country. He invariably made an opening remark implying he was checking on her to ensure she was managing on her own, which Katherine thought amusing as she had been managing on her own for some time before George started calling in, and continued to do so after he left. But she enjoyed his company and the diversion his visits brought.

She had often thought she should invite George to stay, particularly when he was homeward bound at the end of a long ride and the afternoon was at an end. It was, after all, common practice to offer hospitality to a traveller, and it would be no more than that. But she never had. It worried her that George might think she had an interest in him beyond their friendship, which, of course, was ridiculous. Men of his age were interested in twenty year olds — women in the prime of childbearing age. Katherine was twice that. Whenever she looked in the mirror, she found more confirmation of those forty-something years in a face that now seemed to show every line. Or was it just that she'd become more concerned about her appearance of late?

Where had the time flown? It was now more than two years since her Bill had died, and she was no closer to deciding what to do with the farm and her life. When she was widowed, she'd said to herself that she'd give herself two years to see if she could manage alone. Two years to decide if she would go back to Scotland or stay on; perhaps with a man who could offer companionship — hopefully even a little more than that. It was a long time since she had enjoyed the pleasure of a good man's arms around her in bed. However, the two marriage proposals she had received from Oscar Carpenter, a widower, and Paddy O'Sullivan, a drunk, and both senior to her by twenty years or more — were easily and politely declined.

While Katherine was unsure what George might make of an offer to stay overnight, she was equally uncertain of her own motivations. She thought it could be the rare pleasure of agreeable company around the sitting-room stove at night. But since she had experienced the rush of pleasure at George's demonstrative show of gratitude after she had suggested he teach the Maasai English, she had started to look at him with different eyes. Yes, he was a frail man, nothing like her Bill in stature, but George Coll had an inner strength of character. She no longer considered him too serious, as she had first thought; but nor could he be described as playful, although he did enjoy a laugh at her expense when she admitted to some of her mistakes while learning the art of farming. He was certainly inclined towards introspection, which was in contrast to her spontaneity. But the more she learned of him, and his passion for defending the less fortunate souls of the world, the more she was drawn to look deeper into his nature.

Katherine thought that his compassion was rooted in a Christian upbringing. She wasn't a religious person herself, but she admired how people of a religious inclination often made an effort to improve society as a whole. George would make someone a good husband one day — someone closer to his thirty than to her . . . With a shock she realised her forty-odd years would soon be fifty.

Back in the house, while Katherine made the tea and served cake, George began to talk. At first, his manner was light and detached, as was his custom. But as he spoke about the Maasai, their life, and the effect that white settlement had upon them, he revealed himself as he never had before. Katherine was spellbound, not only by his thoughts on esoteric topics such as the effects of religion and education on the Maasai way of life, but also by his concerns about their treatment at the hands of the government. He had seldom discussed his dealings with the Maasai with her, and then only in brief outline. This time it was an outpouring of all his worries and frustrations. Something within him that day allowed him to reveal his innermost thoughts.

He had become quite an admirer of Maasai culture and was dejected about its imminent demise following what he called the alienation of their land. He told her of his friend, Dr Norman Lewis, and how he had risked his career to alert people in high places to the injustices being committed in the name of the empire, but that Lewis had a grander vision than his own more immediate concerns. He described his shame at being an unwilling accomplice by acting as interpreter; his guilt at sitting idly by, and his frustration at his inability to put his point of view forcibly to the governor and others about the Maasai's legitimate claim to ownership of the land they had lost.

'But, George, surely it's not your fault the government acts so shamefully?' Katherine said as he fell into morose silence.

'I don't know. Sometimes I just get too upset to think straight. All I know is that these people have been good citizens of the protectorate, they have even helped the British in years past to pacify the other more unruly tribes, and for all their good deeds they're being driven from their homeland with nothing to show by way of compensation.'

He shrugged his shoulders in a gesture of resignation. 'I'm sorry, Katherine,' he said, standing. 'I've taken up your entire afternoon with my belly-aching. Look, it's getting dark already. I'd better be going.'

With a start, Katherine realised it was indeed late. The room, which glowed with light when the sun was high, had darkened as it disappeared behind the hills. She felt she hadn't shown George the support he needed; they had been cheated by the clock.

'You'll be going then,' she said, aware of the awkwardness as they stood at the door that she had not yet opened for him.

'Yes, I must,' he said, rumpling the broad brim of his felt hat. But he lingered. 'Katherine . . .'

'Yes?'

He looked into her eyes then couldn't hold her gaze. He lifted his hat, making a gesture like a wave as he flipped open the door latch. 'I'll be seeing you soon then.'

'Yes. I suppose so.'

As he walked slowly to his horse she held her breath, but he swung into the saddle, gave another wave and rode off.

Katherine found herself staring into the fire, her knitting forgotten in her lap as the dancing flames carried her back to the day's events. Determined to put George from her mind, she returned to her work, recalling that the fire and the onset of evening often conspired to lure her into a pensive mood.

There had been a period, shortly after Bill died, when she dreaded that time of day. She felt there was something disturbing, even sinister, about the way the sun fell from the sky at six o'clock regardless of the time of year, plunging the farm, the house and the surrounding hills into darkness. There was no such thing as twilight to give a person warning; nothing to alert the body to the imminent and dramatic change in temperature. She felt as if the departing heat of day sucked the very life from her in its haste to be gone. She would stand at the window willing the sun to linger, or at least to depart gracefully. But sunset came with a jolt, and she would be left feeling abandoned and alone.

Things had improved since she had employed Kira as her housemaid. Katherine treated her more like a ward than an employee, teaching her to read as well as speak English. With

Kira doing her studies beside her at sundown, Katherine's fear of the approaching night became more manageable.

'I do not understand the meaning of this word,' Kira said from across the dining table.

'Sound it out to me.'

'I can say it but I don't know it.'

'You mean you can pronounce it but don't understand its meaning.'

'Yes.'

'You should try to increase your vocabulary, Kira. "Pronounce" is a word you know, and, as I've said before, you should practise using words you know in sentences. Remember?'

'Yes, Katherine.'

'Now, what's the word you're having trouble with?'

'Folklore.'

'Hmm, let me see. It might be hard for you to understand, but folklore is a collection of stories handed down over the years. I remember my mother gave me a book of folklore stories when I was about your age. Back home — in fact, in most countries — folklore is important. It's a little like history.'

'The Maasai have folklore.'

'They do? But the Maasai have no books. Nothing written.'

'Does folklore have to be in books?'

'No, I don't suppose it does. But what can you remember of your stories? As near as we can tell, you were about five when you were taken by the Kikuyu.'

'I can remember some. I remember sitting in a circle around my father with many other children. I think they were my brothers and sisters and maybe the children of my father's other wives. He would tell us stories from the before time.'

'You mean from the past. What were the stories?'

'I remember a story about an ostrich. Her chicks were taken away by a lion and the lion hid them. The ostrich called a meeting of all the other animals. She complained very much about what the lion had done. The animals were too afraid of the lion to help the ostrich — I mean, to give her justice — but the mongoose said he would help. He told the ostrich to dig a

hole under a termites' nest. It must have a door at the front . . .
What do you call a door at the front, Katherine?'

'An entrance?'

'Yes, an entrance at the front, and another hole at the back.
He said that when she had done what he asked she must call
another meeting and see that the lion also came. At the meeting,
the mongoose said the chicks could not belong to the lion. Oh,
I can't remember how my father said the words.' Her hand flew
up to cover her smile of dismay.

'That's all right, Kira. Tell me anyway. I'm enjoying it.'

'I know we all laughed very much. I think my father said the
mongoose called the lion a stupid chicken because he had
chicks. So then of course the lion became very angry. He chased
the mongoose, and it ran into the hole under the termites' nest.

'Now the lion waited and waited at the entrance, but the
mongoose had run out the other hole. And the ostrich went and
found her chicks because the lion did not want to leave the
termite's nest. He was afraid the mongoose would come out
when he was gone.'

'Very good, Kira. That's a nice folklore story. Are there
others?'

Kira dropped her chin into her hands and frowned in
concentration. 'I remember a little bit about another one, but
only pieces of it.'

'What is it?'

'It is about a mother. She was crossing a river and her baby
was born when she was still in the river.' She tapped at her head
as she did when trying to remember her lessons. 'I can't
remember what happened. It was a baby boy, yes, and when he
came from the water his mother found that he had a stone in
each hand.'

Katherine put down her knitting. 'How very odd,' she said.
'What happened to the child?'

'I don't know. I think everyone was afraid of him. They
expected he would use his power to possess people's souls. It
was like there was a devil inside him.'

'I think you're getting it mixed up with one of those Bible
stories you've been reading for practice.'

'Maybe I am.' Kira thought about it some more. 'Are there medicine men who can make magic happen in the Bible stories, Katherine?'

'Well, let me see . . . Not medicine men as such, although there was a lot of what people like to think is magic involved in some of them.'

'I think maybe this boy with the stones had some kind of magic. He could help the Maasai against all the bad people. I think.'

'What a pity it's not true,' Katherine said. 'From what George has told me, the Maasai could certainly do with someone like that at the moment.'

Ole Sadera walked quickly past the scene of confusion that was the *enkang*. The women were stripping their huts preparatory to abandoning the village. He expected there would be arguments between the married men and their wives as the women pleaded to take along a favourite cooking pot or a particularly soft calfskin hide. The men would have to resist wherever possible because haste was needed and everything had to be carried on the women's backs or on the few donkeys the *enkang* possessed. The exodus could not be halted because a woman could not keep up.

The men would carry spear, shield, *simi* and a gourd of milk. Their task was to move and protect the most valuable asset of the *enkang* — the cattle.

He could hear a number of heated squabbles among the women. He saw his old friend, Ole Nchoe, with his four wives. They had tied their favourite cooking items into bundles and were loading them onto a donkey. Ole Nchoe was one of the luckier men in the village: his women worked well together, with his first wife able to take charge.

Ole Sadera thanked Enkai that he had many more years before he also became an elder with the dubious joys of marriage and parenting. He would be able to afford several wives because of the cattle accrued from many successful raids, but at times like these he was thankful he was still a bachelor.

When the *enkang* had to move because of the demands of the

season or the condition of the pasture, it was stressful, but things were done in an organised manner. Today they were moving under duress. The soldiers would be back, and if the Maasai had not gone by then, they had made it clear there would be trouble.

Outside the *boma* surrounding the *enkang*, the old men and boys had gathered the sheep and goats into a number of manageable flocks. All seemed to be progressing well, so Ole Sadera headed towards the slopes where the *moran* were herding the cattle together in readiness for the march.

He was surprised to see a white man on a horse under the old fig tree. He chastised himself for not noticing him earlier, and wondered how long he'd been there. He was alone and not in uniform, but Ole Sadera had no inclination to see or speak to another white man.

The fig tree and the man were in his path to the cattle and Ole Sadera's first impulse was to avoid him by taking another route. It made his blood rise to feel he should avoid a stranger who had come uninvited onto his land, and angry to recall it was men like him who were driving him from it.

He hefted his spear and shouldered his heavy war shield and strode boldly towards him. If this greedy white man was so impatient to grab Maasai land, he must wait until Ole Sadera's people and their cattle were gone from the valley.

Coll tugged at the wide brim of his hat, sliding it from his head to wipe the sweat from his brow. Beneath him was the Maasai *enkang* — a scene of chaos as men, women and children scurried about. It was so unlike the usual situation. The Maasai were an aloof and elegant people and the sight of them scurrying about like so many ants on a disturbed nest saddened him.

It disturbed his sense of order. He didn't subscribe to the views of the Socialists and Marxists with their ceaseless ranting that the masses should rise up against oppression. Coll felt there was no need for that nonsense if people acted fairly to one another. In his view of the world, the likes of Delamere and the big organisations like the East Africa Syndicate could be defeated by a just society and the honest efforts of fair-minded citizens. It was the reason he had believed that London would halt the forced resettlement of the Maasai before it went too far. He had persisted in that belief until almost the last moment, when Norman Lewis had told him, only the previous week, that his friends in London could do nothing in the short term to prevent the commissioner driving the Maasai from their land.

In the short term. What did that mean? Was it feasible to allow the white settlers, craving land of their own, to settle in the Great Rift Valley and then tell them some time later that it was only a short-term agreement? The period of the leases was not a short term — ninety-nine years. Even in his extreme naivety, Coll understood that neither the commissioner nor the government would renege on those leases. Here was an act that was simply unfair, and, by the colour of his skin and his tacit involvement in the discussion, Coll felt complicit in it.

A lone *morani* approached him up the slope. He was not very tall, but quite wiry and there was something about his stride and his manner that told Coll he was a person of resolve. He planted his feet firmly with each step he took towards him. As the man drew nearer, Coll recognised the insignia on his shield that defined him as the *olaiguenani* of his age set.

The *morani* stared at Coll until he was almost abreast of him, then turned his eyes away in the direction of his path, intent on ignoring him. In spite of the uncharacteristic rudeness, Coll summoned his courage and addressed the man in Maa.

'Hello,' he said. 'I trust your cattle are well.'

The *morani* stopped and turned back to stare again at Coll, this time in amazement. 'You speak Maa,' he said, his eyes wide in disbelief.

'Poorly, as you can see. I am a student of your language.'

The *morani* remained silent. The lowing of the cattle, which were spilling over the crest of the hill above them, filled the void.

'I am Coll by name,' he said in the absence of the Maasai's response. 'I am pleased to meet the *olaiguenani* of the Il Tuati age set.'

The *morani* allowed his spear point to dip downwards and the taut muscles on his shoulders to relax. He seemed lost for words, but finally said, 'You know the Maasai?'

'I know some things. I know of your age set. I have heard of your age set's bravery.'

The Maasai grudgingly nodded an acknowledgement. 'I am Parsaloi Ole Sadera,' he said, standing erect with his head high, but now without its aggressive tilt. 'Why have you come to this place?'

Coll was himself unsure of the answer. He'd simply felt he had to come to placate his conscience in some obscure way. The words he wanted to use, like 'compassion' and 'injustice', were beyond his Maa vocabulary. 'I come because . . .' He searched for an answer that would make sense but found none. 'I am here to help. If I can.'

The *olaiguenani* nodded slowly. 'Did you come from Commissioner Stewart to tell us we can stay in the great valley?'

'No.'

'Did you come to offer cows in compensation for the loss of our best dry-season grazing land?'

'No.'

Ole Sadera nodded again. 'Then how can you help?' he asked softly.

Coll could think of nothing to say. He felt foolish and impotent in the face of such a simple question.

The *olaiguenani* of the Il Tuati age set raised his spear and shield and continued on his way up the hill to join his brothers herding their cattle towards the north.

PART 2

ENTORROR

CHAPTER 16

1909

Ole Sadera stood on the high bank watching a thousand Purko cattle shuffle listlessly along the riverbed, heads low, their hipbones jutting at sharp angles. A handful of his *moran* were with him to protect the herd from predators. He would have preferred to bring more warriors, to protect them against vigilante settlers who objected to the Maasai leading their starving cattle out of the reserve, but he had bowed to the advice of older heads. They said the mere sight of a large party of *moran* would lead to blood on the Laikipia Plains, and more trouble.

Crossing the Uaso Ngiro River — now a mere scattering of stagnant shallow puddles — was an illegal act that could result in a heavy fine for his men and a prison term for himself. But the Purko could not stand to see their beloved cattle suffer, and this was not the first time they had broken out of the reservation to find the grass and water they needed.

The herd had followed the sandy riverbed for miles until Ole Sadera found a section that provided better cover from prying eyes in the surrounding savannah. The slight rise above the left bank was what he'd been looking for, but he was waiting for the herders to pull an exhausted animal from one of the steep-sided mud pools that thirsty elephants had gouged in the riverbed in a desperate attempt to find relief from the unending drought.

'Which direction shall we go?' one of his *moran* asked him.

Ole Sadera had given it no thought. As they got closer to the river he had been too busy studying the terrain for strong points from which he could mount a counter challenge should they be attacked.

'It is a matter for the herders to decide,' he answered, more brusquely than he intended. 'Now, go to that high ground. Keep the herd in sight and come immediately you see any sign of the settlers or *askaris*.'

Apart from the wrench of being forced from their homeland, in the early years of the resettlement the Purko Maasai barely felt the effects of their relocation to the northern reserve. They set up their villages in clusters of family connections much as they had in the Great Rift Valley. Friends and neighbours were soon reunited. The northern land, which they called Entorror, was at the most distant edge of their territory but not completely unknown to them. In those early years the cattle, sheep and goats had flourished and multiplied. Some had said it was a blessing to move north. They said the pasture was good and would become even sweeter with the constant grazing of their herds.

Now that a string of poor seasons had come one on another, the Maasai discovered it more than usually difficult to find enough pasture for the increased herd. Traditionally, they would have roamed in search of water and grass, but in the more restricted range of the northern reserve they had few choices.

They began to eye the forbidden land beyond their boundaries. The whites' cattle were relatively few and didn't need all the pasture sprawling over those undulating hills. The Purko couldn't understand such waste, and had broken out of the reservation on a number of occasions. The settlers' response had been swift and furious.

Down in the riverbed, the herders had managed to drag the cow from the bog hole. Ole Sadera realised he'd had his hands clasped tight into fists.

As the last of the cattle climbed the bank, a whistle from the hill interrupted his thoughts. His scout came running towards him. His heart sank. He could guess his message.

'How many?' Ole Sadera said.

'Like so,' the scout said, showing ten fingers. 'Shall we prepare to fight?'

Ole Sadera gritted his teeth. 'No,' he said. 'We shall not fight.'

'Hsst!'

The sound came from the small hole in the cell's corrugated iron wall that served as a source of air and light. Ole Sadera got to his feet and put his face to the hole. Mantira, looking drawn and worried, greeted him.

'Ah, you are alive,' he said.

'Yes, I am alive. What did you expect?'

'They said you were beaten.'

'It was nothing.' But his hand went instinctively to his swollen and bloodied eye that had felt the force of one of the *askaris*' rifle butts. 'What are you doing here?'

'Is that all a friend is to receive when he comes to look at a baboon's bum through a hole in a wall?'

'I'm sorry, Nkapilil. Thank you for coming. What news do you have?'

'The elders have spoken to the *askari* captain. You will be released.'

'When?'

'Soon.'

'And at what price?'

'It is not for you to worry about. Enough that you get your ugly bones out of that stinking iron cage.'

'How many cows?'

Mantira looked glum. 'Half the herd.'

'What! That is impossible. I would rather stay in here and rot.'

'No, you wouldn't. And don't flatter yourself. Do you think your skinny hide is worth so many cattle? No, the herd owners were also fined.'

Ole Sadera contemplated the irony of it. They had led their cattle out of the reserve to save them, but had lost them in the process.

'This is Lenana's fault. If he hadn't exceeded his authority and accepted the British demands to leave the great valley, this would not have happened.'

Mantira shrugged. 'The British accept his word as leader.'

'Then if he assumes that authority, let him take responsibility for our starving cattle. Let him demand a greater pasture area for our herds. But he will not, because he doesn't want to offend the British.'

'We don't know that.'

'No. We know nothing of him. He has never come to Entorror.'

Ole Sadera was thinking about the various ceremonies traditionally officiated by the *laibon*. The important *eunoto* ceremony was almost due, but the date was in the hands of the *laibon*. Without the *eunoto*, the next generation of warriors could not graduate from boyhood.

'What are we to do, my friend?' he went on.

'We do what we must. From what I've heard, they are having similar problems at Ngong. I can imagine it is even worse further south. This drought has hurt us all, but it will pass. Like all others.'

'I was not talking about the drought. I mean, what are we Purko to do? We are without a *laibon*. How can he conduct his duties so far from us? What of the *eunoto*? Who will arrange the dates and start the proceedings? He has brought this separation upon us by his own doing. Now he abandons us.'

'It is no use complaining. What can we do about it?'

'We can take his role ourselves.'

'Oh-ho! It is worse in that tin box than I thought. The heat has made you more stupid than before. Do the *laibon*'s duties? You are mad, my friend.'

'Not all of his duties, dunghead. Only those we cannot do without, like declaring the *eunoto* ceremony is to commence.'

Mantira shook his head. 'I swear. Is there nothing sacred? Where do you get these ideas?'

'It matters not where I get the ideas. As I have told you many times before, if the elders do not serve our purpose or the needs of the Maasai, we must take control. That time is near.'

* * *

Lord Delamere, uncharacteristically spruce in his formal evening attire, stepped up to the podium, raised his hands for silence and waited patiently for the clamour of conversation to abate. Assembled before him in the ballroom of the Muthaiga Club were the more well-connected members of the settlers' community in British East Africa, many of whom were the descendants of titled forebears.

When the room was silent, he extended a welcome on behalf of the Colonists' Association. As host, it was his honour to introduce the governor, which he commenced to do without preamble.

'Your Excellency, ladies and gentlemen,' he began. 'On behalf of the Colonists' Association, welcome to the Muthaiga Club. And if I may ask your indulgence before I introduce His Excellency, hasn't the Muthaiga management done a beautiful job decorating this ballroom tonight?'

Polite applause from the crowd.

'I haven't seen such conspicuous extravagance since Lord Worrall's nag won the Nairobi Derby.' He raised his hands to quieten the mirth. 'But to the business of the evening. We are here to pay tribute to Governor Edouard. He has been at the helm of His Majesty's ship British East Africa for just a few months, yet already we have seen his stamp on this country of ours.'

Enthusiastic applause came from all corners of the room.

'And this from a French-Canadian!'

The men roared with laughter.

'And an engineer to boot,' Delamere added above the laughter. 'But seriously, what more could we have asked for in a governor? During my time in the protectorate, I have seen two types in charge. We've had brains and we've had determined administrators. And now we have both in one man. We have been sent an administrator when the protectorate is sadly in need of organisation and an engineer when we so desperately need to get things moving, including our doddering railway line. Consequently, if I might be so bold, I see a governor with exactly the right mix for British East Africa.'

The room hummed with a general murmur of support and scattered calls of 'Hear! Hear!'

'A graduate of Britain's Royal Military College, he served under Kitchener in the Sudan and was later honoured by Her Majesty Queen Victoria with the KCMG.' Delamere raised his hand to his right. 'Ladies and gentlemen, may I present Sir Percy Edouard.'

Governor Edouard strode to the podium amid hearty applause. He was a short, handsome man with a strong cleft chin and an energetic walk; a man who exuded self-confidence and determination. He smiled at the warm welcome, his fashionable monocle flashing in the dazzle of the club's newly installed electric lighting, and opened his address, in a crisp, slightly North American accent, with a vote of thanks to Delamere for his kind words of welcome. He quipped that although of French-Canadian descent he was every bit as much an Englishman as most, but sadly with not quite the pedigree of their illustrious host.

Edouard then quickly came to the meat of his subject, which was the changes he intended to make over the coming months and years. 'Ladies and gentlemen, I am a man of action.' He paused to search the faces before him lest anyone dared to challenge his claim. When he found none, he continued. 'I have completed a comprehensive survey of the state of affairs in this protectorate of British East Africa and, quite frankly, I am appalled. My report on this matter is already with the Colonial Office, but I am not waiting for their imprimatur. My duty is clear. I shall assume I have their blessing until I hear otherwise.'

He went on to recount the shortcomings of his predecessors and other office bearers, of their failure to articulate a policy for the ordered development of the country — particularly the agricultural sector — and the dreadful mess of the land grants made to date. He then spent some time explaining how he intended to redress the issue of the insupportable proliferation of native reserves and land grants in a hodge-podge of overlap, particularly in Maasailand.

Heads were nodding among his audience.

'I believe that one of our difficulties arises from the manner in which the Maasai come to a consensus. As you are all most probably aware, the Maasai have a complicated societal structure with spokesmen for this, that and the other thing. There are also different sectors of their society called age sets, which complicates matters substantially. Now we can't possibly deal with them on that basis. I intend to appoint a paramount chief who will be the spokesman for all the Maasai, and it is through him that we will negotiate agreements.' Edouard paused, then added, 'Of course, I need to be cognisant that it is my duty to respect the natives' rights, including the place they choose to live.'

Someone towards the rear of the crowd called out, 'What about the situation of these huge native reserves on some of the country's best land?'

'The Colonial Office has made it quite clear that preservation of native rights is important. The Maasai — for I suspect it is the Maasai you have on your mind, sir — cannot be moved without their agreement.'

The room filled with a babble of discussion at the unexpected turnaround in the governor's theme.

Delamere was also curious about it, but then Edouard looked directly at him and Delamere immediately understood. Edouard could hardly stand in a public forum — even a forum of keen supporters — and contradict Colonial Office policy. Word would spread and parties more sympathetic to the Africans might get to hear about the governor's support.

In the past, the government had been able to find among the local chiefs one who was prepared to support government policy. There was no reason why the Maasai should be treated any differently. Delamere understood that by appointing a paramount chief, Edouard could handpick the man who would make the decision on behalf of the Maasai to move from their Laikipia reserve, allowing new settlers' land to be created in their wake.

CHAPTER 17

The condition of the cattle on the Laikipia Plateau was the worst Coll had seen them in months. The drought had taken a huge toll — dozens were dropping daily.

He vowed to confront the governor again about the situation. So many Maasai cattle could not be accommodated in the northern reserve. It would not be the first time he had raised the matter. Each time Edouard simply nodded and said he would look into it, and there it would end. No wonder the Maasai felt compelled to break out into the neighbouring land, he thought.

Fortunately the herd was free of any symptoms of disease, but it was hard to go on inspecting them when they were in such poor condition. He checked the position of the sun. It was too low to examine mucous membranes and such.

He waved to the herders to indicate he had finished for the day, and called to them in faltering Maa that he would see them again in the morning.

Halfway back to camp he sensed someone, or something, following him. He stopped a number of times but saw nothing. More precisely, he saw nothing in the moment after he turned, but there were times when there appeared to be a space in his field of vision that had in the preceding instant been occupied. It gave him the eerie feeling of being stalked by a ghost. Stories of the mystical man-eating lions of years before, when the railway was being constructed, came to mind. He chided himself for being irrational and continued on his way to camp where he felt a cup of tea would settle his nerves.

It was while he was pouring his tea that the Maasai warrior appeared as if from nowhere. Coll choked back a startled exclamation, and managed to replace the pot without spilling its contents in the fire.

'Hello,' he said impulsively, then corrected himself. '*Sopa*.'

'*Hepa*,' was the sociable reply.

Coll rummaged around his vocabulary for something sanguine to cover his ungracious start, but at that moment, under the Maasai's steady gaze, he could find none. 'Um . . .'

'You speak Maa,' the stranger said. It was more of a statement than a question.

'I do,' Coll replied. 'But poorly,' he added modestly.

The warrior looked vaguely familiar, but the light was not good. He squinted at him through the waving heat above the fire while the Maasai's intense black eyes bored into him as if he were under some kind of examination.

'I am Parsaloi Ole Sadera.'

'Oh! I remember you. The *olaiguenani*.'

'Do I know you?' the Maasai asked.

The phrase could be translated as either, 'Have we met before?' or 'Is it possible for us to have a reasonable conversation?' He chose to respond to both. 'I am George Coll. Please, let us talk.' Coll resumed his seat and Ole Sadera joined him at the fire. 'We met when the government . . . when you and your people were leaving the Great Rift Valley.' Coll remembered the *morani*'s outrage at being forced from his ancestral land.

There was just a flicker of recognition from Ole Sadera. 'I come to you for help,' he said.

'Certainly,' Coll answered, expecting a question about cattle, which was almost the sole topic of conversation with a Maasai.

'I want to speak English.'

'You do? Very good.'

'You can teach me?'

'Me? Well . . . I . . .'

'You speak Maa like an *entito*. You also need my help.'

His comparison of Coll's Maa to that of a young girl was less than flattering.

'I see,' Coll said. 'Very well, I can teach you. It will take many hours and you must study hard, as I did to learn your language. If you can do that, soon you may learn to speak English, also like an *entito*.'

Coll wondered if his attempt at a joke had fallen flat in the translation, but after a moment of surprise, the Maasai's face broke into a wide grin.

Katherine dropped the reins and let the horse plod down the track to the farmhouse. Kira, sitting beside her in the cart, had probably been as glad as she to see the end of the afternoon's social event.

The small community in the Limuru area continued to invite Katherine to their gatherings as they had in the days when she and Bill would attend. Katherine seldom accepted, but the Robinsons — an elderly couple who also tended to avoid the larger gatherings — sent a note every couple of months to invite her for tea. Occasionally, they invited another guest, who was invariably male and single. Katherine liked the old couple, who had the farm next but one where they grew black wattle for the tanning industry, and appreciated their well-meaning intentions, but she found the whole situation rather uncomfortable. She felt unskilled in the art of social discourse — probably because of lack of practice, as Bill and she had married when she was still quite young. And no matter how well-meaning, the Robinsons' idea of a suitable partner was nothing near what Katherine had in mind. Although she never expressed any interest in the would-be suitor, it usually took some time to convince him that there was no point in continuing to call by.

Fortunately, she had been able to bring the embarrassment of this afternoon to an end by noting the lateness of the hour and the perils of travel after dark.

Kira made for company on the ride, but Katherine also thought it good to expose her to the way white society conducted itself on such occasions. She didn't necessarily want to indoctrinate Kira in the ways of the white population, but she thought the extra knowledge could do no harm.

'What did you think of Mr Calligan?' she asked the girl, referring to the Robinsons' most recent offering.

'He is dull.'

'Really? And why do you think so?'

'He tries to make you like him, but he talks about silly things.'

'I see,' Katherine replied, realising that her young charge was more insightful than she had given her credit for.

As they pulled up at the house, the farm worker who also doubled as her *syce* came from the shed to unharness the horse and rub him down.

She had mixed feelings about whether Kira should stay in the white community and continue her education, or not. She liked having Kira around, but she could understand if she wanted to return to her own people. What would become of her in a Maasai village was another matter. According to George Coll, if Kira had remained with the Maasai she would almost certainly have been married by now, probably to a man twice her age.

Thinking about George made her wonder when he would next visit. He had been spending a lot of time in the northern reserve, attempting to help the Maasai through the difficult times they were experiencing. There had been another incursion into settlers' land and the *askaris* had been quick to crush it.

Ordinarily Katherine would be supportive of the settlers, but since becoming more aware of the Maasai through Kira and George, she could be more sympathetic. In many ways the Maasai reminded her of the Turkana — they had the same elegant stature and haughty self-esteem. She imagined they might have even stemmed from the same ancestry. Times were tough for the settlers, but she'd never been one to compromise her conscience for the sake of personal gain, and from what George had told her, the Maasai had been treated quite shoddily by the government.

In the lamplight of the kitchen, Katherine studied Kira objectively. She was about fifteen and therefore a woman in Maasai eyes. 'What do you think about marriage?' she asked.

Instead of acting bashful about the question, Kira surprised her again by giving the matter some thought before replying.

'I think I cannot marry a Kikuyu.'

'Is there any question of that?' Katherine asked, stunned.

'Some of the boys have been making jokes about it, but I know they are not always joking.'

'Well . . . I'm pleased to hear you're not taking it seriously.'

'I must. Soon I will be too old.' She noticed Katherine's pained expression. 'But not yet,' she said, smiling. 'One day.'

Katherine wondered if George had found any connection with Kira's lost family; if he had, it was quite possible that Kira would soon leave her to rejoin them.

She tried to imagine Kira trapped in an early marriage, with a life of drudgery ahead of her. It was not something she would choose for anyone she cared for, but it was obvious that the girl had been giving the matter some thought. There would come a time when she would have to make up her own mind.

Katherine wondered if she could remain as objective when that time came.

Nashilo pouted, but Ole Sadera paid no attention. She sighed and posed and still he continued to sharpen his *simi*, ignoring her completely. In the end, she had to concede. Her time with him was far too precious to waste it with foolish games to win his interest.

'Parsaloi, will you sit with me and talk, please?'

'I am sitting. And I am also talking, if you want to talk.' He studied a pit on the blade before resuming his steady grooming with stone against metal.

It was true she had nothing in particular to discuss; she merely wanted his undivided attention. It was seldom she could spare the time away from her husband's village, and only managed to win the little time she had with Ole Sadera by the ruse of visiting her family. Her husband had almost lost patience with her, and was probably happy to be free of her for the few days.

The night before had been full of the passion that lovers enjoy after a time of separation. She knew a man needed time to rest after such prolonged activity, but now she wanted more. She wanted his attention. She craved the intimacy that some women enjoyed with their men. Was it too much to hope for in a man with whom she could only spend stolen moments?

'Yes, I want to talk. I want to ask you something about marriage.'

He glanced up from his work. 'Marriage? What do I know about marriage?'

'What I mean is, why am I permitted to make love to my husband's age mates but not to you?'

'Hmm,' he said, lowering his blade. 'Do you not know of the story of the warrior and his two sisters.'

'What does it say?'

She knew the story he was referring to — almost everyone did, having heard it and many others as a child — but she could see an avenue to regain his attention. Ole Sadera set down his *simi* and stone and made himself comfortable on the log he'd made as his stool. She could see that, like any Maasai, he enjoyed relating the old stories.

'There once was an old man who had a son and two daughters,' he began. 'The boy grew up to be a warrior and the two girls remained unmarried.

'War broke out between the old man's tribe and the neighbouring Maasai, where there were few women to take as brides. The old man was afraid to send his cattle to the salt lick, which he was required to do once or twice a month, because it was on the neighbour's land. Soon his cattle grew sick and he wondered what he could do.

'His son, a brave *morani*, said he would go alone to the salt lick with a few of the most ailing cows. If their enemy attacked and the cattle were stolen it would be no great loss. On the other hand, if he was not attacked it would prove they were able to use the salt lick and the cattle would be saved. If this was the case, he said he would make a smoky fire to indicate that his father could bring the rest of the herd to the salt lick in safety.

'The son took his elder sister with him and she erected a hut surrounded by a high thorn *boma*.'

'Was his sister attractive?' Nashilo asked, interrupting.

Ole Sadera thought about it. 'I don't know.'

'I think she was. She was very pretty, in fact.'

He frowned, but continued. 'The next morning he took his cows out to graze, leaving his sister alone in the safety of the *boma*. But a group of young warriors from the enemy tribe came and the girl fell in love with them, so she opened the *boma* and made love to them all.

'When the *morani* returned he saw the enemy warriors' footprints in the dust around the hut, but said nothing to his sister.

'The next morning he took his cattle to graze again, but this time he turned back and hid himself near the hut. The enemy warriors returned and the girl made love to them again. When they were about to leave, he heard his sister say that they should return in the evening and wait for her to sing and dance for that would be a signal that her brother was milking the big red cow and they could then come and take all the other cattle. She would then run away and marry one of them.

'In the evening the *morani* prepared his weapons and pretended to go to milk the big red cow. When he heard his sister singing, he rushed into the *boma* and killed all the enemy warriors. He then made a big fire and burned the bodies.

'The smoke alerted his father who brought the whole herd to the salt lick and they were saved.

'When the son told his father of his sister's treachery, the old man decided to break with the tradition that forbade unmarried women to consort with the young men. He allowed his daughters to sing, dance and spend time with the young *moran* until they were married. After that a woman could only make love to the same group of men that had been her husband's age mates.'

'And the babies?'

'There are no babies in the story.'

'But if there were, who would they belong to? Her husband or one of his friends?'

'Why, her husband, of course.'

'But who can say who the father is?'

'Nashilo, there are many things men don't understand. It is enough to know them.' He studied her with curiosity. 'Why do you ask?'

'No reason.'

The answer didn't satisfy him and he waited for her to say more.

'Parsaloi,' she said, wilting under his gaze, 'I want to have your baby.' She turned her head away from him, suddenly embarrassed by her foolishness.

In the silence that followed, she ached to know what was in his mind, then she felt his hand slip from her shoulder to the soft underside of her arm and he gently pulled her to him.

CHAPTER 18

Delamere reined in his horse and sat, grim-faced, staring across to Lake Elmenteita where his cattle and his land — all one hundred thousand acres of it — extended for as far as he could see.

He had just completed a round of meetings with his white overseers and they had confirmed what he already suspected: he had lost the best part of a hundred cattle over recent months. Soysambu, his Elmenteita ranch, was less than half of his holdings, so he could assume that his total losses were over two hundred head.

It appeared that all his efforts to keep his Maasai herders stealing from him had been in vain.

Many of his fellow settlers might launch a reprisal raid, but Delamere would not consider it; not because it was illegal, but because it was futile. 'They're congenital thieves' was a favourite reference he made to the Maasai. 'Raised in the belief that God gifted all the cattle in the world to them, and that any not in their possession must have been lost or stolen.'

Banishing the Maasai from his property would defeat his purposes, and any form of punishment would only serve to estrange the men he needed if his herd were to thrive. Unlike most of the other ranchers, Delamere appreciated that the Maasai were expert cattlemen. They had knowledge of which pastures were best and when to rest them; they knew the diseases the cattle suffered and the best bush medicines to prescribe for their cure; they could divine the mood of the beasts and how to improve their temper so as to improve the quality of the meat and quantity of the milk.

He didn't want to lose them. But what could he do to eliminate the thievery?

A thought came to him: a memory of a story he had read in an acount of one of the earliest meetings between a white man and the Maasai. He wondered if he could use that secret to retain his expert herders but reduce his losses.

Ole Sadera sat opposite George Coll in the shade of a fever tree. Coll had his back propped against the yellow trunk while Ole Sadera sat cross-legged and upright, keeping an eye on the herd of cattle he was helping to move to new grazing land. The sun was high and they had paused to rest before Coll made his way home via Naivasha.

'It is difficult, Swara,' Ole Sadera said.

'I know it is, but try. As I've told you, it's not enough to learn to speak English, you must also learn to read and write it. Until you can do that, you are only halfway to understanding.'

They were speaking in English, as was the agreed rule during Ole Sadera's study sessions.

'But you not learn to read Maa,' the Maasai retorted.

'But there is no written Maa language,' Coll protested before realising it was a joke, and correctly guessing it was the Maasai's attempt to sidetrack the lesson. 'Come, Parsaloi, what is this word?' He pointed at the children's schoolbook that lay open on the ground between them.

'Man.'

'And this?'

'Woman.'

'Very good. And this?'

Ole Sadera creased his brow and ran a hand under his long braids to scratch his neck. The picture beside the word was not helpful. A woman, made obvious by her long dress, stood with a man in front of a building with a cross on it.

'This is new word.'

'It is, it's called "marriage". See, on the next page there is "children" and then "family". Understand?'

'What of your woman, Swara?'

'What? What do you mean?'

'Where your woman?'

'Where *is* your woman,' Coll corrected him instinctively. 'What makes you think I have a woman?'

'Many Englishman have woman. Even in book, man always has woman.'

'No, they don't. Not necessarily.'

'Why not?' Ole Sadera pressed.

It was his favourite expression. Coll had to admit it was succinct and powerful. And, at times, very annoying.

'Because . . . Well, there's a whole host of reasons. You don't have a woman, do you?' he countered.

'I do.'

'Yes, well . . . but not like this.' He pointed to the book. 'Not married.'

'No, but no matter. I have woman. You, no. Why not?'

'I . . . I've not found anyone.'

'You must, Swara. You must have someone. You not good in here.' He pointed to Coll's chest and thumped his own. 'You need someone take care for you. Make medicine for you.' He smiled conspiratorially at Coll and placed a hand on his shoulder. 'Maybe make bed with you.'

In spite of himself, Coll's imagination found him suddenly in bed with Katherine. He could imagine the feel of her lips on his. He could feel the slimness of her waist and the firmness of her breasts. He thrust it all aside. It had become a habit. At night, with the stars above drawing him into their infinite depths, he thought of her and wondered if he was being fair accepting her friendship while offering nothing of himself in return.

He also wondered at what point the simple friendship between them had drifted into the now more complex situation. There had been times when they stuck to trivial interests. She would tell him about the minutiae of life on the farm. He would discuss his increasing knowledge of the Maasai and their customs. Simple. It brought to mind the matter of Kira and the Kikuyu raid.

'Tell me, Parsaloi, do you know anything of the Kikuyu raid on a Maasai village about ten years ago?'

'Hmm, yes. I know it. That was last time for Kikuyu raid. Then government send *askaris* to make for peace. I know it not from me. My woman was there when the Kikuyu come.'

He told Coll what he knew of the details. Even from an indirect source, it was a bloody account. An earlier raid had enraged the Kikuyu — the Maasai were generally the initiators — creating a series of retaliatory raids. These grew in intensity and savagery until the Kikuyu amassed a large army, apparently intent on settling the matter with finality. They swept down on the offending village and defeated them with such consummate ease that they carried their orgy of blood-letting into neighbouring Maasai settlements. In the carnage, many innocents were hacked to death, including the mother of Ole Sadera's girlfriend. Many lost children who were taken as spoils of war.

It was a heartrending story made more so by Ole Sadera's apparent objectivity as he recounted it. Coll suspected it was the Maasai's way of controlling his emotions. There also appeared to be no resentment against the Kikuyu for their brutality. Coll questioned if he was now able to put the incident behind him.

'This is the way of war. Swara,' he responded. 'Can I forget? No. But I can understand. Inside I cry for this. Inside so much hurt because our enemy did not pay and now the British say we must not make war. So I must learn not hurt all time this thing happen. I know to make war even when our land is taken is not good for Maasai. I know I must be silent on this things. This not Maasai way. But what can I do?' The control he had earlier exerted seemed in danger of failing, but he rregained it to continue. 'Already we lose land. This is so much bad for me I do not know how to stop hurt inside. So I be silent. Maybe I just wait. Maybe there be time when British go home and Maasai make this bad thing better.'

It was the first time Coll had heard the notion that the Maasai — perhaps all Africans — believed that the British were only temporary occupants of the land. It was a revelation to Coll, and his first inclination was to correct Parsaloi's misconception. It was the right think to do, and Coll had always prided himself on his integrity. But having heard that the Maasai believed the only end to his people's plight hung from the tenuous belief that the British colonists would one day leave, he couldn't dash that one hope with the truth — that Britain had already invested a fortune in a railway and other infrastructure and was unlikely to withdraw, certainly not now she had begun to colonise the country on a large scale.

Coll was torn between truthfulness and compassion. He had always believed that his strength of character and integrity were his counter to any of the physical frailties he suffered, but now he realised he was also a realist. He could not dash his friend's only hope for the end to his torment.

Katherine seemed to have the knack of sensing when George Coll might be about to make a visit. At some indeterminate time after seeing him last, she would bake a batch of scones and take a little more care with her appearance than usual. Not that she dressed up as she might when taking the cart to Nairobi for supplies, but enough for Kira to ask if she had been invited to an outing by one of her neighbours.

Around mid-afternoon, after Katherine had completed supervising progress on the new fences, she was indoors with her head in the oven when a knock came at the door. She cast a glance in the mirror and, brushing the wrinkles from her smock, went quickly to the door.

She threw it open with a smile, and was startled to find the man standing there was not George Coll. The fellow seemed equally startled but vaguely familiar. Katherine recognised him as the Robinsons' other guest from the week before and searched her brain to recall his name.

'Katherine,' he said, rather breathlessly. 'Good afternoon. I hope I'm not disturbing you?' He wore a pinstriped jacket buttoned across a midriff that might have once permitted it to close without strain but now caused it to look rather uncomfortable. He held his hat in one hand and a bunch of flowers in the other.

'Oh, um, Allen . . .'

'Arthur. Arthur Calligan.'

'I'm sorry. Arthur. Of course.' She shook his hand. It was warm and moist. 'Forgive me, Arthur, it's just that —'

'I've interrupted you in something important, haven't I? Maybe I should come back some other time.' He began to back away from the door seeming genuinely concerned and obviously nervous.

'No, it's just that I've been busy and my head was miles away.'

'Then I have interrupted. Oh, here.' He shoved the flowers in her direction. 'For you. Now, I think I should go, and I'll —'

'Not at all. Thank you,' she said, taking the sprigs of lavender and small budded roses. She guessed they had come from the Indian couple a few miles up the road, who exported flowers to Bombay for reasons unknown to anyone in the surrounding farms.

'Look,' she said, 'I was about to make tea. Would you like to join me for a cup?'

He brightened. 'A cup of tea. Yes, that would be very nice. Thank you.' He followed her inside.

Kira came from the kitchen annexe and served the tea and scones while Katherine and Arthur chatted. Once started, her visitor could not be contained. Katherine recalled what a bore he'd been that afternoon at the Robinsons' too.

A knock on the door interrupted them. Katherine knew who it would be.

'George!' she said brightly.

'Good afternoon, Katherine. Nice to see you.' He sounded a little more formal than usual. 'I was just passing and thought I'd look in to see how you're managing. But I notice you have guests,' he pointed his hat in the direction of the cart, 'so perhaps I'd better not intrude.'

'You're not intruding. We're just having some tea. Would you . . .' She caught George's gaze drift away to stare over her shoulder.

'Oh, George, this is, um, Arthur. Who just dropped by.' She felt she needed to offer something more substantial by way of explanation, but couldn't think of anything.

Arthur simply nodded.

George's mouth opened and closed again without uttering a word.

The irony of having two male callers arrive simultaneously when otherwise she could go weeks without seeing a soul threatened to cause Katherine to giggle.

'Well, as I say,' George said, 'shan't intrude. I'll come back when you're . . . I'll see you some other time, Katherine.' He turned and walked stiffly down the stairs.

Katherine was tempted to call after him, but thought better of it. After all, what was there to explain? But her amusement at the situation vanished as she realised that the rare moment of intimacy they had shared on George's previous visit, when she had dared hope that he was at last coming out of his shell, would now be lost.

Coll headed home at a brisk clip. For once he was glad he would have the oppressive surroundings of Nairobi and its crowds to distract him from his thoughts of Katherine and her new companion. Still, the ride from Limuru was filled with an endless torment. He knew nothing about the man he'd found visiting Katherine, but over the miles he developed an intense dislike for him. He was a conniving cad, a braggart attempting to convince Katherine of his heroic deeds while hunting elephant in the Congo or being a soldier of fortune in search of noble causes to combat. He had visions of the suave Arthur laughing at her jokes, filling her glass with wine and making clever dinner conversation. When his wicked imagination led him to wonder what might have occurred later, in the bedroom, he had to put it from his mind. Down that path lay madness.

When he wasn't fulminating against the trickery of the artful Arthur, self-pity consumed him. Was it his fault he was suffering a debilitating illness? And righteous indignation followed. Should he imitate the caddish Arthur and ignore what was best for Katherine? Was he the only responsible individual in all of East Africa?

*   *   *

Coll sat brooding over a cup of tea on Norman Lewis's veranda. Lewis came from inside the house carrying a glass of whisky and soda and sat opposite Coll, studying him for a moment before he spoke.

'So, what seems to be the problem, George?'

Coll looked up at him, perplexed. 'What do you mean?'

'I mean, I haven't seen your face for more than two weeks and you've hardly had a word to say since you arrived.'

Coll earnestly studied his teacup but felt Lewis's eyes had not left him. 'It's, um . . . difficult.'

'You know, George, if I didn't know you better, I'd say you had woman troubles.'

'Humph. What would you know about woman troubles?'

'I've had my share. Of troubles, that is. You forget, I was married once.'

'Hardly makes you an expert.'

'Perhaps not, but I'm a willing listener.'

Coll was silent.

'How's the widow Wallace up there in Limuru?' Lewis asked.

Coll slowly shook his head and took a sip of tea. 'I . . . Well, I don't know.'

'Come on, what's up?'

Coll sighed. 'I wonder about Katherine . . .' He glanced at Lewis before continuing. 'I mean, I wonder if there should be more than just friendship between us.'

'I imagine Katherine is thinking the same.'

'What do you mean?'

'George, you're up there almost every other week. What is the poor woman supposed to think?'

Coll frowned.

'Don't you like her?'

'Of course I do. Why would I bother seeing her if I didn't?'

'Then what's the problem?'

'The problem is I can't — I won't — get involved.'

His ire was rising, fuelled, Lewis suspected, by his inability to explain himself. Perhaps he didn't even understand his own mind.

'It's . . . unfair,' Coll added.

Lewis nodded, now beginning to understand him. 'You're afraid that because you have TB it would be unfair to get involved in a long-term relationship.'

'Yes.'

'Yet you have been prepared to go along with it, letting her believe there might be more to it.'

'No.' He paused. 'Yes,' he added softly. 'I suppose that's it.'

Lewis put his glass on the table between them. 'George, I'm going to say something you may not like, and it's this. You're not the only man out here with a grave illness. You're probably not even the only man out here with an illness who's fallen in love. But if you don't get over this false sense of martyrdom, I can honestly say that you're probably the stupidest fellow in all of British East Africa.'

'You shouldn't preach on matters you don't understand,' Coll shot back at him.

'I think I understand your medical condition well enough. But as to what's in your head, I'll admit to being at a complete loss. Let me remind you of something you told me about yourself. Or have you forgotten?'

'What?' Coll said, irritated.

'Do you remember when we first discussed your condition, and I — being the ever-helpful medical practitioner — tried to take you under my wing and convince you to take care of yourself? You said you had sacrificed enough for your illness and that you would make no more concessions to it. Do you remember that conversation, George?'

'I do, but this is different.'

'Why?'

'Because this is not about me. It's about Katherine. She's already suffered the loss of a husband. How can I put her in the situation of nursing an invalid — an invalid who will be lucky to have a few good years left in him?'

'For Christ's sake, George. You can't play God with her life. And what makes you so sure you're not going to come through this? Medical science is full of stories of remissions, or even spontaneous cures. It's not for you to speak for Katherine. She may be prepared to love you unconditionally.'

'I can't do that to her, Norman. I've been down this road before, back in Scotland. Jennie and I were going to be married, but I found out about the TB and I called it off. I had too much love for her to condemn her to an uncertain life, a life where she would watch her husband slowly die.'

Lewis shook his head. 'George, you've got more religion than me, but doesn't the Bible say that only God can pronounce the hour of a man's death?'

'For an irreligious man, you have a good selection of misquotations to call upon when they suit your purposes.' Coll pushed himself up from his chair. 'And I'd rather you kept them to yourself, thank you.'

CHAPTER 19

Lord Delamere wrapped his handkerchief around the handle of the blackened iron kettle and poured its boiling contents into a battered teapot sitting on the edge of the wood stove. After adding a handful of tea leaves, he waited a moment before filling the two cups that sat on the slab table between him and his neighbour, Gilbert Colchester.

Delamere's house on the edge of the Great Rift Valley bore no resemblance to his ancestral home in Cheshire. It was little more than a lean-to with a canvas annexe. He planned to build something more substantial in due course, but there was never the time. Surprisingly, his wife seemed also content to wait, although she regularly spent time with friends in Nairobi, which was the present case.

Colchester added three spoons of sugar to his tea and sipped silently, watching his host tear apart a loaf of bread. Delamere knew it would be up to himself to initiate any conversation. Although their properties shared a boundary, the two men lived many miles apart and met infrequently. Colchester reminded him of a feral sheepdog rather than a wealthy landowner and cattle rancher. This impression was heightened by his habit of giving a kind of growl before he spoke, as if the effort of speech was too much trouble. He also had enlarged adenoids, which gave his voice, when he deigned to use it, an odd whine.

Colchester had the habit of wandering off for days to camp

with his Maasai herders, sharing their food and joining them in their meat feasts. At home, he chewed their snuff and burned leleshwa leaves to ease his adenoids. It was this familiarity with Maasai customs that had caused Delamere to invite him to his house that day.

In spite of Colchester's taciturn nature and odd habits, Delamere respected the man. He thought it a pity that Colchester was not more forthcoming with his ideas, which, when explored, could be surprisingly insightful. Instead, one had to prise them from him. His redeeming feature was his willingness to spend the enormous amounts of energy and money needed to grow a pastoral empire from the uncompromising soil of British East Africa. Like Delamere, he believed that only large estates could produce the efficiencies needed to prosper in a land with soil and weather so unlike that experienced by any English farmer. Both men were not afraid to experiment, developing new methods in their armoury of defences against the unexpected. They knew that unless their farms were very profitable, there would be no capital to reinvest to continue to battle until Africa was subdued. They were two unlikely comrades in the same mammoth quest.

'Tell me, Gilbert,' Delamere began when they had eaten most of the bread and drained their cups, 'what do you know about the business of blood brothers among the Maasai?'

'It happens.'

Delamere waited in vain for elaboration. 'Why do they have it? When is it used? Who can become a blood brother?' he probed.

Colchester simply blinked at him and lifted his cup to his lips. Finding it empty, his eyes went to the teapot on the stove. Delamere retrieved the pot and refilled his cup.

'Why do they have blood brothers?' he asked again.

Colchester made that growling sound. 'Urrr . . . to make friends.'

'And can anyone become a blood brother?'

Colchester was silent for so long Delamere thought he might need to repeat the question. Eventually his neighbour said, 'I suppose so.'

'I have an idea,' Delamere said, leaning across the table on his elbows. 'If we were to become blood brothers to the Maasai in these parts — I mean the ones we use as herders — do you think it would stop them stealing our cattle?'

Colchester's teacup paused on its journey to his lips. 'No,' he said.

'Why not?' Delamere asked, crestfallen. 'I've read that Lugard used it to win the cooperation of the tribes all those years ago.'

'The *olaiguenani*,' Colchester responded. 'Only if it was with the *olaiguenani*.'

Delamere nodded. 'I see.'

He knew the role of the *olaiguenani*. In fact, he knew the Maasai quite well, although not to the extent his neighbour did. It made sense to involve the *olaiguenani* in the blood ritual as they had the strongest local influence on the *moran*.

'Why don't you go and have a little chat with the *olaiguenani* around these parts? See what they think about it. Maybe they'll agree to it.'

Colchester nodded slowly, sipping at his tea.

Delamere became more enthusiastic as he realised his neighbour could see merit in the plan. 'As we build our stock we'll need a lot more herders. It could be very profitable to take out some insurance against theft, Gilbert.'

The feral sheepdog smiled.

Ole Sadera and Mantira watched Gilbert Colchester ride away. When he had passed from sight into the cedar forest, Mantira said, 'What do you make of this plan, Parsaloi?'

'You know him better than me. What do you think?'

'I think he is a man who understands the Maasai. I think it is possible he is telling the truth.' He turned to Ole Sadera. 'But why do you ask? Surely this is the very same idea you put to me when we were waiting to be arrested at the edge of the great valley. You said then that we should share the brisket with the whites so that they could not attack us.'

'Yes, I know. But I have come to believe that any idea the whites have is better for them than for the Maasai. Now I must question my own thinking.'

'Thinking, thinking. Do you never rest? Me, I have never been at ease with the idea. The *en-kiyieu* has never been shared with whites.'

'That is true, but these men are the leaders of the whites. If they are prepared to share the brisket, the future for our people is safe.' Ole Sadera could see that Mantira was wavering. 'These are difficult times, my brother. We must choose what to keep from the past and what to change. Just as we may need to declare the start to the *eunoto*.'

'That is clearly the *laibon*'s duty. Now you go too far.'

'The young men grow restless to graduate into the ranks of the *moran*. It is time for the age sets to move forward. If Lenana does not do his duty and declare the *eunoto* very soon, then we must.'

'This is not our way, Parsaloi. I can agree with the *en-kiyieu*, but to change the way we induct our warriors . . . I fear we may unleash powers that will in the end destroy all of us.'

Gilbert Colchester took his seat under the African fig and tucked a wad of tobacco snuff up into the space between his cheek and jaw. The strong essence rushed from his palate to his brain giving his disposition an immediate lift.

It was Delamere's idea to have two chairs brought up the hill from his house after it became apparent that the killing and preparation of the bullock would take some time. Colchester could have told him that, but preferred to let Delamere muddle through with his blood brotherhood ceremony, rather than get involved in a protracted discussion.

Colchester had arranged the ceremony with the two Maasai after Mantira and Ole Sadera had sent word that they were agreeable. This came as a surprise to Colchester who thought it curious that the Maasai would be prepared to make such a solemn undertaking. From what he knew about the blood brotherhood relationship, it was one between equals with roughly equal benefits clearly seen for both sides. The Maasai might have suspected it was Delamere's hope that they would henceforth respect his property and treat his cattle as his, not theirs, but from the Maasai side, he could see nothing beneficial for them. Later, from the circuitous, polite manner of the Maasai when discussing important matters, he realised that the two men had made an assumption about Delamere's position that was quite at odds with reality. But he had quickly come to the conclusion that it would do his and Delamere's cause no harm to permit the Maasai to continue with that false belief.

The bullock was on the cooking fire and would soon be ready for their purposes. Colchester knew the meat would be next to raw, but he had become accustomed to it from his experience in similar ceremonies and feasts.

Delamere seemed content to keep the silence between them intact, and Colchester relaxed and let the snuff carry him into a place of tranquillity — a mood he seldom enjoyed around his fellow white men.

He had always felt that this place above Delamere's farmhouse, under the shade of the fig, was special. It sat in a hollow on the side of the hill surrounded by an amphitheatre of boulders. Sometimes, while passing it, he had believed he sensed a presence there, as if he had been shrouded in a soft blanket and some hidden force had hushed the air. The tree itself was an ancient, gnarled thing. The Maasai called the African fig the *oreteti* tree and revered it for its longevity and toughness — characteristics they aspired to in their own lives. They commemorated the *oreteti* in prayers and blessings. This one on Delamere's hill was especially regarded by the warriors as it had surely seen the glory days when the *moran* were answerable neither to family, nor elders; to no one but their fellow warriors. From the deserts north of Mount Kenya to the Aberdares, from the Aberdares to Kilimanjaro, the Maasai warriors had raged unstoppable across their enormous territory. Such was their dominance that no other tribe dared to keep cattle in case it brought the Maasai to their land. They even kept their sheep and goats hidden in the valleys and forests. They were the days when Colchester would have loved to be a *morani* too.

Mantira and Ole Sadera approached. Delamere and Colchester stood to meet them, and Colchester formally greeted them. The two *olaiguenani* responded, then Ole Sadera began to speak in a flat monotone — almost a chant. He spoke of brothers and responsibility; respect and unbreakable vows. Colchester understood him perfectly. Delamere's Maa was not quite adequate to follow the formal discourse.

An attendant produced a knife and the four men ran the blade across their forearms one after the other. Four thin lines began to weep blood.

Ole Sadera and Mantira were each handed a lump of bullock meat. They wiped the meat over the white men's forearms.

Ole Sadera said, 'Hereafter, our blood runs in your veins. Your blood runs in ours. Our children will inherit your blood, as yours will ours. In this way we show our respect for each other's land, for each other's property, for each other's beliefs, for each other's lives.'

The two *olaiguenani* ate part of the bloodied meat.

The Maasai handed the meat to the two white men who copied the action while Colchester repeated the words in Maa.

It was done, and the meat feast commenced in earnest.

Delamere returned to his seat under the fig tree. Colchester wrestled with the choice of joining the *moran* or observing tiresome obligations. Reluctantly, he returned to sit beside Delamere.

'Well, Gilbert,' Delamere said, studying his hunk of meat, 'that's a good day's work, what?' He turned the meat this way and that until he found a suitable piece and took a tentative bite.

Colchester took a mouthful of meat and said nothing.

'I expect that little performance of ours will save us quite a few head of cattle, eh?'

Colchester again made no comment. If he had chosen to, he might have said, *yes, the blood brotherhood will probably reduce the number of cattle stolen*. He might have also disclosed his discovery of why the Maasai had agreed to the ceremony and what their expectations might now be from the new kinship. When he heard the Maasai using the title *olaiguenani* in reference to Delamere, he realised they believed Delamere was a spokesman for the white tribe — in other words, a member of the government administration.

It was clear to Colchester that the ceremony had marked a profound change in the Maasai's relationship with the two white men. Importantly, both Ole Sadera and Mantira — the two most influential leaders in Entorror, the northern reserve — now expected that he and Delamere would act in their best interests, just as true brothers would, and, further, that Delamere would use his power as a member of the government to see that those best interests were observed.

Delamere was at the forefront of the settlers in their often intense arguments with Edouard and his administration. For him to be mistaken as a member of the administration was the supreme irony. Delamere would have been amused had Colchester had the mind to inform him.

Colchester was quite sure that Delamere had no intention of assisting the Maasai, blood brotherhood or not, except in the unlikely situation where their interests coincided with his.

CHAPTER 20

Governor Edouard drummed his fingers on his desk as he read the report from the German authorities on the outbreak of east coast fever in one of their provinces.

'Who is this Herr Flehmig, Wadley?'

'He's the equivalent of a district commissioner, Sir Percy,' Wadley said. He sat across the desk from the governor, nursing a bundle of business correspondence. 'He's in the Mwanza Province which is just over our southern border.'

'I know where it is, man, but what I want to know is, what the devil does he think he's doing sending through piffle like this? Doesn't he think we have inspectors of our own? Bloody impertinence. Well, I suppose we'll have to send Coll down there to investigate.'

'Yes, sir.'

When Wadley had scanned the German DC's report earlier, he'd known Edouard would not be pleased. East coast fever was a contagious and deadly bovine disease. It had been slowly moving up the continent following an outbreak several years earlier in South Africa. There were plans, drafted a year or so earlier, to move all the Maasai out of the Laikipia area to an extended reserve in the south. Knowledge of an ECF outbreak would make that move difficult to justify.

'Are you sure you want to send Coll, Governor?'

'Hmm, I know what you're implying, Wadley.'

Coll was a diligent operative, but a trifle too close to the Maasai to be trusted with confidential information.

Wadley cleared his throat. 'Perhaps we should send someone, ah . . . someone aware of the sensitivity of the information?'

Edouard thought about it for a moment. 'Good idea. But what about Coll?'

'Mr Coll has done fine work as stock inspector, Sir Percy. Perhaps he's due for promotion? A position as game warden in the northern region might be appropriate.'

'Hmm, I think you're right, Wadley. Game warden in the north. Draw up the paperwork for me. In recognition of outstanding service to His Majesty's government, etcetera, etcetera. Perhaps we can interest John Hull in going to the southern reserve. He understands these things. Ask him to pop in for a chat.'

Wadley made a note. Hull was the manager of the East Africa Syndicate — the largest landholders in the Great Rift Valley, and keen to expand their interests on the Laikipia Plateau.

'In the meantime, shall I take the usual precautions and proclaim it a quarantine area, Sir Percy?'

Edouard touched a finger to the deep cleft in his chin — a habit Wadley had learned usually presaged something of importance.

'Rather than quarantine,' the governor said, 'we'll close the corridor.'

Wadley was careful in choosing his words. 'The corridor between the north and south Maasai reserves is mentioned in the 1904 agreement, sir.'

'I don't give a damn, Wadley. East coast fever must be stopped. We can't have infected stock wandering all over the Great Rift Valley. The settlers will have a fit. Anyway, didn't you tell me the Maasai were already in default of that agreement by not moving out of the Naivasha area?'

'Well, I wouldn't like to swear to the legality or otherwise of a few natives lingering longer than was stipulated. Anyway, they've now moved to the northern reserve.'

'But technically they were in default. Let's not make it any more difficult than needs be, Wadley. I'll have someone tell Lenana of the changed arrangements in the next few days.'

Edouard fell silent again. The finger found its way back to the furrow in his chin.

'And another thing, Wadley, we'd better put a hold on that big *eunoto* festival the Maasai are about to have. Any time those people get together for one of their shindigs, they're bound to bring hundreds of cattle. Can't seem to go anywhere without them.' He nodded, obviously pleased with his plan. 'No, it'll never do. Draw up something for me to put a stop to it. Say it's for the safety of Maasai stock during the drought. Until further notice, etcetera, etcetera.'

He headed off any further discussion by shuffling through the other papers on his desk, becoming irritated, as he usually did, halfway through the correspondence.

'Look at all this rubbish about funding. What is it about British East Africa, Wadley? I had none of these problems with allocations when I was commissioner for South African Railways. Damned if I did. We needed new rolling stock to support the drive into Boer-held country. I got a million pounds. Now, here we are, it's East Africa's chance in history, and what do I get? Prevarication and red tape. Where's the money to fence the southern reserve? How am I expected to encourage commercial development on a shoestring?'

It was a rhetorical question and Wadley held his tongue. He understood Edouard's frustration. There was a group within the Colonial Office who were very conscious of the strengthening political climate sympathetic to natives' rights and who used the budget to ensure their voice was heeded. Various do-gooders spurred them on. To make matters worse, there were some within the protectorate who shared those views. Edouard knew better than to ride roughshod over these people. British East Africa had been the burial ground of some very promising careers. Nevertheless, Wadley was fairly certain the governor would have behaved in a far more decisive fashion, as had been his style in the past in Nigeria and South Africa, except for the unsettling knowledge that somewhere within the administration was a spy — an insider with knowledge of confidential matters and the ear of important people in London.

The matter had worried Sir Charles Eliot too, and he had expended a lot of energy to discover the source, but had ultimately failed. Later, he had resigned in disgrace.

Somewhere in Eliot's confidential papers would be his suspicions about the person or persons involved. Wadley had not read those papers, but he knew that Edouard had, and believed it would not be long before the person feeding the pallid penpushers in London would be exposed. Edouard was a man of great energy, drive and ambition. He would not rest until he had found the traitors and dealt with them.

Dr Norman Lewis bounced around on the seat of his cart, cursing his aching posterior and, what was in his view, his overly developed sense of generosity.

His three-day tour of the medical facilities in Naivasha had been routine — an annual inspection — but George Coll had convinced him to accompany him afterwards to his camp in the Great Rift Valley, where he would sleep in a tent, of all things! Upcountry accommodation in government employees' guesthouses was notoriously uncomfortable. He had hardly slept a wink in Naivasha with the biting bedbugs and mosquitoes that seemed unerringly to find the holes in his bed-net and attack every square inch of his exposed skin. He could understand why George Coll avoided the guesthouses, choosing to pitch a tent instead, but Lewis was not a camper.

Coll was in the area on an inspection of his own and they had met by chance in Naivasha. When he asked if Lewis would like to join him in camp, Lewis had emphatically declined. But as they chatted, Lewis realised his friend seemed in need of a sympathetic ear. In a moment of weakness, he changed his mind and accepted the invitation. It was now two hours into the torturous journey to Coll's camp and he was regretting the decision.

'How much further is it?' he called to Coll, who was riding ahead of him.

'Not far; past the next bend in the river.'

'And who is this Maasai chap you want me to meet?'

'It's the fellow I've been telling you about — the *olaiguenani* — the one I've been teaching English.'

'I see. And why is he here? This is not the Maasai's land any more, is it?'

'Unfortunately, no. He's returning from Ngong. I came upon him by accident while out inspecting game animals in the valley. He's escorting some cattle. I thought it was a great opportunity for you to meet him before he heads north again.'

Lewis thought it typical of Coll that he would strike up a friendship with a Maasai. It seemed he had never quite got over their failure to save the Rift Valley for them. Lewis supposed that by devoting most of his free time to teaching one of their leaders English, Coll felt he was compensating for that failure. As Lewis considered the issue, he concluded it was probably fortunate for Coll that he had this interest in the Maasai to occupy him. He was by nature a solitary person, and his job, which ensured he was out in the field more often than in the towns, did nothing to help expand his range of acquaintances. Lewis had tried to encourage him into a closer friendship with Katherine Wallace, without success. Coll could be a very stubborn man on certain issues, and when it came to the matter of Katherine, he was adamant about keeping his emotional distance. There was ample evidence that he was in love, but equally evident was his self-denial of that fact. Lewis couldn't even convince him to take him to meet the woman, such was his determination to prevent any interference in the matter.

They came upon the cattle first — about fifty head. Three Maasai herders were scattered among them. Coll greeted each and exchanged a few words with them. The third man he introduced as Parsaloi Ole Sadera.

'Dr Lewis,' the Maasai said, 'I am pleased meeting with you.'

'And I, you,' Lewis replied, impressed by the extent of the young *morani*'s English. 'George has told me you are a very good student.'

He smiled, showing a row of white teeth. 'But Swara's Maa is better than my English.'

'Swara?' Lewis said, looking from Ole Sadera to Coll.

'It's my nickname,' Coll said. 'The Maasai love nicknames and that's mine, I'm afraid.'

'I see.' Lewis nodded, waiting for an explanation. It was obvious Coll had no intention of further enlightening him, so he asked what it meant.

Ole Sadera answered. 'It is the word for gazelle, what you call impala.'

Lewis looked at Coll, the least likely gazelle he could imagine.

Coll smiled bashfully. 'I know what you're thinking, Norman. It's not because of my abundant energy and sleek muscular body as you may well expect. It's because of the way I sometimes clear my throat.' As if on cue, he gave a nervous cough.

Ole Sadera grinned. 'Swara. All same, *swara.*'

Lewis smiled in spite of Coll's embarrassment. He obviously didn't realise how often he punctuated his conversation with the little cough. It was a habit created through his illness but adapted by him as a kind of verbalised pause. The Maasai had perceptively recognised the similarity between it and the impala's little grunt of alarm.

Coll suggested they go on to camp to give Lewis some merciful relief from hours sitting on the hard seat of his cart. Shortly before dusk, Ole Sadera joined them, saying he would take the midnight watch over the cattle. The three men chatted for some time about the grazing conditions around Ngong, which was less than a day's ride from Nairobi.

'Ngong is not so bad,' Ole Sadera said. 'But further to the south I hear that the land is weak these days. Not like Entorror in the north.'

'But the Loitai live in the south. They seem to manage,' Coll said.

'Yes, they know its ways. We Purko do not have such knowledge. It is better the Loitai stay there and we stay in Entorror.'

Lewis asked how the Maasai were coping without access to the pastures in the Great Rift Valley.

'Look around you, Dr Lewis,' Ole Sadera said, sweeping his hand westward. The rolling grassland undulated in and out of long shadows formed by the now setting sun. 'This place was Maasailand — our home. Between the north and the south.

Maasai cattle grazed all these lands. This is why we Maasai came to this place maybe three, four hundred years before, maybe more even than that. Even now, when I am only passing through, my heart is happy to see it again.'

Lewis said he understood how he must feel to be forced to live somewhere else.

'Yes, it is sad. Sad also for the young men who not yet become warriors. Where will we make the graduation ceremony now that Kinangop is lost?'

Lewis nodded in sympathy. Coll had explained a few of the important ceremonies to him. The graduation ceremony from boyhood to warrior had always been held in the Aberdares, now part of the alienated land.

'But it is not you I am . . . What is the word, Swara?' He and Coll exchanged a few words in Maa. 'Yes, I understand,' he said to Coll before continuing. 'It is not you I am complaining to. Swara told me you try very hard to save our land. All the Maasai people need to say thank you, Dr Lewis.'

The sombre expression of gratitude embarrassed Lewis. He demurred, saying that although he and Coll had done their best, they had ultimately failed to prevent the loss of the valley to the Maasai, for which they were sorry.

'No,' Ole Sadera said, 'do not say sorry. You have tried very hard. The Maasai do not know you and Swara try so hard, but I know. I say thank you, Dr Lewis. You are a very good man.'

Lewis nodded, confused by the unexpected show of emotion. He mumbled some words of appreciation. With the human face of the Maasai cause now before him, his efforts to save their land took on a more personal complexion. Initially, the battle to prevent the government from taking over the Rift Valley had been one of principle for him. As he had done all his adult life, he had defended the needy against the greedy. There hadn't been a philosophical argument or social issue upon which he didn't hold a passionate view — one way or the other — but they had been fought on an essentially intellectual level. Now the injustice of the displacement of all those people more than four years ago seemed all the more scandalous. Curiously, he thought it also all the more important. He wondered if he might have fought even harder back then had he known the individuals involved.

No Maasai had ever visited Katherine's farm. Kira once noticed two old men standing at the head of the track above where the Kikuyu field workers were reaping the maize. She thought they might be Maasai, but they remained for only a few minutes before turning away to resume their journey.

She knew from George Coll's account to Katherine that the Maasai were no longer in the Rift Valley — the nearest part of Maasailand to the farm. The valley was where she had lived before the invading Kikuyu warriors had carried her away, singing songs of victory and bravery as they climbed the escarpment.

The last glimpse Kira had of her homeland was when the war party reached the ridge and paused, exhausted by the climb. The warriors' voices had faded into silence, perhaps because they, like Kira, were in contemplation of the bloody events that had transpired on the valley floor.

She could still see the breathtaking sweep of space as her eye travelled into the shimmering distance on that day. The wind carried the sweet tang of dry grass, cattle dung and hot mouldering earth. An eagle rode the updraught sending yellow weaver birds into twittering panic. With their departure came a profound silence. Only the wind, warm and evocative, brushed her face and whispered in her ear.

Sometimes at night, with only the mournful call of an eagle owl or the distant below of a buffalo to fill her thoughts, she would recall that dimly remembered time. The words the wind had whispered that day were that she could never leave, but in time the memories faded. One part of her was content to see them go. Katherine had shown her the ways of the whites and Kira could appreciate the many benefits such a life could offer. Another side resisted that call. If she chose to forego her Maasai side, who would she ultimately be? The dilemma made her head spin and the answers — if any existed — remained as elusive as the eagle owl's prey.

CHAPTER 21

Coll reined in his horse at the turn-off to Katherine's farm. He had been wrestling with the notion of visiting her — 'settling the matter with her' was how he termed it during his attempts at sleep. But sitting there, dithering with indecision, he realised there was nothing to settle. Katherine was her own person; she was not beholden to him in any way. Why should she be? And anyhow, wasn't that how he wanted it? The questions flowed, but he had few answers.

If he took the turn-off to Katherine's he had two problems to overcome. First he had to consider the possibility that she would not be pleased to see him. He had acted like a petulant child last time, storming off when he found her entertaining her new friend. Would she even want him to continue his visits under the changed circumstances? For his part, he didn't wish to arrive and find this person, Arthur, still there. The idea of them sharing a bed together caused his gut to churn.

'Something wrong, George?' Lewis asked, drawing the cart to a halt beside him.

'No, nothing at all. Just waiting for you to catch up.'

Coll berated himself for stalling so long. Norman's presence was the second problem. He could hardly disappear without some explanation, and even the explanation would require explaining. He simply didn't want to discuss it. Nor could he invite Lewis to join him. Lewis had often expressed the wish to meet Katherine, and Coll imagined he would arrange it one day, but not today. It would be difficult enough to speak with her without another person there to complicate matters. He felt he would simply have to forget the whole thing, and return another day — alone.

'Nearly there,' Lewis said.

'Where?'

'Nairobi, of course.'

'Oh, yes. Nearly there. Shall we press on?'

'Your friend Katherine lives around here somewhere, doesn't she?'

Coll shot him a glance before mumbling that she did.

'She'd be disappointed if you didn't visit. Being so close.'

'Oh, I don't —'

'Why don't you drop in on her since you're passing? Unfortunately, I can't stop. I've a busy afternoon ahead, preparing my reports.'

'Well . . . perhaps I should just pop in for a moment.'

'Indeed. Give her my regards and tell her I hope we can meet some day soon.'

'I will.'

Lewis bid him goodbye and flicked at the reins.

His friend's abrupt departure surprised Coll. He called a 'goodbye' after the disappearing cart, then he looked down the track to the Wallace farm. Once it had been so familiar that he hardly had to think as he trotted his horse down it. Now it seemed strangely foreign.

Lewis smiled, pleased with himself. Without a little encouragement, he doubted whether George would have gone to visit Katherine Wallace.

From observing him at close quarters over recent days, Lewis could tell his friend had something on his mind. By his reticence to discuss it, Lewis assumed the matter of Katherine was coming to a head.

He hoped George would see some sense and allow himself to follow his heart.

* * *

Coll shifted his weight from one foot to the other. There was no visitor's cart hitched to the gatepost. If there had been, he knew he would not have had the nerve to proceed. He had now knocked twice. After the first rap he'd seen the curtains move and, after a second, heard a muffled voice say, 'Just a moment'. But several moments had passed and nobody had come to the door.

Just when he felt she had decided not to see him, the door slowly opened. Kira stood there.

'Oh, Kira,' he said, almost relieved it was not Katherine. 'I was just passing and —'

'Please come in, Mr Coll. Miss Katherine will come in a moment.'

'Thank you,' he said, stepping through the doorway with his hat brim curled into a tight roll in his sweaty palm.

Kira stood smiling at him, which didn't help. He had no idea how to make conversation with a young Maasai girl. He wasn't even sure how well she handled the language other than taking orders for tea and cake.

'Hello, George.'

Katherine emerged from her bedroom. She wore a long creamy-yellow pleated skirt that brushed the floor. Just above the hem was a floral frieze set against a background of the same grey as the broad belt of dark grey fabric that banded her narrow waist. The high collar of her blouse had a simple stitched edge that kept the bodice tucked snugly to her breasts. Her enigmatic smile gave him no clue to her thoughts.

'Hello, Katherine.'

'So glad to see you, George. You'll have a cup of tea?'

'Yes, please.'

'Kira, would you pour the tea, please?'

'I hope I'm not intruding . . .'

'Not at all, George. Why would you say that? Won't you take a seat?'

'Thank you.'

He knocked his knee on the table leg as he sat. The pain made his eyes water. He tried to ignore it by covering his discomfort with a smile, but it only served to give him a pained expression as he struggled to answer her question. 'I mean, last time I came, it appeared as if . . . I mean, you had a visitor, and I didn't want to . . . Oh, thank you, Kira.'

The arrival of Kira with the tea salvaged what was becoming a very awkward situation. The conversation was not proceeding as he'd planned it. He decided to change the subject while he regathered his thoughts.

'Kira, I have a piece of news for you,' he said.

Kira blinked at him, a little startled by the attention.

'I asked my Maasai friend about the Kikuyu raid — the one when you were stolen from your village.'

The girl looked to Katherine, uncertain of his meaning.

Katherine explained that she had mentioned the abduction to George, and that he had agreed to help them trace Kira's family if possible.

'Yes,' Coll continued, 'and my Maasai friend, Ole Sadera, said he knew of the raid. It was made on a Purko village on the eastern slopes of the Rift Valley. His own village was far away so he had no details, but the mother of his friend was lost in the same raid. He has agreed to visit you and see if he can help.'

'That's wonderful news, George,' Katherine said. 'Isn't it, Kira?'

'Thank you, Mr Coll,' the girl responded, her eyes bright with excitement.

Katherine nodded her approval at her good manners. 'Thank you, Kira,' she said. 'That will be all for now.'

When she'd gone, Katherine said, 'I appreciate your efforts, George. And so does Kira, I'm sure. Even knowing we are trying to find her family will make her feel better.'

'I didn't want to say that the woman Ole Sadera knows has lost touch with her original family. I'm sorry I had no better news. Just between you and me, it's like finding a needle in a haystack. They could have moved a dozen times since then. Ole Sadera said the Purko section is very big and he has no idea where they might be by now.'

'I understand, but thank you anyway.'

'You're, um, welcome, Katherine.'

A silence emerged, and grew. After a few moments they both began to speak at once.

They smiled.

'You first,' he said.

'No, please. After you.'

'Well,' he began, 'I was just going to say, I hope you'll forgive my behaviour the other day when you had your visitor here.'

'Who? Arthur? Oh, I didn't mind. He was just about to leave as you arrived.'

'There was no excuse for my rudeness.' He was determined to speak his piece before he lost his nerve.

'I don't think you were —'

'Unforgivable. I mean, you have your friends. I have mine. There's no need for us to be uncomfortable if we, as it were, stumble in when they're visiting, is there? No. Surely we can keep in touch. If you want to, I mean. And if your gentleman friend doesn't mind.'

'Why would he mind?'

'You know. If another man . . . that is, I . . . come calling.'

'For goodness sake, George, Arthur is a casual acquaintance — not even that. I was introduced to him at a neighbour's house and he was merely making a courtesy call. So far as being a "gentleman friend" as you so quaintly put it, he's nothing of the kind.'

'He's not?'

'I very much doubt he'll be back.'

'Oh. I see.'

He fidgeted with his teaspoon, trying to conceal his relief. And wondering if he could fulfil the promise he'd made to himself should it turn out there was a simple explanation for Katherine's caller.

When he was harbouring the notion that Katherine had taken a lover, he had chastised himself for his reticence in making his feelings known to her. He realised then, at the moment that he felt he had lost her, how stupid he had been to let such a woman slip from his grasp. He swore that if he had the chance again, he would declare his interest and take his chances with her response.

He summoned up all his nerve and began to speak. 'You know, Katherine, we've been friends —'

Suddenly there was a constriction in his chest, as if a belt had been tightened about it. He just had time to snatch his handkerchief from his pocket before the coughing fit erupted. He struggled to control it, and through his watery eyes saw Katherine's startled expression.

'George!' she said. 'Are you all right? Kira! Come with some water! Quickly!'

He tried to say he would be all right in a moment, but all that emerged was a series of suffocating sobs.

The Maasai girl appeared holding a tumbler of water. Katherine took it and pressed it into Coll's hands. 'Take a sip, George,' she said.

His chest was bursting with the effort to breathe and the room seemed to close in on him. The glass fell from his hand. He reached to catch it, but saw it hit the floor, shattering into a hundred tiny sparkling shards.

At the 'Tobermory' signpost, Coll drew his horse to a halt and looked back down the track to Katherine's house. His retreat had been hasty and as undignified as his frightful coughing fit.

By the time he had regained control he had lost all confidence in himself. Despite Katherine's protestations that he should at least rest a little before making the journey home, he had thanked her for her concern and taken flight.

He realised he had almost made a terrible mistake. It was clear that he had not defeated his illness and therefore had no right to ask Katherine to consider a closer friendship.

Under the circumstances, he wondered if it was wise even to see her again. It would be almost unbearable to spend time with her now that he had lowered his defences and admitted how much she meant to him.

CHAPTER 22

Smoke hovered above the dwindling embers of Lenana's fire. He sat cross-legged and alone inside his hut, fingering the sacred stones given to him by his father. He put the irritations of the day — his squabbling wives, arguments about a bride price, and myriad other annoyances — from his mind and took refuge in contemplation, making his escape to a peaceful place where he would listen for the voice of his forefathers and hope for words of advice.

That night he was troubled by Ole Sadera's threat to hold the *eunoto* outside his authority. He hummed an old song and opened his mind to the departed ones.

Whispered words came indistinctly from the void. Snatches of forgotten conversations from other times spent with the ancestors flitted by. A familiar voice imposed itself over the others.

'Lenana, my son,' it said.

'Supeet?' Lenana asked. 'I hear you.'

It was the voice of his grandfather. A man he could scarcely remember from his childhood, but one who had come to him in the past when he had asked the spirits for counsel.

'You have summoned me with your song,' Supeet said from beyond the smoke. 'What is it that troubles you?'

Lenana told him of Ole Sadera's intention to hold the *eunoto* in Entorror.

'This one, this Ole Sadera,' Supeet said, 'I see him leading the Maasai against the whiteman. He will stand against your enemies while others fall away. He has strength beyond what eyes can see. Be aware of what he says. Heed his words, for he holds the future of the Maasai in his hands.'

'But how can I agree for Ole Sadera to hold the *eunoto* in Entorror without my blessing?'

'You cannot. The answer lies in uniting the Maasai once again — north and south together in one place.' The voice wavered in the smoke. 'Ole Sadera has won the hearts of the Maasai in the north while you have kept close only to those in the south. You must unite the two or you will lose both.'

'But it is the British who have cut Maasailand in two pieces.'

'It is difficult, but it must be done.'

'Will the *moran* then be satisfied? Without the *eunoto*?'

'They will not. You must convince the whites to allow the *eunoto* to proceed. Ole Sadera and his Il Tuati will then respect you. Without it, he may turn the *moran* against you.'

Lenana shook his head in misery. 'Why would Governor Edouard listen to my wishes? He needs nothing that I have to give in return for such bounty.'

'Do not doubt your skills, Lenana,' the voice said. 'You are the *laibon*, the son of my son, the Great Laibon.'

'Will you help me? Will you show me the way?' Lenana pleaded.

'Find a way . . . Find a way . . .' The voice grew fainter and fainter until it melded into the *hoo-too-way* call of an owl.

CHAPTER 23

Wadley showed Delamere into Governor Edouard's office.

'Ah, Lord Delamere,' Edouard said, as he stepped from behind his desk to greet him. 'Good of you to come.'

'My pleasure, Governor.'

'Please,' Edouard said, indicating a pair of comfortable armchairs facing each other on opposite sides of a low table. 'Let's take a seat here, shall we? Tea?'

'No, thank you.'

The governor waved his hand to dismiss Wadley.

'I know we have our regular formal meetings, but the matter I'd like to discuss with you is probably best done between us, rather than involve the Colonists' Association and all those minutes of meeting, etcetera.'

'If you wish,' Delamere said. He was gaining the impression that Edouard was more of a political beast than he had at first appeared. But Delamere recognised something of his own character in Edouard's gritty determination to get things done and was prepared to work with him in whatever mode he chose.

'It's about land on the Laikipia Plateau,' Edouard said.

Delamere's eyebrow rose. The Colonists' Association had indicated that the highlands of the Laikipia Plateau were ideally suited for development by settlers because they enjoyed a white man's climate and could be farmed using white men's farming techniques. Many of his constituents had complained that the agreement granting such excellent grazing and farming land to the Maasai had been too generous. They had begun referring to the plateau as the White Highlands.

'On a confidential basis, if I may,' Edouard added.

Delamere nodded. 'Of course.'

'Lord Delamere, I feel it's my duty, as governor, to maximise the use of productive land. People like you and Mr Colchester are ideal settlers and should be given every encouragement to farm the land, just as people like Captain Grogan should be granted forestry concessions to fill the demand for timber.'

Delamere acknowledged the compliment with a nod.

Edouard went on. 'I have tried unsuccessfully to encourage the Maasai to move out of the northern reserve. I had thought that by offering to extend the southern reserve massively, I could convince them of its attractions. But as soon as I convince one group of leaders, I lose another. Or the elders agree and the *olaiguenani* do not. It's like dealing with a multi-headed serpent — you cut off one head and another one rears.'

'That's unfortunately the way of the Maasai,' Delamere said. 'I don't know how they get to make any decisions with all the palaver they go through.'

'Quite. But I have an idea that might address some of those issues.'

'Oh?' Delamere asked, leaning forward.

'All in due course, Lord Delamere. Returning, if I may, to the matter at hand. We all agree that moving them south is for their own good. The northern reserve is overcrowded. They have frequently broken out of the Laikipia reserve in periods of severe drought, such as this. Why, only a few months ago I had to heavily fine a bunch of *moran* and incarcerate the leader.' Edouard touched a finger to his chin. 'I want to call a meeting with the Maasai to get to the bottom of it all. I was wondering if you might have a word with the northern bunch, who seem to be a law unto themselves these days. You appear to have some influence. Perhaps you can convince them to come to the meeting. They might listen to someone less . . . official than me.'

'What do I have to offer them as an incentive to come?'

'The *eunoto*. You may not have heard, but I've been forced to ban it.' He hesitated before continuing. 'Unfortunately, recent stock inspections in the southern Maasai reserve have confirmed our worst fears. East coast fever is endemic.'

'What?' Delamere sat upright in his chair. 'Are you sure?'

'Quite. My man was down there recently. I have closed the corridor between the reserves.'

'What about quarantine?'

Edouard hesitated again. 'Lord Delamere, we all know that the Maasai seem able to manage stock diseases in ways we don't quite understand. ECF is therefore more of a problem for us than for them. Hence I'm closing the corridor as a quarantine measure. But I don't want to use that word at the moment. I wouldn't think it prudent to make it generally known about the outbreak. I think we all agree that moving the Maasai to where they will be under better scrutiny and control will, in the long run, provide a more useful outcome for all of us. Not least the Maasai. Announcing a quarantine and drawing attention to ECF will only get the settlers a little excited, and it would hardly enhance our chances of moving the Maasai there, would it?' He looked pointedly at Delamere.

Delamere nodded sagely. 'I see what you mean, Governor.' He allowed himself a smile. He felt he would have no difficulty convincing his new blood brothers to attend the meeting. 'If you can convince Lenana to consider the move, I'll see if I can get the northern lot to come along,' he said. 'See if we can agree on some helpful solutions.'

As Coll rode his tired mare across the rolling hills of the Laikipia Plateau, he was once again reminded how resilient the high plains were. Compared with the drought elsewhere, Laikipia was surviving reasonably well. While obviously dry, it was not totally desiccated, as was the case in the southern reaches of the Great Rift Valley.

The sweeping Laikipia plains had an eerie light on them, with the sun trapped between a cloudbank and the hills. The odd glow increased his sense of isolation. Nothing existed between him and the horizon but the soft warm wind and swaying grasses.

The Maasai called this part of their territory Entorror. It derived from the Maa verb *a-rror*, meaning to fall to the ground. As far as he could interpret it, the word referred to an abundance of grass, so much that a man with cattle need never move on.

The Maasai's custom of moving their cattle to reduce the stress on the land was key to their success as pastoralists. Coll thought that many of the settlers could learn from their practices. It was the main reason that the Laikipia Plateau's grass had improved over recent years, and official figures showed that the Maasai's herd had trebled to nearly two hundred thousand cattle since they had moved there from the Rift Valley in 1904. During difficult times, the smaller stock animals were of equal importance to the survival of pure pastoralists such as the Maasai. The Purko section had amassed nearly a million sheep and goats.

Entorror was huge. Coll estimated it was at least ten thousand square miles, although no definite boundaries existed. The northern reserve was a much-reduced portion of it — at around half of that area. But in spite of its size and relatively good pasture, the first few months of 1910 had been particularly trying. The Maasai had the previous year broken from their reserve in many places along the Uaso Ngiro River, incurring penalties and fines of cattle. It had proved to Coll that there was a need to extend the reserve. He had been able to convince Governor Stewart to extend it some years earlier, but had so far been unable to convince Governor Edouard of the need to extend it again.

He was in Laikipia at the governor's request. Edouard wanted to make sure that the leaders Ole Sadera and Mantira were aware of the ban on the *eunoto*. Coll had been promoted to game warden, but even so he thought it an odd mission for him. The Maasai *laibon* usually conveyed all administrative orders of that kind. Still, he didn't mind making the journey. The high dry air was good for his chest, and might help his sleep, which had been disturbed by his unresolved relationship with Katherine.

He rode into the *moran*'s *manyatta* in Rumuruti and soon found Ole Sadera.

'Swara, my friend. You have come,' the *olaiguenani* said, clasping Coll by the shoulders.

Coll returned the gesture. 'I trust your cattle are well,' he said.

Amid the uncertainty of whose salutation and greeting to use, Ole Sadera had at an early stage suggested they invent one of their own — a compromise between the white man's handshake and the Maasai's spray of spittle. Clasping each other's shoulders had become their personal greeting.

'You are well?' Ole Sadera asked. His inflection gave it a deeper meaning.

'Thank you, Parsaloi. I am.' Coll didn't want to enter into a discussion about his health. 'How did you know I was coming?' he asked, deflecting the conversation.

Ole Sadera smiled. 'The grass has ears.' It was a Maasai proverb that rolled wonderfully off the tongue in Maa.

An old woman brought a gourd of fresh milk and handed it to Coll. The two men sat on low stools and Coll took a sip of the warm milk. He was still not quite accustomed to the odour of Maasai gourds, but was relieved to have overcome the tendency to gag as he drank.

Coll and Ole Sadera chatted comfortably together for some time. In spite of Coll's efforts, Ole Sadera returned to the matter of his health and mentioned that he looked pale.

'I am just tired,' Coll replied dismissively. 'I have had a long, tiring month. It is nothing to worry about.'

'The bark of the red thorn tree, boiled and mixed with ghee, is very useful for a cough.'

'It's nothing, really.'

'I can have one of the women make some for you. It takes little time.'

'No,' Coll said in exasperation. 'Thank you, Parsaloi. I have all the medicine I need.'

Ole Sadera changed the subject. 'What news from Nairobi?' he asked.

Coll had hoped to break the news gently, but launched into it. 'The governor has banned the *eunoto*, my friend.'

'Yes.'

'You know about it?'

'I do.'

'But how?'

Ole Sadera just shrugged.

'I'm very sorry,' Coll said. 'I know the *eunoto* is important to you.'

'There is no need to be saddened, Swara. We will have our own *eunoto* here in Entorror.'

'But surely Lenana will not permit it?'

'Lenana has not shown his face in Entorror. He is a stranger here. Many of the young men have never seen him. Mantira and I are the only leaders they recognise. We *moran* will not be deprived of our graduation. We will paint our bodies with ochre, we will dance and we will have our meat feast.'

'Surely it would be better if the *laibon* gave his blessing?'

'I will send word to the *laibon*. He may come if he chooses or he can remain in Ngong. It is of no consequence.'

Coll sat silently, picking at a dry grass stem.

'You are worried, Swara. You have more news for me?'

Coll glanced up at his friend. 'Yes, I have.' He paused before adding, 'The governor has closed the corridor to the southern reserve.'

Ole Sadera appeared shocked. He turned his head to the south and stared into the distance for a long time before speaking. 'How will we keep our Maasai family together?'

'I'm sorry, Parsaloi. I have no idea why he has done this.'

'Do you know, Swara, my friend Mantira taught me a proverb when I was a young *morani*. It is: *Clever is the eye that has travelled*. He told me it was every warrior's duty to see all of Maasailand and, in so doing, to learn as much as he could from his fellow warriors.' He shook his head. 'I have done this. I have been to the south many years ago, and I have learned from my distant brothers. How will our next generation of warriors learn what they must?'

He turned again towards the south and, after a moment's silence, asked, 'Are we to lose Entorror?'

'Entorror? Entorror is your homeland, Parsaloi. Of course not. You are safe here.'

Ole Sadera was not reassured. 'Do you not remember, Swara? The Maasai once had a homeland that spread from sky to sky.'

Coll fidgeted on his seat. 'Yes, but you still have two huge reserves. And, as the treaty says, you have them for as long as the Maasai exist as a people. Everything is well here in Entorror. You are safe here; your herds and flocks grow bigger every day. What could be wrong?'

'Why has the governor closed the corridor?' Ole Sadera asked abruptly.

'Why . . . I'm not sure . . .' Coll's voice caught in his throat and he coughed. 'I'm sure it's for the best, my friend,' he added lamely.

'Something is wrong, Swara. I feel it.' A troubled expression clouded the *olaiguenani*'s face. 'Something is very wrong.'

CHAPTER 24

Shortly after returning from his meeting with the northern Maasai, Coll was summoned to the governor's office to again act as interpreter for a meeting with Lenana.

Governor Sir Percy Edouard, resplendent in the stiff, high-collared tunic of his Royal Engineer's uniform, drew out his chair on the other side of the desk from the diminutive Lenana. Coll had noticed that Edouard always wore his full dress uniform under these circumstances. It made him appear even more intimidating and he suspected it was another of the governor's tricks to add to his prestige and authority in the natives' eyes.

As the governor took his seat, Lenana seemed to shrink further into his navy greatcoat — a present given him upon his appointment as chief cattle judge at the Nairobi Agricultural Show. Coll sat at the end of the desk on the governor's right side. Lenana's interpreter, one of his fellow elders, sat opposite.

Coll was still feeling guilty about delivering the bad news about the closing of the corridor and the ban on the *eunoto*. He knew it was illogical but he couldn't help feeling tainted by his involvement.

After the exchange of pleasantries, Edouard wasted no time in getting down to business. 'Tell Lenana we are not pleased with the way some of the young *moran* are acting at present, Coll.'

Coll did as he was asked.

Lenana sat silent and composed as first Coll, then his own interpreter, translated the message.

'Remind him that it is illegal for his *moran* to go about spearing lions for a lark,' continued Edouard.

When that had passed through both interpreters, he added, 'And that the number of incident of cattle stealing is growing.'

Finally, the governor came to the point. 'Tell the *laibon* that it is his duty to keep matters under control and that I will hold him personally responsible if this lawless behaviour continues.'

In reply Lenana told Coll that he was having difficulty with the young *moran*. He said they were far away and in no mood for restraint.

'Lenana says his *moran* are proving difficult to control,' Coll said in translation.

Edouard's smirk revealed he had heard the answer he wanted.

'Tell the *laibon* that His Majesty's government are here to support loyal chieftains. Tell him we have no such trouble with the Kikuyu, the Kamba, the Luo. And it is our wish that the *laibon* should assume greater control over his people, in the interests of peace.'

Coll translated.

Lenana sucked his teeth in agreement.

'Tell him I strongly recommend he accept an appointment as paramount chief. Let him know the position would come with the full weight of British justice to enforce his legal rulings in all matters associated with the Maasai tribe.'

Coll hesitated, searching Edouard's face to confirm he had heard correctly.

'Get on with it, man,' Edouard admonished.

When Coll translated it, Lenana's bright dark eyes went from Coll to Edouard and back again.

'What is this paramount chief that the governor speaks of?' Lenana asked.

'I believe he means you are to take a similar position to that created for the Kikuyu and others.'

Lenana sucked his teeth again. 'I agree to it,' he said.

Coll turned to Edouard and, with a look of disbelief, said, 'Your Excellency, Lenana agrees.'

Edouard seemed as surprised as Coll. 'Do you think he understands?' he asked.

'I . . . I think so, sir. Perhaps I'll repeat the details?'

'Yes.'

It took some time for Coll to fully explain the position and stress that it would mean the end of the traditional roles of *olaiguenani* and several others. 'Are you sure you want to do this, Lenana? Are you not concerned this will cause trouble among your *moran*? Your elders?'

Lenana, always softly spoken, said he understood. He also added a request.

'Sir,' Coll said, turning back to Edouard, 'Lenana agrees. He says it is important that the Maasai be united. However, he does have a condition. He is agreeable to accept the position of paramount chief if you allow the *eunoto* to proceed.'

Edouard kept his expression guarded. 'Hmm, I suppose that can be arranged. Provided there is a separate *eunoto* for the southern reserve. Tell him that I don't want cattle traipsing all over the Great Rift Valley.'

The governor gently touched his slender white fingertips together as Coll made the translation.

'Lenana agrees with having two *eunoto* ceremonies, Sir Percy,' Coll said.

'Very well. Now, Coll, Lenana and I have other matters to discuss. You may leave us.'

Coll got to his feet and moved to the door, still struggling to comprehend the magnitude of the changes that had been set in motion. In a few short sentences, the governor, with the Maasai's spiritual leader in full agreement, had changed the way the Maasai would conduct their dealings with the outside world.

A tradition that had endured for thousands of years had been shredded in a few short moments.

Edouard waited until the door had closed behind Coll before continuing his discussion with Lenana through the Maasai interpreter. He was pleased with Lenana's agreement to accept the position of paramount chief, and suspected his masterstroke of banning the *eunoto* had something to do with it.

The old man had been surprisingly inflexible when Edouard first broached the matter of moving the northern Maasai to an extended southern reserve. The *laibon* had said it was unlikely that he could get the other elders and leaders to agree, and would risk his reputation if they formally opposed him. With the new power arrangements he would now put in place, Edouard knew he only had to get the old man's agreement and it would be done.

He had decided to dismiss Coll on an impulse. The leak of information from his office was beginning to develop a pattern and, although an unlikely suspect, Coll was one of several possible links to recent embarrassing disclosures.

The matter he wanted to discuss with Lenana was not one he cared to have Coll, or anyone else, witness. It would greatly increase the risk of failure if his plan to move the Maasai from the north became public knowledge before he had a chance to get Lenana's agreement on paper.

The sun climbed above the Laikipia like a blood-red ball. It turned the morning mists into diaphanous veils of pink silk hovering like spectres above the dark earth. They wavered and were soon gone. What remained appeared to be a blue carpet with highlights on the rises and soft shades of purple in the indentations in the plain. Moments later the sun dissolved the illusion and what emerged was the grey soil and dead grass stubble of another unforgiving, rainless day.

Gilbert Colchester rose from his seat and strolled to the edge of the veranda where the morning sun fell flush on his face. Squinting, he saw the outlines of the Maasai *moran* — two wavering, arrow-thin shapes — ambling out of the sun. He sent a stream of tobacco juice into the dust and grunted at Delamere, seated against the wall of the Rumuruti district commissioner's outpost building.

'Are they here?' Delamere asked.

Colchester inclined his head towards the two men and gave another grunt. 'Yah,' he replied.

The previous day, he and Delamere had met the two *olaiguenani* and spent most of the time observing the minutiae of Maasai social customs. However, Delamere was able to indicate that on the day following he and Colchester would discuss with them the suggestion that the northern Maasai consider abandoning Entorror and moving to the south. He said he hoped they would agree, as this was their recommendation as their friends and blood brothers.

Delamere appeared anxious to avoid protracted ceremony, and as soon as the Maasai arrived he immediately got down to the crux of their visit. Skilfully sculpting his arguments, he began a long, meandering speech in faltering Maa, explaining that he believed the proposal to move the Maasai was in their best interests and, as a friend, he encouraged them to give the matter favourable consideration.

'The government will give three acres for every two you have here in Laikipia, and they will irrigate the southern reserve so that your cattle will not go without water again.'

He told them that the government was concerned about their friends, the Purko Maasai, and wanted them to have a good life.

'The governor has asked me to invite you to Ngong, where we can discuss the situation with Lenana. We know this land,' he continued, indicating himself and Colchester, 'as you do. The dry years come and go. It would be good if you took your stock from here while the drought lies heavy on you. One day the Laikipia Plateau will bring forth rich grasses as it does in the good years, and you may wish to return, but if you stay now a great many cattle may die.'

Delamere was in his element, wielding words like a swordsman. His orational skills were formidable and well known — Colchester had seen him in action several times. He was not tall but he had the bearing of a giant. When he spoke he was more often heeded than not. He was a man who, regardless of whether one agreed with his point of view or not, could never be ignored. Most men knew not to antagonise him, as his temper was legendary. He was as quick with his hands and whip as he was with his words.

As Delamere talked and the Maasai politely listened, Colchester could see he was growing in confidence. As it was on the floor of the Legislative Assembly, the podium of the Colonists' Association meetings or around the bar at the Norfolk Hotel late at night, Delamere was unstoppable when passionately committed to his subject.

He told the Maasai the whites were not necessarily interested in claiming the Laikipia Plateau, and might even soon quit the country entirely. Colchester knew that the men, believing Delamere to be a member of the government, would see this as official policy.

Impressive though it was, Colchester knew that his oratory alone could not convince them. Delamere may have quickly discarded the blood-brotherhood ceremony as a ploy to stop the Maasai stealing his cattle, but to the Maasai it was a lifetime bond, and an important one. And it was this relationship and trust, rather than his oratory, that would win Delamere his case.

Colchester had no doubt that the Maasai would not only go to the meeting, they would also sign the agreement based upon that trust.

Ole Sadera lay in the darkness listening to the scuttle of a mongoose's small feet as it hunted outside his hut for scraps. Beside him, her body pressed against his bare skin, was Nashilo, breathing heavily. The fury of their lovemaking had tested her too.

'You are thinking again,' Nashilo said into the darkness.

'I am,' he replied. 'How do you know?'

'You are always thinking, my love.'

'Mmm.'

The cooking fire, now a small mound of red coals, threw just enough light onto the roof struts so that if he stared hard he could see warriors in a row, spears raised and *simis* drawn. He began to relive battles past, and the spectre of Maasai against Maasai appeared among the shadows. Then the struts became guns and the wafting smoke made white figures move ominously through the darkness.

'Some say it is better to release the nightmares while awake rather than have them disturb your sleep,' Nashilo whispered. 'What nightmare would you release, Parsaloi?'

He thought for a moment. 'The uncertainty. The doubt I have about questions for which I have no answers.'

'What questions?'

He sighed. 'Questions like: Is it worth losing your land to find peace? Or, if the land you have is vast, if it takes you many days to walk its boundaries, even all the days between moons, would it be worth fighting for?'

'The *moran* have fought many wars to defend what is ours.'

'What if you had already given away much of it, so that what remains is no more than a shadow of what it was, is it worth losing the peace to keep what is left?'

'If peace is more important than the land, then you must lose it.'

'And what if, after losing almost all you have, and finding you cannot live there now because it is small and poor and bereft of water, they ask for more?'

'Now, Parsaloi, this is no longer a game, or it is a game you play in your mind. Only you know those answers.'

'Do I? Nashilo, you are foolish if you think I know these things. I am in the middle between the Maasai and the white man; between the *moran* and the elders. How can I know what is right?'

'You must. You are the *olaiguenani* of the Il Tuati — the warriors of the right hand. The future.'

He lay there in silence, listening to her breath, trying to regain the tranquillity that was lost when the fiery red figures appeared among the dark roof struts.

'I have not eased your mind with my silly game, have I?' she asked.

'As well as anyone can.'

Her hand came from the darkness and touched his arm. 'Then should I go?'

He knew she would have to return to her hut that night. Her husband was with another of his wives, but he would expect to find Nashilo in her hut when he returned in the morning. He ran a hand down the silken skin of her arm, and then found her breast. 'Soon,' he said in a voice thick with lust.

She touched the sensitive skin on the inside of his thigh and slid her hand upwards to his engorged penis.

He cast out the nagging thoughts of doubt and responsibility. In the morning he would face them again, but at that moment he could think of nothing but the delirious pleasure of Nashilo climbing on him, spreading her warm thighs across his hips, and the breathtaking pleasure as she eased her body down on him.

CHAPTER 25

Katherine had permitted herself the treat of taking the cart loaded with maize to Nairobi, instead of having her usual buyer collect it from the farm. The outing gave her a chance to mix with the townsfolk and to admire the new styles the women were brave, or foolish, enough to wear. The dress designs from London were far removed from the practical realities of life on her farm, but Katherine hadn't lost her eye for fashion.

She hoped to have time later in the day to indulge herself with a stroll down Bazaar Street, shopping for nothing in particular. Among the Indian stalls with their exotic fragrances and rich fabrics she might find that elusive item missing from her sitting room or kitchen; things she didn't realise she'd needed, but which became absolutely essential when she found them — like a gadget to make threading a needle easier, or a moulded baking dish for cupcakes.

Her first task was to deliver the maize to Fazal, the produce merchant, and she headed the horse towards the purple and yellow façade of the Jeevanjee markets.

At the end of Stewart Street, she halted. A large crowd had gathered around the main market building, flowing onto the road and blocking traffic. Katherine tied her horse to a post and went to investigate.

The crowd was almost exclusively Indian. Many of the women were in elegant silk saris and headscarves, or richly embroidered trousers, frocks and caps. Others wore ankle-length skirts tied at the waist, a short blouse and *aurhni* — a long muslin scarf hanging loosely around their neck and shoulders. She recognised these women as members of the Bohra sect, having learned a little about the Bohra from old Fazal as they chatted during his visits to the farm.

A speaker was addressing the gathering in some Asiatic language from the first floor stone parapet of the market building, from where, it was said, the peaks of Mounts Kenia and Kilimanjaro were visible.

Katherine was the only white woman present and felt a little conspicuous. She got more than a few surprised glances, but the colour and excitement drew her in. The crowd was well behaved despite a frisson of tension in the air.

She felt a gentle touch on her arm and turned to find Fazal at her side. 'Good morning, ma'am,' he whispered, nodding to her and revealing large protruding teeth as he smiled. Katherine liked old Fazal. He could haggle with the best of his race, but he was gentle and more than once had shown her a kindness when she needed some help to get her produce to market.

'Hello, Fazal,' she said, wondering why they were whispering. The man on the parapet was bellowing his indecipherable message into the street, which had now become even noisier with the angry voices from a group of white men standing on the opposite pavement.

'Mrs Wallace, I didn't know you were a supporter.'

'A supporter of what?'

'Why, the Indian cause, of course.'

'I . . . I'm not sure I understand the Indian cause.'

'We are protesting against the laws that prevent us from enjoying the privileges and the great honour of being part of the British East Africa society.'

It was typical of Fazal's quaint manner of expressing himself. Katherine enjoyed it. It made her think of him as a gentleman of the old world where, she wistfully hoped, rajas still ruled in sumptuous splendour.

'What privileges?' she asked.

'Oh, very basic ones, I assure you, ma'am.' Fazal's head bobbed in emphasis. 'The right to serve on a jury; the right to bear firearms — not that I would want to do that, oh, no; and a place for Indian representatives in the Legislative Council.'

The group of whites — settlers by the look of them — were now shouting at the crowd as well as the speaker. The party mood started to fade.

'I'm sorry, Fazal, did you say something about the Legislative Council?'

'I did. I was saying that we twelve thousand Indians have but one place in the Legislative Council, whereas the Europeans — numbering no more than three thousand — have the rest.'

'Really?'

'Indeed, Mrs Wallace. Very much indeed. And I am not even mentioning the problem on the steamers, which is very important to myself. We get no blankets, you know, not even for full second-class fare, whereas the whites get not one but two very fine blankets. You know, Mrs Wallace, it is quite unfair.'

Katherine nodded, trying to concentrate as the white settlers pressed, red-faced, towards the nearest group of Indians, some of whom were telling them to hush.

Suddenly a stone hit the iron roof above the speaker's head. Another immediately followed, striking him on the cheek. His hand flew to his face and a trickle of blood appeared between his fingers.

A clamorous roar went up from the crowd.

A policeman's whistle sounded and, as if from nowhere, a dozen regular and railway policemen charged at the assembly.

'Oh, my goodness!' Fazal cried. 'The police! Mrs Wallace. Come, we must run.'

Katherine stood rooted to the spot, unable to comprehend the turn of events. The pleasant atmosphere of not five minutes before had turned into an ugly riot. Rather than trying to restrain the white troublemakers, the police stood side by side with them, hitting out at men and women alike in the panicking Indian crowd.

Fazal came rushing back to her. 'Mrs Wallace, I beg of you. For the love of Allah, come with me! Come quickly —'

A truncheon smashed into old Fazal's face, shattering several of his prominent teeth. He fell to the ground screaming, his head buried in his arms, but the policeman continued to viciously beat and kick the old man where he lay.

Katherine was lost in a swirling nightmare of unimaginable violence. She heard herself screaming hysterically, and began to hit the policeman ineffectively about his shoulders, trying to stop his attack on the now motionless Fazal.

The policeman swung about, catching Katherine on the cheek with his looping truncheon. She fell into a black void of unconsciousness.

Kira brought a cool, dampened cloth to replace the one Katherine held to her bruised eye. The room had the soft warm glow of later afternoon and she suggested Kira go to check that the yard boy had secured the calves in the barn for the night.

She was still in shock at the brutality of the attack on the Asians the previous day, but had begun to wonder why she had been unaware of the disparity between the laws affecting the two communities. Of course, she was aware of their different ways of life, but completely ignorant of the kind of barriers that Fazal had mentioned. Until she saw Fazal lying battered and bleeding, she had not known how deeply the prejudices ran between the whites and the Indians.

She realised she lived a sheltered life on her farm.

She was deep in thought and didn't hear the cart draw up outside. She jumped when George Coll appeared in the doorway, the evening sky blood-red at his back.

'I came as soon as I heard,' Coll said. He gently took Katherine's hand holding the damp cloth and drew it from her face, gasping when he saw her bruised eye. 'My God! What did they do to you?'

His concern was touching, and as he continued to hold her hand in his she realised they had never actually touched like that before — not even in greeting.

'An over-enthusiastic constable,' she said, replacing the cloth to conceal the ugly blue-green contusion. 'The swelling's going down. I'll be as good as new in a few days.'

He demanded to know the details, and shook his head in disbelief and anger when she reached the part about old Fazal being viciously beaten.

'They took him off to hospital in quite a bad state,' she said. 'I haven't heard anything, but I must get in to see him as soon as this eye goes down.'

'And what about you?' he asked, taking her hand again, patting it. 'How did you get such a terrible knock?'

'The policeman was in a fury,' she said. To her surprise, the palm of George's hand was not at all soft and his grip firmer than she'd imagined. 'I do believe he swung about in self-defence, fearing he was about to be attacked.'

'There's absolutely no excuse! The police are supposed to be able to control themselves under those conditions. We'll press charges.'

'To be honest, George, I don't think I could recognise him. It all happened so quickly. Anyway, it's done.'

He really was in a state, she thought. It was endearing to see him fussing about her.

'You know, Katherine, this incident only proves the total insensitivity this government has to their people. I'm speaking of the Asians and the Africans, of course. Take the Maasai. Sir Percy Edouard is hell bent on moving them out of their reserve.

'Oh,' he added, taking his hand from hers to search in his coat pocket, 'I have some ointment that Norman gave me. I'm to rub it on over the bruise. He says it will help clear it up.'

He unscrewed the lid.

'I need some light. Here will do, if you just sit back a little, Katherine — under the lantern where I can see what I'm doing.'

She leaned back and George, beside her on the sofa, raised himself on a knee to look down on her. He hovered there, studying her eye. She winced as his finger brushed her cheekbone.

'Sorry! I'm too heavy-handed for this. I should have brought Norman along.'

'I think you're doing very well, George.'

'Do you think so?' he said, smiling with relief, and resumed his ministrations.

'I only witnessed one incident,' she said, thinking how softly he smoothed the ointment, 'but it's made me consider the whole matter of justice in this place.'

'It's so encouraging to hear someone else with these same thoughts,' he said. 'Do you think it's only you and I who are concerned?'

He was absorbed in rubbing the medication on her eyelid and brow and didn't notice her studying him. His eyes were a much warmer colour and brighter than she'd previously thought. He ran the tip of his tongue over his lips as he worked, lost in concentration.

'There,' he said, smiling. His gaze met hers, and she held it, no longer afraid to reveal her attention to his eyes, his nose, his face.

'Green rather than grey,' she said softly.

'What's that?' he asked, not moving from his position above her. She could feel the warmth of his breath.

'Your eyes. They're more green than grey. Perhaps it's the light of the paraffin lantern.'

'And yours are . . .' He leaned back a little but his hand remained on her shoulder. 'Yours are blue, maybe a touch of green.'

He moved towards her again and she met his lips with hers. The kiss was gentle and his hand moved from her shoulder to softly cup the back of her neck. When the sweet embrace ended, he moved his hand to her cheek and caressed it.

She was afraid to speak. Her heart thumped in her chest so strongly she was sure he could hear it. The moment might have held them there forever, but George broke the connection and turned his eyes away. When she again caught his expression, it had changed from affection to a sad acceptance of some hidden command. *Please, no!* she thought. She might have even vocalised it, such was the strength of the emotion. He moved away from her, this time in retreat.

'This can't be,' he said, struggling to get the words from his throat.

'George —'

'I'd better go, Katherine.'

He was at the door, but although she had followed him there she was incapable of opening it for him. Instead, she just stood there, trying to comprehend what had happened between them to change his manner so dramatically.

'It's late,' he said, reaching for the door handle.

She wanted to hold him; to let him know that whatever it was that had occurred, it could be made right.

'George, please. Tell me.'

He opened his mouth to speak, then pressed his lips together again. She felt like shaking the words from him.

'George, you shouldn't go down that road so late. It's dangerous.'

He drew back from the hand she placed gently on his arm. 'No,' he spluttered, bumping into the doorframe as he retreated from her. 'I . . . I can't.'

He fumbled with the latch. 'I've got to go,' he said, swinging the door wide and striding briskly to his horse and cart.

'George,' she said, but so softly he couldn't possibly hear it. He was in the cart and heading into the gathering darkness. She watched him go, biting her lip.

Coll spent the whole day following his flight from Katherine — there was no other way to describe it — in the small gloomy sitting room of the house he rented overlooking the railway shunting yards. He had no energy to move. It was only when a train rumbled along the cutting gouged into the hill below him, a half-mile from the Nairobi station, that he realised it was mid-afternoon and he hadn't eaten.

He stood and took a step towards the box-like cooking annexe, and his head spun, caused either by hunger or the impossibly long, sleepless night infused with the bitter taste of all the poor decisions he had made in his life. When he did fall into fitful sleep, he was tormented by vivid dreams laden with fantasies. In one he was a leopard, and fought off his rivals for the attentions of a sleek, spotted gold female, but when he was about to consummate his victory he found, to his horror, he had resumed his human form. The leopardess turned on him and savaged him. He awoke in a lather with a cry on his lips. For a long time thereafter he lay in the darkness pondering the meaning of the dream, wondering if he had gone quite mad.

He pumped up the pressure on the paraffin Primus stove, lit it, and filled the kettle. While he waited for it to boil, he sat at the table and returned again to the events of the previous day, painful as they were, in another attempt to untangle them.

It had been a bad decision to let his guard slip when he found Katherine bruised and in need of his help. She was too fragile; he was too overcome with concern; she was too close. There was a moment when he could have stepped back, avoiding the inevitable, but then their lips met. Now it was too late to return to how they had been.

In truth, he didn't want to, but he just couldn't risk a romantic involvement. In the intimacy of the moment, she had crept under his guard, catching him unprepared for the many emotions that rushed through him in that instant. At first, there was an overwhelming joy. And, strangely, relief — that he was not a completely undesirable individual; in fact, was so desirable that a woman like Katherine seemed to want him just at that moment. But the pleasure quickly passed and then came the fear. This was dangerous ground. He could not be loved — not even desired.

Finally, there was sadness. He had permitted, even encouraged, Katherine to join him in that headlong rush to intimacy. She had kept her feelings locked away until then. Once she had revealed them in the eagerness of her kiss, the pretence of mere friendship had dissolved in an instant. It must have taken great courage to shed the disguise of years and reveal her most hidden self to him. When he so rudely retreated in disarray, he must have left her feeling shocked and humiliated.

It would never be the same, and he knew, as surely as the sun would rise in the morning, that he could not face Katherine again.

He went to pour the boiling water into his teapot, but found he had forgotten to put the kettle on the stove.

CHAPTER 26

The *eunoto* celebrations began almost immediately after the women had built the *manyatta* at Ngong. Six hundred Maasai *moran*, now gathering from all corners of Maasailand and dressed in full battle regalia, gathered in preparation for the event.

The *moran* were adorned with beaded anklets and amulets, headbands and earrings, made for the occasion by doting mothers and fiercely jealous girlfriends. They carried buffalo hide shields painted with the insignia of their age set and clan, and long bladed spears. Short brutal *simis* hung in leather holders at their waist and they all wore the brief red *shuka* of their warrior status, barely covering their nakedness and often exposing their buttocks as they trotted in columns across the savannah. Many *moran* wore a lion's mane *olewaru* headdress, adding impressively to their physical stature as well as to their status, because only a warrior who had killed a lion with his own spear could take its glory for his own. Others, less fortunate, wore an *olewaru* of flamboyant ostrich feathers.

Building the traditional forty-nine huts and central ceremonial house had taken the women over a month. All six hundred *moran* who would take part in the four days of festivities came from three different age sets, each with a unique part to play in the *eunoto* depending upon which stage of Maasai life they would occupy in the time ahead.

The youngest group were the men recently circumcised. They would replace the junior *moran* of Ole Sadera's age set. It was a proud moment for them, as they would carry the responsibility of the young guard for the next seven or so years.

Ole Sadera's age set, the Il Tuati, would move up to replace Mantira's men as the senior *moran* — considered to be the wise heads on the battlefield and the most influential in preparing battle tactics. These two younger groups therefore had much to celebrate.

For those in Mantira's age set, it was a sometimes traumatic time when lives took a dramatic turn. At best, it was a day of mixed emotions. As they left *moran* status and became elders, they would be permitted to marry, to set up a household, and to raise a family. Their cattle, often held in trust for them by other family members while they lived their warrior's life, would be returned to them. They would augment their herd by gifts from their clansmen, and later with cattle won in raids. But their celebrations were tempered because they would never again be members of the brotherhood of warriors — free to indulge in all manner of games; to fight for the glory of the section; and, when necessary, to wage war on those who would dare to defy their supremacy. They would acquire status within the tribe by their wealth and wisdom rather than their courage and fighting skills. There would be no lion hunting to test them in the future. They would have to find satisfaction in the respect given to them as elders.

At sunrise on the morning of the fourth day, Ole Sadera joined Mantira in a secluded culvert with scores of their comrades to paint their torsos and faces with white chalk. They mixed red ochre with fat and painted it on their long legs then scoured patterns into it with their fingernails. Red — symbolising the warrior's fiery temperament — was a favourite of the Maasai in clothing, body paint or beads, and was in abundance during the *eunoto*. Each warrior went to great pains to decorate himself in a manner likely to catch the eyes of the young women who came to watch the *moran* dance. In the case of Mantira's age set, it was also an opportunity to catch the eye of a prospective wife. But, unknown to Mantira, that would not be the situation for him.

Ole Sadera was in possession of some important news that he could not reveal. Mantira's peers had chosen him to be the *aulononi* — the one who would lead his age set into elderhood. It was the greatest honour a *morani* could receive, even better than that of *olaiguenani*, because the *aulononi* represented the entire population of elders about to graduate.

The *morani* chosen to be the *aulononi* had to have been an exceptional warrior and be unblemished either physically or morally. Therefore, he had to be tall and have perfect physical features as well as good health. He must be a pure blood Maasai and not have slept with a married woman nor have killed a man, and both parents must be alive. He must never have had a curse or evil omen placed upon him. If a man failed on any one of these characteristics, he could not become the *aulononi*.

Ole Sadera took grim consolation from the fact that when the time came, he could not be his age set's *aulononi*, as he failed all conditions.

As the *aulononi*, Mantira would be presented with a girl from a highly regarded family whom he would be obliged to marry. Ole Sadera knew this would not please Mantira, who had already chosen his beloved Sirita to be his first wife. The girl chosen for the *aulononi* would also have to forego any engagement plans she had, and the other warrior she had chosen would be obliged to surrender his sweetheart for the sake of tradition.

It was important to keep the *aulononi* news secret until the group presented Mantira with the paraphernalia of office, because the responsibilities and restrictions upon normal life were so onerous nobody wanted the position. Given the chance, most men would find some way to disqualify themselves by self-mutilation or by hurting another. Ole Sadera had been given the confidential information so he could keep an eye on Mantira in case he became aware of the age set's plans for him.

Mantira had been silent for some time as they prepared their body with chalk and ochre. Ole Sadera had received nothing but grunts and monosyllabic replies to his attempts at conversation.

'Are you not pleased to be graduating today, old friend?' Ole Sadera said. 'You have been quiet all day.'

'Have I? Perhaps it's this chalk; it refuses to sit well on my body.'

'I see. Or is it approaching elderhood that doesn't sit well?'

Mantira glanced at him. 'Perhaps.'

'Another perhaps.'

Mantira made an effort to smile at his friend's chiding. 'Yes, perhaps this, perhaps that. Perhaps I have only one thing to be pleased about, and that is that Sirita and I can now get married.'

Ole Sadera thought it best to change the subject. 'You and your Il Talala will be fine elders.'

Mantira gave him an incredulous look.

'I mean it, Mantira. You will be able to confidently give advice on proper behaviour because everyone knows that you and your whole age set have behaved so badly over these long years that your experience will be greatly sought after.'

This brought a chuckle from Mantira, who added, 'And in a few years we will have to step aside as your even more experienced Il Tuati join us.'

The humour had lightened the moment, and they were silent for a while, finishing their markings.

'Parsaloi, I have heard rumours that you are seeing Nashilo in places that you should not be seen,' Mantira said.

'You should first see such things for yourself. Is it not true that flies have ears?'

'Yes, flies have ears, but I myself have seen you.'

Ole Sadera felt ashamed at his attempt at deception. 'I did not want to tell you in case it offended you,' he said, chastened.

'Offending me is not a concern. What does concern me is that others have seen you. If Nashilo's husband also discovers the truth, it will be a scandal. You are not of his age set and have no rights to her.'

'And how would you, an elder, judge me in that scandal, my friend?'

'No, please, do not make a joke of it, Parsaloi. It is not amusing. I would not want to judge you in such matters.'

'I understand.'

Ole Sadera wanted no further scrutiny of the matter. In spite of his guilt and remorse, he could not end his relationship with Nashilo and he didn't want it to become an issue between him and Mantira.

'The *moran* are gathering,' he said. 'They are ready to return to the *manyatta*.'

Mantira nodded, and they joined the long line of warriors marching back to the *manyatta*, accompanied by braying kudu horns. Bells tied to their thighs marked the beat of their march. Mantira's group carried no weapons, only long white poles that signified the transition from might to wisdom.

The main events occurred around the large conical ceremonial hut constructed in the centre of the forty-nine dwellings, called *osingira*, where the women had stored the milk, roasted meat and honey beer.

Mantira had one more important task to complete before he gathered with the other *moran* to receive Lenana's blessing. He asked Ole Sadera to go with him.

They headed to Mantira's mother's hut, where he would undergo his last ordeal on his path to elderhood. The old woman formally greeted the two warriors, and Mantira sat at her feet so the old woman could shave off her son's braids using a small blade and a lotion of milk and water.

Mantira sat silent and resolute as the crowning glory of his warrior years fell to the ground around him. It was a poignant moment for both mother and son as it signified the degree of separation that would occur between the man and his family. As an elder and a married man, Mantira would be tied equally to his wife's parents as to his own. For his mother, shaving her son was the last loving duty she would ever perform for him.

When his head was bare, his mother used the milk and water to wash him before coating his gleaming scalp with a red ochre mixed into a paste with mutton fat. Mantira then gathered his *shuka* around him, keeping his face expressionless. It was important that he not succumb to the emotion of the moment for it was not fitting for a *moran*, shortly to become an elder, to reveal too much of what was in his heart.

His mother understood this too, and after Mantira had formally thanked her for all the things she had done for him in his life, the old woman merely nodded in acknowledgement. But as he turned to go, the old woman grabbed his hand and kissed it. An awkward few moments passed as Mantira tried to retrieve his hand from his mother's fierce grasp, the agony of it clearly drawn on his features.

Mantira whispered something to his mother and was then able to peel away her bony fingers. Even so, as he and Ole Sadera walked away together, the old woman's racking sobs followed them.

'You look unwell, George,' Lewis said as they rode together along the Ngong road. 'Is your chest condition worrying you?'

'No, my chest is well enough.'

'Then are you getting enough sleep?'

Coll sighed. 'Yes, doctor, I am. Now can we please change the subject? It's far too nice a day to dwell on boring topics such as my health.'

Regardless of the denial, Lewis knew Coll was not well. He was breathing heavily and, although the day was warm, was sweating more than could be expected. Lewis suggested they take a rest, saying he needed to stretch his legs. They brought their horses to a halt on a rise that gave them a view over the hills that marked the south-western boundary of the Nairobi district.

'My God,' Lewis said, sitting upright in his saddle. Beyond the spread of grey-green trees, shimmering grasses rolled out like a yellow undulating carpet to the horizon. Above it all was an astonishingly blue sky dotted with flawless, white clouds. 'Amazing,' he added. 'I had no idea . . . I'm glad you asked me to come today, George. You know, I've never been out to Ngong before.'

'Nor seen a *eunoto* festival, I suppose.'

'Quite.'

'Nor have I. What a relief Edouard lifted the ban.'

They climbed down from their mounts and tied them to the bare limbs of a woody shrub.

'I don't know what he's up to,' Lewis said, straightening his back and stretching. 'He seldom does anything for altruistic reasons, but I've kept my eyes and ears open and have seen nothing in his correspondence to indicate he's up to one of his tricks.'

'I hope you're taking care while prying around his office.'

'I'm sure he doesn't suspect a thing.'

They found a fallen log in the shade and took a seat.

'Look at this beautiful country,' Lewis said. 'I should get out into the bush more often, but there's always a mountain of damned paperwork.'

Bees from a nearby wild hive buzzed among the grass stalks.

'Have you seen Lenana since he was made paramount chief?' Lewis asked.

'I haven't,' Coll replied. 'Edouard worries me with this appointment.'

'Lately I've become suspicious of nearly everything he does. What is it that concerns you?'

'It's so wrong. Appointing tribal leaders as spokesmen seems to have worked with the Kikuyu, but it's not the Maasai way.'

'What's the difference?' Lewis asked.

'I don't know much about the Kikuyu, but they're basically farmers. Maybe that's the difference. Perhaps they have chiefs in their own tribes. I think Edouard would like to change the Maasai into farmers so he could keep an eye on them. But they hate farming. They believe that the use of tools is demeaning. Edouard just doesn't understand. And he refuses to take advice. I honestly believe he doesn't want to hear anything that might be contrary to what he has already decided to do. Only last week —'

Coll paused for breath. Lewis had often heard him wheeze and struggle for breath when he became upset, but this time the congestion seemed to sit deep in his chest. He wished he'd brought his stethoscope.

'Sorry,' Coll muttered. 'Only last week I suggested to him that if we wanted to get the Maasai more involved in production, we should import merinos from Australia to cross-breed with the Maasai sheep. They could sell the wool.'

'What did he have to say to that?'

'He thought it would only encourage the Maasai to start stealing sheep as well as cattle. That's his attitude. But that kind of change wouldn't be too hard for them to accept. They simply don't want to become farmers, and really, isn't it their choice? All they want is to be left alone to live as they have for the last thousand years.'

He fell into a coughing fit.

Lewis watched him struggle to resume control and, when it had eased, said, 'George . . . your bouts are getting worse. You should —'

Coll held up his hand to stop him.

Lewis sucked the inside of his cheek. 'Very well. But are you at least taking the syrup I gave you?'

'Yes, Norman, I am.' Coll swallowed and took a tentative breath. 'But getting back to the matter of the paramount chief . . . I don't trust Edouard's intentions. He just seemed to pull it from the air. The Maasai don't really have chiefs. They elect spokesmen to represent their age groups, but otherwise everything seems to be done on some sort of consensus among the leaders. A paramount chief makes no sense. Lenana, like any *laibon*, is a spiritual advisor. That's about all.'

'It makes no sense unless you remember that this is the way we British do things. We can't cope with the cultural complexities of the many people we rule. We boil it all down to one simple formula: deal with the top man, or if there isn't one — such as in the case of the Maasai — appoint one. It simplifies matters.'

'Why would Lenana want such a position?'

Coll seemed to be talking to himself more than expecting an answer, but Lewis gave one anyway.

'I'd say, power. Influence. Perhaps he'll be given some official duties that will add prestige.'

'That's all well and good, but it begs the question: why — after all the land negotiations have been settled — does Edouard now want a paramount chief?'

'I'll keep an eye on things around the government offices,' Lewis said, 'as you will undoubtedly do among the Maasai. If we find any indication of what he's up to, I'll get in touch with my friends in Whitehall.'

Coll had a little more colour now that his attack seemed to have passed.

'How are you feeling?' Lewis asked. 'Well enough to continue?'

'Of course,' Coll replied, getting to his feet.

They rode on in silence until the small Maasai village of Ngong came into view. Surrounding it was a huge herd of cattle that extended across the plain and up the hillside.

'My God!' Coll remarked. 'Look at that herd. There must be, what? Five thousand? Ten?'

Lewis nodded. 'Closer to ten, I'd say.'

'What are they doing here? The Maasai travel with their cattle, but this looks to be far too many for the ceremony. What's going on?'

They slapped their mounts to quicken their pace down the hill into the village. In the centre of the *boma* they found Lenana standing at the calves enclosure with a few of the other elders.

Coll exchanged greetings and blessings with Lenana and waited impatiently while the *laibon* and Lewis completed formalities. He then engaged in a long-drawn-out conversation with the *laibon* in Maa. In contrast with Lenana's dispassionate tone, Coll was very agitated. Lewis was concerned to see his friend begin to sweat and struggle with his breathing again. Then the racking cough returned to the extent that he could not continue his conversation.

Lewis tried to insist that Coll take a rest, but his friend shrugged him aside. Coll's distress grew until he could hardly breathe.

'George, for God's sake. Take it easy. What in heaven's name is wrong with you? You have to rest.'

'The *eunoto*,' Coll gasped, struggling to draw breath.

'Never mind the *eunoto*, George. I want you to sit right here while I get the horses.'

Coll brushed his hand aside and took a long careful breath. 'I knew there was something afoot. Lenana has agreed with

Edouard's proposal.' He took another gasp of air. 'After the *eunoto*, they will go south.'

There were flecks of blood on Coll's lips, which were turning blue. Lewis, absorbed in loosening Coll's collar, was only half listening.

'Damn it, Norman!' he spluttered, grabbing the hand at his collar. 'Don't you understand? The northern Maasai. All of them. They're moving *south*!'

Coll's hand went limp and he slumped into Lewis's arms.

The assembled *moran* filled the hot still air with six hundred booming bass voices.

'*Hhuunh*!' they chanted. '*Hhuunh-huh*!'

The Ngong Hills reverberated and, whether Maasai or not, everyone in the township of Ngong was compelled to stand spellbound at the sight of the red-robed wall of warriors gathered on the wide plain, bobbing, thrusting their shoulders forward and chanting.

Only Norman Lewis was impervious to the compelling power of their pageant. Having made Coll as comfortable as possible, he made a dash to the few scattered shops in the town and borrowed a cart.

Sweating profusely under the deadweight of his friend's inert body, he suddenly felt it lift as Ole Sadera, in his body paint and ceremonial regalia, took the unconscious man into his arms. Lewis helped the Maasai heave Coll into the back of the cart.

'I will come with you,' Ole Sadera said.

'No. There's no need. I will take him home and tend to him.'

The Maasai seemed torn by indecision.

'You have your duty here,' Lewis said. 'George will be all right as soon as I get him home. Come to my house in a few days. Everyone knows where I live.'

Lewis flicked the reins and the cart clattered over the rocky track back towards Ngong and the road to Nairobi. As they climbed the slope to leave the small valley where the assembled Maasai were observing the rite of passage that would change their lives, Lewis felt it a great pity that one of their greatest admirers was unable to witness the majesty of the occasion.

CHAPTER 27

Mantira found Ole Sadera standing on one leg, stork-like, looking out over the herd, which spread up and over the stark slopes of the Ngong hills.

'There is little pasture remaining for such a large herd,' Mantira said, following Ole Sadera's eyes.

'Yes. We must move them soon or they will lose more condition. They have already grown thin over the long journey here.'

'There is little remaining to keep us here. The *eunoto* is complete. Lenana is to give us his final blessing, and we may go.'

'Your age set has given you a great honour, my friend,' Ole Sadera said, acknowledging Mantira's appointment as *aulononi*. 'I cannot believe how times are changing for us. You, of all people, to become married. Without doubt, you will have a little one around your feet within a year. That long sword of yours has slain more women than an army of *moran*.'

Mantira was appreciative of his friend's attempt to revive him from his despondency. He made an effort to smile, but the disappointment of losing the chance to marry the woman he loved was too raw. To avoid any further discomfort to either of them, he decided to broach the matter he had come to discuss with Ole Sadera.

'You were not happy with our decision to move to the south, Parsaloi.'

'I said I would sign. I have spoken to my age mates and they agree to move.'

'They would never refuse what you ask of them. But that is not what I asked.'

'If you are asking if I can celebrate surrendering yet another part of our homeland, then no, I am not happy about it. But I accept what must be.'

'Everyone knows of your strong feelings, but you have said little. Why?'

From out on the savannah the *wot-wot-wot* call of a red-billed hornbill filled the silence while Ole Sadera pondered his answer.

'Sometimes I feel I cannot carry all these strong feelings. They weaken me, Mantira. I grow tired of them. They haunt my heart through the days and trouble my dreams at night. I wonder if I have been truly cursed at birth as some would have it.'

Mantira searched for words to console him while the hornbill continued its forlorn call. 'I know your life has been difficult for you, Parsaloi. I have watched you grow. I watched as the other children teased you because your mother was a Laikipiak. You were smaller than others were, and weaker in some ways, but there was strength in your manner. You refused to be defeated by anyone. Yes, there were beatings and you would be left bloodied, but never defeated. It was in your eyes. In time, others were to see what I saw, and you were accepted. It was your strength. I wondered if it was the same strength that made you grasp those stones at your birth. Or why you tried harder and succeeded at every trial put in your path. I could never understand you. You have always seemed . . . different.'

'I am *not* different,' Ole Sadera said forcefully. He opened his clenched palms and stared at them. Holding them up, he asked. 'How different are these hands? Do they seem different to you? What does a newborn infant know about grasping at stones, and of omens or curses?'

Mantira was surprised by the outburst. Ole Sadera had never revealed his feelings so openly. The *eunoto* and the end of their time together as brothers-in-arms had obviously provoked many emotions.

'If I appear strange to you, it's because I . . . I see things that others do not. It . . . worries me.' Ole Sadera lowered his voice. 'Sometimes it frightens me.'

'What do you see?'

'In dreams . . . Are they really dreams? I don't know. But I see the Maasai stumbling on a long journey. I see our cattle falling. There is hunger and death.'

'That is all from our past, my friend. You must not give in to such thoughts. You should listen to the words of the elders. They have seen many dark days but they have passed.'

'The elders,' Ole Sadera said dismissively. 'They say our move to the southern reserve will bring us prosperity and happiness. They say that by abandoning Entorror we will gain more land, better land.'

'They are right. The whites have made it better for those in the south. We have heard it from our own blood brothers.'

'In the past I have travelled to the south. I do not believe it can be made good for us there. But can't you see what has happened? We have moved from the great valley to appease the whites. Now we move from Entorror. I see no end to it until we are all finished.'

Mantira put a hand on Ole Sadera's shoulder. 'Listen to me, Parsaloi. Put these nightmares out of your mind. The evil spirits that were at your birth send them. Try to be guided by the elders, and our friends. Would our blood brothers lie to us?'

Ole Sadera nodded, acknowledging the advice, but still unsure. 'Why am I the only one to see these problems?'

'Maybe you do not see far enough. Delamere has said this move to the southern reserve will be good for us. He says the whites will not stay here for long. He gave his word as a blood brother and a leader of the whites. We must believe it.'

Mantira could see that Ole Sadera was coming around to his view. 'Entorror will come back to us when the whites tire of it and return to their own homeland,' he continued. 'Entorror and the great valley will then be ours again.'

Dr Norman Lewis sat back, unhooked the stethoscope from his ears and considered his patient. Again, he worried if he were doing the best thing for him. If he had any sense at all, he would order George Coll back home to England and into a sanatorium for complete rest and treatment for his tuberculosis, but he knew he couldn't do it. There was no provision under the protectorate's health regulations to do so, and even if there were, he knew Coll would resist it with all his undoubted determination. He had said he would make no more concessions to his ailment, and Lewis knew him well enough to believe him.

'You should be in hospital, George,' he said gravely.

'I thought I was, doctor.' A wan smile creased Coll's pallid features.

'Seriously, you need more care than I can give you in my spare bedroom. If I didn't think the climate would kill you, I'd have bundled you off to Mombasa the minute I got you back from Ngong. One of these days we'll get a bloody hospital here in Nairobi,' he muttered.

'I don't much care for a seaside holiday at the moment,' Coll said, still trying to make light of the situation.

Lewis would have none of it. 'How long have you been coughing up blood like that?'

'Not long,' Coll said dismissively, but when he caught sight of Lewis's stern expression, he added, 'About a month or so.'

Lewis slapped his hands on his thighs and rose from his chair with a sigh. He took a few paces to the window and gazed out to the gum trees in the crook of Ngong road. He needed some space to gather his thoughts. The mystery of the gum trees often helped.

He had treated difficult patients in the past, but in the case of George Coll he had also to deal with the added burden of his own guilt. He felt that he had given impetus to Coll's obsession to help the Maasai by his own strident anti-establishment credo. He had allowed his friend to believe that his political contacts back in Britain could solve the land resettlement issue in a trice. In fact, the Maasai were almost an insignificant sideshow in a far bigger philosophical debate.

Lewis could trace his own obsession back to his early days as a doctor in the slums of Glasgow. He knew how draining the struggle with oppression and privilege could be. In a purely altruistic society, even a socialist one, would there be any need to protect a stubborn, desperately ill friend from worrying himself sick about injustice?

There were so many unanswered questions in life. It made the mystery of the very un-African gum trees pale into insignificance.

Turning back to Coll, he said, 'George, I want you to listen carefully. You fainted because your lungs are failing to supply your blood with enough oxygen. And as you lose blood because of the haemorrhaging in your lungs, your system is dangerously compromised. You are at risk of contracting a number of opportunistic diseases, such as pneumonia, and other complications.'

Coll merely nodded.

Lewis felt repentant for allowing his exasperation to overcome his normally professional conduct. 'I'm sorry,' he said. 'I'm trying to get you to realise that you can't go on in this fashion. You have to let go of some of those responsibilities that are dragging you down.'

Coll seemed to sag into the bed, as if the strength that had kept him buoyed was exhausted. 'If I had known of Edouard's secret plans to move the Maasai southward . . .'

'You couldn't possibly have known, George. He kept you at bay. It was obviously a matter he wanted to keep secret between himself and Lenana until the move was under way. And, realistically, what could you have done anyway? This is precisely the kind of thing I'm warning you against. You can't continue to fight —'

'I had my suspicions, you know. When I left Edouard's office, I intended to see Lenana after the meeting, but something came up and I was called away. I should have been more mindful of the dangers. Edouard is a scheming scoundrel. I feel sick when I think of how he manipulated that old man.'

'You're not listening to me, George. I want you to rest here for a few days. And I don't want you to become distressed about what's happening out there in Maasailand.'

'And if I don't care about what's happening out there, who will?'

'Me, for one. You're not alone. I'll write to our friends in London. They'll raise the matter in the House.'

'It's too late for anyone in London to help us. By the time your letter reaches them, the Maasai will be in the south and they'll be stuck there. It will be like a prison. Edouard will have carved up their northern reserve by the time the politicians get wind of it.'

Coll had seen through his floundering excuses. Lewis knew that if he were to remove the damaging stress his patient was suffering, and in the process assuage the guilt he felt for worsening his illness, he would have to take direct action — dangerous though it may be.

Late afternoon sunlight sent slanting beams through the dirty window of the post office, falling on the Indian signalman's twitching hand as he *rat-a-tatted* on the Morse key.

Norman Lewis watched in fascination, imagining his words being flung out across the world like a lightning bolt. He pictured the English signalman in London checking the incoming message, reading the address — to Mr Ramsay MacDonald — and calling a boy to race helter-skelter across London on his bicycle to Whitehall, bell ringing all the way.

Lewis and the signalman were alone in the room, giving Lewis some comfort. He had ridden hard for two hours to send his message from Machakos rather than risk being recognised by the post office people in Nairobi. Even then he was careful to keep his message cryptic, hoping it would not easily be deciphered by the Indian signalman or raise his curiosity.

Our friends under duress heading south. No papers for travel. Early agreements ignored. Implore your immediate assistance in the white place. Explanatory letter follows but do not wait. Matter of utmost urgency. Repeat urgent. Norman.

The signalman barely gave him a glance as he took Lewis's payment and handed him his copy of the telegram.

Lewis thought the telegram was perhaps the most unusual medicine he had ever prescribed for TB. He also thought it was his one hope of keeping George Coll at home and at ease until his damaged tissue had a chance to repair itself. It was the only thing he could do for his friend as he now understood that Coll had made his decision that the Maasai's cause was his cause — one worth fighting for and, if necessary, dying for.

'A telegram! Are you mad, Norman?' Coll threw his hands in the air in disbelief. 'How could you possibly send a telegram to London? Edouard will know about it before it reaches your man's desk.'

'It was a private telegram.'

'I don't care. It's not safe. Nairobi's a small town. The post office people know you.'

'Calm yourself, George. And please sit down again.'

Coll did as he was asked. His strength had picked up but sudden movements made his head spin.

'You shouldn't have done it, Norman. It's far too —'

'That's why I used the post office in Machakos. Nobody knows me down there. Anyway, it's done, and what's more, I've seen the response.' He grinned at Coll. 'I intercepted the telegram as it came in on the morning's correspondence. The move south has been halted.'

Coll stared at him for a moment before realising what Lewis meant. 'Halted? You mean, it's been *stopped*?' His mouth fell open. 'Norman, are you saying the order has been reversed?'

Lewis, grinning, said he was.

'You've done it! We've won!' Coll's voice choked and he made a grab at his handkerchief to stifle his coughing.

Lewis handed him his glass of water, and stood beside him, patting his shoulder. 'Steady, George,' he said. 'I don't want you having a relapse just as we're turning the corner.'

'Turning the corner?' Coll smiled through the tears brought on by his spasm. 'We've more than turned the corner; we've won the race, Norman.'

'I was talking about your health, dear fellow.'

Coll blinked his eyes clear. 'We've done it! We've beaten the bastards.'

It was the first time Lewis could recall Coll swearing.

'Yes, George,' he agreed. 'For the moment, we've got the bastards on the run.'

Governor Edouard's jaw tightened into a hard line. The telegram Wadley had handed him was a slap in the face to his authority in British East Africa. He felt frustrated and angry. It was an intolerable situation that decisions were made by men in London on matters quite beyond their understanding. He had difficulty controlling his urge to crush the offensive paper with its crisp, autocratic tone:

> ... *therefore believe it imperative to delay or if necessary reverse any movement of the Maasai southward until legality of alteration to 1904 agreement has been clarified, or an appropriate alternative agreement obtained.*

It smacked of meddlesome bureaucracy at its worst.

'You've read this, Wadley, of course?' he said through gritted teeth.

'Yes, Sir Percy, I have.'

What made Edouard livid was that the order from the Colonial Office inferred he had overstepped his mark by not informing London of the move. But what fuelled his rage — even more than the effrontery of the Colonial Office's directive — was the suspicion, now confirmed, that someone within his administration had secretly and maliciously informed London behind his back. He struggled to maintain his composure.

'Very well, then,' he said, taking a slow, deep breath. 'Wadley, draft an acknowledgement for the Colonial Office, and a note to send by messenger to Lenana. We will meet again to formalise the resettlement. Let us say, the day after tomorrow, Thursday. In the meantime, he is to defer the movement of all Maasai and cattle. Understood?'

'Yes, sir.' Wadley scribbled a note on his pad. 'Oh, and there's this, sir.'

Wadley handed him what appeared to be another telegram, but was in fact a facsimile copy. Edouard gave him a look, but snatched the paper from him.

'I thought you should see it,' Wadley hastened on. 'Given the circumstances of the, um, other telegram.'

The addressee's name caught the governor's eye immediately. 'How did we get this?' he asked brusquely.

'Mr Smythe, the ADC in Mombasa, stumbled upon it at the post office. He noticed it was addressed to Mr Ramsay MacDonald and . . . well, I suppose his curiosity was aroused, being it was a private correspondence and not one of ours.'

'How does Mombasa get to have a copy of it?'

'Every telegram from here goes to Mombasa first before being relayed to London, sir.'

Edouard read the missive again.

Our friends under duress heading south. No papers for travel. Early agreements ignored. Implore your immediate assistance in the white place. Explanatory letter follows but do not wait. Matter of utmost urgency. Repeat urgent. Norman.

His eye went to the signature line. *Norman.* There was a William Normoyle up in Kisumu. No one else came to mind.

'Thank you, Wadley,' the governor said placidly. 'Leave this with me for a while.'

'Yes, sir,' Wadley said, and left the office.

Edouard took a key from his waistcoat pocket and fumbled it in the lock on the bottom drawer. Removing a folder, he opened it in front of him on the desk and ran his finger down Eliot's list of suspects: Branson, Keith; Somerville, Brian; McGuire, Andrew. Near the end of the column, his finger stopped at Lewis, Norman.

CHAPTER 28

The settlers drew their mounts to a halt overlooking the valley. A group of Maasai herders had crossed the Uaso Ngiro and were grazing their cattle outside the reserve. It was not the first time it had happened and, in light of the administration's inattention to police its own rules, the settlers had formed a vigilante group to enforce the law.

Their leader glanced around his men — fourteen gritty farmers and cattlemen driven to their wits' end trying to scratch a living from the unforgiving land. He caught and held each pair of eyes for a moment, seeking acknowledgement that they were still prepared to break the law to defend what was theirs from the intractable Maasai.

When it was done, he urged them forward, down the slope to the unsuspecting herders.

They drove their horses among the cattle, scattering them from their path. They swung at the Maasai, old men and boys, with *sjamboks* and *kiboko* whips. There were angry yells arising from the dust, cries of frustration and screams of pain.

The Maasai tried to defend themselves with their herding sticks. A few of the old men, not yet incapable of hurling a spear, made ineffective attempts at retaliation. They were beaten until they fell in the dust. Most fled after their cattle to the river.

The settlers gave up the chase as the last of the intruders scampered across the Uaso Ngiro's shallow sandy pools.

The cloying scent of incense tickled the back of Katherine's throat and she stifled the urge to sneeze. Isher Vidyarthi held the meeting in his compelling grasp as he railed against the latest atrocities the administration and its officials had inflicted upon the Indian community. Vidyarthi was a prominent member of the Punjabi Hindu community, and, if the stories in the press could be believed, a charismatic revolutionary leading the Indian population into sedition.

Katherine glanced around the room where she and the large group of Indians were gathered. It was huge, and peering down from garish oil paintings were various Hindu gods and goddesses, some bug-eyed and others in all manner of unlikely, if heroic, poses. Religion had never been among the pressing needs in Katherine's life. Bill and she had managed with their own system of beliefs borrowed and adapted from all they'd seen and experienced in their long years of travelling. It was only when she met George Coll that she'd briefly entertained a notion of understanding any one god, Christian or otherwise.

But she hadn't come to Vidyarthi's house that Sunday afternoon to study religion. She had come after one of Fazal's daughters, Shirin, had explained to her the objectives of the Asian and Native Progress Association.

Katherine had met Shirin, Vidyarthi's wife, at Fazal's funeral, and in endeavouring to understand the brutality and prejudice she had witnessed the day Fazal met his death had become aware of ANPA and its work. During her visits to Nairobi — now more frequent due to the loss of Fazal's carrier service — she met with Shirin and others and learned more. The more she learned, the more she became incensed by the injustices suffered by the Indians and Africans.

She began to take notice of newspaper reports and advertisements discriminating against Indians and the natives. The Land Board posted a resolve that 'Indian immigration is discouraged as much as possible for the purposes of settlement and that no government land is allotted to them'. Another, a week later, read: 'Although it is open to any person to bid for any of the town or residential plots in Nairobi, Parklands or Ngong Road, Asiatics or Natives will not be allowed to reside there.'

Who was behind this travesty, she wondered. It soon became clear when she read a report in a Nairobi newspaper quoting from a speech by one of the leaders of the Colonists' Association: 'Colour distinction is the base of every British social system which comprises various races. The very existence of the white race depends upon the relentless maintenance of this colour distinction. There can be no intelligence or wealth test here. Let us be honest and call a spade a spade. Our boundary line is colour.'

Isher Vidyarthi was an impressive man — tall, rather aesthetic in appearance, with long limbs, delicate hands and piercing black eyes. His distinguished silver hair and neatly trimmed beard might have placed him in academia, but he was a successful businessman and lawyer. His speech continued to address some of the issues affecting native Africans.

'The *kipende* laws, which require all African adults to carry an identity badge showing permission from their employer to move outside the native reserves, have long been hated. Now the native is effectively being forced into labour for no other reason than to earn cash to pay his taxes — taxes that are unjustifiable given the fact that the native receives virtually none of the benefits that the white farmers do. The natives have their own land to till; their own families to feed.

'Did any of you see this morning's *East African Standard*?' He looked over his glasses to find a few heads nodding. 'Well, for the remainder of you, let me read Sir Percy Edouard's speech of last Friday as reported this morning:

'"We consider that taxation is the only possible method of compelling the native to leave his reserve for the purpose of seeking work. Only in this way can the cost of living be increased for the native, and as we have previously pointed out it is on this that the supply of labour and the price of labour depend.

'"To raise the rate of wages would not increase but would diminish the supply of labour. A rise in the rate of wages would enable the hut tax or poll tax of a family or tribe to be earned by fewer external workers, and as the payment of this tax is avowedly the reason the natives seek employment, it follows that if we increase the rate of remuneration of the individual we decrease the number of individuals necessary to earn a given sum."

'Friends, do you see what is happening here? Unlike in Europe or America, where governments try to secure agricultural workers in homes and on land that is their own, here in British East Africa the government is trying to turn peasants into wage earners. But not even for the advantage of becoming wealthy. Many people such as the Maasai shun the dubious appeal of trade goods and so have no need for money — except for the sole purpose of paying tax. What is the logic in opening up more and more land to the settlers if there is no labour to work it?'

This brought a brief but enthusiastic round of applause.

'This then is our challenge, ladies and gentlemen. We must fight for the rights of the most numerous residents of this country — the Asians and the Africans — against the oppressive Europeans.' Vidyarthi raised his hands above his head. 'Equal rights for Asians and natives. Land rights for the Africans, and commercial rights for the Asians.'

The crowd were on their feet, shouting 'Hear! Hear!', which gave Katherine her first chance to view the entire audience. There was a majority of Asians, a sprinkling of whites, but not a single African. And, surprisingly, considering the rumours coming from the northern Maasai reserve, there was not a word said about the recent murders of Maasai herders who had strayed onto white settlers' land.

Ole Sadera looked uncomfortable in Norman Lewis's sitting room. He was by no means a large man, but the room seemed to constrain him like a sleek cheetah caught in a trap.

Lewis had taken him in to see Coll. The warrior appeared startled by his friend's pallid features. After his brief visit, which was all that Lewis would allow, he immediately asked if he could bring Coll some of his Maasai medicine. Lewis explained that what Coll needed was complete rest and that was all that could be done. The *morani* didn't appear convinced and pointedly probed Lewis until he appeared satisfied that Lewis was doing everything possible to return his friend to good health.

'He goes home in a couple of days,' Lewis said, shaking his head.

'But he is still ill.'

'He insists. And I'm afraid that when our friend makes up his mind, no amount of logic or pleading can change it. But he should be all right so long as he gets his rest over the next few weeks.'

'Who will see to him? Who will cook his meals and care for him?' Ole Sadera asked.

'That is a problem, I admit,' Lewis replied. 'But if Coll takes it easy, he will be able to manage on his own. I'll be taking a look at him every other day; more if I can.'

Ole Sadera nodded. 'He should have a wife to care for him,' he pronounced solemnly.

'Indeed, it would help.'

'Why does he not have a wife?'

Lewis sighed. 'I'm afraid it's a little complicated and not easily explained,' he said. 'George *had* a friend — a very good friend — and I think she would have liked the friendship to go further, but George would have none of it. I suppose the easiest way to explain it is that he pushed her away.'

Ole Sadera looked puzzled. 'Pushed her away?'

'It's an expression. It means he showed he wasn't interested in a closer relationship. You probably find this confusing, Parsaloi. It's something quite personal between George and Katherine — Katherine Wallace — she has a farm out on the Limuru road. I don't think I can explain it in a way you could understand.'

Ole Sadera nodded. 'Swara is ashamed to be sick. He is a proud man who feels that the woman, Katherine Wallace, will pity him, and he doesn't want pity, he wants her love.'

Lewis gaped at him. 'Why, er, yes. You may well be right.'

'And he does not know how to find out her true feelings for him.'

'Quite. He's almost said as much to me.'

Ole Sadera nodded. 'I could see it in his heart. He is not happy about this problem.'

'You don't think so?' Lewis asked, now deferring to the Maasai's opinions.

'No. This Katherine Wallace must come here, see Swara.'

'No. Absolutely not. Not in the condition he's in. Perhaps in time, when he is stronger, it would be a good idea. But not now.' He thought about it for another moment. 'Even then he may forbid it. He's so stubborn.'

'What is stubborn?'

'Stubborn? It means George won't listen to reason because he believes only he knows what's right for him.'

Ole Sadera considered this for a moment, before nodding. 'Yes, very stubborn.'

Lewis hauled on the reins, bringing the horse to a halt at a fork on the red murram road where a sign said 'Tobermory'. The remainder of his homeward journey was an easy ride of about fifteen miles downhill to Nairobi. His tour of the missionary health clinic at Kijabe had been routine and he was glad to be heading home earlier than expected.

The branching track led to Katherine Wallace's farm. He remembered it from the last time he had travelled through Limuru. In spite of Lewis's encouragement, Coll had not returned to Katherine's farm. Coll remained adamant that it would be unfair to her.

Lewis felt that his friend had become emotionally diminished, retreating further into his work and caring little about filling the gap Katherine had left in his life. After an initial recovery, his physical condition had deteriorated too. Coll had thrown himself into his work with a fury and it had affected his health. He ignored Lewis's lecturing on the matter. Coll's sense of loyalty — misplaced in Lewis's view — caused him to push beyond what was wise for someone in his condition. As a game warden, which was a promotion of sorts, he spent too much time living rough in the highlands and in the unhealthy moist atmosphere of Lake Victoria.

Lewis considered the sign for a moment more, then turned his horse onto the track between the two fenceposts.

The house was modest, typical of the small allotment farms in the area. A flock of chickens fluttered ahead of his cart and an old dog gave a desultory bark as he pulled up beside the veranda.

An African girl came shyly to the door as he climbed down to stand at the bottom of the steps.

'I'll get it, Kira.' The voice came from behind him.

He turned to find a fine-looking woman approaching. She might have been anywhere from her mid-thirties to late forties. He knew that many settlers' wives aged quickly under the harsh conditions of climate, childbirth and years of ceaseless toil. But this woman had retained a good portion of what would have been a classic beauty when she was younger. Katherine Wallace could thank her Celtic forebears for her fine, unblemished skin, he thought. There was also a touch of Scottish pride in the way she held her head high and chin cocked aggressively forward. The light cotton skirt and blouse emphasised her trim figure.

She was aware of his frank appraisal and pressed a loose strand of hair into place before giving him a defiant look as she spoke. 'If you've come for the tax, I sent it in last week.'

Lewis smiled. 'I've been on the road all day but I didn't think I looked that bad. A tax collector indeed!' he said with mock outrage.

The woman appraised him through narrowed eyes. 'If you're not a tax man, who are you?'

'Dr Norman Lewis,' he said, removing his hat.

Katherine's mouth opened, and she hesitated a moment before taking his offered hand. 'George's friend,' she said softly.

'Yes. And you're Katherine Wallace, I presume.'

She nodded, gazing at him even more intently. After a moment she said, 'Won't you come in, Dr Lewis.'

'Thank you.'

In the comfortable atmosphere of the kitchen — which reminded him very much of a country kitchen back in Scotland — Lewis attempted to engage Katherine in small talk about the farm and the need for rain. She answered politely, but kept her guard up.

As soon as Lewis paused, she said, 'Forgive me for asking, Dr Lewis . . . but I don't suppose this is a house call.'

'No, Mrs Wallace, it's not. Or perhaps it is, in a manner of speaking. I want to talk to you about George.'

She seemed to have experience in keeping her feelings hidden, because he couldn't read her eyes. He pressed on regardless. 'I'm a friend of George's. Probably one of the few close friends that he has.' He placed his hat on the seat beside him. 'I'm concerned about his health, Mrs Wallace.'

She leaned forward. 'I knew it,' she said. 'He's ill, isn't he?'

'Well, yes and no. He's not getting much worse, but then again he's not much better. You probably already know, or have guessed, that George has tuberculosis.'

When Katherine didn't give any sign one way or the other, he continued. 'But what I'm more concerned about is his state of mind.'

'What do you mean?'

He took a deep breath. 'Mrs Wallace, from what George has told me about you, I believe I can speak plainly. As a doctor of many years, I've learned that the best way to approach delicate subjects is head-on. I hope you don't mind.'

She nodded, clasping her hands together in her lap.

'George is ill. We both know that much. Even George knows it. But what he won't admit, or doesn't want to contemplate — because I've told him as much — is that he may not have too many years left.'

Katherine dropped her gaze to her hands for a brief moment, then lifted her head again.

'I might be sounding a little pessimistic — we doctors are sometimes given to that condition — but let me say, at best, it could go either way.'

'You mentioned his state of mind.'

'I did.' He paused, not so sure he should have embarked upon his mission but also determined to see it through. 'It's been a long time, mind you, but I still think I can recognise such a situation when I see it. I believe George loves you, Mrs Wallace.'

'Is that a medical condition, doctor?' Her voice was guardedly unemotional, but a hand went to the collar of her blouse and fussed with it nervously.

'I'm sorry, I'm not handling this very well. The point is that George has this misplaced valour that won't allow him to engage another's feelings in case it causes grief should his condition worsen.'

'Surely he knows we must all leave sometime?'

'I'm sure he does. But you can see the problem.'

Katherine shook her head. 'I'm afraid I don't.'

'He needs to get some sense about him. He should get on with his life, and live every day of it.'

'Agreed. But why are you telling me this?'

'Because . . .' he began, but found he could not go on under that cool gaze. She spoke for him.

'Because *I* know he should live his life, and *you* know he should, but if bloody George Coll can't, or won't, take it to heart, what can we do?'

Lewis sighed. 'You're right, of course.'

'Yes . . . I'm right.' She touched a handkerchief to her nose. 'Tea?' she asked.

'Thank you, but no. I'll be going.'

He stood, and she followed him to the door.

Lewis took her hand in his. 'Mrs Wallace, I'm pleased to have met you. I think I can appreciate what George sees in you, and I just hope one or the other of you can overcome whatever is holding you back, and does something about it.' He smiled grimly. 'George may not know it, but he needs you, Katherine Wallace.'

She smiled, her eyes glistening.

Lewis climbed wearily into his cart, waved goodbye and flicked the horse into a quick walk.

Katherine stood at the fireplace staring at the black iron oven door, lost in her thoughts. The last shafts of afternoon light slanted through the window, sending long shadows across the floor and its eclectic collection of rugs.

Minutes passed, until a faint burning smell roused her and, with a start, she remembered she had gone to the oven to remove her cake. She searched the shelves for the cloth she used to open the hot door, and found it already clutched in her hand.

When the oven door dropped open, a cloud of sugar-sweet smoke rose into her face. In her haste, she lost her grip on the cloth and burned her fingers as she made a grab at the hot baking dish.

Looking down at the smouldering ruins of her sponge cake, she realised it wasn't a great loss. Without a visitor to help eat the cake, most of it would be wasted anyway.

She slumped to a chair, her eyes brimming with tears, and put her blistered finger in her mouth. She realised how many of her days had been built around the chance that George Coll might visit as he passed her farm.

She felt foolish sitting there in the gathering shadows, crying. She told herself it was just the time of day that did it — that time when, after the day's work was done, she had nothing to look forward to other than a simple meal and an empty bed.

A flush of anger welled up within her. Why had Bill been so thoughtless? Why had he gone out against that lion? Why didn't he consider what would happen to his wife if she were left alone?

She brushed away her tears. She shouldn't allow bitter regrets to cloud her memories. Life was too short for such foolishness.

But she could not escape the fact that she *had* been foolish. And selfish too.

She was selfish to tarnish Bill's memory with her own mistakes. It was she who had pushed him into the activity that led to his death.

And it was she who had foolishly pushed George Coll too far.

CHAPTER 29

The Amala was no longer a proud tributary of the Mara River. It had been reduced by the drought to a series of muddy water holes connected by long stretches of sand, which made the long walk north difficult, but Leboo Ole Kipetu knew if he kept within the rubble-strewn river banks, the *askaris* would not find him.

Leboo and his boy had been driving his twenty-two cattle and handful of goats northward for days. They were all that remained of his once sizeable herd.

Leboo had chosen to move to the southern reserve when the white governor chased the Maasai out of the great valley. His first wife was a Loitai Maasai whose family lived in the Loita hills of the southern reserve. She had come to him from a family with many cows, and he thought it good business to stay close to them where he might gain more stock through kin connections.

But the years in the south had not been lucky for him. His second wife was barren, so he returned her to her family. Then the rains failed for three consecutive years, and when he and his wife's family moved west to find better pasture, the hostile Sokit set upon them, killing his wife and stealing many of his cows.

It had cost him a fine young goat to receive advice from the Loitai *laibon* that he would be more prosperous and find a suitable wife if he went back to his Entorror homeland. And so it was that Ole Kipetu had decided to risk all and make the forbidden journey across the floor of the great valley to Entorror, where he would find his Purko kin.

He had also heard that the *ol-milo* — the deadly new cattle fever that the whites referred to as east coast fever — was spreading across the entire southern reserve. He was tired of the difficult life and decided to risk all to be in Entorror again.

CHAPTER 30

Lord Delamere could stomach the evidence no longer. He turned from his Maasai herdsman, who was holding the heifer, and climbed onto his mare. He paused and studied the animal again, to see if he could have been mistaken, but the signs were irrefutable. He kicked at the mare's flanks and sent her off at a brisk gallop, away from the sickening sight.

Perched on the low rise ahead, one of many in the folds of the Great Rift Valley, was the headquarters of his Elmenteita estate, all one hundred thousand acres of it. Soysambu Ranch was the place, among all his properties, where he and his wife had chosen to settle.

He had built up the property over the years. Soysambu — the Maa word meaning the brindled rock — was now his main source of income; the place where he spent most of his time and money doing battle with the elements, the terrain, the animals, the occasionally fractious natives and the many diseases that could, and did, attack European livestock and agriculture. He had decided to concentrate his efforts on sheep, but his cattle were a sizable proportion of his overall investment.

He had laid twenty miles of pipeline to bring lake water to his livestock, and spent a fortune breeding strains of wheat resistant to rust. He had identified the missing minerals in Nakuru soil that were essential to the health of his stock and had rectified the deficiency.

During that time, he had received little cooperation from frequently obstinate bureaucrats, and absolutely no support, financial or otherwise, from the government.

To fund his enormous investment he had mortgaged Vale Royal, his family estate in England. The bank was now muttering threats of foreclosure if he didn't make a contribution in the near future. He was determined to let all his assets in England go if necessary. Africa and his future were inextricably tied, and it was impossible for him to think of any other way of life.

At the top of the rise he reined in the mare. She was blowing hard and he was momentarily regretful of having pushed her so cruelly. His gaze followed the downward slope to his herd of over a thousand cattle, dotted here and there with Maasai herdsmen. He felt unable to believe what his eyes and his experience had told him.

At first he'd thought it was merely one of the many minor ailments found in Africa. But he had not been a pastoralist for so many years without picking up a thing or two about veterinary science. After only a cursory study of the first dozen or so ailing beasts, he knew this was something far more deadly than redwater infection or gallsickness. He first detected a swelling in the lymph node under the infected animal's ear, which soon appeared in other parts of the body. A fever occurred at about the same time as there was a loss of appetite and general lethargy. The cow began to show difficulty in breathing and developed a cough as fluid built up in the lungs. Within a week or so the truly horrible symptoms began: diarrhoea at first, sometimes tinged with blood; wasting muscles; white discolouration of the eyes and gums. In the last stages the nervous system was attacked and the animal became unable to stand or, more commonly, staggered in circles. Others became paralysed. Mercifully, death quickly followed.

The tragedy would soon be played out in every other ranch and farm throughout the Great Rift Valley. Delamere could only shake his head in resignation. After all his years fighting to survive everything that Africa could throw at him, it was an almost invisible organism that would bring him to his knees.

East coast fever was an insidious ailment. The experts said the brown tick was the vector, which was probably a very appropriate term in a laboratory environment. What it meant out here in the African savannah was that the grass held a deadly menace, one that could ambush a passing healthy beast and render it a suppurating mess in a matter of days.

Although he was a tenacious fighter, Delamere was realistic enough to know when he had met his match. ECF was incurable. Morbidity was almost a hundred per cent, and mortality was somewhere between ten and ninety per cent, depending upon inherent resistance. He expected eighty per cent of his four thousand head would die.

It was an unmitigated disaster.

He knew very well where the infection would have begun, but he had been confident that the closure of the corridor to the south and the effective quarantining of ECF to that region would protect him against an outbreak in the northern Great Rift Valley. Somewhere, somehow, the quarantine had been broken and brown ticks had infested the grasses in the Great Rift Valley. The evidence pointed to an itinerant Maasai herder, someone who had crept into the valley with his small herd of zebu cattle, travelling to see kin in the northern reserve.

The answer was clear to Delamere. He would have to severely purge his herd — possibly destroy them all — and start again.

He had never been in doubt about the need to move the Maasai to a single containment area. If there was anything positive to be taken from the ECF outbreak it was that the disaster would finally convince the doubters that there was no choice but to close the northern reserve and send the Maasai immediately to the south.

Governor Edouard's suspicions about George Coll arose when, quite accidentally, he saw him in the company of Dr Norman Lewis. As occasional interpreter, Coll was privy to some of Edouard's discussions with Lenana and others. It wasn't that Edouard felt Coll might have used the information from those discussions to do damage to the government's plans — he had always been careful not to disclose anything particularly confidential while Coll was present — but seeing him with Lewis reminded him that his game warden had all the attributes of the native-rights do-gooder he so disdained. Coll tended to put his own interpretation on events, which invariably meant a sympathetic slant on matters affecting the natives. It was people like Coll back in London who were raising hell on all manner of petty details and disrupting the business of empire. The combination of Coll the bleeding heart and Lewis the educated conspirator struck a chord and Edouard decided to keep an eye on both. He was a patient man, prepared to bide his time. Eventually he was confident that one or the other would make a fatal and defining mistake, and he would pounce.

His suspicions had led him to forego bringing Coll to this meeting with Lenana at the camp at Ngong. The *laibon* had uncharacteristically asked for the meeting. Usually he avoided discussions unless pressed into them.

With the outbreak of ECF in the valley, Edouard had finally been given the full support of the settlers to formalise the earlier agreement with Lenana. He expected some resistance from the old man, but was determined to achieve an outcome with which the Colonial Office could have no dispute.

A number of small children were playing a game with pebbles on the approach to Lenana's hut. A bigger boy, of an age to be tending goats and sheep, was sitting listlessly in the dust, a mass of flies invading his eyes and nose. They didn't seem to bother him, but Edouard had the almost irresistible urge to brush them away. He shuddered at the sight and waited for Lenana to emerge from his hut.

When Lenana greeted him, Edouard was shocked at his condition. Normally a very frail man, Lenana seemed to have shrunk even further and appeared weak and lethargic. The elder who acted as interpreter agreed with Edouard that the *laibon* was indeed ill, which was the reason he had asked the governor to see him. There were matters that were now becoming more critical. He said there had been days when Lenana had not been himself and had taken to wandering away from the *enkang*. The elders were becoming very concerned.

Lenana refused to have the meeting outside in the daylight, so Edouard and the interpreter joined him in the tight and smoky confines of his hut. Lenana had to lower his head under the low ceiling while Edouard had to bend deeply. They sat around a small fire with a single sputtering oil lamp providing additional illumination. Soon Edouard's sight became accustomed to the gloom and his eyes ran around the hut. A couple of calfskins and what appeared to be a wooden pillow sat on a simple bed platform. A small cooking pot hung by a plaited leather thong from one of the ceiling struts, and a large gourd was propped against a wall. Above the sickly sweet tang of curdled milk was the all-pervasive odour of cow dung. Edouard swallowed and tried to keep his breath shallow. It was not what he had expected in the home of the Maasai's paramount chief.

With the long-winded preliminaries over, Lenana began a tortuous path to the crux of the meeting. He was dying, he said, and was concerned about his son and his succession to the position of *laibon*.

The interpreter inclined his head as he translated the *laibon*'s next words. 'Lenana says we have heard that Sendeyu's son is saying he is the rightful heir to the position of *laibon*. This son is now grown and of an age where he is prepared to fight for what he believes was stolen from his father.'

'What does Lenana want me to do about it?' Edouard asked.

'He asks that when he is dead, you appoint Seggi, his first son, to the position of paramount chief.'

'I see,' Edouard said, running a finger down the cleft in his chin. 'Tell Lenana this is possible, but there are some arrangements between us that are unfinished, and they should be attended to before any decision on succession is made.'

The interpreter went into collaboration with the *laibon*. After a moment he said, 'Lenana says he will hear them.'

Edouard explained that it would be helpful if Lenana agreed to the consolidation of the Maasai into a single southern reserve.

The old interpreter said, 'Lenana asks, did we not already agree to move from Entorror to the south, and did you not tell us to go back?'

Edouard, miffed at being driven into admitting a distasteful failure, blustered, 'It's not sufficient for you Maasai to go wandering off of your own volition. The government requires certain protocols, a degree of substance in the matter.' He explained that if the Maasai truly wanted to move they would have to make a new agreement replacing the one signed with Commissioner Stewart in 1904.

'Lenana says there are many who worry about the water in Ngatet,' the interpreter said.

'We have discussed that, Lenana and I. We have even sent his representative down there with my man, Mr Hull. I have agreed to build dams and channels to bring the water from the Amara River.'

Edouard waited for the translation before adding, 'There will be no more discussion of matters we have already talked about and agreed. I will draw up a new agreement and Lenana, the elders and the *olaiguenani* must sign. Only then will I see to it that his son Seggi is appointed paramount chief, after he . . . when it is time.'

Determined to have the last word, the old man insisted that Edouard send a representative of the government to the northern Maasai. He said it would show that the *laibon*'s order to attend the signing ceremony had the backing of the government. Edouard agreed, and made his farewells, leaving the diminutive old *laibon* in the semi-darkness.

Taking a deep breath and blinking in the harsh sunlight, Edouard decided he should meet the young man whom he would be dealing with as paramount chief after the *laibon* passed away. He asked the elder to bring him to meet him.

'But he is here,' the old man said, indicating the boy sitting in the dust. The swarming flies remained untroubled and determinably in place. 'This is Lenana's son, Seggi.'

'Seggi,' Lenana said into the gloom of his hut. 'Are you there, my son?'

'Yes, father, I am here,' the boy answered from the foot of the *laibon*'s bed platform.

Lenana tried to lift his head and focus upon him, but it required too much effort and his eyes were too weak. He wondered how long it had been since he had called for his son. He must have drifted off into another troubled dream as he waited. Was it an hour ago? A day? But he remembered it had been only days ago that he had spoken to the leaders about the need to sign the agreement with the British. It had been difficult with Ole Sadera demanding compensation. But nobody opposed him and the clan leaders dispersed, agreeing to return for the final signing ceremony. After that, he was uncertain about the passage of time, and whether his thoughts were real or the stuff of dreams.

The image at the end of his bed wavered behind a wisp of smoke. 'Seggi,' he asked again, 'is that you?'

'Yes, father. It is me, Seggi.'

A vision came to the old man of himself in his own father's hut many years before, when his deception had won him the position of *laibon*. He chuckled at the irony, but his laugh came out cracked and brittle like the sound of dry sticks crushed underfoot.

The humour quickly evaporated as the importance of the matter he wished to discuss with his son came vividly back to mind. 'Listen to me, Seggi,' he said into the silence. 'Are you listening, my son?'

'I am, Father.'

'Good. You must listen to what I say, Seggi. It is important, because soon I will die. What I tell you now may not be said again.'

'Yes, my father.'

'I give you my blessing. You are hereby anointed as the *laibon* to succeed me.' He pointed to the place beside the bed where his wife had put the calfskin bag. 'Here by my hand are the stones and the iron club. Show them to the elders. They are the insignia that my father gave me, and I now pass on to you. You will be the *laibon* from my passing until your own, at which time you will have appointed your own first son as successor.'

'Yes, Father.'

Lenana nodded. Seggi was a good boy, if a little slow. But he had been a vigilant student. Lenana believed he would carry out his duties to the best of his abilities.

'You will also be the Britishers' paramount chief, as I have been. It is their duty to guide you on all matters to do with the whites, as the elders will guide you as the *laibon* on matters to do with the Maasai. Listen to the British, for they are more powerful than any enemies of our past. But that is of no consequence. They are our friends and can bring us benefits. Be strong, my boy. Soon you will be of age and will stand on your own. Until then, listen to the advice of the elders.'

Lenana's head began to swim and he had to surrender to the tiredness that swept over him. As he fell through the darkness of approaching deep sleep, he heard a distant voice calling. It was familiar, but lost in time.

'Do not leave our land, for if you do, your cattle will perish, your children will die of a terrible disease, and you will face a powerful enemy, and you will be defeated.'

The vision wavered and was lost for a moment, but it returned to his half-sleep. The words came as if from a great distance.

'Do not leave your land, Sendeyu. Do not leave your land, Sendeyu, because . . .'

He remembered the words of warning, but wondered why his father was speaking to him using his brother's name.

CHAPTER 31

Galbraith Collins swung into the saddle on his high-spirited black stallion like a man born to a life as a cattle farmer in British East Africa. It was true that he sat a horse well, but he hadn't learnt his skills on his hundred thousand acres in the Great Rift Valley. It was in Fermanagh County, on his family's estates in Northern Ireland, that he first rode as a young boy. Collins was the third son of the Earl of Enniskillen and had arrived in British East Africa in 1903, shortly after his neighbour and brother-in-law, Lord Delamere.

He'd slipped his .303 into its leather sleeve as he headed out from his farmhouse. He had loaded the rifle with soft-points, which he didn't usually use for hunting table meat as they badly bruised the meat and made an exit hole as big as a loaf of bread. He had another quarry in mind. Like his neighbours, Collins had become enraged by the amount of stock taken by cattle thieves, and had vowed that if he caught the culprits they would pay dearly.

Within a few miles of the house, he came upon the dead sheep as reported by his foreman. He swore as he dismounted to inspect the partially butchered carcass. There were no signs of mauling, as would be the case following a predator's attack. And it was a recent kill, too recent even for the scavengers to have found it.

Collins climbed back into the saddle, his blood boiling, and nudged the stallion into an easy canter. Within a quarter of an hour, he spotted three figures ahead of him. As he drew nearer he recognised their headdresses and ornamentation to be those of the Maasai. They were walking north, most likely taking some of his best mutton back to the reserve.

He gave them a shout to hold up. The men glanced briefly back at him before making a dash towards a patch of thornbush. Collins cursed, and for a moment considered galloping his horse in to prevent them escaping into the scrub. Instead, he shouldered the .303 and fired at the closest of the three.

The man fell as if struck by a bag of wheat.

Collins slowly walked the stallion to the fallen warrior. His friends were gone, lost in the thornbush.

He dismounted and, with his rifle at the ready, stood above the Maasai lying face down on the ground. 'That'll teach you, you thieving *bastard*!' he cursed. A dark circle was slowly spreading around a small hole in the back of the Maasai's red shuka. Collins hoped he'd try to rise so he could have the satisfaction of sinking his boot into his belly. But the man lay still, with only a low groan to indicate he was conscious.

Blood was pooling beneath the prone body. Collins rolled him over, none too gently, with the toe of his boot. The Maasai swallowed a cry and clutched at his abdomen. A portion of his intestines escaped through his cupped fingers. Although obviously in pain, the *morani* glared defiantly up at Collins with ill-concealed hatred.

Collins smiled down at the wounded man, nodding in satisfaction. 'That will take the sting out of you for a while, *boyo*,' he said, waving the point of his rifle in his face.

The warrior didn't flinch, which annoyed Collins who at least expected the Maasai to beg for mercy. If there was one thing he couldn't tolerate in the natives, it was insolence, and this Maasai had too much for his own good. A murderous rage engulfed him and he squeezed the trigger to within a hair of firing, but then had a better idea.

He returned to his horse, mounted and walked the stallion back to the *morani*, now sweating and shaking in the early stages of shock. He moved the horse perilously close to him, its hooves stamping dust into his face.

'I don't think you're the type to die of shock, are you, boyo?' he sneered.

He peered out over the thornbush. The remaining two Maasai were nowhere in sight.

'And it looks like your companions have turned tail and run out on you. Bad luck, that. Can't say I'd hold out much hope for passing Samaritans either.'

The *morani* needed no translation to know he was being taunted. He glared at Collins.

'Looks like you'll have to make it home on your own. Don't want the hyena to finish you off, do we?'

Collins laughed and rode off.

As the two Maasai *moran* crested the ridge, the Great Rift Valley came into view below them, running far away into the southeast. Nestled under the eastern escarpment was Lake Nakuru, where half a million flamingos formed a pink rim that almost completely encircled its jade waters.

The two men had come in search of their age set brother who had not returned from a raiding party to the valley the day before. The missing man's companions said they had lost sight of him when the white farmer, whose property they had been raiding, fired on them. They fled, believing he was dead, but their *olaiguenani*, Ole Sadera, nominated the two *moran* to go in search of him so as to have proof of the matter.

The Maasai herdsmen working on the whites' cattle farms in the Great Rift Valley conveniently ignored the Maasai's incursions, and the farms had been a good source of quality mutton for those with the daring to risk discovery by the farm owners. The chances of being found in their huge acreages were slight, and many of the *moran* believed it was worth the risk.

The *moran* had only a sketchy idea where their brother was last seen, but the circling vultures gave them a clue where to start their search.

They found the partly consumed body smothered in a blanket of blowflies at the edge of a thornbush thicket. Marks in the soft earth indicated the warrior might have dragged himself to the thorns before he died, probably in a vain attempt to find protection from the scavengers that finally overwhelmed him. It would not have been a good way to die.

They collected his shield, which was his badge of honour showing his various exploits and brave deeds in its vivid markings, and his spear. One of the Maasai found a flattened pellet of metal among the gory remains. He showed the strange object, which could fit into the palm of his hand, to his companion, who agreed it was worth taking back to show Ole Sadera.

It was a solemn mood that greeted Coll when he arrived at Ole Sadera's *manyatta*.

'I grieve with you, Parsaloi,' he said when they met.

'We all grieve when a warrior dies an inglorious death, Swara. It was not fitting. He was a brave man. To die without a chance to engage his enemy is a terrible dishonour.'

'The police have arrested the man. Galbraith Collins. He's the owner of the farm where your men found the body.'

'And what will happen now?'

'Why, he'll be put on trial. Your men will be called as witnesses, of course, and I suspect he'll be punished severely.'

Ole Sadera nodded.

'I know that you have your concerns about the government's shoddy treatment regarding the matter of your land,' Coll went on, 'but if there's one thing we British do well, it's upholding our criminal law. I promise you, this fellow Collins will be dealt with.'

'Even me, I have seen your justice.'

'You have?'

'Many years ago. I saw Mr Frederick Jackson making British justice.'

'Really? Well, that's very interesting.'

'Will he be there to see justice is done with this man, Galbraith Collins?'

'No, Jackson's not here any more.'

Ole Sadera considered this for a moment. 'Then it will be Delamere?'

'Lord Delamere? Good heavens no. He's not in the judiciary.'

'But he is in the government, yes?'

'No. Not at all.'

'But he has many cattle. How can he have so much land?'

'Hmm, that's probably a good question, Parsaloi. But I can assure you, he's just a civilian like me, albeit a much richer one.' Coll was amused by the idea that Delamere — at times one of the government's fiercest opponents — could be mistaken for one of their number. 'My word, wouldn't the governor be amused to hear that?' he said, smiling.

He turned to Ole Sadera to see if he shared the joke, and found him ashen.

'Parsaloi, what's the matter?'

'I must find Mantira,' he said, and stalked off.

'Why did Delamere have us believe he was one of the whites' leaders?' Ole Sadera demanded of Mantira. They had been discussing the matter for some time and had reached no agreement.

'Did he say he was, or was it our wish to believe he was?' Mantira countered.

The answer didn't appease Ole Sadera, who felt he'd been deliberately misled.

'And what does it matter?' Mantira continued. 'He is a brother of the blood.'

As usual, Mantira was able to prick Ole Sadera's bubble of intuition with piercing logic.

'All I can say is that I sense something wrong,' the younger man insisted. 'What about the reports from Ole Kipetu?'

'How can you listen to an embittered old man, Parsaloi?' Mantira said, shaking his head in disbelief. 'You don't know this Leboo Ole Kipetu. I do, and I tell you he has never been a happy one.'

'From what he has told me about life in the south, he has no reason to be happy.'

'Exaggeration!' Mantira insisted. 'You know it is the habit of the idle. Leboo Ole Kipetu is only a junior elder but he is already famous for tall stories.'

'Have you seen his herd? Have you seen his boy? He has no need to exaggerate. The evidence is there before your eyes.

Anyone can plainly see these last few years have not been good for them in the south.'

'Nonsense. Who would look fat and prosperous after such a long journey? There is not enough water anywhere. And he has come across the great valley and over the Mau Escarpment.'

Ole Sadera paused. To some extent, he shared Mantira's scepticism about Leboo's story, but it gave new life to his concerns about the wisdom of agreeing with Lenana's proposal. At the time, with the realisation that the new cattle disease would infect the great valley and, eventually, Entorror, he had been prepared to give up the northern reserve and move to safety and a much larger area in the south. But Leboo's story had again unsettled him. Something inside told him there was a danger concealed.

He tried another tactic.

'Tell me this, Mantira,' he said. 'Why is it we now need something written before we make the journey? How is it we were allowed to go before, and now we cannot unless we make a mark on the governor's paper?'

'You know these whites, ah? Parsaloi, think about it. You have seen enough of them to know they can so easily find new ways of doing the same thing.'

'But the papers,' he persisted, 'what do they mean? I don't understand why they are sometimes important and at other times forgotten.'

'It's just as your friend Swara says, it's their custom. Putting the words on paper makes it clear to everyone what is being agreed.'

'But if I cannot understand them, or you, or any of us, why do we need them? If it is only the whites who can understand them, what can it mean to us?'

Mantira jammed the shaft of his spear in the soft dirt. 'Ai, ai, Parsaloi. Listen to you. It's always *Why? Why?* You are the most difficult . . . obstinate . . . Do you know that?'

Ole Sadera stuck his jaw out defiantly. 'And if I am? What is an *olaiguenani* if he does not become difficult when his brothers' wellbeing is threatened?'

'You talk of wellbeing! Here we are in Entorror with how

many cattle? There is not enough space for our herds here. How many times have we been fined because we have been forced over the river in search of pasture? It is impossible to manage with what we have here.'

'And didn't this impossible situation arise because we placed our mark on another white man's papers?'

Mantira didn't bother to reply. He watched as Ole Sadera walked briskly away, wondering what lately troubled his young friend's head. There didn't appear to be anything anyone could do without it raising his suspicions and fears.

Norman Lewis stalked the veranda of his Ngong Road house. 'I don't understand you, George,' he said. 'How can you possibly support this latest push by Edouard?'

'Because,' Coll said patiently, 'it's what the Maasai want.'

'Utter rot! They're being pressured into it, as usual.'

'I don't believe they are, Norman. I went to Ngong after the governor made the announcement, and the elders agree with the plans. Maybe the outbreak of east coast fever in the Rift Valley has convinced them. I don't know, but if I thought there was any resistance to it, anything at all, I'd agree with you.'

'What did Lenana have to say?'

'Well, he's unfortunately not well. I only spent a brief time with him, and then I was introduced to his son, Seggi.'

'His son? Why?'

'I understand he's to be the new paramount chief.'

'So now we have a dynasty of paramount chiefs,' Lewis said with disgust.

Coll looked uneasy. 'Apparently.'

'Frankly, I don't believe a word of it. What about the others? Do Ole Sadera and the other fellow agree with this?'

'He and other leaders met Lenana last month. As far as I know they have decided to go ahead with a formal agreement. And if that's their wish, we must respect it.'

'And you heard this from Lenana?'

'Briefly, but as I say, he's not well, and it was Seggi, or more correctly, one of the elders who is acting as his advisor who gave me the details.'

'Who can you trust in this situation? All our experience points to another round of manipulation by Edouard.'

'We'll soon know. Seggi has called all the elders and the *olaiguenani* to a meeting. In the meantime, I am going north to arrange the meeting with Lenana and Edouard.'

'What's this fellow, Seggi, like?' Lewis said, taking his seat again.

Coll rubbed his jaw. 'Just a boy really. When Lenana goes — which may not be very much longer — he will have the say about any move. He's . . . not very outgoing, I'm afraid.'

'Oh, my God,' Lewis moaned. 'That's the end of it then. Edouard will annihilate him.'

'Norman, for goodness' sake! Aren't you letting your political philosophy get in the way of your common sense? We've been through the process, and the Maasai have actually asked to be allowed to reunite in the south, so why can't you accept that? Can't you ever see any of the good that's being done here? Look at the improvement in health that we've seen by educating the Maasai in simple sanitary methods. And peace — there hasn't been a tribal war in years. All of this, and yet you continually denigrate our efforts.'

'*Our* efforts? Since when are you a partner to Edouard and his ways?'

'I don't necessarily agree with everything we've done, but I will support anything that allows the Maasai to be the masters of their own destiny. I repeat, this is their choice. Who are we to inflict upon the Maasai our interpretation of what is best for them?'

'We seem to have done plenty of that to the other tribes. It's only a matter of time for the Maasai. They're already in a reserve. Next thing, we'll be sending in the missionaries to tell them how to think. That's hardly allowing them to be masters of their own destiny.'

'I see nothing wrong in the advancement of civilisation and Christianity.'

'Oh, please! Let's not include religion among the benefits of civilisation. The last thing these people need are more gods to whisper in their ears; or in the case of your precious

Christianity, the clergy who will take what grubby coins they can get for a few words from the good book.'

'I won't hear that sort of talk, Norman. While I don't happen to be a churchgoer, it doesn't mean I am not a believer in the Almighty and His work for the greater good of mankind. You and your medical associates can't claim to have the solution to all the ills of the world.'

'Spare me your sermons, George. I've had my fill over the years.'

'That's perhaps the best suggestion you've made today.'

'What is?' Lewis asked as Coll stood and went to the stairs, where he paused to regain his breath and composure.

'Sparing you my sermons,' Coll threw back over his shoulder, and marched down the steps into the garden, where the bougainvillea began its wild rambling ways. 'I've had about enough of your cynicism for now,' he added from the path. 'Good day to you.'

'You're getting yourself all upset, George,' Lewis called after him as Coll went storming off down the hill. 'It'll do your chest no good!'

CHAPTER 32

George Coll didn't want to appear conspicuous, so he sat among the idly curious at the back of the courtroom, albeit more interested than most in the trial that was now in its third day of hearings. Standing before the judge was the prosecutor, Herbert Wallis — a balding, slightly paunchy man with an ill-fitting suit and sweating profusely in the airless courthouse. In the dock, on trial for murder, was Galbraith Collins, a leading member of the settler community; a man with powerful friends both in British East Africa and abroad. It was clear by his deferential cross-examination that Wallis was well aware of that fact.

'If you please, Mr Collins,' Wallis said, 'you have heard the testimony given by Sergeant Dutton OIC of the Nakuru police station that the mutilated body of the Maasai warrior, Toiran, was found on your farm in the Great Rift Valley. Through the court's interpreter you've also heard from the Maasai witness who found the deceased that he recovered a metal object from near the body, which he gave to the police when he went to report the murder.'

'Objection!' the defence attorney cried.

'Sustained,' the judge said, looking over his glasses at the prosecutor. 'Mr Wallis, may I remind you that we have yet to determine if the matter on trial here is indeed murder, or even if a crime has been committed. At this stage we cannot rule out anything, including death by misadventure.'

Wallis mopped his brow with a large white handkerchief. 'I thank Your Honour for the reminder, and apologise to the court and my learned friend.' He nodded towards the defence attorney and his three assistants. 'Let me rephrase the question.' He cleared his throat and turned again to the dock. 'Mr Collins, you have heard that the Maasai warrior returned a small bimetal pellet to Sergeant Pearson of the Nakuru police station who gave his opinion that it was, or had been, a projectile from a .303 rifle.'

Collins nodded. 'Yes.'

'Could you please tell me, Mr Collins, do you possess such a weapon?'

'I do.'

'I see. And I presume that you, like any farmer in the valley, use it from time to time to shoot meat for the table?'

'That's correct.'

'Very good. And would you say you're an accomplished marksman with this weapon of yours, Mr Collins?'

'I can shoot the knobs off a giraffe at a hundred yards,' Collins answered with a smirk.

The jury and gallery burst into laughter.

'Order,' the judge warned, rapping his gavel.

'Mr Collins, you've said in your deposition to the court that you were out riding on 3 April 1911 when you came upon what looked like a raiding party of Maasai on your land. Can you tell the court how you arrived at that conclusion, please?'

'All three had on war paint and lion's mane headdresses.'

'And was it only their dress that made you believe they were on a raiding party?'

'I had earlier found what remained of one of my best rams. The bastards had cut it up and taken hunks of meat. Ignorant buggers don't have the faintest idea how to do a proper butchering job on a carcass. It was all chopped about.'

The courtroom buzzed and heads nodded.

'Order,' the judge growled. 'Order in the court. And I'll remind you, Mr Collins, not to use profanities in my courtroom.'

'Mr Collins,' the prosecutor continued, 'you said in your deposition that you found the men you suspected were the raiders. What did you do then, may I ask?'

'I called for them to stop.'

'And what were your intentions at that point?'

'I was going to give the thieving b— the thieving beggars a good thrashing with my *kiboko* whip and run them into Nakuru to be locked up.'

'But that didn't happen, Mr Collins, did it? Instead of stopping, the three men ran off. And this infuriated you, didn't it?'

'You're damn right it did!'

'It made you very angry, didn't it, Mr Collins?'

Collins glared at Wallis. 'You're not a farmer, are you, Mr Wallis?'

'Just answer the question, please,' Wallis said.

'Because if you were, you wouldn't ask such a stupid question.'

There was a rumble of agreement around the courtroom. Wallis looked to the bench. The judge appeared unmoved, and Coll noticed several nodding heads among the jury.

'There isn't a farmer in this protectorate,' Collins continued, 'who hasn't been driven mad by thieving natives. And the Maasai are the worst. No one is spared. You people here in Nairobi think we settlers are just a bunch of complaining toffs. Well, I'm telling you, there isn't a settler hereabouts who'd not do exactly the same as me if he'd seen one of his best stock cruelly slaughtered as mine was by these . . . these heathen thieves.'

'What you're saying, Mr Collins,' Wallis said, drawing himself up and sucking in his belly, 'is that for the sake of a mere dead sheep — a farm animal — you fired on three men, hitting one, the Maasai man Toiran, while trying to warn them off?'

'No, Mr Wallis,' Collins sneered, 'I'm sick and tired of warnings. I fired on the bastard, yes. But I shot to kill!'

The tall, elegant, severely handsome figure of Douglas Fenwick rose from the defence attorney's table and paused to look down at his papers as if considering whether he needed them for his final address to the jury. He seemed to decide against it, instead striding nonchalantly towards the jury box, thumbs tucked into his waistcoat pockets, looking down at the floor in thought.

When nearer the jury box he lifted his gaze and nodded to the members of the jury — white settlers to a man — making eye contact with each one while a small friendly smile played on his lips.

'Gentlemen,' he said, nodding as if he shared some amusing secret with them. 'Gentlemen, we all know why we're here in this courtroom, don't we?' He again quickly ran his eyes around the twelve men. 'We're here because your friend and neighbour Galbraith Collins has caught a thief. He's caught a thief, and in desperation has dispensed justice summarily.

'The prosecutor will tell you that Mr Collins committed a crime in punishing that thief. He will tell you that if Mr Collins had acted responsibly and obeyed the law, he should have apprehended the villain and dragged him before this court. My learned friend, Mr Wallis,' he waved his hand dismissively at the prosecutor's bench, 'might even be able to quote you chapter and verse from some policeman's notebook describing those procedures in excruciating detail. If the jury will indulge me in a small flight of fancy, let me imagine what it might say. Perhaps it would go something like this. The suspect should be asked to stand fast, to listen attentively while his wrongdoings were listed and his rights explained to him, and then he would be politely invited to accompany the officer to the nearest police station where he may, or may not, be charged.'

Some of the jurymen nodded and smiled grimly.

Fenwick smiled with them, then his mood changed. He grew stern. Leaning on the rail of the jury box, he said, 'We all know that out there on those empty windswept plains of the Great Rift Valley that procedure is impossible. I'm sure every one of you has had something of his stolen by a native. It might be a cow, a sheep, a basket of corn, or even a set of underwear off the clothesline. Every one of you knows too well it is a fight to survive. Because, out there,' he threw an arm dramatically towards the courthouse window, 'you and I know, gentlemen of the jury, that the law in this regard cannot cope. It is indeed an ass.' He had every one of the jury captured by his steel-grey eyes. The courtroom was perfectly silent.

He turned from the jury and took a pace or two away, rubbing his jaw in thought. 'No,' he said, and turned back to them. 'Let me not say the law is an ass. Let me rather say that it needs to be adapted to the peculiar circumstances of life in Africa, among people who have little knowledge and care less about British law. Let me say there isn't a man or woman in this courtroom who doesn't have compassion and concern for his fellow man; who isn't mindful of his Christian duty of charity. But survival out here, so far from Mother England, demands vigilance.'

He searched the jury's eyes for understanding. Heads nodded in mute agreement. Hearts had perhaps been touched by Fenwick's eloquence.

As if satisfied with what he'd seen, he continued. 'My client, your friend and neighbour, Galbraith Collins, overrode his Christian charity, his compassion, and did what the law has been unable to do. He has dealt out justice and made a statement for all other transgressors to heed. He said, *Abide by the law or you will be punished*. Gentlemen of the jury, I believe we owe Galbraith Collins our sympathy that it was he who had to make that pronouncement, but also our gratitude for taking such a brave stand against lawlessness. He has my sympathy and gratitude. I trust he has yours.'

With that, Fenwick returned to his seat.

A murmur spread around the courtroom as the judge cleared his throat and called for order. He addressed the jury, reiterating their responsibilities and the procedures they were bound to follow after retiring to consider their verdict.

'In this case,' the judge said, peering over his glasses, 'I am instructing you that regardless of Mr Fenwick's opinion that the law needs to be adapted to Africa, that is not your duty here today. Nor are you to take into consideration what penalties the court might impose. Despite the inference of Mr Fenwick's eloquent address to you, this court is not wanting in compassion. Your profoundly important duty is to assess the simple facts of the case. The Maasai warrior Toiran was shot and killed by the defendant. He has admitted as much and shows no remorse. You have no other option than to return a verdict to that effect.' He gave his gavel a sharp rap, saying, 'The jury will retire to consider its verdict.'

Ten minutes later, the jury returned.

The judge invited the foreman to address the court on behalf of the jury. 'How do you find the defendant, guilty or not guilty?'

'We find the defendant,' the foreman said, standing upright, his eyes towards the wall opposite, 'innocent of all charges.'

CHAPTER 33

Norman Lewis's cynicism about the Maasai's move south played on George Coll's mind and he decided to ride out to Rumuruti village on the Laikipia Plateau to satisfy himself that all was well.

He also had the unpleasant duty, which he had been avoiding for days, of advising Ole Sadera of the recent court decision regarding Collins and the murder of the Maasai *morani* in the Great Rift Valley. His own reaction had moved from disbelief, to anger and finally to guilt. He had assured the Maasai that justice would be done, which was now manifestly, incredibly and nauseatingly untrue. He used his time in the saddle to compose the words that might explain this turn of events, and how he had also felt cheated by the decision, but Coll knew that no matter what he said, the words would ring hollow.

After an exchange of greetings, Coll followed the elders through the village, where Maasai women were busy with their weaving and beading, to their meeting place in a shady cedar thicket. Ole Nakola, a man who seemed to wear the creases and contours of the Great Rift Valley in his wrinkled face, courteously welcomed Coll and invited him to speak.

Coll told the elders the governor had sent him to prepare them for the meeting called by Lenana, where he expected they would sign a new resettlement agreement. He asked them to confirm they were agreeable to the plan.

The elders began to speak in turn, mentioning such things as the need to have the Maasai in one place, the benefits of the additional land granted in exchange for the northern reserve and the advantages of being located with their *laibon* in the south.

Coll breathed a sigh of relief as one after another confirmed their agreement.

'I thank you for your words,' Coll said. 'If there are any among you who still have any remaining concerns, I believe the governor would approve an inspection visit to the southern reserve should the Purko desire it.'

'We do not want to send anybody to look at any part of the country,' Ole Nakola said on behalf of the others. 'Between us, we know all of it . . . We know the country offered is not good for our cattle. We know it is bad and waterless, and we have no faith in what the government says.'

Coll was dumbstruck. Were these the same men who had just moments ago given their full endorsement of the move? 'I don't understand, Ole Nakola,' he stammered. 'I thought you were pleased about the move.'

'We wanted the great valley, but if we can't have it, we shall have to do without it. We would rather stay here in Entorror, but if we cannot, we will go.'

'But . . . you know the problems here in Laikipia. There is little water, and the governor has promised to build water storage in the south so that you and your cattle will not be wanting.'

'We are not sure of these things, but we are prepared to go.'

'We do not want any more conferences on the matter,' said one of the other elders. 'We will just go.'

'If the British say we must go, then we will go,' said another.

It was hardly the ringing endorsement that Coll wanted to hear, but the elders would not be drawn further.

'What are the views of Ole Sadera and Mantira?'

The elders exchanged glances.

Pointing beyond the *boma* gate, Ole Nakola said, 'Mantira is with the Il Talala in his *manyatta*. They share our opinion, but you can see for yourself.'

'And Ole Sadera?' Coll asked.

Ole Nakola looked uncomfortable. 'The Il Tuati have gone to the bush.'

The elders appeared disinclined to discuss Ole Sadera. It was not in their custom to air bad news. Coll was uncertain how much he could ask of them, and how much they could tell him. Finally, Ole Nakola offered to find a boy to lead Coll to Ole Sadera's meat camp, where the *olaiguenani* himself could answer all his questions.

News that it was a meat camp confirmed to Coll there was something unusual happening among the warrior group. The *moran* set up a meat camp to slaughter and feast on the meat of one of their cattle in the belief that it would give them strength and courage. A meat camp was usually held on the eve of some important event, and often preceded a battle.

The significance of the camp and the manner in which Ole Nakola and the elders had concealed it caused Coll's chest to tighten. His breath came in short gasps and he had difficulty controlling a rising feeling of trepidation.

Many had said that they could push the Maasai only so far before they mounted a retaliatory expedition. The first settlers had terrifying tales of the Maasai's notorious blood lust.

He and Lewis had been struggling for white reform. Coll now feared they were about to witness a black revolution.

Long before he reached the forest where Ole Sadera held his meat camp, Coll could hear the reverberating chant of a hundred droning bass voices. From a distance it might have been an aspirating engine, with the forceful rush of expelled steam followed by the gushing intake of air on its return stroke.

Hhuunh-huh!

As he drew close to the forest where the elders had said he would find Ole Sadera, the chant grew louder until it became all-pervasive — a part of the dark Lariak hills themselves. It was as if a giant had taken up residence and his breath filled the forest.

Hhuunh-huh!

After pushing through a patch of particularly thick bush, his guide — a small Maasai boy — abruptly stopped and Coll tumbled over him into a clearing. Gleaming black bodies of near-naked warriors, decorated in red, yellow and white ochre, circled a blazing fire. After each step, there was a dramatic pause, exaggerated by the thrusting of chests and shoulders in time with the chant.

Hhuunh-huh!

With a cry of '*Yip! Yip! Yip!*' one of the *moran* sprang from the circle and began to leap effortlessly into the early evening air. His body glistened in the firelight and his red *shuka* flapped around tightly corded leg muscles.

The surrounding warriors thumped their war shields in time with his leap.

The power and beauty of the spectacle enthralled Coll.

An unseen figure came from the darkness behind him, and a hand grabbed his arm, drawing him from the clearing.

'Parsaloi!' he gasped, shaken.

'Swara, you are here.' But the greeting was not welcoming.

'When you were not at the *enkang* I worried that you were ill,' Coll said, wondering why he felt it necessary to fabricate an excuse.

Ole Sadera smiled wryly. 'Perhaps I am, my friend.'

'Oh? How so?'

'What brings you here this evening, Swara?'

The question was a little more abrupt than the usual Maasai courtesy. It caught Coll unawares and he stumbled over his reply. 'I . . . I wanted to . . . to speak to you about the meeting at Ngong. The meeting called by Lenana.'

Ole Sadera turned from Coll to the dancing Il Tuati. 'I see,' he said.

'Well . . .' By now Coll knew something was amiss. 'You are coming, are you not?'

'No.'

'*No?*'

'I will not stand against the others, but I cannot sign.'

'But why? I thought all the Maasai were in agreement. I heard it said that it was time for the Maasai to unite for the good of the tribe. And that there was too little grazing land in Laikipia. What . . . what is it you fear?'

'The Il Tuati fear nothing.'

Coll studied Ole Sadera's profile. The light of the fire picked out the muscle and bone structure of his jaw, which flexed and rippled.

'Yes, Parsaloi, but what is it *you* fear?'

Ole Sadera glanced at Coll and for a moment let the tension in his jaw relax. He took a deep breath before answering.

'I fear the decisions I must make, Swara. How can I be sure what is best for my brothers? If we stay in Entorror when all others leave, what will happen to the Il Tuati? What will happen when it is time to move on to become elders, to marry and begin a family? Who will make the blessing? Who will celebrate with us? Where will we find wives? And even if it is the right thing for the Il Tuati to stay here, alone, what will the remainder of the Purko section do without the strength of the senior *moran*?' He bit his bottom lip and his face again grew tense as he wrestled with his thoughts. 'I fear being herded like cattle across the great valley. To be counted and prodded. It is shameful. But after all these things, and more than any of them, I fear losing what it is to be Maasai.' He turned to Coll. 'Do you understand me? Can you know what it means to be Maasai and face losing everything that is yourself?'

Coll tried to understand. 'I think so.'

Ole Sadera dropped his head. 'I am sorry, Swara. I burden you with problems you have no way of solving for me.'

'You are right. Only you can make the final decision on what to advise your Il Tuati. But you are wrong to imagine you are alone. What of the advice of the elders?'

'The elders are weak. They neglect their responsibilities. It is the Il Tuati and our brothers the Il Talala *moran* who must carry the burden of this decision.'

'What does Mantira say of these things?'

Ole Sadera was silent, his face closing against hearing any more of Coll's words.

Coll tried to reach him again. 'Is it not good to hear other views before deciding your answer?'

The rapport was lost. Ole Sadera grew angry again.

'Men can talk. Stupid men never listen. Sometimes a *morani* must stand alone and do what is right.'

He stormed off towards the firelight and the dancing warriors. Coll followed him.

'But what is right, Parsaloi? What will you do?' He was frustrated now that the argument had come full circle. 'I must have an answer for the governor.'

Ole Sadera swung around but his expression was lost in the silhouette. 'The governor?' His voice was thick and barely audible over the chanting *moran*. 'Tell the governor the Il Tuati would rather die in battle than be chased from their land again!'

Nashilo watched the white man leave the meat camp and waited as Ole Sadera paced the outskirts of the *moran*'s dancing circle. Shortly after, he walked off into the darkening forest.

She crept after him, carefully placing her footsteps to avoid any sound that would alert him to her presence. She had no plans to reveal herself, for he would know she had followed him from the camp and it was forbidden for a woman to observe the *moran* when they took meat. She wasn't sure why she was there; maybe it was the conversation she'd had with Ntooto that day.

'One more *eunoto* and he will join the elders,' Ntooto had said in a voice full of doom. Nashilo heard the unspoken message and disregarded it. Ntooto was reminding her that in a few years Parsaloi would be expected to marry and take his place among his age mates as a family man. She was saying that Nashilo might as well give up her relationship with Parsaloi now because, inevitably, he would take one or more wives and she would be forgotten. Nashilo had faced the possibility of this outcome herself and didn't care to be reminded of it. So long as she lived, she said to herself repeatedly, Parsaloi would be her greatest love. And she, his.

But if Nashilo were perfectly honest with herself, she had to admit to being completely ignorant of Parsaloi's true feelings. Love was something she imagined lurked behind those troubled eyes, but it never actually managed to show itself, in either word or form. The best she had come to expect was a fierce passion and an occasional glimpse into his heart. She was never more content than when he shared his hopes and dreams with her. She had long ago accepted that if these were all he could offer her, then they would have to suffice.

Parsaloi stopped in a small clearing where the surrounding forest muted the sounds of the *moran*'s camp. It was dark there and Nashilo wasn't sure exactly where he was, until his soft voice rose in song. As her eyes became accustomed to the darkness she could see him standing in the centre of the clearing, his head raised to the sky.

'*Leeyio, Naiteru kop,*' he sang.

'*Lord, who was the beginner of the world,*
Guide me as I go to do battle
Guide me as you have guided the cattle of the sky
Let me see my enemy so I may strike him before he strikes me.'

From somewhere nearby came the loud shriek of a hyrax. It startled her and she stumbled, her foot snapping a twig.

Ole Sadera grabbed his spear and turned towards her in a single movement. Motionless, he peered into the darkness to where she had hidden behind a bush. His form was clear against the lesser darkness of the sky. Her heart beat like a drum until she was sure he could hear it.

After breathless moments, he slowly raised his spear, the iron point towards where Nashilo hid in her bush.

'Parsaloi!' she piped. 'Wait! It's me.'

He lowered his spear arm. 'Show yourself,' he said.

She came sheepishly from her hiding place. As she drew nearer she tried to read his expression in the dim light, but he wore his enigmatic face — the one he put on whenever she tried to plumb his deepest thoughts.

'What are you doing here?' he demanded.

'I want to be with you.'

'It is forbidden.'

'I know. I didn't want you to know I was here.'

'Then why be here?'

'I always want to be near you.'

'You cannot always be with me. Can a woman have two husbands?'

'No.'

'You must go.'

She waited for him to relent, and his silence again allowed the tree hyrax to fill the night with its raucous shrieks.

'You harden your heart to me these days.'

Her words caused him to pause. He planted his spear haft in the ground before answering. 'These are difficult times, Nashilo. There is much that a man must do.'

'Are you and the Il Tuati moving south with the *enkang*?'

He took a deep breath and allowed it to escape slowly. 'No.'

'Then how will I see you again?' she said, her voice rising in concern. She'd heard rumours that the *moran* were resisting the calls of the elders, but she couldn't — daren't — believe it.

Ole Sadera moved a few paces from her.

She followed, placing her hand on his shoulder. 'How can I live without you?' she pleaded.

'It is something that must be endured.' He turned to face her. His eyes caught the faint light. 'No matter where I am, no matter where you are, we will know how it has been between us. We also know it must pass. You are married, and one day I must also marry.'

The unfathomable face was gone and she could again see into his heart.

'Nashilo, what we have is not forever. There are things that must be done. I have . . . responsibilities.'

'My love,' she said, throwing her arms around him.

His arms briefly encircled her, but then he let them drop to his sides. 'You must go,' he said.

Through her tears, she studied his face. He had retreated to where she could never go. He had arrived at a decision and would hear no dispute. She knew it was pointless to argue.

The shriek of a second hyrax came from a great distance.

It was not easy for her to take backward steps from him, but she knew she must. He was a strange, unknowable man, as strong as a leather thong but never so pliable.

CHAPTER 34

Kira was very unhappy. She always felt unhappy when she had to disagree with Katherine, but it was important that she do so. She couldn't face another meeting with the Indian women of the Asian and Native Progress Association.

'But, Kira,' Katherine said, 'the ANPA ladies love you. Don't they always say hello and give you little presents from time to time?'

It was true. On the face of it, the women seemed to accept Kira. They would gush over her whenever she appeared among them. She was, after all, the only black African at any of their meetings.

But Kira had developed a finely tuned ability to detect ill feelings directed against her. Before arriving at Katherine's kitchen door, Kira had not only been an orphan, she'd been an outcast. The Kikuyu who took her in had many children. Kira served as a menial servant, cleaning, harrowing, weeding, cooking. She kept out of people's way and escaped attention and the attendant troubles it might bring by her ability to read the mood behind people's expressions. What she'd detected behind the smiles of the ANPA women was not friendliness but animosity concealed by a veneer of cordiality. In her mind, they were two-faced.

The term was one Katherine had used to describe her former white friends who nowadays snubbed her for her support for

ANPA. Katherine could detect hubris in the whites, but it surprised Kira to realise that she couldn't see it in the Indians. Kira kept her thoughts on these matters to herself, as Katherine appeared to be genuinely interested in the ANPA cause. As it included indirect assistance to her own Maasai people, she couldn't be offended by her employer's good intentions.

'It's good for you to get among other people,' Katherine said. 'Even if they're not your own kind. It's good practice for when you must make your way in life.'

'Make your way in life' was another of Katherine's expressions — one she used as a means of filling the void that was Kira's future. She still fervently believed Kira could find a place in white society, but she'd never actually been able to articulate how it could be done. Kira remained apprehensive about ever achieving that level of acceptance. At seventeen, she had developed into a striking young woman. She was lithe and leggy, but although Katherine tried to instil in her the confidence to move among the whites and other groups in Nairobi, she remained painfully shy.

Katherine waited expectantly for Kira to speak. In response to the silence, she said, 'Well, I've always said you must be true to yourself. I can't go back on that advice even though I believe you're being foolish thinking the ANPA ladies don't like you. I think it's all in your head, young lady. In time I hope you'll gain the good sense to realise when people are genuinely trying to help you, and ignore your prejudices.'

Kira wondered if Katherine was hinting that she didn't appreciate her efforts either.

'Now, what do you say?' Katherine entreated.

Kira could not refuse.

Katherine spotted the women up ahead and turned to Kira to remind her how to quietly deal with the situation. 'Keep your head up, Kira. We've nothing to be ashamed of. Be proud of who you are. Just look straight ahead. Don't forget to smile.'

She then straightened her back as they marched towards the group of white women gathered outside Weatherby's Haberdashery on Government Road. They were whispering among themselves, and pointedly turned their backs on Katherine and the girl as they approached.

'Good morning, ladies,' Katherine said in a firm voice, determined to make the point that they could not intimidate her by their rudeness. She expected no reply, and got none. Since her involvement with the Asian and Native Progress Association, many of the women she had previously considered her friends shunned her company. Her habit of bringing Kira on her shopping expeditions seemed to confirm their suspicions that she had 'gone over to the other side'.

Katherine imagined their animated conversation when she was out of earshot. They would whisper about her foolish involvement with natives, Indians and other socially undesirable individuals. They might compare her to the reformist churchmen who were presently preaching equality for all races. There was no doubt that their husbands' opinions would be recited parrot-fashion and without an iota of dissent. It was all very well, they'd say, to abolish slavery, which was certainly an evil practice, but extending the sentiment to include rights to land, equal pay, education and labour reform was quite another matter.

Katherine blinked back the tears of rage that threatened her resolve to be resolute in the face of their small-mindedness. She told herself she could manage without fair-weather friends. She still had one or two like-minded individuals among her acquaintances, who shared at least some of her views.

Just as she regained control of her temper, Governor Edouard and his wife came strolling towards them along the row of shops. It was an omen. Katherine would never have such an opportunity again to tackle the governor over Galbraith Collins's atrocious court case.

She stepped boldly into Edouard's path, leaving Kira a few paces behind.

'Good morning, Governor,' she said. Nodding to his wife, she added, 'Lady Edouard.'

'A very good morning to you, madam,' Edouard said, smiling cautiously.

'I hope you'll forgive my forthright manner, Sir Percy. I am Katherine Wallace. I have written to —'

'I know who you are, Mrs Wallace,' he said, his smile intact. 'I have seen your name more than once on correspondence to my office. I always thought it odd — I mean, a Wallace among all those Patels and Guptas and Husseins.'

'And you'll continue to see it among them until justice is done, Governor.'

'Justice?'

Lady Edouard took his arm as if to lead him away, but he patted her hand reassuringly. 'It's quite all right my dear. Mrs Wallace is a member of that Indian group we've been hearing about. The ones who are always sending such interesting letters to the *Standard*.'

He returned his gaze to Katherine. 'What justice, or lack of it, concerns you today, Mrs Wallace?'

'The court case, or lack of it, against Galbraith Collins.'

'I see. And you feel that we somehow serve justice when an honest farmer is hounded for defending his property? I think it would serve your interests better to stay at home and darn your husband's socks, Mrs Wallace, rather than meddle in matters to do with the land and the good men who till its soils to put meat on your table.'

'For your information, Governor, *I* am the one who puts meat on my table, but what, may I ask, has that to do with the murder of an innocent man?'

Edouard was unflappable. 'I suggest you leave matters of government to His Majesty's appointed officials, madam,' he said stiffly and began to move away.

'It might interest you to know that ANPA has done just that. Our plaint against Galbraith Collins is with the Colonial Office.'

Edouard turned and glared at Katherine. For a moment, she thought he might explode with rage, but with great control he said, 'Mrs Wallace, the black population of British East Africa totals some three million. We whites are but three thousand, while your friends, the Asians, are twelve. You would do well to keep those figures in mind before you bring about the social revolution you and your friends seem to favour.'

* * *

273

Katherine sat in her cart outside the printer's office waiting for
Vidyarthi who was inside collecting the ANPA posters and
leaflets that she would help to deliver in the town and
throughout the surrounding settlements.

She had resolved that the white population would not
intimidate her into giving up her support for the Asian and
Native Progress Association. Their snubs only made her more
determined to donate her energies to Shirin and her husband,
Vidyarthi. She spent considerable time away from her farm so
that she could attend their outdoor protest meetings, where the
presence of a white woman was almost guaranteed to get
coverage in the *East African Standard*.

It was high noon and Katherine's double terai made her feel
hot and a little faint as she sat in the cart in the hot sun. She
climbed down and took a seat in the shade. She had not been long
there when she saw George Coll approaching down River Road.
For a moment she was unsure if it was him, as River Road, being
the centre of the Indian business area, was far removed from the
administrative buildings. But it was, and for a silly moment she
wanted to run and hide. But she stayed where she was, affecting
a nonchalant attitude as he drew nearer.

'Katherine,' he said, when he had almost passed her. From his
expression it appeared that he had spoken involuntarily, and
might have continued walking past without comment had he
had time to consider it.

Katherine feigned surprise. 'George! How nice. How are
you?'

'I . . . I'm quite well. I didn't expect . . . I mean, it's nice to see
you too. What are you doing here? That is, I mean, are you, er,
shopping?'

'Not really. Are you?'

'No.'

She could see he was thinking the same thing as she — why
were they there?

'I'm here with a friend,' she offered.

'Oh.'

'He's collecting some notices.'

'I see.'

'From the printer.'

'Yes.'

She wondered if he felt as awkward as she did.

Vidyarthi came striding out of the printery, and stopped short at finding Katherine no longer in the cart.

'I'm here, Isher,' she said.

Vidyarthi spun around. 'Ah, so you are.' When he realised she had been speaking to Coll he turned on one of his brilliant smiles. 'Oh, I'm sorry. I am interrupting you.'

'No, not at all,' Katherine said.

'Not at all,' responded Coll.

'Isher, I'd like you to meet, er, a friend of mine. George Coll. George, this is Isher Vidyarthi.'

The two men shook hands and exchanged pleasantries for a few moments before a numbing silence fell over all three of them.

Coll shuffled his feet and gave one his nervous coughs.

Katherine smiled ineffectually.

'Ah, so, Katherine,' Vidyarthi said. 'Shall we go?'

'Yes.'

'Then would you excuse us, Mr Coll?' Vidyarthi said pleasantly. 'It was nice to meet you. We have to rush.'

'Certainly. Of course.'

'Goodbye, George.'

'Yes. Goodbye, um, Katherine.'

As Vidyarthi handed her up into the cart, Katherine had the awful feeling that George had got the wrong impression about the dashing Indian. She hesitated a moment then turned to Coll, only to see him walking hurriedly down River Road without a backward glance.

Lord Delamere tapped his riding crop on the podium in the Muthaiga Club's library and called for silence.

The murmur of collective voices slowly ebbed. Delamere waited for complete silence before speaking.

'Since this is an informal gathering I'll not be following the Colonists' Association's usual meeting procedure, but instead call on our governor, Sir Percy Edouard, to give us an off-the-record summary of some important developments.' He extended a hand towards Edouard. 'Sir Percy, if you please.'

The governor strode to the podium amid polite applause. 'Good evening, gentlemen,' he said, smiling. 'Thank you for inviting me to your gathering this evening.

'Before I get to the topic at hand, perhaps I might take a moment or two to make a few personal observations upon matters that seem to have attracted some attention in the press, both here and at home. I am referring of course to the hullabaloo about the use of Crown land here in British East Africa. You, more than anyone, would be aware of how scarce land of any description is here in the protectorate.'

Edouard pulled a monocle from his waistcoat pocket and glanced down at his notes before continuing. 'It wouldn't surprise you, for instance, to hear that more than four-fifths of BEA is desert, and that most of the arable land exists above five thousand feet.' He looked out over his audience. 'What I believe many of you have begun to call the White Highlands.

'My point, gentlemen, is that while some sections of the press bleat about alienating land from the natives, what they don't understand is that there's precious little of it worth a damn, and what good land exists must be well husbanded if it is to make a return on the sizable investment our government has made in it.'

A murmur of agreement came from the audience.

'Let me quote Mr Joseph Chamberlain, in my view one of the finest colonial secretaries we have seen in recent years.'

He coughed to clear his throat. 'Chamberlain said, "I believe that the British race is the greatest of the governing races that the world has ever seen . . . It is not enough to occupy great spaces of the world's surface unless you can make the best of them. It is the duty of a landlord to develop his estate." Accordingly, Chamberlain advocated investment in Africa. Gentlemen, I unashamedly subscribe to Chamberlain's point of view.'

Applause rippled around the room.

When it had subsided, Edouard said, 'Now, to more salient matters. I'm pleased that during the introduction Lord Delamere labelled this little chat as an "off-the-record summary". What I have to tell you this evening has not been completely ratified, but I have every confidence in saying it will be concluded in the next few days.

'Most of you know that the Maasai wish to leave their northern reserve so as to be co-located with those in the south. The new agreement we have now drafted calls for some four and a half thousand square miles of the Laikipia Plateau to be given up in exchange for nearly half as much again in the southern reserve. A very generous offer, I'm sure you'll agree.

'The movement that got under way some months ago came to a premature end because of some, shall we say, mix-ups in London. However, all is falling into place and I expect that the Laikipia Plateau will be vacated for use for more productive activities very soon.'

A buzz of excited chatter filled the library room. Edouard raised his hand for silence.

'This means that there will be large movements of Maasai and their stock through the Great Rift Valley and environs. We estimate that about ten thousand Maasai will move south, with around one hundred and seventy-five thousand cattle and more than a million sheep and goats.' He let the figures sink in for a moment. 'A sizable operation, you'll agree. I will have *askaris* and troops in place to marshal the movement, but I am hoping — nay, let me make it clear — I am expecting every one of you to do your part.

'After we start the resettlement, we must not allow it to lose momentum. The Maasai will want to dawdle to allow their cattle to feed on the better pastures. In many cases this will mean they will want to graze on your land.'

He ran his eyes around the settlers.

'I am not proposing we forego all charity, gentlemen, but be sparing with it. Don't let them stay longer than is absolutely necessary. View it as your Christian duty to speed the Maasai to their goal in the southern reserve.'

*　*　*

Norman Lewis found the government offices empty except for a sleepy *askari* at the front door. It was a Friday and he imagined the senior officers would be at the Nairobi Club with their gin and tonics, while junior men like himself, with the inclination for an ale, would be at Wood's or the Norfolk.

He passed through Wadley's outer office into the governor's suite. The correspondence tray was on the desk. It was usually locked away, but on the few occasions that Lewis had had the opportunity to scan its contents he'd found they revealed interesting insights into the machinery of government. He looked to the outer door, where the *askari* sat nodding over the truncheon he nursed in his lap, then started to flip through the papers.

A memo near the top of the pile caught his eye. The handwriting was familiar, so he turned to the last page to find the signature: G Coll, signed at Rumuruti. Lewis had not heard from Coll since their quarrel more than two weeks beforehand, so was unaware that his friend had gone upcountry. It was dated just three days prior so must have come by runner. The sense of urgency piqued his curiosity. He stood at the desk and read it.

> *Your Excellency,*
> *Re: Report on Discussions with Purko Maasai*
> *At your behest, I arrived at Rumuruti in due haste, arriving Monday last, 6 March 1911.*
> *I immediately made contact with Purko elders at their village.*
> *I enquired about Lenana's decision to move the Maasai into one reserve, being the one in the south. At first they agreed it was a good idea, given the shortage of land and the difficulty in accessing water in these dry times.*
> *However, upon further discussion they seemed to change their stance. They were then of the view that the move would be a disaster and quoted a number of objections including stock deaths and doubts that the government would honour their promise to improve water storage. They then admitted that they would move if the government said they must.*

In short, the elders are indecisive, but it is clear that their present agreement to the move cannot be said to be totally without a feeling of duress. They need more time.

Of the moran, *I can be more specific. Ole Sadera is clearly against the move. He is deeply concerned about the effects upon their wellbeing and flatly refuses to sign any new agreement.*

Mantira also has concerns about the move, but does not share Ole Sadera's strident objections. I believe he may be convinced in due course, but it must be said that at present he is of a similar view to that of the elders.

May I therefore strongly recommend that the matters concerning the Purko be clarified before any agreement is signed. I will await Your Excellency's further instructions that I beg be sent here as a matter of urgency.

Attached by a pin to the bottom of the page was a tiny square of paper and a word written by another hand: *Hold*.

Lewis angrily thrust the memo back onto the stack of papers.

'Maddening, isn't it?' The voice came from the doorway, where Edouard stood, an icy smile on his lips. 'Imagine if you can, Dr Lewis, dealing with such drivel every day of the week.'

Lewis was lost for words. He felt like a schoolboy caught stealing plums.

Edouard sauntered into the office, resplendent in his colonel's dress uniform with its royal blue and red tunic and its tiny sparkling escutcheons on the epaulettes and cuffs. He peeled off his white gloves and slapped them in the palm of his hand to flatten them before throwing them on the desk in front of Lewis.

'Imagine . . .' Edouard said, turning from Lewis to wander around his office, 'imagine the frustration of doing one's best for king and country while playing nursemaid to a spoiled bunch of titled layabouts.' His hands were clasped behind his back as he strolled, studying the portraits of previous governors and commissioners. He paused in front of the portrait of King George V. 'But worse than that, my good doctor,' he turned towards Lewis, 'far worse than that is finding oneself in a rats' nest of traitors and informers.'

Lewis, stung into action, finally found his voice. 'How would you characterise a traitor then? Is it someone who sees a wrong being committed in the name of that king and country and seeks to redress it?'

'I see miserable little men unable to aspire to the heights they believe to be their calling, who instead trade in lies and ignorance to bring down those more talented. I see —'

'More talented? Hah!' Lewis's humiliation had transformed itself into a burning antagonism. 'How much talent does it take to convince natives — at the point of a gun — to comply with your edicts?'

'It may have escaped you, Dr Lewis, while you're dispensing tea and sympathy to your patients, that I am trying to manage — with all its competing demands — our government's estate here in British East Africa.'

'That's it, isn't it, Edouard? To you it's just another British estate, to be governed in the best interests of an absent landlord. Tell me this — and a man of such undoubted talent as yourself should find no challenge in it — how can the British Government justify its alienation of all this land? I dare say it's bad enough when we conquer a country by force of arms, but here, why, we're nothing more than caretakers of a land still owned by others.'

'When those owners, as you call them, are incapable or unwilling to work it so as to make contributions to those who have provided the benefits of civilisation, then yes, it is our duty to expropriate the means of production.'

'Who asked for such benefits? And at what price was their provision negotiated?'

'I have no doubt you are a man learned in matters of science, doctor, but leave matters of state to those who can understand their intricacies.'

'It takes little skill to understand the situation here.'

'Ah! An insight from the good doctor. Do enlighten me.'

'It was not to dispense the arguable benefits of European life that we entered into this part of Africa. Oh, no. It was to spread our various and competing ideas on religion.'

'Oh, ho! A holy war,' Edouard scoffed.

'Not quite, but once Livingstone had enflamed missionary zeal at home with his unfortunate but heroic death, the race was on to win souls — the French with their Catholicism and we with our Protestantism. When the natives were less than enamoured of Christianity and broke a few heads, we sent our troops in to convince them to behave. Of course, the military presence soon developed into a military confrontation.'

'Dr Lewis, don't tell me you're now going to suggest you are also an expert on geopolitics?'

'You don't have to be an expert to trace what followed. To forestall the French, who, we believed, had their sights set on the headwaters of the Nile, we built a railway line to Uganda. And it was the railway corridor — a half-mile wide strip — that introduced the concept of Crown land to British East Africa. With that as a precedent we found it was easy to increase it by gradually stripping traditional land from its rightful owners. This so-called *protectorate* means nothing in either fact or law. No one is protected from the avaricious demands of the settlers. Nor from their biased governor.'

'I've heard just about enough of your pontificating, but nowhere in all your fanciful theories have you justified your appearance in my office this evening.'

Edouard's abrupt change of attack brought Lewis to a halt.

'I see you have fewer ideas on that matter, Dr Lewis. Perhaps I can give you the benefit of my thoughts on this one. May I suggest that, having been thwarted in your recent attempts to defame my administration at home, you are now attempting to find more material to send to your confidant, the leader of the Parliamentary Labour Party. Do you deny it?'

Lewis decided to avoid any discussion of the matter. 'I have never made a personal attack on you, Governor Edouard. But I quite simply abhor the ruthless, secretive decisions you hide under the pretext of enlightened governance.'

Edouard's face coloured. 'If it is character we are now discussing, Dr Lewis, what can be said about a man who professes strong moral convictions about those decisions, but is too weak and fearful to voice them? Instead he sneaks about like a coward, whispering in other ears in the hope that someone else, presumably with enough dignity and fortitude, will take up the battle for him.' He drew himself up to his full height. 'But character matters aside, I demand to know this. Did you, or did you not, convey confidential information, illegally obtained, to Ramsay MacDonald about government decisions in certain matters? Matters that were intended to restore justice for the hard-working residents of British East Africa?' He took a pace towards Lewis, his chest thrust out. 'These decisions, whether they agree with your jaundiced view of equity or your pathetic opinions on what is best for the people of this land, are my right, nay, my duty to make. Are you so much of a coward that you will still deny that you informed MacDonald?'

'You're *damn* right I did!'

Edouard's tension immediately evaporated. He sniffed and tried to conceal a smile.

'Well,' he said, unable to keep the smile from widening. 'I'm so pleased we've at least agreed on one point this evening, doctor. I shall have a file note of our conversation drawn up for your signature in the morning.'

The governor walked to the other side of his desk and took his seat. Without looking up from his papers he said, 'Now get out, I have work to do.'

CHAPTER 35

Women paused in their shopping to stare and wonder. Businessmen and shopkeepers sneered, while the many natives at work or simply idling away the day watched the marchers pass with incomprehension.

About a dozen Asian men, led by Isher Vidyarthi, and three women, including Katherine Wallace, marched with discipline and reserve down Sixth Avenue towards the governor's offices. They carried crudely built and painted placards. *Justice for the Maasai*, one proclaimed. *Gaol for Murderers*, said another.

Katherine carried nothing but her parasol and a fear that she would find herself in another mêlée, but the march, unannounced and carried out in the heat of the day, went almost unnoticed.

After climbing the hill, they halted, sweating and hot, ten paces from the veranda steps leading to the governor's front door. They waited for five minutes. Then ten. Members of the group started to exchange glances and look to Vidyarthi, who remained ramrod straight and grim-faced. After a further ten minutes a man with pince-nez spectacles and carrying a mailbag came out, gawped at the crowd, and then scuttled back inside. Shortly after, an *askari* came through the double timber doors and scowled. Two members of the governor's staff followed, and finally the governor appeared. He ran an eye over the gathering before speaking.

'And to what do I owe the pleasure of this visit, Mr Vidyarthi?' Edouard said, looking down his nose from his elevated position on the veranda. As he spoke, a few more officials came out, arranging themselves to the right and left of him.

'We wish to draw Your Excellency's attention to a petition, Sir Percy.'

'Do you now,' he said with a smile. 'Very well, let's see it.'

As Edouard waited for Vidyarthi to mount the steps, his eyes swept over the crowd, pausing on Katherine for a long moment. Katherine glared at him, but a movement among the officials distracted her.

She gaped. George Coll had eased his way through the crowd to stand next to the governor.

Coll had been collecting the paperwork for his upcoming field trip when the ripple of excitement coursed through the governor's offices. As one after another of the office staff moved to the windows and other vantage points he became mildly curious, but quickly stuffed his papers in his bag and headed to the door to leave.

He was surprised to find the governor and others standing on the veranda. He eased his way through the door and saw the reason for all the excitement. A group of Indians holding little painted banners had congregated in the garden.

Coll glanced over them in mild curiosity before his eyes fell upon Katherine Wallace, who was staring at him. He read the horror in her eyes to find him aligned against her on the parapets of power.

Wadley found it difficult to sit astride a horse when his haemorrhoids gave him such trouble, but sitting in an open buggy, with every pothole reminding him of his medical condition, was not much better.

In spite of the topee perched on his cranium, which caused sweat to trickle down under his collar, and the protectorate's standard-issue sun umbrella above him, he felt, or imagined he could feel, the deleterious effects of the actinic rays of the sun, as had been the warning in every publication he had read on the dangers of travel in the tropics.

Before leaving for the coast on official business, Governor Edouard had given Wadley instructions to attend to the matters with Lenana as a priority. But Wadley had delayed his departure, first hoping that the poor weather would soon clear, and later that his haemorrhoids would settle down. Neither had gone his way.

He peered from under his brolly at the unremitting sun. He knew it was a trick of the tropics. Before the day was done, the heavens would open in a typical wet-season downpour. He hoped that his decision to make an early start would at least spare him from being trapped by the rain.

The reason for the visit to Lenana's camp at Ngong was another cause for irritation. Edouard was worried that Lenana would die before making a public statement in support of the proposed resettlement agreement. He also wanted a date set for the elders and leaders to come together for the ceremonial signing. In Wadley's view, the old man was in no hurry to die, and he believed the whole matter should be left to take its natural course, as was the usual procedure in the civil service.

Before his driver had turned the buggy into the Ngong *boma*, Wadley could tell there was something odd happening there. A group of old women were gathered outside the *boma* gate, their wailing voices making an ungodly cacophony. Inside, the signs were similarly ominous, with a cluster of elders looking glum outside Lenana's hut.

He found the *laibon*'s interpreter and learned, to his horror, that the old man had died that very hour.

'But that's . . . that's impossible!' Wadley spluttered. 'There's no . . . We haven't . . . Where's Lenana's son?' he asked. 'Where's Seggi?'

He was hoping that Lenana had given the boy instructions for the signing ceremony.

'He is inside helping the wives prepare the *laibon*'s body,' the interpreter said.

'I must speak with him,' Wadley said, making towards the hut.

The old man restrained him. 'Please, sir, let me call him for you.' He entered the hut before Wadley could respond.

Wadley paced up and down in the dust of the *enkang*, lamenting his decision to delay his trip. What would Edouard say if he learned Wadley had postponed the trip for no other reason than his own convenience? How could he explain it was because of the weather or, worse, his itching haemorrhoids? The thought of them made for an almost unbearable urge to scratch. He tried to stand still, and turned his eyes to the heavens. The sun had mercifully gone behind a big black cloud.

The boy, Seggi, came from the hut and looked apprehensively at Wadley. The interpreter was behind him and nudged the boy closer.

'He is here, sir,' he said.

'Good . . . very good. Ah . . . ask the boy if he received any instructions from his father before he . . . before he passed away.'

The interpreter was silent.

'Well?' Wadley asked.

'Seggi is now the *laibon*, sir. He is not a boy. Also, you can ask him what you will. The *laibon* speaks English, a little.'

'I see,' Wadley replied, peeved at being admonished.

The boy had given no hint of having heard the question, so Wadley rephrased it. 'Did your father tell you that the Maasai should move to join the southern Maasai?' he asked loudly in a slow, deliberate voice.

The new paramount chief shook his head, 'No,' he replied.

Wadley's heart sank. 'Are you sure?' he prompted.

'Yes.'

Wadley studied the boy, a lad no more than half his own modest height, and realised he would have to be more imaginative if he were to save the day.

'Did your father tell you the northern Maasai must *not* move?'

'No,' the boy answered after a moment's thought.

'Ah, so he must want the move to go ahead?'

Seggi remained silent, trying to unravel the words.

'If he didn't say no to it, then he must want you to approve it, yes?' Without waiting for a reply, Wadley continued. 'Tell me this, Seggi. Did your father explain to you that you would be the paramount chief when he died?'

'Yes.'

'And did he tell you that the British Government gave you this honour and we are your friends?'

'Yes.'

'Do you know that the British Government has already asked your father to move the Maasai to the south?'

A pause. 'Yes,' he answered.

'Very good, Seggi.' Wadley nodded, pleased with his progress. 'So he must have told you that you were to respect the British Government — your friends.'

'Yes.'

'I thought so. I can see you are the kind of man who can be trusted to carry out his father's wishes. Very good, Seggi.'

The boy appeared confused.

Wadley span the conversation through a number of turns until he had Seggi agreeing that it had been his father's dying wish to see the northern Maasai reunited with their southern brothers. He hinted at presents from the governor, and important new roles for Seggi within the protectorate's administration. Then he lowered his voice and, in a conspiratorial tone, added, 'A little advice, Seggi. The governor admires a man who can move things along. I suggest that you do not wait too long before you issue your first orders. I suggest you call the elders together immediately. If you do, I suspect that Governor Edouard will be very pleased with you.'

Before long, Seggi had agreed to a date for the signing.

Wadley pumped the young paramount chief's hand, and those of the elders watching from nearby. Then he climbed into the buggy, satisfied that he had achieved his mission. As his driver gave a flick to the traces, the first heavy drops of rain hit the top of his big sola topee.

Sitting comfortably in his rocking chair on the veranda, Norman Lewis stared out at the flimsy grey sheets of drizzling rain that wafted like clouds over the township of Nairobi, sprawled in disarray at the bottom of his hill.

The town had grown since he'd arrived nearly eight years ago. He often wondered if it had improved with age, but couldn't really recall the image from those days. The only changes he had noticed over the years were to the gums growing in the bend of Ngong Road. The trunks had lost their adolescent coarseness and were now sleek and smooth. Their branches proudly stretched thirty feet above the road towards the flat grey sky. In the rain they looked like svelte young bathers fresh from the water, with pale skin and smooth glistening torsos.

He wondered how many times he had sat alone on that veranda wrestling with the mystery of those particular trees. He often tried to picture the planter of the seedlings, John Ainsworth, and imagine why he had put them there in that inexplicable bend in the road. George Coll had told him the Maasai said they soaked up ground water, but there was no swamp on the Ngong Road hill. It was not black-cotton soil — the bane of Nairobi residents in any weather, wet or dry. The hill had the rich red loam typical of the Kikuyu food gardens further west. Why would anyone plant such exotic trees so far from their home? Didn't Ainsworth have anything better to do than to plant trees for no particular purpose?

Lewis had walked often to the gum trees in the hope of finding a clue to their presence there. The wind moved their lithe young limbs from side to side and whispered through their slender grey-green leaves. But they told him nothing.

When Edouard sent him official word of his transfer, he had decided to settle the matter finally by finding John Ainsworth and posing the question directly. As luck would have it, Ainsworth was passing through Nairobi from his home district on the shores of Lake Victoria, and Lewis invited him for a drink at the Muthaiga Club. The answer, when Ainsworth told him, was quite remarkable.

'Hello!' came a voice from the bottom of the garden.

'George!' Lewis called. 'Come up!'

Coll paid the buggy fare and made a difficult journey of the fifty paces up the garden path, stopping twice to catch his breath. He was wearing a mackintosh against the soaking rain. When he arrived on the veranda Lewis shook his hand warmly.

As his friend helped him out of his coat, Coll said, 'You'll appeal of course, Norman.'

'I don't think so.'

'But you must! It's outrageous.' Coll threw his arms about and paced the length of the veranda until he began to splutter and cough.

'Please sit, George. And try not to get too excited. You know it only makes your chest congestion worse.'

Coll took a seat across the small coffee table from his friend. 'I heard about it only yesterday. Where are they sending you?'

'To Nyasaland.'

'Nyasaland! My God, Norman, that's hundreds of miles away.'

'Over a thousand, to be precise. And, for my sins, full of Scottish Presbyterians.'

Coll shook his head and stared miserably at the rain.

'A cup of tea, George? It'll soothe your chest against this damp air.'

'No, thank you.'

'Well, I'm having a whisky and be damned about the time of day.' He disappeared inside the house. 'Are you sure you won't join me?' he called from the kitchen. 'For a cup of tea, I mean.'

'No,' Coll called back.

Lewis returned with a large glass from which he took a sizable gulp as soon as he was again seated.

'I'm sorry we had that disagreement, Norman,' Coll said after a moment.

'So am I,' Lewis replied.

'It did no good, you know. The Maasai are moving to the southern reserve anyway.'

'I know,' Lewis said, clasping one fist inside the another. 'Damn that Edouard!'

'Damn him indeed,' Coll replied. 'Maybe it was foolish of us to think we could have changed the way things turned out.' After a moment's silence he said, 'I saw Katherine yesterday. She was protesting against the Collins court case.'

'Another disgrace.'

'She looked wonderful.'

Lewis remembered the fine-looking woman he'd met at Limuru when trying to patch things up between the two of them.

'I say, Norman, do you mind if I take a wee glass of that whisky myself?'

'You? A whisky?'

'If you don't mind.'

'My pleasure.'

Lewis went back indoors and returned with Coll's glass and his own refilled. They clinked glasses. 'Cheers,' Lewis said.

'Good luck,' replied Coll, taking a careful sip. His eyes watered and he struggled to avoid coughing.

'She's quite a woman, that Katherine,' Lewis said.

Coll took another sip. 'She certainly is. Pity you never met her.'

'But I did.'

'You did? How? I mean, when?'

'A couple of years ago. I didn't want to tell you. I thought you'd think I was interfering.'

'Norman! How could . . . How dare you go behind my back like that?'

'Now, now, George, don't get excited. It obviously did no good. If it had, you wouldn't be the miserable old sod you are at present.'

Coll's outrage quickly turned to grudging recognition of the truth of his friend's words. 'I suppose you're right about that. I often wonder . . .' He didn't finish the thought. 'But tell me, when do you leave for Nyasaland?' he asked.

'Thursday's train, then a couple of days later a ship to Chinde.'

'Good old Chinde again. That's where I met you, in '03.'

'You're right. At the railing on board that old tub. If I remember correctly, it almost sank before we got halfway to Mombasa.'

Coll smiled and nodded.

Lewis turned his eyes to the gum trees, admiring their fine shape again. 'He did it for the simple beauty of it, George.'

'Who did what?'

'Ainsworth. I asked him. About the gums, I mean.'

'Oh.'

'Don't you find that amazing?'

'Not really,' Coll said, carefully taking another sip of whisky.

'If I hadn't heard it from the man himself I could scarcely believe it.'

'What's so extraordinary about that? People do things all the time for the beauty of it.'

'Aye, but here in Nairobi? Perhaps years hence, when the place grows out of its ugliness, people will start to think about beautifying it. And for no other reason than that. Can you imagine a time like that, George? But by then those trees will be sixty, eighty, feet tall and people will probably wonder, like I did, why the hell they were planted there in the first place.'

'I don't find that strange at all,' Coll said. 'It's something I would do myself.'

Lewis looked at his friend and smiled. 'Yes. I suppose you would, George. In fact, I'm sure you would.'

The two men sat in silence then, contemplating the gums as the rain dripped from their sad, grey leaves.

CHAPTER 36

Ole Sadera was irritated. Mantira had been a friend for many years, but during that time there had been occasions when he had strained the friendship by his habit of mercilessly badgering Ole Sadera to win his way. Today was such a day.

'Mantira, what is it you want of me?' Ole Sadera asked, exasperated. 'I have told you the Il Tuati will not move. It is our final decision. Now leave me.'

'Maybe Entorror is now no better than the south. The *ol-milo* has struck our cattle as it has in the south. At least in the south we will have a larger range. And what will you do if the British come to Entorror and insist you go?'

Ole Sadera simply turned his back on him.

'I agree the British are breaking their promises,' Mantira continued, undeterred. 'I also believe it is wrong that we must move our people and herds with such haste.'

'You do not mention British justice. Do you also agree it has failed us? Remember it was the great benefit available to all Maasai; all Africans? Didn't we once think it a most wondrous thing? Where was it when the settler Collins was accused of the murder of one of our people and then released?'

'Yes, it was wrong. Maybe we were foolish to believe that British justice would always be in our favour, but is it worth losing everything for the life of one *morani*?'

Again Ole Sadera refused to answer, turning his attention to his age set brothers who were making preparations for a mock battle among themselves. He would have preferred to join them had Mantira not demanded his attention.

When he and Mantira were merely friends, he would have already made a rude remark to end the argument, or challenged him to a contest to decide the issue, but following the *eunoto* ceremony Mantira had received the great honour of being appointed as the chief elder, the *aulononi*. Custom dictated that Ole Sadera was obliged to pay him due respect. So he listened, and desperately tried to hold his temper in check.

'Would you go to war for this matter, my friend?' Mantira asked.

Ole Sadera turned from his feigned study of the activities in the camp and said through gritted teeth, 'Is there nothing worth fighting for these days? There have been times when we have gone into battle, you and I, uncertain of our chances of success. We knew it was no disgrace to lose, but to lie on one's belly when all that is important is taken from us, truly is. I have not forgotten those days.' He glared at Mantira. 'Have you?'

Mantira bristled. 'No, I have not forgotten. Nor have I forgotten Lenana's dying words. Do you forget that his father — the Great Laibon — also made a prophecy on his deathbed? The iron snake came, as he said it would, bringing white men with their diseases and their power. Lenana also predicted trouble if we ignore the governor's request to move to the south. We do not dare ignore it.'

Ole Sadera returned to sullen silence.

'If I cannot convince you to take my advice as a friend, will you not take it to save my reputation among the elders as their *aulononi*?'

'What is it you are saying now?'

'All the Purko know we have been friends these many years. Wasn't it I who stood for you when your childhood age mates made your life a hell with their taunts? Now they know my thoughts in favour of the move, and yours against it. They also know that I have come to your meat camp with the intention of advising you to change your mind. What will they say if I return without your agreement and with the prospect of war and disgrace as a consequence? They will rightly say, *What kind of wisdom is this from the new chief elder — our* aulononi? *How can we continue to honour him in this position if his childhood friend cannot hear the wisdom of his words?'*

Ole Sadera's anger grew. It was infuriating that Mantira would so flagrantly exploit their friendship in such a cowardly manner. He turned away.

'You are not listening to me, Parsaloi.' He grabbed Ole Sadera and turned him around to face him. 'This is important to all the Purko Maasai. It is important to our age sets, to the *moran*'s dignity. Are you so selfish that you would sacrifice our peace to your pride? Listen to me. If I cannot have your heart, I must have your ear.'

Ole Sadera pulled his *simi* from its sheath and held it before Mantira's startled eyes for a moment, then he grabbed his own ear lobe and slashed it off. Mantira recoiled as blood spurted from the wound.

Ole Sadera solemnly handed him the piece of severed flesh. 'You have my ear and, if you must, you will have my agreement to move from our land.'

Coll arrived at the Il Tuati's *manyatta* and found Ole Sadera in earnest discussion with a group of his fellow *moran*. He spotted Coll standing at the *boma* gate and left the group to greet him.

'Swara. You are back.'

His voice conveyed no enthusiasm. Coll suspected he guessed why he was there. Then he noticed the Maasai's blood-caked left ear.

'Parsaloi! What has happened? Were you in a fight?'

Ole Sadera's hand went involuntarily to his ear. 'It is of no consequence,' he said dismissively. 'These days you are coming often to Entorror.'

'I am,' Coll said, stepping back to examine the ear from another angle. He knew it was useless to query the cause of the injury. 'I sometimes feel Laikipia is my home away from home.'

Ole Sadera nodded. 'Soon it will be more your home than mine.'

'No,' Coll said. 'I understand what you mean, but the government has not promised Laikipia to anyone.'

Ole Sadera refrained from comment.

'I am here again because Mantira said I should talk to you.'

'And so we are talking,' Ole Sadera said. His face revealed nothing.

'He says he has been unable to convince you of the benefits of moving to the south.'

'Mantira and I have had many different opinions during our lives. In this matter we can agree that the choice of moving to the south or staying in Entorror is difficult.'

'I would like to know if you will go of your own free will.'

Ole Sadera pulled a blade of grass from the ground and split it with his thumbnail, studying it as if the answer was hidden within it. 'Your Maa is quite good, Swara, but I wonder if you understand "free will". Is it free will if I fear the consequences of my agreement but still agree? What if a friend begs me to do something I fear may be a dangerous mistake? Is it free will if I say yes to please him? And if I want to stay here but all those I love leave, is that also free will?'

Coll had no answer and the questions hung in the air between them.

Ole Sadera had shredded the blade of grass in his hand. He threw it away and pressed both hands to his head. 'No one can answer these things for me, Swara.' His face was contorted as if in pain. 'No one can help me decide.'

CHAPTER 37

The representative elders and age set leaders of the northern Maasai, an honour guard of *moran* and a contingent of wives converged on Ngong for the signing of the 1911 resettlement agreement. The wives drove herds of goats and sheep, which made for a noisy and dusty convergence of colour and people.

Coll had been waiting all morning when Governor Edouard, resplendent in full military rig-out, rode into the village accompanied by his senior officials and an impressive display of soldiery.

His troops were on loan to British East Africa from Rhodesia, the Sudan and South Africa. They would act as *askaris,* or policemen, for the movement of the Maasai and their herds under a Rhodesian company sergeant by the name of Ploog, who appeared to be acting as the governor's batman for the day.

Ploog was an enormous man with black bushy eyebrows and piercing coal-black eyes. He wore a cap formed from the skinned head of a leopard complete with snarling fangs.

Ploog's second-in-command — the only other white man in the group — was a nondescript Irishman with a sour look and bad body odour by the name of O'Rourke. He marched in the dust behind the mounted officials at the head of the twenty-man *askari* contingent.

Coll stood with the warriors and elders like a stagehand caught amongst the cast in an elegantly staged theatre production. Edouard dismounted and acknowledged Coll's greeting with a slight nod.

Coll had noticed a definite cooling in Edouard's attitude since Norman Lewis was discovered to be sending confidential information to opposition members of the British government. Edouard had never shown Coll any favours in the past, but now it appeared as if he had decided to make life as difficult for him as possible. Coll had resolved not to give him the satisfaction of complaining and took all of the so-called 'special assignments' with as much grace as he could muster.

'I have all the necessary signatories gathered here, sir,' he said. 'Ready for the signing.'

'Where is the table?' the governor demanded.

'I have set up a platform over there under the tree, Sir Percy.'

'Hmm,' Edouard replied, and walked towards it, peeling off a glove as he went. Ploog followed without offering a word to Coll.

'You! Boy. Get out of the way,' Edouard said, flicking a glove at a boy standing by the calfskin-covered platform.

'Sir, that's Seggi,' Coll offered discreetly. 'The paramount chief.'

Edouard raised an eyebrow. 'Really?'

Coll stepped forward and made the introductions. 'Sir Percy Edouard, may I present Seggi, *laibon* for the Purko and paramount chief of the Maasai.'

The boy nodded and smiled shyly.

'Scrawny little chap,' the governor said, nodding a casual greeting at him.

'Um, sir, Seggi is quite clever as you shall see. He, um, speaks English quite well.'

'I see,' Edouard replied. 'Interesting. Well, shall we make a start? Wadley will do the honours.'

While Wadley read out the agreement, and the Maasai interpreter repeated it for the gathering, Edouard stood stiffly, scanning the assembly. 'Who's that, Coll?' he asked out of the corner of his mouth.

'That's Parsaloi Ole Sadera, sir. Spokesman for a section of the warriors.'

'Surly blighter. Is he the one who's been giving us all the trouble?'

Coll said that the age set leader had had some early difficulties understanding the proposal, but was now agreeable to the move.

To Ploog, Edouard said, 'Keep an eye on this one, sergeant. He may be a troublemaker.'

When Wadley had finished, Edouard said he would have Ole Sadera sign first. 'Ask him if he agrees to the terms,' Edouard demanded of the interpreter.

To Coll's shock and amazement, Ole Sadera said, 'No, I do not agree with the move.'

'Parsaloi! What are you saying?' Coll hissed in strangled Maa as the interpreter translated his answer to the governor.

Edouard turned from the interpreter to Coll, to Ole Sadera, and back to Coll. 'What nonsense is this then, Coll? You told me they were all in agreement!'

'I'm sorry, Sir Percy. A misunderstanding. Let me have a few words with him for clarification.'

'Well, be quick about it.'

'Parsaloi, you know what the governor is saying, and you have already agreed. You are acting like a child.'

'If I am treated as a child, I shall act as a child,' Ole Sadera answered with a frown. 'And why is it necessary to sign this paper anyway?'

'It is the custom,' Coll begged. 'It's how all agreements are made between the government and the tribes.'

'I have learned that a mark on a paper means nothing. Do you not remember when we were moved from the great valley? When we were offered Entorror? We signed a paper then. Like this one. It is foolish to believe a mark on paper matters. And it is demeaning to be asked to play such childish games. We will go because the British say we must go, not because we agree it is right or just. And not because we sign a paper.'

'It is to protect both parties. If the government does not stand by its promises in this paper, you can use it to prove you have been unfairly treated.'

'How will a paper help us?'

'You can get a lawyer — a man who knows our laws and can represent your case in the courts. The British justice system protects all its people.'

'Coll!' Edouard said through tight lips. 'What the blazes is going on here?'

'A moment more, Your Excellency.'

'Where was the British justice system when my age set brother was killed?' Ole Sadera said.

Coll looked uncomfortable. 'There were extraordinary circumstances, hideous circumstances, at play in that trial,' he said. 'I don't have time to explain right now, but believe me, British justice is usually much better than that.'

This did not convince the *olaiguenani*.

'Parsaloi,' Coll continued, 'you once told me of a time in Naivasha when you were a young man. You had been accused of killing the men who raped your women and stole your cattle. Do you remember?'

Ole Sadera nodded.

'The British judge agreed that the white man was wrong, and he let you go. You said that the wisdom of that judge and the justice you received that day had surprised you. That was British justice at its best.'

'Will it also be at its best if this agreement is broken?'

Coll glanced at Edouard. 'To be honest, Parsaloi, I don't know. All I can say is that justice is intended to be fair to everyone; always.'

Ole Sadera studied him.

'If you are ever harmed by this agreement,' Coll continued, 'I will personally help you get a lawyer to act for you. I promise you.'

Ole Sadera studied Governor Edouard and the big man with the cold eyes and the leopard fangs on his head. To Coll he said, 'Do you think I should sign, Swara?'

'I do, Parsaloi. It will be the best thing for you and your people. Governor Edouard has made big plans for the move to the south and has brought in all these men to make sure you do not have any trouble from the settlers when you pass their farms.'

'Is that why the big ugly one is here?' he asked, nodding at Sergeant Ploog.

Ploog glared. He knew they were discussing him.

'Yes, he will be in charge of the *askaris*.'

'And do you trust the governor and this big monkey?'

'I didn't trust him at first, but now the government in London, and our friends, know all about the Maasai. They will see to it that the move goes well and you reach the southern reserve safely.'

Ole Sadera still looked uncertain, but he said, 'Swara, tell the governor I will sign.'

Coll breathed a sigh of relief. 'Ole Sadera will sign, Sir Percy.'

'Well, tell him to get on with it.' Edouard turned to his batman. 'I told you, Ploog. A troublemaker.'

'Yes, sir,' Ploog growled. 'What we call a funny bugger back 'ome, sir. But don't you worry, this 'un won't give me no trouble once we get started, sir.'

As Ole Sadera made his thumb mark on the paper, he stared intently at Edouard. But Coll wasn't watching that exchange. His eyes were on the big Rhodesian standing beside the governor and glaring at Ole Sadera. Coll recalled a similar feeling of revulsion when staring into the yellow eyes of a hyena.

PART 3

NGATET

CHAPTER 38

1912

Nashilo watched him as she often did whenever he was near. She wondered if it was only she who could feel Parsaloi's presence, or whether everyone experienced that almost imperceptible sensation like a slight pressure on the skin. She sometimes had such a feeling when she was naked, bathing, and the warm wind came from the savannah to press gently against her. A touching without a touch. She smiled at her foolishness; perhaps it was the baby growing within her that prompted such thoughts.

Parsaloi was in a meeting with a group of elders, including, ironically, her husband. There had been a number of meetings among the leaders in preparation for the Purko's move to the southern reserve. She picked up her water gourd and sauntered towards the *boma* gate, where Parsaloi and the elders stood.

'You should leave on the next new moon,' Parsaloi was saying. 'You will need the full moon's light when you reach the crest of the Mau.'

'What of you and the Il Tuati?' her husband asked.

'The *moran* will not act as herd boys on the whim of the whites. We will drive our cattle and take our own path to Ngatet, in our own time.'

The conversation continued as she walked slowly past the group. Parsaloi gave no indication that he had seen her, but soon after she reached the water hole he was there, standing some ten paces away, drinking and throwing water onto his body in preparation for his long journey back to his *manyatta*.

Nashilo kept her eyes on her water gourd. 'You are going back so soon?'

'Yes,' he said, sluicing water into his mouth.

'And you are not making the journey south with us?'

'I thought your ears were small and pretty, but they must be the size of a donkey's.'

She didn't want him to play games with her. She tried to act hurt and sad. 'Who will care for me on that long walk?'

'Why, your husband, of course.'

'He has many wives.'

'He has four. And you the prettiest. Why would he not see you safely over the escarpment?'

'I am to have a baby,' she said.

After a moment's pause he asked, 'What is that to me?'

'It is your baby.'

'Now you speak only foolishness. It is your husband's baby. Now go home to him and tell him. He will be pleased to hear it.'

'Are you one of those who believe it is impossible for a woman to have a child unless it is to her husband?'

'It matters not. A child is a gift enjoyed by all. Be thankful for your blessing.'

Her joy at her news turned sour, but she wouldn't retreat. This could be her last time to see him before the trek south began. She changed her tactic. 'Who will keep us safe from the lion and leopard if not your Il Tuati?'

Parsaloi was annoyed. 'The Il Tuati refuse to be the *enkang*'s wet nurses,' he said, then frowned and shifted his gaze from her. 'And I cannot convince them otherwise. But we will not be far. The rains are upon us. I have already told the elders that you must move quickly.' His expression softened. 'I will keep an eye on you from time to time.'

Comforted by the knowledge that he *did* care, and had thought of the problems they might have crossing the high crest of the escarpment, she softened her tone. 'Will you miss me?' she asked.

He lifted water to his mouth, made gurgling sounds and sprayed it out. 'Are you well?' he asked. 'The baby . . . do you feel it?'

'Not yet. But soon, I think.'

'You will be careful, Nashilo. The Mau Summit can be very cold. Be sure to make camp early each night. Make time for a proper shelter.'

She thought his voice had softened, but she needed to see his face before being sure.

'It is getting late,' he said before she could respond, and picked his way across the stream using a line of rocks.

'Parsaloi?' she pleaded.

He turned to her from the other bank. If they extended their arms they might just touch fingertips. But she daren't try.

'Yes?' he said.

'I will miss you.'

He made a clicking sound with his tongue — an acknowledgement, no more. He turned to leave.

'Will you miss me?'

He glanced back at the *enkang*, then briefly at her before diverting his eyes. 'Yes.'

He had taken a dozen steps before he turned back to her. For a breathless, silent moment she thought he might add something more, for there were words unsaid in his eyes, but he turned his back again and was soon gone.

Thursday's train from Kisumu was late into Nairobi. A notice scrawled on a blackboard informed travellers that the delay was due to a rhino charging the locomotive and derailing it.

Lewis found a steward to see to his belongings and convinced Coll — who had come to the station to see him off — to join him at Wood's for a farewell drink while they waited.

They sat alone on the veranda watching the rain fall from a leaden sky in relentless vertical sheets, exploding in the muddy potholes on Government Road. It was not one of Coll's better days. The damp had affected his chest, bringing on an incessant cough. Lewis was worried that Coll would not take care of himself when he was gone, and told him so.

'I'll be all right,' Coll insisted.

'I have spoken to Dr Ribiero about your condition, and he's agreed to see you. He's a bit odd, but a good doctor nevertheless.'

'I can't imagine how you, a graduate of the medical college at Glasgow University, can take seriously a fellow who rides a zebra around the town.'

'As I say, a little unconventional, but better than some. And whatever you do, stay off the highlands as much as you can during the wet. It would appear from the way the season's started we're going to get more than our share of rain this year.'

Lewis finished his whisky and called the Swahili waiter to bring him another.

Coll appeared deep in thought, nursing his cup of tea.

'You're worrying, George,' Lewis said.

Coll sighed. 'I've just been recalling all the things you've done for the Maasai, and how it's led to your undoing. The irony is that while the Maasai may feel the whites have treated them harshly, they know nothing about you and the price you've paid on their behalf.'

'Let's hope they won't need any further help from people like us, and that the government is the one giving them support. If the Maasai are in agreement, as you now believe, everything should go well. However, unlike you, I don't trust Edouard to manage what must now follow. It's an enormous undertaking, and he's never shown much inclination to invest in native matters. He prefers to throw money at the problems brought to him by the settlers.'

A blast of a steam whistle made them turn to the station. The train was pulling in.

'If that's the case, I don't know who I can turn to,' Coll said, cracking his knuckles and fidgeting in his chair. 'Unlike you, I can't call on powerful people in London if I need them.'

'If I'm wrong and you're right, you won't need to.'

'I'm sure all will be well. Now that the Maasai have put their mind to it, it will all work out for the best.'

'That's what I admire about you, George. Ever the optimist. However, as a precaution, I'm going to contact a lawyer while

I'm in Mombasa. Just in case. I'll send you his name.' Lewis stood. 'Now, I must go else I'll miss my train.'

Coll rose to follow him, but Lewis insisted he remain at Wood's until the rain stopped. He would hear no argument on the matter, and Coll conceded. They shook hands and, after an uncertain moment, hugged briefly. Lewis patted Coll on the back, unable to find any words.

The train whistle sounded a warning of imminent departure.

'George, I want you to take care of yourself,' Lewis said.

'I will, Norman. Hurry, you'll miss your train.'

'And George.'

'Yes?'

'Why not go and see Katherine?'

'Norman —'

'Just for a visit. She's a good friend. And you never know when you'll need one.'

Coll shook his head with a sigh, but made no commitment. 'Keep in touch, Norman.'

'Yes. And I'll send you the legal fellow's name from Mombasa.'

'Very well.'

Lewis made the short dash across Government Road to the station and jumped aboard the train as it eased into motion. The small carriage was empty. He took a seat and pushed up the shutter.

The train passed the station building, giving him the dismal view of Nairobi in the rain. On the veranda of Wood's hotel he could see Coll's narrow frame. He was where he'd left him, holding the rail, watching the train depart.

Lewis pushed open the window to make a final farewell gesture, but at that instant Coll doubled over, pulling a handkerchief from his pocket and holding it to his mouth, while his other hand clutched at his heaving chest.

Edouard contemplated with disgust the man standing on the other side of his desk. Sergeant Ploog was a soldier whom any officer would have whipped for the condition of his uniform, not to mention the reeking malodorous state of his person.

But Edouard had to be pragmatic. Although it offended his strict sense of military decorum, he allowed the outlandish leopard cap with its snarling fangs, suspecting it would make an awesome impression on the Maasai. And he knew he needed Ploog's cooperation to carry out the complicated task ahead.

'I understand Mr Wadley has handed you your orders, sergeant?'

'Yessir. 'E 'as.'

'And do you have any questions?'

'No, sir. I'm to make sure the niggers keep movin' through the Rift Valley and over the escarpment without causin' a bother.'

'Quite. And I'd like to make it clear, if Mr Wadley hasn't already mentioned it: I can be a generous man when my instructions are carried out to the letter. Something for you, understand? You can choose to include your men in it or keep it to yourself.'

Ploog grinned. 'Yessir. I understand what you're sayin', sir.'

'Good. Now you'll get your warrants from Mr Wadley to draw necessary stores for you and your men in Nakuru. There'll be additional warrants for yourself in Naivasha, plus emergency rations we'll make available for the Maasai should they need them.'

He paused, waiting for the details to sink into Ploog's quite obviously thick skull.

'Is that perfectly clear, sergeant?'

'Yessir.'

'Very well. And don't forget my words. And the bonus if you can accomplish your mission in quick time. Now, good luck and be off with you.'

Sergeant Ploog sat at the rough-sawn bench that served as a table in the Green Carpet Tavern. It was a fancy name for the corrugated-iron and canvas construction in the Indian bazaar, where the owner — a huge, turbaned Sikh — served illegal spirits to the jetsam of Nairobi. The rain came out of a grey sky in a fine, drifting mist. Large fat drops fell from the leaking iron roof to the table and the chancy wind ruffled the loose canvas around them.

'Look at us, O'Rourke,' Ploog said to his corporal sitting opposite him. 'What are we doing in a shit hole like Nairobi?'

O'Rourke gave a desultory nod and looked glumly at the rain.

'Cold and wet,' Ploog continued. 'We should be in Uganda with the rest of the unit, instead of playing nursemaid to a bunch of bloody niggers.'

'Yar,' O'Rourke replied.

'That's where we'll be when we're done here, corporal,' Ploog said, raising his drink to his lips. 'We'll be back in Uganda. In the sunshine. Where it's hot and the women likewise.' He guffawed at his own joke. A trickle of spirits glistened on his chin.

O'Rourke grinned. 'Yar, women, hot,' he slurred.

'Damn right, corporal. So you know what we're gonna do?'

O'Rourke was staring into the rain again.

'O'Rourke! You bastard, look at me.'

The corporal made an effort to focus.

'Do you know what we're gonna do, corporal? We're gonna get this job finished quick. Quick, I say! No wastin' time while these bastards dawdle along on a Sunday picnic, eh? No. We get 'em movin', we do.'

O'Rourke had the presence of mind to nod.

'That's right. We move the bastards along double-quick time. Then get the 'ell out of 'ere.' He drained his glass. 'Boy!' he called to the proprietor. 'Get me some more of this piss you call whisky. Two glasses and be quick about it.'

The sikh eyed the *askaris*, but poured two glasses of slightly milky liquid from a Glenfiddich bottle.

The waiter, a Kamba boy of about fourteen, approached the two men cautiously, carrying the drinks. Ploog bellowed again and the boy, who was by then immediately behind the sergeant, almost dropped the glasses. His hands shook as he moved towards the bench.

'About time, you lazy nigger!' Ploog said, slamming his hand on the table.

The waiter fumbled the glasses, spilling their contents onto the bench and into Ploog's lap.

Ploog, his eyes bulging with fury, grabbed the boy by the ear and dragged his face to within an inch of his. 'You little shit,' he hissed. 'You useless fuckin' shit.'

The boy whimpered in pain.

'Clean the table,' Ploog growled.

The boy fumbled around the belt of his *kikoi* and produced a grotty piece of cloth, which he used in an attempt to mop up the whisky.

With surprising speed, Ploog whipped a knife from his belt and, grabbing the boy's wrist, impaled his hand on the timber bench.

The boy screamed in pain, but Ploog was on his feet, a handgun drawn at the sikh, who made a rush at him. Ploog fired into his belly and watched the Indian fall in a writhing bundle at his feet.

O'Rourke stared bug-eyed first at the boy, then the owner, before Ploog grabbed him by the collar and reefed him out of his chair.

Before the neighbouring shopkeepers had gathered their senses, the *askaris* had left the bazaar.

CHAPTER 39

Governor Edouard strode vigorously along the pathway leading to the Nairobi Club, where he intended to have lunch. Only an occasional puddle remained as a reminder of the morning shower that had now long gone, leaving a cloudless blue sky. He gave his cane a twirl. He was feeling in excellent spirits, as he usually did when a seemingly intractable problem had been overcome. The Maasai had caused him more than their share of setbacks over the previous few years, but now they were on their way south, opening up the enormous resources of the White Highlands.

He was full of energy at the prospect of yet another contest. For a long time the Indian group calling themselves the Asian and Native Progress Association had been a niggling irritant. The Indians had a stranglehold over commerce, particularly in Nairobi, but still they demanded more.

Given the political climate in Great Britain, Edouard knew he would eventually have to concede some ground. But he had no intention of doing so without extracting something of value in return.

It was bad enough dealing with the Indians' insistence on what they called reforms for their own community, but they had broadened their platform to include the Africans, doubtless to give them more political leverage at home. Edouard knew he had to break that platform down or risk having a far more serious set of restraints forced upon him.

At the club he would meet Lord Cransworth, a prominent member of the settler community, whom he would ask to be his broker with the top people in ANPA.

Edouard began to whistle. The day was bright and his mood optimistic. He loved a good battle.

The house was like nothing Isher Vidyarthi had seen before. Two storeys high, with gables and a towering widow's watch, it belonged in a snow-covered eighteenth-century landscape rather than on the verdant slopes above tropical Nairobi. A liveried servant met him at the door and he followed the man into a long tiled entrance hall, admiring the high domed ceiling and the sweep of the distant staircase winding itself out of sight into the upper levels.

The hall was hung with paintings — watercolours — all famous, he imagined. The extraordinary golden light they captured reminded him of his brief time in England as a student. He leaned closer to one as he passed, trying to catch the artist's signature, but was startled by a voice from the end of the hallway.

'Ah! Doctor Vidyarthi!' It was his host, Lord Cransworth, landowner, prominent member of the Colonists' Association; a friend of the governor and other leading members of the settler community.

'Your Lordship,' he replied, taking the extended hand and feeling his thin fingers succumb to the older man's iron grip.

They had met previously at several official functions where Vidyarthi was one of the token representatives of the Asian community. Cransworth had never shown any interest in exchanging more than perfunctory remarks, so it was with some surprise that Vidyarthi had accepted the invitation to the big house for what the calling card described as 'tea and a chat'.

In the drawing room the tea soon arrived, after which Cransworth immediately came to the point of his invitation. It was to discuss what the Asian community considered to be their most important issue: approval to set up stalls in the city's municipal market.

'You know, doctor, I personally have nothing against Asians selling their cloth, their pots and pans and whatnots in the market,' Cransworth said. 'The restriction goes way back to the early years when the traders — the white traders, that is — felt they needed some kind of protection against the sale of shoddy goods. No offence. Well, between you and me, those chaps that are there at the moment don't seem to have their heart in it. Don't seem to give a tinker's damn about what and how much they sell. We believe it might be time for the city council to reconsider the matter.'

'I am very pleased to hear it, Lord Cransworth. Am I to take it, then, that you are speaking here officially for the Nairobi City Council?'

'No, no. Not at all,' Cransworth said, reaching into his pocket for a match to light the pipe he had pulled from his waistcoat.

'The Legislative Council?'

Cransworth shook his head while sucking the flame into his pipe.

'The Colonists' Association then?'

Cransworth shook the match out and took a couple more puffs to satisfy himself that the pipe had taken. 'Nothing like that, Dr Vidyarthi. Please, this is an informal chat. Nothing more.'

'An informal chat is pleasant, sir, but if we are going to take this discussion any further, I must have something to tell my committee.'

Cransworth eyed him for a long moment. 'I'll be perfectly frank with you, doctor. There are one or two of the larger issues that your Asian and Native Progress Association is pushing that worry us.'

Vidyarthi wondered whom the collective pronoun referred to, but let it pass.

'We're prepared to meet you on the markets matter. We're even prepared to reconsider Asian ownership of residential plots in the Parklands area.' Cransworth paused to let the importance of these concessions sink in. 'What we find difficult to handle is this double-headed monster.'

'Double-headed monster?'

'In a manner of speaking, you understand. The double-headed monster is your organisation's representation of such a widely diverse group of people and issues. Asians and Africans. How can anyone — the Legco, the Colonists' Association or the council — deal with so many, often conflicting, demands?'

'We are simply asking for equality. Fair treatment on a non-racial basis. Where is the conflict, Lord Cransworth?'

'Where is the conflict? My dear fellow, it's everywhere you look. You speak of equality, but with all your rhetoric, you Asians aren't farmers or ranchers. I don't see you charging off into the bush to plant maize and milk cows. But in aligning yourselves with the natives for land in the White Highlands, you're making a rod for your back.'

Vidyarthi could see what he was driving at. The whites wanted to offer a minor concession against a major threat. Market stalls for uncontested laws governing rural land. It was a blatant attempt at a bribe.

The Asian and Native Progress Association had been constituted on the issue of universal representation. There were those among the foundation members who believed that linking the two disadvantaged groups was both a moral and political imperative. The philosophy had persisted in spite of the lack of involvement by the Africans. But he could see that Cransworth was offering an important carrot to split the bond. How would the committee take it? Vidyarthi had little doubt they would find it very difficult to walk away from the two major concessions offered to them.

'If I were to take this to the committee — and I must say, I don't know how it will be received — what promise, what assurances, do we have that you speak for the controlling interests in the appropriate bodies?'

As he uttered the question, he suspected he knew Cransworth's answer.

'You have no need to doubt my sources, doctor. I can assure you, if ANPA drops the natives' land claims, the people who matter will back your request for the market and Parklands.'

Nashilo felt the warmth of the morning sun on her shoulders as she strolled through the waving grasses. The sickness she had felt early that morning had left her, and there was no need to hurry. Her husband was pleased that she was at last pregnant, and in an unusually benevolent mood had allowed her to rest from the routine chores directed towards maintaining his personal comfort. She had decided to take a leisurely walk towards the stream that fed the cattle's watering hole and allow thoughts of Parsaloi's baby to fill her heart.

She spotted Okelia, the youngest son of her father's third wife, watching over his small herd. He was a gangling boy, too young by a mere year or so to be inducted into the ranks of the *moran* at the last *eunoto*. He would now have to wait many years for the next opportunity. As a consequence he'd been in a sullen mood ever since, with most of the family assumed to be collaborators in a conspiracy to deprive him of his manly aspirations. Nashilo was a favoured half-sister, however, and escaped the worst of his wrath. She joined him on a rise in the meagre shade of a euphorbia tree, which stood as stiff and aloof as Okelia himself. But Nashilo's exuberant nature drew him out of his uncommunicative mood and they were soon chatting about the imminent move south.

'I will join the men driving the cattle,' Okelia stated with conviction.

Nashilo thought it unlikely as she had already heard her husband agreeing with the other elders that Okelia would accompany the women and help with the goats and sheep.

'I'm sure you will,' she said.

'And help to defend them against lion, of course.'

'Of course.'

'It will be a very long journey,' he said, looking to the south where a hilly rise confined the outlook to a mere ten or so miles. 'Do you think we will pass through Kikuyuland?'

'I don't think so. But we may be close to it.'

'I hope so, then I can raid all the Kikuyu villages. I shall kill many, and bring my half-sister back to our family.'

The Kikuyu raid had been a devastating blow for the family. Several lives had been lost, but the uncertainty of little Lokatira's fate made it the most poignant story recalled at almost every family gathering. Death was an accepted consequence for a people living among hostile neighbours and wild animals, but to know that a despised enemy had taken a loved one to endure a life immeasurably different from her own was unbearable.

'I wonder how she looks now,' Nashilo said wistfully.

'I have even forgotten what she looked like when she was taken,' Okelia said sheepishly.

Nashilo smiled. 'You were not yet past your first season then, Okelia. Of course you can't remember.'

'Really? Then how do I know so much about her?'

'I don't know. Maybe it's because we speak of her often.'

'Then I shall rush into the Kikuyu villages and call her name.'

'What about the Kikuyu warriors?'

'I shall kill them all first, of course.'

Nashilo recognised that even Okelia knew his plan was mere bravado, but she didn't want to dampen the convivial atmosphere.

'If it makes your raid any easier, people say she looked like me at that age.'

'Then I shall search for a girl with big feet and skinny legs,' he said with an impish smile.

Nashilo laughed and gave him a friendly cuff on the ear.

Katherine paused at the front door of the Vidyarthis' house before giving the knocker an assertive rap. After a moment, a young Indian girl wearing a plain white apron over a dark blue sari opened the door. She enquired if she could be of assistance.

'You can,' Katherine said in a businesslike manner. 'You can tell Mr Vidyarthi that Katherine Wallace is here to see him.'

'Yes, ma'am,' the girl said and disappeared inside.

Minutes passed. Katherine took a few paces along the veranda. Vidyarthi's new T-model Ford — his pride and joy — was in its usual place at the side of the house. She returned to the door and listened for any sound of voices. Nothing.

Eventually, the maid reappeared in the doorway. 'I'm sorry, madam, but Mr Vidyarthi is not at home.'

'Nonsense!' Katherine said, taking a punt on the fact that Vidyarthi never went anywhere on foot.

The girl's eyes widened.

'Complete rubbish,' she added.

The girl's mouth fell open and she glanced over her shoulder, confirming Katherine's guess that she was acting under instructions.

'Tell Mr Vidyarthi that I am not leaving this doorstep until he sees me.'

The maid was on the brink of tears. 'Madam, I . . . I . . .'

'It's all right, Asma, I'll see Mrs Wallace.'

The maid scuttled past Vidyarthi before he reached the door.

'Please come in, Katherine,' he said, waving her inside. He closed the door then led her into a sitting room to the side of the wide entrance hall. 'Please,' he said, indicating a chair.

Katherine took her seat and Vidyarthi sat opposite her, leaning forward in his chair with his elbows on his knees. She glared at him before pulling a sheet of paper from her purse.

'What is this all about?' she said, brandishing the notice of meeting at him.

He knew what it was and needed to do no more than glance at it. He dropped his gaze to his hands and studied his long thin fingers as he weaved them into each other like a magician trying to make them disappear.

'We had to do it, Katherine.'

His dejected tone took the steam from her anger. 'Isher . . . why?'

'ANPA has always prided itself on its trans-ethnic philosophy, Katherine. I, for one, see it as God's wish for all men of all faiths to share the spoils of the earth.'

'Then what is this motion about?' She read the subheading aloud. '"A motion to rescind the inclusion of African interests in the Articles and Constitution of the Asian and Native Progress Association until" —'

'— "until a framework is established to facilitate the objectives of the organisation for the substantive membership." I know what it says, Katherine. I wrote it.'

'You! I thought it was some group of bigoted dissidents among us. Why? How could you do this?'

'We have always argued that if our policy discriminated against non-Indian groups simply by virtue of their racial

317

differences, we would have no chance to win the debate against racial policies perpetrated by the whites. But it was more than a moral question for some. It was a matter of politics. There's a social reformation sweeping the world. People are talking about equality, social conscience, democracy. Many of us in ANPA believed we would gain moral support from these new socialists, if not financial support. This support has not manifested. Meanwhile, we have struck major obstacles in achieving many of our aims because we have spread our efforts over a playing field too wide for us to compete effectively. Our membership asks, where are the Africans? Why do they not join us in the fight? Why do we have so few natives in ANPA, and why are they not at the forefront of the battle for such things as land rights and labour law reforms — matters that affect them directly?'

'Some of the younger, educated ones are.'

'Too few, too late, I'm afraid.'

'But it's not too late. We'll defeat this motion at the general meeting.'

Vidyarthi slowly shook his head. 'It is already won, Katherine.'

'What do you mean? The meeting's not until next week.'

'Under the Articles, the executive hold forty per cent of the voting rights in matters such as this. Even if we didn't have that significant minority, I can tell you, there is not a voice out there that will defend the status quo. Our membership is tired of waiting and, as you will hear on the night, if you are foolish enough to attend, we have strong indications that the government will grant the newly constituted organisation significant benefits as an inducement to the changes we will be making. Incidentally, I shall deny that if you should repeat it.'

Katherine was flushed with anger and frustration. 'I'll fight this, you'll see.'

Vidyarthi sadly shook his head. 'Katherine, Katherine. In appreciation of all your support and good work over the years, I'll tell you this in confidence. If you stand against this motion, every Asian in Nairobi will vilify you. They will see you as a vandal, spoiling what is being offered. I understand you have already lost many of your friends in the European community because of your association with ANPA. You don't want to alienate what remaining friends you have, do you?'

Katherine could have laughed off the threat if she had not been so downhearted. Friends were never as important to her as principles. She had already demonstrated that once. But she was sufficiently pragmatic to realise that Vidyarthi's assessment of her chances of changing the situation were probably true.

She stood, determined not to reveal the hopelessness she felt. 'Well, we can't have that, can we, Isher? We can't have your precious trans-ethnic philosophy sullied by an anti-racial argument on your big night.'

At the door she turned to him, unable to resist a final barb. 'I hope the thirty pieces of silver you receive can sweeten the bile that will rise from your gut when you lower your flag to the likes of Edouard.'

CHAPTER 40

'Ah, Coll. Good of you to come,' Sir Percy Edouard said as Coll entered the office.

Coll nodded. 'Yes, sir,' he replied, wondering what option he'd had when summoned by the governor.

Edouard continued to scratch out something on a paper in front of him before replacing the pen in its mount. 'I have a new appointment for you,' he said. He didn't ask Coll to sit.

'Yes, sir.'

'I want you to be the resettlement supervisor on the Maasai's move to the south.'

'Me?' Coll had a vision of nights on the freezing Mau in sheeting rain. He could imagine what Lewis would have to say about such a posting. On the other hand, he'd thought a lot about the risks such a perilous journey held for both the Maasai and their stock. It could go disastrously wrong without proper administration.

'Promoted from game warden to field supervisor,' Edouard went on. 'How's that sound?'

'Well . . . I'm —'

'Eminently qualified. Plenty of field experience. Speak the language. Why, there's not another in the protectorate who can hold a candle to you.'

Edouard's flattery caused Coll to wonder about his motives.

'No extra salary, I'm afraid,' the governor went on. 'No

budget for that sort of thing. Those twenty *askaris* have stretched the coffers to the limit.'

'I don't expect you'll have any trouble with the Maasai, sir. After all, the leaders have signed off on the agreement.'

'A native's idea of getting moving and mine are quite often worlds apart, Coll. My *askaris* are there to remind them we have a timetable. And a budget. I can't go on feeding them survival rations as they dawdle along at their leisure.'

'It will be an enormous task, Sir Percy. I'm not sure you're aware of the difficulties of moving more than ten thousand Maasai and millions of livestock.'

'Look here, Coll, I was an engineer before I sat behind this desk, you know!'

Coll's cheeky comment had slipped out, but the governor's relatively restrained rebuke caused him again to analyse the situation. He realised that Edouard was right. Coll *was* eminently qualified for the job, and it was quite likely that Edouard was keen to get him to agree to do it. He decided to press his advantage and, if he must take the position, have some of his concerns addressed at the outset.

'I didn't mean to imply anything by it, Sir Percy, but, with respect, moving so many people over such distances — men, women and children — is not like shunting rolling stock.'

'Don't be so damned impertinent, Coll. I'll remind you —'

'And I was wondering about the water situation in the south. Are you sure it's adequate? I mean, are there decent flows in the rivers and enough water holes?'

'As I was just saying, Coll,' Edouard said through gritted teeth, 'I was an engineer. So I think I should know something about water supplies. However, since you're so damned concerned about them, I can tell you I've had a dozen new water holes constructed.'

'Moving that amount of people and stock is going to take time and a lot of care.'

'All the more reason for them to shake a leg.'

'But you've missed my point, sir,' Coll said. 'We'll have to arrange three or four different routes to spread the grazing impact. Not to mention food supplies for all those people strung out —'

'Coll —'

'There are old people among them. And they can't move faster than their stock can feed —'

'Coll —'

'We'll have to coordinate their movements by setting up checkpoints and food depots. If we don't, there could be a very nasty situation. And if the weather turns bad, we —'

'Coll!' Edouard's fist came down on the desk.

Coll spluttered and gasped for breath. He plunged a hand into his pocket to find his handkerchief as he began to cough.

'Do you want the position or not?' Edouard said icily. 'If not, I'll just have to give it to Corporal O'Rourke.'

Coll had a vision of the poor Maasai struggling on under the tender mercies of Ploog, O'Rourke and the Sudanese *askaris*. 'I'd be happy to accept, sir,' he said.

Edouard's mood changed immediately. He beamed. 'Good for you, Coll. Well done.'

'On one condition, sir.'

Edouard frowned again.

'We can't have the Maasai begin the move until I've put the necessary depots and stores in place. In fact, there's another issue.'

'Yes-s-s.'

'I'll need to take a tour of inspection of the southern reserve to make sure.'

'To make sure of what, exactly?' Edouard said, losing patience.

'The condition of the water holes, the pasture stocks. After all, we're moving over a million animals.'

Edouard drummed his fingers on his desk. 'Have you finished?'

Coll smiled, relieved. 'Yes, sir.'

'Splendid.' The governor swept around his desk and patted Coll on the back as he escorted him to the door. 'Now, better get a move on. I want to see the Maasai well and truly on their way over the Mau Summit before the end of the month.'

Coll began to protest that it was unlikely he could move them so quickly, but Edouard cut him off.

'I've heard the weather blows a gale up there,' the governor continued. 'Better take your mack.'

The governor had made a joke. Coll made an effort to smile.

'Mr David Morrison?'

'Yes. Can I help you, Mr . . . ?'

'Lewis. Dr Norman Lewis. And I think you can.'

'Please, won't you take a seat, doctor?'

'Thank you,' Lewis said, and stepped into the office, which was not what he had expected of a solicitor in the country's biggest town and commercial capital. It was large enough — probably the size of three or four London solicitors' premises combined — but it was the furniture that made it unusual.

'I wasn't sure I was in the right place,' Lewis said, as he settled into an ornate padded chair with red inlay running from its curled golden feet to the tops of its high back. Standing to one side on a platform was a wrought-iron candelabra of impressive size. It had gnarled eagle's talons for feet, and to light its many-tiered candles would have risked a conflagration.

'You mean the warehouse downstairs?' Morrison asked. It was obviously not the first time a client had enquired about the premises.

'Um, actually, yes.' Lewis had glanced into the warehouse as he made his way to the staircase. It was crammed with bric-a-brac.

'Practicalities, Dr Lewis.'

The answer did nothing to calm Lewis's rising concern about the wisdom of engaging an eccentric as a legal representative.

Morrison must have noticed his alarm. 'I rent both the warehouse and this space above it, Dr Lewis. I find that collecting antiques — furniture, principally — provides an interest as well as sometimes being the only practical way to collect one's fees.'

'I see,' Lewis said, before admitting to himself that he didn't see at all. 'I'm sorry, Mr Morrison, I might be wasting your time. I was led to believe that you were a solicitor, but I've clearly been misinformed.'

'You are not misinformed, doctor, but perhaps confused, for which I apologise. I should have explained my situation properly. I usually do with new clients, but I assume the people who make it through the warehouse to this office know about me. I am indeed a practising solicitor, and what you see around you, and in the warehouse downstairs, is my accounts receivable, if you like. It's a practical way of securing payment for services rendered.'

Lewis remained silent.

Morrison continued. 'Granted, the situation is less than ideal, as you can imagine. It comes from my weakness for defending unpopular causes, and perhaps choosing clients who either can't or won't pay. Most of my clients are Arabs and Indians who might have many assets but not a lot of cash, as they tend to send it home by the bucketload.'

'Ah,' Lewis said. The clarification rang true. Lewis's contact in Mombasa had recommended Morrison as possibly the only solicitor in British East Africa brave enough to consider the case. 'I think I understand.'

'Splendid.' Morrison looked relieved to see his prospective client still in his seat. 'I've actually become quite accomplished in evaluating old Arab furniture. Take this desk, for example.' He patted the palms of both hands on its lacquered top. 'It's actually an emir's bed from the island of Lamu, about a hundred and fifty miles up the coast. And this . . .' he got to his feet and walked to the far wall where what could only be described as a throne stood, 'used to belong to Sultan Seyyid Humoud bin Muhammad of Zanzibar.'

'You have Arab royalty among your clients?' Lewis asked, incredulous.

'Sadly, no. But some of my clients have obviously had connections to people with access to the cast-offs from a palace renovation. There seems to have been a deal of argy-bargy among the Arab nobility hereabouts.'

Lewis nodded. 'Interesting.'

Morrison returned to his seat. 'I can assure you, it's a welcome change to have a European sitting in the client's seat, doctor,' he said with a broad smile. 'Now, how may I help you?'

Lewis paused, wondering how best to break the news that it was not he but a Maasai warrior who would be his client, that they had no sultan's furniture to offer by way of collateral, and that the only way they could make payment was with enough stringy zebu cattle to meet the bill.

Coll was at the door, about to leave for his reconnaissance of the southern reserve, when the telegram from Norman Lewis arrived. It advised that the solicitor, David Morrison, was prepared to accept the Maasai's case.

'Morrison certain second resettlement illegal,' Lewis wrote. 'Decision re any action in your hands.'

Coll took the telegram inside and sat at his kitchen table, staring at it. *Why now?* was his first thought.

The Maasai, although not pleased with the order to move, were at least reconciled to it. Ole Sadera and the other leaders were awaiting his word before transporting their people and possessions a hundred miles to the south. If Coll were to disrupt that massive undertaking on a single legal opinion, he had better be sure it was for the best. But how could he know?

Perhaps Lenana was right. Maybe it was in the Maasai's best interests to be reunited with their tribesmen in the south. The southern reserve was huge and at least had the advantage of being free from east coast fever. Until he made his inspection of Ngatet, he had no evidence to disrupt the present arrangements.

He decided to make a hurried trip to the southern reserve. If it was not yet ready for the influx of the northern Maasai, he could advise Ole Sadera to remain in Entorror and contest the order in court.

If, on the other hand, all was well in Ngatet, then the Maasai could commence their migration under his supervision as planned.

The SS *Cananore* ploughed the grey choppy sea into foamy furrows, honking a despondent farewell to Fort Jesus as it headed out from Mombasa harbour. In the northeast a black tropical storm was lifting into the sky, rumbling angrily as it gathered strength for its assault. Smaller clouds scuttled airily over the whitecaps on the reef, running like obedient emissaries of an approaching potentate.

The trade winds, fresh and crisp from the northeast with the smell of spice and ocean on them, tugged at Norman Lewis's trousers as he stood clutching the ship's railing.

The *Cananore* veered to starboard, giving him a last glimpse of Mombasa. Lewis would have liked the guns of Fort Jesus to thunder an appropriate farewell, or for an escaped beam of sunlight to catch the white coral-rock buildings lining the shore, making them glow as they had when he first arrived. But like so many things in his eight or more years in the protectorate, his departure failed to meet his hopes, much less his expectations. The town merely faded in a misty gloom and was soon lost from sight behind the headland.

He left behind many regrets, but not his anger. Leaving the protectorate in such a state of social injustice was greatly regrettable, and his anger was at having allowed the people with power and privilege to believe they had won the war when in fact they had only won another short-term battle.

Lewis believed that people like Edouard, who served only the powerful and privileged, would find no place in the new order. The empire was approaching a crossroads. Old warriors like Commissioner Stewart, who, like any soldier, relied on the philosophy of military might to resolve issues, would be obsolete. Even the engineers like Edouard would find their ambitious building programs, which promised the undoubted benefits of civilisation, insufficient to calm the conquered. Lewis was convinced the 'fight them, then fix them' approach would ultimately fail. If Britain didn't engage the population in a partnership of development, there would never be peace. A man may tolerate the theft of all his possessions, but if an invader stole his homeland, it could never be forgiven or forgotten. Eventually there would be a massive rebellion that no amount of force could defeat in the end.

Lewis was disappointed he would not be in the protectorate to witness a Maasai victory against the government. David Morrison believed they had a case that he could take to the highest court and win. Lewis sighed. That would have been one fight he would have loved to contest.

With Mombasa now gone, he began to contemplate the long sea journey to Nyasaland, where he would begin all over again. How would it be this time? He already knew that the Presbyterians had a good hold on the country, with hundreds of mission-controlled plantations where he would no doubt find the kind of exploitation that he had railed against in British East Africa. But he would not flinch from his duty to harass and pursue the exploiters, whether they were private, religious or governmental. And he knew his socialist friends back home in Great Britain would continue to raise the flag for changing society to a more equitable one.

He already felt better about his banishment to the British colony in Nyasaland. Perhaps it was the fresh sea air that gave him new life. He would soon forget British East Africa and all its frustrations. He turned his head to where he felt sure he would find many opportunities to spread again the seeds of the new socialist philosophy; hopefully this time to find more fertile soil for it to take root. Behind him the thunderclouds rumbled.

CHAPTER 41

In the beginning, the trek from their home on the Laikipia Plateau presented no insurmountable difficulty to the people of Rumuruti village. As they began their long journey to the south, their path followed the undulations of hills and valleys, but the general trend was downward and the walk was not too demanding on the old and the frail.

Mothers toted babies on their backs and small children were propped on donkeys amid wobbling piles of pots and gourds. Older children shared shepherding responsibilities under the guiding eye of Okelia. Elders fit enough to toss a stone at a hyena helped where they could.

Children of an age to know the customs of their people asked why they were moving so far, and why they couldn't set up village right there. As far as the eye could see, the grass was good and water available. Some even wondered why they had moved from the good grazing land of Rumuruti at all.

But as the days dragged on, the simple daily chores of finding a camp site, erecting a makeshift *boma* to keep it safe from predators, and feeding children and animals consumed more and more time and the questions became fewer. The distant grey line of the Mau Escarpment — the gateway to the southern reserve — seemed as far away as it had the day they left Rumuruti. Their progress became laboured and slow.

It was not the long days of walking followed by hours

searching for firewood that caused Nashilo's heart to ache. Nor the visits by the *askaris*, who scowled at them should they stop to rest; nor the nights, when lions roared and children became fretful and in need of comfort. It was the faces of her people. Bereft of any understanding of the reasons for their move, and torn between their desire to remain in Rumuruti and the orders of their leaders to embark on a seemingly mindless, endless trek to an unknown land, their usually bright and optimistic outlook crumbled. As she scurried up and down the long thin line of people and animals, assisting first one struggling family group then another, Nashilo could see the usual stoic determination to overcome whatever hardship befell them fade from their eyes.

To worsen the sense of wretchedness, she knew that all across the wide Laikipia Plateau similar human sagas were repeated as thousands of her Maasai people drifted across the savannah like bundles of dried weeds, torn from their roots and flung into the wind.

Nashilo seldom saw or heard from her husband. By day he was herding cattle, and at night he would sleep near them to fend off predators. His other wives — Nashilo's three sister-wives — all had small children and Nashilo did what she could to assist. It was a familiar pattern among most of the women journeying south. In the absence of their menfolk, the women, children and elderly had to fend for themselves.

Parsaloi, accompanied by a small group of warriors, kept an eye on their small caravan in the early days of their move. She would occasionally see him on a distant hill. How she knew it was Parsaloi she couldn't say, but she felt his presence. There came a day when she sensed he had moved on. Days passed and he did not appear, even at a distance. She tried to stop wondering where he was and why he had suddenly disappeared. She tried to put him from her thoughts, but couldn't.

With Okelia busy with the sheep and goats, Nashilo had only Ntooto for moral support. The old woman's strength was flagging and she could do little to help, but her presence helped to keep Nashilo's mind off her loneliness.

The *askaris* visited every few days to hand out small food parcels from the government. There was never enough, but the women supplemented it with what they had carried with them and what they could find in the bush.

The *askaris*' visits were a mixed blessing. As well as the food, they handed out stern warnings about the pace of their journey. It was always *faster, faster,* no matter the difficulties, the weather or the terrain. They didn't care when an older member of the clan was ill or exhausted. In one instance, the caravan had to wait while a woman gave birth. Nashilo became very distressed when the baby was stillborn. She could only be thankful that her own time would come at the end of their journey to Ngatet.

There was another disturbing aspect of the *askaris*' visits that had only recently become apparent to Nashilo. The soldier called Ploog had started to pay her some uninvited attention. He often touched Nashilo as he handed her the meagre portions of *posho* for herself and Ntooto, and it made her flesh creep. But she made light of her fears, because Okelia had sensed her nervousness and now watched Ploog with ill-concealed disgust.

'I do not like that one,' Okelia said, nodding towards the sergeant who was standing with his companion, guffawing at some shared joke. 'Big and fat and ugly,' he muttered.

'Be very careful, Okelia. He has a bad temper. Be like me. I am just ignoring him.'

But it was hard to ignore Ploog. After a particularly threatening display, where he seized her by the arm and drew her into his foul embrace, she asked one of her sister-wives to collect the food while she stayed out of sight, minding the smaller children.

Nashilo began to have bad feelings about what might lie ahead.

The dry, featureless expanse stretched to the horizon. Had he been asked, George Coll would have said that neither man nor beast could live in such utter desolation. But the local district commissioner had confirmed that this was indeed the land the Maasai called Ngatet; the land promised to them in place of the rich Laikipia Plateau.

Coll found some of the new water storage dams, but they were empty. The DC told him that the rains had not yet arrived in the south. He said that sometimes they failed to arrive at all. It was not uncommon; the seasons were whimsical and even in good years the water and feed were scarce.

Coll was very worried. The grass was all but gone. No European farmer would attempt to make a living from such poor pastureland, but to the Maasai, it was not profit but life itself that depended on their cattle's survival.

In previous droughts, the Maasai would lead their cattle to one of their several dry-season grazing lands. If these also failed, as it appeared they had on this occasion, they would drive their cattle north through the Great Rift Valley, perhaps as far as Entorror and the Laikipia plateau. In principle, the mile-wide corridor linking the northern and southern reserves, as promised in the 1904 agreement, still allowed this migration, but the corridor had never been officially proclaimed and the governor had allocated some of the land to settlers. Maasai herders were forbidden to take their cattle across any settler's land.

In what had appeared to be a featureless plain, a small rise concealed a shallow valley where Coll discovered a herd of cattle scattered over a large expanse. At the centre of the herd were a handful of huts surrounded by a thin thornbush *boma*.

He headed his horse towards a group of men who were branding a cow. They greeted him cautiously. A visit by a member of the administration usually meant trouble for them, but he gained their confidence by chatting to them in their own language. He enquired about the branding operation. The cow appeared well past the age when she should be branded.

The men shook their heads and said it was not for branding. Their medicine man was attempting to cure it of a strange disease, which had recently killed many of their cattle.

Coll felt a touch of apprehension.

The government had not yet replaced the stock inspector responsible for the south since the incumbent had quit some months ago. It was a dangerous situation because the buffalo crossing from the Serengeti Plains on their seasonal migration carried various exotic bovine diseases. Coll walked over to the cow, which was down on its haunches and having difficulty holding its head up.

He didn't need his veterinary training to identify the cause of the cow's illness. Even a knowledgeable layman could identify the disease causing the enlarged superficial lymph nodes, increased body temperature, dullness and respiratory distress. Coll recognised it as the dreaded, highly contagious east coast fever.

His immediate thought was to dash home to halt the Maasai's move, but then he remembered that the agreement with Edouard, meant the move would not commence until Coll had finished his report on Ngatet.

The conditions of the dams made it absolutely impossible for the Maasai to move to Ngatet until after the rains, but now, with the presence of east coast fever, Coll knew he had to talk to Ole Sadera about challenging the order in court.

Coll raised his collar against the gusts from the northeast that repeatedly tried to grab his hat and fling it down the thirty-mile-wide continental fracture that was the Great Rift Valley.

He had been riding into the wind and occasional rain for three days, anxious to get word back to Nairobi about the situation in the southern reserve as soon as possible. He was heading to Naivasha, where he could telegraph his report to the governor. He didn't trust Edouard's promise to wait until he returned to make his report. The governor was often praised as being a man of action; 'impetuous' was another description Coll used in private.

Coll planned that Naivasha would be the main checkpoint and source of supplies for the Maasai's trek, and he thought it might be wise to show the governor he had made some progress in that regard while he was gone. So while he was in Naivasha, he would meet the district commissioner and begin the complex arrangements that would ensure a reliable supply chain for the convoy. He needed to be in the governor's good graces, as his immediate task on return was to convince Edouard to delay the start of the move until the rains replenished the dams in the southern reserve. The thought of confronting Edouard filled him with trepidation, but it had to be done otherwise the resettlement would be a disaster.

He had given a great deal of thought to the move during his long ride. He wanted to use four main routes from Laikipia to the southern reserve so as to spread the grazing pressure over a larger area.

They would only use the short, hazardous route over the Mau Summit if the weather held up. Even then it was only suitable for the younger ones. The other three routes would be via the more gentle slopes and good water supplies around Lake Naivasha.

Even given the best of planning and the most benevolent conditions, the movement of such a multitude would require good luck if they were to avoid a debacle.

CHAPTER 42

The long snaking lines across the valley floor were like grain fallen from a leaking bag. One pathetic little caravan followed another, many miles apart, as numerous villages were emptied to obey the order to move south. Only occasionally, after crossing the valley floor and beginning the undulating climb towards the western side of the escarpment, was Nashilo reminded of the other Maasai's existence. When her Rumuruti group crested a ridge they might see in the distance — one, two or three valleys beyond — another dark line on the grassy plain; another column of dust rising from tired feet and hooves.

Ahead of them lay the Mau Escarpment, sometimes looming on the horizon, sometimes beyond the next rolling hill. The younger people in the clan, including Nashilo, had never seen the Mau as they saw it now. Nor had they experienced such cold, biting rain. The wind came in with a chill from the east, where the jagged snow-capped teeth of Mount Kenya hid among the swirling clouds.

The children had lost their enthusiasm for the adventure. They plodded along, enduring the tedium of the walk and the ever-present nagging hunger from bellies too seldom satisfied by the infrequent deliveries of food.

Nashilo's husband came one morning to say that the pasture had been hard to find on their path to the Mau, and it was becoming worse as they drew nearer to it. The heavy concentration of cattle from other villages as they converged towards the pass over the summit was the reason. This forced him and the other men to range further afield to find the grass. He said it was unlikely they would meet again until after they had crossed over the escarpment.

In the following days, they climbed steadily higher and, as they did, the weather worsened.

The old people could not keep up. Ntooto refused to admit it, but even she found it almost unendurable to continue in such appalling conditions. The Rumuruti villagers slipped further behind schedule as they stopped for a day's rest to allow the old folk and children to regain their strength.

Ploog was very unhappy about this and made his camp nearer to them so that he could keep an eye on their progress. Whenever Nashilo's group stopped to erect a temporary village, the *askaris* harassed them to press onward.

Nausea increasingly troubled Nashilo. As the air grew thinner, her stomach churned and she fought bouts of faintness. The other women told her it was common in early pregnancy, and that only rest could ease her discomfort. But the *askaris* would have none of it, and Ploog's frequent appearance did nothing to help her peace of mind.

The Naivasha district commissioner, Gordon Gower, greeted Coll perfunctorily, barely looking up from his paperwork, which covered his desk and every other flat surface in his office. Gower was a former employee of the Imperial British East Africa Company, and when the Foreign Office had taken over administration in 1895, they had offered him a position in the newly proclaimed protectorate. Coll knew Gower quite well, having met him several times previously, but was never able to like him. He was a heavy drinker, and when he discovered that Coll didn't touch a drop declared that his dearly departed father had advised him never to trust teetotallers. At first Coll had thought he was joking, but in all the many occasions that he had passed through Naivasha in his travels to Rumuruti and places beyond, he had found Gower true to his father's advice. He had never offered Coll so much as a cup of tea.

Coll had already dispatched his telegram to the governor and expected to be soon on his way to the government guesthouse where he would take a much-needed rest before heading off to Nairobi in the morning. He merely had to advise Gower of the arrangements he proposed for the supply of food relief to the Maasai as they passed Naivasha.

'What rations?' Gower asked when Coll had outlined his plans.

'The rations you will draw on the warrants I'll be supplying you.'

'Already got those. And already met the first two consignments.'

'Who to?'

'Army bloke. Ploog, I think he said his name was.'

'Ploog!' Coll's breath caught in his chest and he immediately began to cough. He covered his mouth as he spluttered and gasped for air. When the coughing had subsided, he found Gower staring at his bloodied handkerchief. Coll quickly stuffed it back into his pocket.

'When did you last supply him with the rations?' he demanded.

'Three or four days ago.'

'Where did he take them?'

'What's this all about, Coll? I can't see how it's any of your business. It was a standard warrant issued from the governor's office.'

'The governor has appointed me as field supervisor for the resettlement.'

'Has he now? Well, you'd better get a move on. Sergeant Ploog is off to the Mau Summit with it all. He could be after your job,' he said, smirking.

Coll gathered his notes together and packed them hastily into his bag. A line of perspiration trickled down his nose.

'Here,' Gower said. 'Are you all right?'

Coll resisted the urge to mop his face with his handkerchief. 'Perfectly fine,' he spluttered, wiping his arm across his forehead and heading out the door to his horse. He had to stop the Maasai before they became trapped on the Mau Summit.

*　*　*

Neither the horse nor Coll could keep up the pace. Coll collapsed on the horse's neck, gasping for air. The mare was blowing hard and sweat foamed down her flanks. Even sitting astride his mount took more energy than Coll could spare, and he slipped from the saddle at the side of Lake Naivasha as the horse drank heavily of its water.

He strained his eyes into the west, as if seeing the extent of his day-long journey to the Mau Escarpment would make it seem less demanding.

A hippo surfaced nearby, noisily blowing water from its nostrils. The mare skittered back, refusing to stand at Coll's command. He chased her for half a mile before snaring one of the reins and falling to the ground, gasping for air, wheezing and coughing up flecks of blood. He tried to take slow, calm breaths as Norman Lewis had instructed him to do whenever he felt the rising panic of suffocation, but he began to sweat and his heart pounded in his chest. With all his willpower he fought the unbearable need to cough and clear his chest. Slowly the attack subsided and he was able to remount and resume his journey.

He kept the pace at a steady walk, knowing that if he didn't carefully conserve his strength and his mare's, he would never reach the Mau Summit.

As the day dragged on, his imagination tormented him with the vision of thousands of Maasai struggling across the summit with little or no food and water, and Ploog's heartless *askaris* driving them forward. The endless hours of riding, however, did afford the chance to plan his course of action when he arrived.

He would stop the move. He would turn the Maasai back towards Naivasha, where they would stay until the rains reached the south. In the meantime he would establish the supply lines as he had originally intended. He would simply have to accept Edouard's wrath, because it was inconceivable that the Maasai should attempt the crossing without this assistance.

During the afternoon, clouds began to roll in from the east. They formed into galleons above Mount Kenya and a dark armada sailed towards the Mau, filling Coll with dread. If a storm were to catch the unprepared Maasai on the summit . . . He shuddered at the prospect.

Towards sunset, he had only just begun the climb up the slopes towards the escarpment, but his horse was exhausted. He had to give her rest or risk losing his only means of transport.

As he set up his small tent, a light rain came in on a chill wind, flapping the canvas and ripping the tie lines from his numb fingers. He took a cold dinner of beef jerky to bed with him. Exhausted and feverish, he lay on his back, which made the constriction in his throat worse, and spent the night desperately trying to get the rest he needed.

In the dark he listened to the sounds of the approaching storm. Above the noise of flapping canvas, the wind moaned in the hills. He was glad of his decision to make camp when he did, but was filled with guilt as he imagined how the Maasai might be faring some thousand or more feet above him on the exposed flanks of the escarpment.

The slopes rose above them, bleak and dark. To the east, late afternoon storm clouds loomed in an ashen sky, and the wind — like a cold, steel blade — slashed a swathe through the grass. The Maasai women of Rumuruti cowered against it in calfskin cloaks and thin woollen shifts, hugging their children to them. Even the elders in their hyrax fur coats felt the chill cut into their bones.

Every step was an effort of will. Ahead lay the Mau forest, and some relief from the biting cold and rain. But the light would soon fail, and Nashilo felt a night on the windswept slopes might be the last for some of the weaker members of their group.

Okelia was up ahead with the milking cows, sheep and goats. The stock were on their last legs, heads bowed against the rain, but their survival was essential if the villagers were to complete the journey.

The younger women coaxed the fallen older ones who were too exhausted to rise from their protective huddles, finally threatening them to get to their feet or die beside the track.

Nashilo did what she could, but the stabbing pains in her belly warned her that the new life she carried would not tolerate any further demands on her strength.

She positioned herself at the tail of the caravan, vigilant for any stragglers — urging them on when they fell behind. The going was heavier there, and she took brief but frequent rests, fighting nausea and an aching head that only worsened the higher they climbed.

Bent against the wind and rain, she didn't see Okelia come from the dimness of evening. He startled her when he took her arm, shouting at her, but the wind snatched the words from his mouth and hurled them into the gathering gloom. He was pointing ahead, up the hill, but she could hardly see for the rain in her face.

He stretched to reach her ear. 'The summit,' he said, pointing ahead. 'Not far.'

Nashilo wiped the streaming rain from her eyes. She tried to smile and nodded her understanding.

'I will help you,' he said, and took her arm.

'No, you must stay with the stock. The milking cows.'

Okelia knew she was right, but he hesitated, concern and doubt in his eyes.

'Go on ahead,' she said. 'Get the stock to shelter and then come back.'

Again he hesitated.

'Go!' she ordered.

Okelia went swiftly to rejoin the elders and children controlling the herd.

What little light existed was soon gone. Nashilo wasn't sure if she was still following the others or had become disoriented by her vertigo and nausea. As she was stepping over a log in her path, she misjudged her footing and fell. On her hands and knees she stifled a sob of despair. She was exhausted, and wondered if she could make it to the top of the rise or would surrender to the mud and manure of the rain-battered hillside.

She had sent Okelia away — her only chance of assistance — and had nothing but her own failing willpower to help her survive. Her despair threatened to overwhelm her, but she gained strength from the knowledge that a new life existed inside her. She would survive if for no other reason than to save Parsaloi's baby.

She used the log she had fallen over to get some leverage. But it was not a log; it was a body, cold and stiff under her hand. It was Ntooto.

In darkness and stinging rain, the desperate band from Rumuruti reached the forested ridge of the Mau Summit, not in convoy but as a rabble, arriving in small, dejected clusters of misery. The last thousand paces had been an enormous effort as they clawed their way up the slope, falling and rising, covered in mud and filth, sometimes on hands and knees.

The Mau forest floor where they arrived was a complete morass. There was nowhere to set a shelter. Mothers pulled skins and blankets from the pack donkeys and gathered their children into shivering huddles under trees and bushes. There was no fire and no food to be had that night.

Okelia took some time to locate his village among the many hundreds of people attempting to find shelter on the Mau. When he did, he was shaken to find Nashilo was not among them. He went immediately down the hill, headlong into the rainstorm.

He thanked Enkai that by some miracle he found Nashilo not far from where he'd last seen her. She was sobbing as she tried to drag a corpse up the hill through the quagmire.

She emphatically resisted his suggestion that they leave Ntooto's body in the rain. 'I cannot leave her!' Nashilo screamed at him, shivering with cold and exhaustion.

Okelia pleaded with her to come away. He reasoned; he threatened. She wouldn't listen. He was angry with himself. He was angry with Nashilo. It was not his fault that he was still a boy, unable to do what was right. If he had been made one of the *moran,* as he had so desperately wanted, she would have been compelled to listen to him.

With tears of frustration in his eyes, he grabbed her cold hands from her hold on the old woman's clothing. 'Nashilo, you must listen to me,' he begged her. 'We cannot stay here.

There is nothing we can do. Ntooto is dead. And so will we be if we don't get away from here.' Tears were now streaming down his cheeks, mixing with rain. 'Look at you. Look at me. We are finished unless we leave Ntooto here. Have you forgotten our ways? There is no disgrace for her to be left here in the night.'

He drew closer to her, trying to engage her with his eyes. 'If we don't find shelter, we will die.'

His half-sister suddenly seemed to understand him. She hugged him to her, weeping uncontrollably. He could feel the tremors of her chill.

'You are right, Okelia,' she said when her sobbing had subsided. 'Of course you are. But let me make my mother ready for the night.'

She turned to Ntooto's muddied corpse, wiped the mire lovingly from her face and set to arranging the old woman's clothing and turning her so that her body lay straight.

Okelia helped her. It was fitting that Ntooto appear composed and ready for the hyenas when they came for her.

CHAPTER 43

When the dawn came creeping through the forest, the Rumuruti people counted their missing and dead. An old man had died in the camp during the night, and two more women, perhaps merely lost, had not made it to the forest. Two cows and five sheep were dead.

Nashilo and Okelia walked through a slippery mire of dung and mud to a thinly covered ridge where they hoped they would get a view of their surroundings. They avoided peering down the path they had trodden the night before, but followed another ridge to get a view into the valley.

The sun rose under a low, flat cover of clouds. As it climbed into the leaden sky it sent thin golden shafts into the forest surrounding them. The Great Rift Valley appeared below, where the cattle, sheep and goats covered the grassy slopes in a patchwork quilt spreading up and into the forest. There was hardly a piece of land unclaimed by a herdsman and his stock. Nashilo imagined that somewhere among them were her husband and all their worldly wealth, yet to make the attempt to cross the summit. Or perhaps they had already passed and were free to spread across the relatively untouched pastures on the other side.

She found a few thin, curling trails of smoke lifting from the forest surrounding them. There were many people out to study the dawn from the nearby ridges and hills. She and the other members of the Rumuruti group were one small part of a massive log jam of people stuck in the morass on the Mau Escarpment; all of them cold, wet, and half-starved.

Nashilo and young Okelia exchanged glances. They knew that their people had to rest for a few days before attempting to cross the escarpment, but it was obvious that neither man nor beast could find food enough in the mud of the Mau Summit.

About two hours before dawn Coll slipped briefly into sleep, only to toss and turn in the throes of vivid dreams.

He saw Katherine running through a field of yellow dandelions carrying a basket of picked flowers. She reached him and danced around him looking absurdly young and pretty. She was teasing him, asking why he wouldn't dance with her. Coll wanted to dance; with all his soul he wanted to join this youthful, beautiful Katherine in her dance, but his feet inexplicably felt like lead. He tried lifting them using both hands, but they were too heavy. Katherine playfully threw a handful of dandelions over him in a yellow shower. He laughed, and felt a strong urge to kiss her, but she disappeared.

The scene changed and thousands of bright red cattle surrounded him. They lowed and contentedly milled about in knee-high grass, but Coll wanted them to move. He got behind them and pushed and pushed. He had no idea where he wanted to move the cattle, or why, but he became very agitated when they wouldn't budge. He wept with the frustration of it.

Then he realised why he was unable to herd them: his feet were stuck to the ground, encased in cow dung, but instead of it being light and easily crumbled, it was a solid ball, as heavy as stone.

Suddenly the cows were gone, and Katherine came skipping back with her flower basket. 'Dance! Dance with me!' she called to him, and threw handfuls of dandelions over him. But the flowers were now blood red and Katherine began to cry because he refused to join her.

Coll wept too. He wiped his tears away with his handkerchief. To his horror, he found it saturated in red dandelion juice. It covered his clothes and ran down to the leaden cow-dung boots that still held him.

After a struggle he at last freed himself from the boots and ran after Katherine, now a small dot on the horizon beyond a vast red field of dandelions. As he ran, his feet became entangled in the flowers. They curled up his legs and stuck to him. In a panic he tore them from his body, releasing a flood of what he thought was a sticky sap, but was in fact blood. Now he despaired of ever catching Katherine. He couldn't allow her to see him in such a state, and he had no way of cleaning himself. He stood there, staring in horror at his bloody hands.

He awoke in a feverish sweat, coughing and gasping for air.

When his heart rate dropped and his breathing returned to normal, he slumped into a half-sleeping, half-awake state, exploring the fading memory of his dream. He realised it had been a metaphor for all his recent mistakes. He had assumed that the British Government and the protectorate's administration would act in the best interests of its native peoples. When given evidence that they would not, he had failed to warn the Maasai of this, naively assuming that he and Norman Lewis could change events by their lobbying.

Even when he received legal advice that the Maasai could make a successful challenge to the resettlement order, he had decided that he knew best and had made the decision for them. He had failed his friend, Ole Sadera, and his people.

And there was Katherine . . .

Outside, the wind had dropped and the pre-dawn was eerily quiet. He was now fully awake, but Katherine remained in the remnants of his dream. Here was perhaps his most heartbreaking mistake. He had rejected a woman who had shown interest in him. By his own stupid obstinacy, Katherine was nothing but an aching memory; an unobtainable treasure.

Nashilo and her fellow villagers tried to make the best of a situation that was quickly becoming unbearable. Almost all their food reserves were gone although the journey was clearly far from over, and the thousands of cattle that had arrived, and continued to arrive, fouled the streams.

And still more cattle came, flowing through their improvised camp like driftwood in a flooded river, bumping into flimsy huts, trampling fireplaces and unsettling the pack animals.

More people arrived too. The Maasai from all over the Laikipia Plateau continued to flood in, looking bewildered, and finding no habitable space available to stop and rest. No one was in charge. Everyone was hoping that someone would bring order to the chaos.

Nashilo became fretful that they would be marooned there for days while the elders argued for and against continuing.

The *askaris* barked at them. They warned the Maasai that they couldn't settle there; that there would be no reliable food deliveries while they remained on the Mau. At the same time, they threatened them not to retreat.

Faced with days on the summit, the Rumuruti people searched for suitable material to build rudimentary huts. They found nothing, and had to improvise with skins and branches stripped from the forest.

Firewood was almost nonexistent. The young children whimpered, and the elderly — with all the many ailments that exhaustion worsened — grew weaker.

Around noon, Nashilo's husband arrived looking haggard. He told his wives he had tried a number of times to drive their herd through the forested ridges without success. There was total confusion among the hundreds of herders and many thousands of stock animals. He said he would return when he had found grass for their herd, but made little acknowledgement of their complaints other than to give a resigned shrug of his shoulders. 'I will leave another milking cow,' he said.

Nashilo realised they were stuck in the Mau forest. The menfolk could drive the cattle no further without risking further heavy losses, and the Maasai were unable to go forward because of the wall of cattle. Neither was able to return the way they had come because the *askaris* threatened violence, brandishing their weapons whenever the Maasai made a move to retreat.

From deep in her heart she cried for Parsaloi. He could rescue them, or at least tell them they must go or retreat, but she hadn't seen him for many days. Her anxiety made her sick and her back ached.

Suddenly she felt a movement inside. The baby had stirred — a fluttering touch of something in her, but distinctly other than her. The baby — Parsaloi's baby — was inside her belly. She found a seat on a fallen cedar and eased herself onto it, afraid to do anything that would bring a halt to the wonderful sensation. She placed a hand on her abdomen. The fluttering strengthened into a kick.

Amidst the squalid mire of their temporary camp, Nashilo felt elated. Even the rain, which had started again, could not spoil the moment.

Now the life inside her had assumed a reality she had hitherto been unable to comprehend. More than anything, she wanted the baby to survive the hell they were enduring. And no matter how bad the southern reserve might be, she didn't want to have her baby out there in the bush, lonely and miserable. She wanted peace and a place to settle before her time came.

A new spirit emerged to replace the old one lost on the previous night.

At the first glimmer of dawn Coll peeped out from under the simple fold of canvas that was his tent. In the east the sun was an indistinct ball in a misty half-light. He crawled to where he had left his saddlebag and dragged it back to his tent to escape the light rain while he searched for something to eat. He found a can of beef, and struggled to open it with his knife. His breath came in short gasps and his hand shook as he used the knife to spoon the food into his mouth.

The top of the escarpment was invisible in the misty rain, and his night-long fears of not being able to complete his mission resurfaced. It was an impossibly high climb even on horseback, but he felt so weak he thought it equally unlikely that he could make it back to Naivasha without help.

He decided to try to reach Ploog and get his assistance to alert the Maasai before seconding one of his *askaris* to take him back to Naivasha.

With a great effort he saddled his horse. He considered packing his tent and camp items, but couldn't manage it.

An early morning breeze stirred the mist as he began his climb, giving him a view ahead of some two or three hundred yards. A number of animal carcasses were scattered across the undulating slopes. It was common enough to find a zebra or wildebeest carcass from a predator's successful kill of the previous night, but finding so many was unusual.

He reached the first carcass and found it to be a heifer. The next was a goat and then another dead cow. They were intact so he surmised it was the weather and their poor condition that had killed them, not lion or hyena. He looked back down the slope and realised he had camped among a field of dead animals.

The next corpse was that of an old Maasai woman. For a moment Coll hoped she was simply exhausted, lying there as if waiting for the sun to rise to warm her before she continued on her journey. But she was cold and rigid; dead for probably no more than a day or two.

He briefly considered returning to his camp to retrieve his shovel to make some kind of grave for the poor old woman, but he knew it would take all his strength. He did what he could with some stones, but before he could construct anything that might deter the scavengers, his strength gave out. He had to sit and wait until he felt strong enough to continue.

His mare was favouring a leg and he decided it prudent to walk for as long as he could. Within a hundred yards he found another corpse — an old man curled against a large rock as if trying to draw what little warmth it offered before the night claimed him.

A cool sun broke through the last of the mist and Coll looked back over the sprawling breadth of the escarpment, wondering how many more were lying out there, victims of this enormous folly.

He coaxed the mare on and, by taking a grip of the saddle strap, let her help him up the hill.

He tried to concentrate on the difficult task of placing one foot in front of the other, but couldn't put the nagging thought from his mind that he was responsible for this situation. If he had been able to insist that Edouard wait until he was in position to arrange and supervise the movement of people and animals, this looming disaster might have been avoided.

CHAPTER 44

Nashilo crept like a timid gazelle towards the *askaris'* tents where the water canisters hung from a guy wire. Ploog and his *askaris* had arrived earlier that day, bringing some minor relief to the Maasai's dire food situation. The water was for the Maasai's use, but Nashilo seldom ventured anywhere near the *askaris'* camp in case Ploog and his smaller companion, O'Rourke, were there. There was no sign of them, but she still would not have taken the risk had her sister-wife not urgently needed water to soothe her baby's fever.

The silence reassured Nashilo that the *askaris* were out scouting among the other groups within the vicinity, but it added an eerie atmosphere to the approaching dusk.

Her hand shook as she decanted the water into her calabash. When she had almost filled it, a sound from behind her made her drop it, spilling the water over herself.

She spun around to find Ploog leering at her, a whisky bottle in his hand, his leopard skullcap snarling. 'Well, well,' he said. 'What have we here?' He was shirtless, revealing a filthy undershirt. 'A water nymph. O'Rourke! Look here, we have an intruder.'

O'Rourke's ugly face appeared through the flap of the tent. Nashilo backed away a step or two as Ploog advanced. She made a grab at her calabash, but the big man was quick, snatching a handful of hair as she stooped. She stifled a squeal of terror, determined not to give him the satisfaction of knowing how much she feared him.

'Has she paid you for the water, sergeant?' O'Rourke asked, now at Ploog's side. He took Nashilo's arm in a painfully tight grip and twisted it behind her back, making her straighten and look up into Ploog's face. He stank of spirits, and his eyes were wild and red-rimmed.

'God's oath, O'Rourke, she hasn't. And look, she's made a mess of herself. She's wasting our water.'

Ploog let go of her hair and flicked at the top of Nashilo's dress. In one swift movement, he pulled out his knife and cut the cords that held it together.

Nashilo screamed as Ploog pulled the dress away, leaving her naked. She dropped her head to hide her face, but then Ploog's rough hands were on her breasts, painfully squeezing them, and from behind she felt O'Rourke's body pressing on hers and his hot putrid breath on her neck.

She threw her head back, hitting O'Rourke's nose, and at the same time swung her sandalled foot at Ploog's crotch. O'Rourke smothered a snarl of pain, but Ploog took the kick on his thigh.

'You little bitch!' he snarled, and brought the back of his hand across her face.

Nashilo struggled and bucked and threw a flurry of kicks in Ploog's direction before a mighty blow to her head knocked her into a grey oblivion.

She lost a moment's consciousness, and as she opened her eyes she saw Okelia charging at the men from behind a tent, howling a war cry and brandishing his herding stick like a sword. Fearing for his life, Nashilo climbed to her feet and made a feeble attempt at another attack, but Ploog's blow sent her to the ground and O'Rourke fell heavily on top of her. A searing pain ripped through her abdomen and she screamed in pain.

Something exploded near her head. She saw Okelia's feet leave the ground, as if he was a bird flung backwards while attempting to take flight in fear.

She only indistinctly felt the small stones tearing at her skin as Ploog dragged her towards the tent. She reached out to Okelia's broken body. But he lay still, with frozen, unseeing eyes.

Ole Sadera approached the camp with dread. It was a poor site, caught in a shallow swale among scattered cedars. The cattle had churned the ground into muddy pools awash with dung. The huts were mere collections of forest refuse thrown over tree branches. There was no fenced area for the protection of the kids and lambs, and there had been no attempt to construct a secure *boma* for the protection of the huts.

He had seen many similar camps in his search to find Nashilo and the other villagers, so was less shocked than he might have been. But the wailing dirge of the women warned him of an even more distressing situation.

From what he had witnessed as he and his companions made the climb from the valley floor, he should not be surprised that one of the old ones had died. Many bodies littered the slopes and many more were missing from the camps he had passed during his search of the ridges for the Rumuruti villagers.

The old women sat around two bodies. One was of a herd boy, fresh-faced and appearing almost as if asleep except for a sinister black hole in the middle of his chest.

The second body lay beside the boy, covered by a white calfskin. Only the lower legs of the corpse were visible under the covering, but they were not those of an elder.

Ole Sadera stared at the feet. He knew those small, rounded toes. His heart gave a thump that caused him to bring a hand to his chest.

The women sat in silence as Ole Sadera raised a corner of the calfskin, then slowly removed it from the body.

Nashilo's face was barely recognisable. The women had cleaned away most of the mud, but the swelling so grossly distorted her beautiful features that for a moment he felt hope that it was not her.

He tried to swallow, but it came out like a choking sob. He reminded himself that Nashilo was another man's wife, and he must not disgrace himself or her by an inordinate display of grief. But his legs suddenly felt weak, and he had to lower himself to his knees beside the naked body.

Her swollen eyes drew his hand to her face as if to soothe the bruising with the soft touch of his fingertips. Her skin felt as brittle as the windswept rocks of the Mau. He snatched his hand away, stared at it in disbelief, and knew that no matter how much he wanted it otherwise, that last touch of her skin — as if it were cold, hard stone — would be the one that he remembered. He wanted to sob and pound the thought from his head.

He caught the women's puzzled glances and willed himself to climb to his feet.

Now he could see the ravages to other parts of her body — the scratches and bruises on her breasts, the torn skin on her legs, bloodstains on a short length of coarse rope still tied to one wrist, and, below the small rounded belly, the curled, matted redness between her legs.

It took little time and few words for the women to convey what had happened.

Ole Sadera plucked his spear from the ground, waved away his companions who had made as if to follow, and stormed from the scene.

At the outskirts of the crude village, he met Nashilo's husband, ashen-faced and hurrying towards the women who had resumed their lament. The men's eyes met briefly without either acknowledging the other.

Ole Sadera loped through the forest to the edge of the escarpment, where he paused for a moment to check his bearings. Below him the bare hills rolled away to the Great Rift Valley, still hidden in the morning mist. He knew that somewhere down there he would find Ploog and his *askaris*.

He hoisted his shield to his shoulder, balanced his spear in the loose grip of his hand and set off in an easy gait that could see him cover the breadth of the valley in what remained of the day. If Ploog was heading back to Naivasha, Ole Sadera knew he could find and kill him before dark. He moved downhill at a slow trot. As the morning mist rose he could see his day's journey roll on ahead of him. The Great Rift Valley spread like a giant's table, its golden covering of grass marked here and there by dark green clumps of foliage and the faint line of a creek bed. Only the old volcanoes of Suswa and Longonot, standing like sentinels at its middle, relieved the eye of its apparently limitless spread to north and south.

On the other side of a fold in the escarpment he caught sight of a pack animal moving uphill. A man was clinging to its flank. Ole Sadera came to a halt to study him further.

It was George Coll. He recognised him by his slight build and his tendency to curl his shoulders as if to protect his chest. He appeared to be having difficulty climbing onto the horse and was clearly in need of help.

The Maasai's hatred burned with such intensity that he could think of nothing but vengeance, swift and powerful. The idea that Ploog might go unpunished for a moment while he indulged in other matters tormented him. He had to leave Coll with his problems and continue his journey of revenge. He could almost taste the satisfaction of sinking his blade into Ploog's barrel chest; almost see in his eyes the horror as he realised he faced certain death.

He continued down the slope at pace, glancing across to Coll in spite of himself. He had fallen, but the horse continued to plod ahead.

Ole Sadera stopped. His hatred was like an itch that would eat at him until the delicious moment when he could satisfy the urge to scratch viciously at it. But he couldn't leave Coll in such a state. He would see what he could do to help before continuing his journey down the valley.

When he reached Coll, he was shocked at his appearance. His friend had never been a strong man, but now he seemed dangerously frail. There was blood on his vest.

'Swara,' he said, squatting beside him. 'Let me help you.'

Coll seemed unable to recognise him at first, then a wan smile creased his lips. 'Parsaloi. What are you doing here?' His smile faded. 'Your people . . . they have already reached the Mau. A disaster. I must turn them back. A change of plan.' He struggled to get to his feet.

Ole Sadera helped him up. 'I will take you to Nairobi, Swara,' he said. 'You need your doctors. You are not well.'

'No!' Coll spluttered. 'Let me go! I must turn them back. Parsaloi, they are on the Mau. With nothing.' He pulled himself free of Ole Sadera's grip and staggered a few paces trying to regain his balance. 'People are dying. Come with me. We must hurry.' He stumbled up the slope.

Ole Sadera looked down at the Rift Valley, imagining Ploog sitting jauntily on his horse, his vile crime already forgotten. He agonised over his situation, detesting his need to control his rage while he helped his friend.

He caught up with Coll, lifted his arm over his shoulder and half-carried him up the slope towards the summit.

CHAPTER 45

Coll was a dead weight by the time he and Ole Sadera reached the first group of camps on the Mau Escarpment. He sat at the base of a huge cedar, seeming on the verge of complete collapse, but he rallied some strength and asked Ole Sadera to find as many of the *askaris* as he could and bring them to him.

Ole Sadera squatted beside him with a water gourd. 'In time, Swara,' he said. 'You need to rest.'

Coll stopped the Maasai's hand as he lifted the water to his lips. 'Parsaloi,' he said with a look of near panic in his eyes, 'we have no time to spare.'

For a moment Ole Sadera wondered if he was referring to the Maasai or to his own dwindling energy.

'I have to reissue their orders,' Coll explained. 'We can't let this madness continue.'

'Very well, Swara. I will go.'

'And, Parsaloi . . .' Coll's hand remained on his, the grip stronger than he could have imagined possible. 'I want you to gather the people from around here into a group. I must tell them to get off this high ground; return to Entorror if they wish, or press on.'

'I can send my *moran* to tell them. There is no need for you to do so. We must get off the escarpment. You must see a doctor.'

'No! They must hear this from me. Please, bring them here.'

He nodded. 'I will, Swara.'

As Ole Sadera turned reluctantly away, Coll called after him. 'Then you must take me to the next group. And the next. I won't leave the Mau until I tell them all that we have made a terrible mistake.'

The exhausted horse plodded head down and listless along the murram road towards Nairobi. Leading it by its reins was Ole Sadera, almost as tired as the horse but unable to relax his vigil on Coll, who was in constant danger of sliding limply from the saddle. Coll's mission had kept him going in defiance of his physical capability. Once accomplished, the iron grip of his mind over his body loosened, and he had hardly spoken since leaving the highlands.

The sign by the side of the road caught Ole Sadera's eye and he stopped to study it. He remembered the word from the time he had first become aware of the severity of Coll's chest condition. It was in a discussion with Dr Lewis about Coll and his need for care when he was so ill. Lewis had written the word, 'Wallace', for him. It had a symmetry that Ole Sadera found pleasing, and he'd practised copying it from Lewis's paper so he could impress Coll with his new skill.

But Coll had not been pleased when he wrote Katherine Wallace's name for him, and became disturbed and angry when he went on to lecture Coll on the need to find a good woman to care for him. Coll had said he could look after himself, and anyway, how could a bachelor, a man with only fornication and cattle raiding on his mind, give him advice on marriage?

Coll's vociferous reaction had taken Ole Sadera by surprise. It was completely uncharacteristic of the softly spoken, considerate man he knew. Ole Sadera knew that Coll was a troubled soul, but only at that point did he realise how deeply his pain ran.

Now, Ole Sadera made a decision for which he felt sure Coll would not thank him. But he knew his friend needed rest for his damaged body, and also the touch of a woman as a more lasting cure for whatever else was troubling him.

He led the horse off the Nairobi road onto the track to Katherine Wallace's farm.

The Kikuyu workers in the maize fields stopped work to stare as the strange procession passed. Some followed the Maasai at a short distance, but Ole Sadera disdainfully ignored them.

Coming from the house, with a food basket for the field workers, was a young Maasai woman. He knew she was Maasai not from her clothes, which were foreign, but from her stature and bearing. She walked with her shoulders back and head high, ignoring the watching Kikuyu. Her eyes went from Coll mounted on the horse to Ole Sadera, and she held his gaze.

Ole Sadera's heart made a thump within his chest. She was beautiful, but also proud — as a Maasai woman should be in the presence of the Kikuyu.

But what made him gasp was that she was also the image of Nashilo, in everything but the years.

'No, no, Wanjira,' Katherine said, her hands on her hips, shaking her head. 'That is not the way to prepare a calf for branding. He'll bolt on the first whiff of the iron and you won't be able to hold him.' She pushed up the sleeves of her blouse. 'You grab him here,' she said, demonstrating the starting position by reaching around the calf's neck and grabbing its chin. 'And here,' she added, pointing to its leg. 'Then you just pull him down.'

Wanjira nodded and smiled. The boy attending the brazier smiled too.

Katherine stepped back. 'Now, let me see you try it again.'

Wanjira made another feeble effort, but the calf stepped through it, trotting to the edge of its tether line.

Katherine shook her head and lifted her head to the hills to await the return of her composure. On the track leading from the Nairobi road was a Maasai warrior — obvious by his red cloth and towering headdress. He was talking to Kira beside a mounted horseman.

As they resumed their path towards the house, the mounted figure seemed familiar, but she refused to speculate. More than once she'd mistaken a traveller seeking directions for the man she most wanted to see come riding down from that Nairobi road.

Now even the horse looked familiar.

She touched a hand to her hair, and brushed invisible spots from her smock, daring to hope.

By the time they had reached the gate she was sure, but could also see that something was wrong. George was having difficulty remaining upright in the saddle as he rode.

She ran to the gate and swung it open. She tried to reach George's eyes as he passed, but his head rested on his chest.

The Maasai said nothing, but drew the horse to a stop beside the porch.

Katherine rushed up and put her hand on Coll's knee. 'George?' she said looking up at him. 'George!'

'He is not well, Missus Wallace,' the Maasai said. 'He has not slept, and he is very weak.'

He gently tugged at Coll's leg. Coll stirred, and looked around him. He tried to focus, and seemed surprised by his surroundings.

'Katherine . . .?' he said when he found her standing beside Ole Sadera.

'Yes, George. It's me,' she said, risking a smile.

Coll slid down from his mount and, standing unsteadily on his feet for the first time all day, reached for her.

'George! Oh, George,' she said as she hugged him to her.

Katherine offered Coll more oxtail soup. 'Enough?' she asked.

'More than enough . . . as usual,' he said, lifting himself to a straighter position on her best sofa. 'Thank you.' His words came squeezed between breathy gasps.

'There's more on the stove.'

'No doubt,' he said, smiling. 'It wouldn't be Katherine Wallace's kitchen . . . without a gallon of good soup.'

'I must have known something,' she said as she took a seat beside him. 'I haven't made soup, or anything else for that matter, for a long time. People don't call around much any more.'

'I'm sorry, Katherine.'

'Oh, I didn't mean you, George. I meant the neighbours. When I was involved with ANPA and their various causes I —'

'I know what you mean, Katherine. But I'm sorry all the same . . . I shouldn't have left you like that . . . With no explanation.'

She shrugged. A smile played on her lips, but didn't quite make it to her eyes.

'It was wrong of me. And foolish.' He pulled himself up to face her. 'I didn't realise how foolish until I got to thinking about you . . . and other matters, while up there on the Mau Escarpment.'

'It's all right, George. No need to explain.'

'There is. I'd . . . I need to, Katherine.'

She indicated by a nod that she understood.

'Up on the Mau I became a bit . . . a bit disoriented. But I discovered something about myself. It must have been the altitude or the fever or . . .' He took another breathy swallow of air. 'Anyway, I got to wondering about myself — about the way I've been so . . . consumed by this illness. It affected my life more than I realised. Out there on those cold, windy hills I realised I had been living under a delusion . . . It came about because I was afraid to risk getting close to someone in case the illness got worse. I can give it its name now — it's TB. Tuberculosis.'

Katherine nodded.

George studied her for a long moment. 'Yes . . . well, I always promised myself I wouldn't involve anyone else in my situation . . . I had even managed to convince myself . . . that I broke off with the woman I loved, so that . . . well, you know . . . when I passed away . . .' He swallowed painfully and stifled a cough. 'The strange thing — the really odd thing — is that I had got it completely wrong . . . I didn't break it off with Jennie to save her from hurt. It was her idea. She said she couldn't be tied to someone with such poor prospects . . . She asked me what would happen if we had a family. How would she survive on her own?'

He fell silent, lost in his recollections of that day.

'Maybe Jennie didn't really love you after all, George?'

Coll nodded. 'That's quite possibly true.'

358

Katherine gave him a small reassuring smile. 'Well, it's good that you've been able to come to grips with the truth of it.'

Coll nodded again. 'But apart from my foolishness in deceiving myself all these years . . . about my noble gesture to protect Jennie, what do you think about it, Katherine? Don't you think I did the right thing, telling her? Isn't it the responsible thing to do? I mean . . . wasn't I right to deny myself for her sake?'

Katherine took a deep breath. 'Yes. You did the right thing by telling her. But letting Jennie's rejection of you affect how you live the rest of your life was foolish.'

'Affect my life? I didn't let it —'

'By keeping your condition to yourself; by denying yourself what might be a happy life, no matter how short you thought it might be, does yourself — and anyone who would love you — no good at all. In fact, I'd say you've taken enormous liberties with such a person by making decisions on her behalf. Who made you God? How do you dare decide what is best for another intelligent person? How —' She caught herself, and dropped her eyes to her hands clasped in her lap. His leaving had hurt her more than she had realised.

'Is it too late, Katherine?'

'Too late?'

'Too late to undo all that foolishness?'

Katherine's eyes brimmed and her smile spread. 'Never too late,' she said, and took him awkwardly into her arms.

CHAPTER 46

The paraffin lantern threw barely enough light for them to find the bed. It was exactly how Katherine wanted it. She took George's hand. She was nervous. Nervous enough for both of them, she suspected.

Beside her she could hear George's short, laboured breaths. He bumped into the large chest at the bottom of her bed.

'You've never seen inside my bedroom, have you, George?' she asked.

'No,' he whispered in reply. 'It has your scent.'

She wanted to say that for a long time now she had always wanted him in that room with her, but she was becoming concerned. Turning to him, she said, 'George . . . I'm not sure about this.'

He drew her close and pressed her to him. 'My darling . . . we've waited so long for this moment.' He kissed her, gently at first, then with eagerness.

She moved back so she could see his eyes as they caught the dim light. 'We can wait a few more days.'

'Days?'

'You're exhausted, George, and you're not well.'

'Just a little short of breath, my love. Nothing to worry about.'

'You need time, and . . . maybe I do too.'

He kissed her nose. 'I don't want to be alone another night. May I at least sleep here?'

'You may. But only to sleep.'

'If that's all I can have, then I accept, although it will be difficult with you beside me.'

'Isn't it strange? I've often thought about you being in this room with me one day. And now I'm saying we should wait.' She smiled. 'You climb into bed. I'll get changed in the sitting room.'

She took her nightdress and closed the door behind her. When she returned, George was asleep.

Quietly slipping into bed beside him, she lay in the dark listening to the sound of his breathing. Each breath seemed drawn at great cost; when he exhaled it was shallow and fitful. She felt the effort must surely wake him, but he slept for some time before awaking with a start.

Katherine rolled towards him and put a hand on his chest, whispering, 'Hush . . . hush,' as she gently coaxed him back to sleep.

He mumbled something indecipherable and fell asleep once more, his hand clasping hers.

Katherine thanked whatever gods had sent him home to her, and begged them to make him well so they could share at least something of a life together.

When Ole Sadera arrived at the farm, leading George Coll's horse and carrying his spear and war shield with its painted insignia, Kira had known he was different from the Maasai she'd occasionally seen in the town. She didn't quite know how she knew, but something in her forgotten past told her he was a man of importance. Later, she realised she really didn't need anything from her past to inform her; the *morani*'s bearing and demeanour was evidence enough. He frightened her by his mere presence on the farm. To be in the same room as him sent shivers down her spine.

So this is what it is like to be with a real Maasai, she said to herself, for she had often wondered how she might adapt to the life that had been stolen from her as a child.

Katherine was wise enough not to press her to make a decision either way about her future, but sometimes Kira wished she would. It was too difficult to sift through all the possible scenarios between life with the Maasai, which pulled at her through some kind of link of the blood, and life with the whites, which she at least, to some extent, understood.

From what she could remember, Kikuyu village life was not much removed from her Maasai home. She wondered if she could again return to such primitive surroundings.

Too many unanswerable questions. She wished she had the courage to speak to the Maasai *morani* to discover what it was that made him seem more interesting than others.

She had finished her housework early, and should have been studying the reading books that Katherine had set for her, but couldn't be bothered. She sauntered to the window and pulled the curtains aside again, just a chink, to peer at the *morani* standing in the shade of the barn, sharpening his short-bladed sword on a piece of flat rock.

'What is it, Kira?' Katherine asked from behind her.

Kira, startled, said that nothing was wrong. She hadn't realised that Katherine had come in from the bedroom.

'You're wearing that bandana I bought you. It looks lovely. Now, if you've finished breakfast, why don't you read the passages I set for you?'

'I have,' she answered.

'Then why don't you take yourself off somewhere?' she suggested before going into the kitchen annexe. She returned with some cheese and bread from the pantry. 'If you don't want to, I can find something for you to do.'

'I would, but . . .'

'But what?' Katherine said, planting her hands on her hips in her no-nonsense pose.

'It's nothing, Katherine.'

Seeing from Katherine's expression that she could not avoid an explanation, she continued. 'It's just that the Maasai man . . .' She turned to glance out the window again. 'He keeps staring at me.'

Katherine peeped out the window too.

'Does he? He's a close friend of George's so I don't expect there's anything to worry about, dear. We'll find out more about him when George comes out for breakfast.'

Coll arrived freshly shaven and with a damp towel still around his neck. He went to where Katherine was laying the crockery on the table.

'Good morning,' he whispered, softly touching her hand as it lay on the back of the kitchen chair.

She covered his hand with hers. 'Good morning,' she replied, then slid the towel from around his neck. Studying him more closely, she found he was still pale, but not as haggard as he had been the previous day. His hand slid around her waist. She indicated with a nod towards Kira that they were not alone.

'Kira and I were wondering about your Maasai friend,' she said.

'Oh, good morning, Kira. You look very pretty this morning. What a beautiful bandana.'

Katherine was pleased that George had made the compliment. She had been trying to increase Kira's self-confidence by encouraging her to wear more attractive clothes than her usual drab housecoat. If Kira didn't appreciate the difference, the young bloods among the local Kikuyu had. They showed a lot of interest in the attractive young woman. Katherine was constantly on alert, but fortunately Kira had shown no indication that she reciprocated their interest.

'My Maasai friend?' Coll said, returning to Katherine's remark. 'He's still here, I hope.'

'He is.'

'I need to talk to him about the problems we had on the Mau.'

'Not before you have breakfast,' she said.

He smiled, and took a seat at the table. 'As you say, my dear.'

While he ate, he told her what he had planned to avoid the disaster that had occurred during the Maasai's move to the southern reserve. He explained there should have been proper checkpoints and food supply depots. The move should have been done in phases, not allowed to turn into that mad dash in such dreadful weather.

'I honestly believed the move was for the best,' he said. 'But I've been misled. The Maasai have been misled. Ngatet is a wasteland with insufficient water, and the cattle fever that's plagued the north is there too. In fact, it probably came from the south. We have to reverse the decision. The government must be forced to reconsider.'

'Edouard is a determined man,' Katherine said. 'I spent some time with ANPA, as you know, and while there I learned the best way to deal with this bullying administration is to play them at their own game. Use the law to fight them.'

'I've had some advice on the matter, but . . . the Maasai in court? I'm not sure . . .'

'Why not? They can sell a few head of cattle to cover the costs.'

'Maybe. We've tried everything else we can think of. My old friend, Norman Lewis, told his contacts in London about the goings-on out here. Maybe he knew it would come to this because he went so far as to brief a lawyer in Mombasa about a possible Maasai case. I was hoping that it wouldn't be necessary. I suppose I always thought — hoped — that the government would act in the best interests of the natives, but now . . . Of course, getting the Maasai to agree to it might be another matter. We can only try.'

'Who will push the case?'

'Certainly not the *laibon*. He and the elders would normally be the leaders in this situation, but he's just a boy.' He thought about it for a moment. 'The only person who might be persuaded to take such drastic action is Parsaloi Ole Sadera.'

'Who is he?'

'He's the Maasai man standing outside your barn, my dear.'

Kira quietly entered the kitchen, avoiding eye contact with the Maasai leader, resplendent in his traditional red robes and beads. Nevertheless, she felt his eyes follow her as she carried the teapot to the table and filled the cups.

The two white people had been talking to the *morani* about legal matters all morning. Kira could hear them from the small kitchen annexe where she had taken refuge from the overpowering presence of the *morani*. Now their conversation had come to a pause as she moved among them, making her feel even more conspicuous than before.

Coll said, 'Kira, let me introduce my friend to you.'

The girl shot a glance towards Ole Sadera, then dropped her gaze to the floor.

'His name is Parsaloi Ole Sadera of the Purko section.'

Kira dared a brief glance to acknowledge him, but when she remained silent, Katherine explained to him that Kira had not met many members of the Maasai since leaving her village.

'What is your name, girl?' he asked her in Maa.

The language had all but disappeared from her memory. It was strange hearing the lyrical cadences of her mother tongue after such a long time. Memories of her mother and life in the *enkang* came flooding back to her. With horror, she found herself on the brink of inexplicable tears.

'Your name,' he repeated for her in English. 'What is it?'

'My name is . . . Lokatira,' she said.

'What are you saying, dear?' Katherine corrected. 'Your name is Kira.'

Kira smiled apologetically. 'No, Katherine, my real name is Lokatira.'

'How so? You told me it was Kira.'

'When you took me in, you called me Kira by mistake. But I didn't correct you.'

'Why didn't you tell me? I think Lokatira is a perfectly lovely name.'

'I wanted to please you,' she replied, now feeling guilty for her deceit. 'And I also liked Kira.' She remembered feeling that a new name would augment her new life.

'Well, I never,' Katherine said, taking a deep breath. 'Kira it is after all,' and she turned back to Parsaloi. Something in his expression made her pause.

Kira saw it too. All his threatening power had dissolved and for a fleeting moment she could see through his harsh exterior to something inside him, quite vulnerable.

He spoke to her in Maa. 'I know you, Lokatira,' he whispered.

'How do you know me?' she replied in English, almost afraid to ask.

'I know you,' he repeated. 'I know about you. More than you can imagine. I know of your family. I knew your mother, Ntooto . . .'

'You knew her? Where is she?'

He hesitated only briefly. 'Her spirit has passed.'

Kira felt a sudden tightness in her chest. It startled her, as she had always thought that the loss of a mother she'd hardly known could not affect her if she ever found out the truth. After all the years, she realised she had always held out a hope that she would see her mother again. The threatening tears finally escaped down her cheeks. She brushed them away with the back of her hand.

'My other family? My father?'

'Your father died fighting the Kikuyu when they took you away.'

'My brothers? My sisters?' she asked hopefully.

'I knew none of them. Only your half-sister, Nashilo.'

His cold, distant expression returned. 'Also dead,' he added.

He was once again the intimidating warrior, with darkness in his heart. Without another word, he pushed away from the table and stormed from the house.

Coll was at the door after him. 'Parsaloi, where are you going?'

Ole Sadera marched up the track without a backward glance, his spear in one hand and his war shield in the other.

'Parsaloi! What do you want me to do about the lawyer?'

But the *morani* broke into a trot and was soon out of sight.

CHAPTER 47

Pointing at the distant rise, the Maasai herder in the Great Rift Valley told Ole Sadera that the *askaris* had passed by that very morning, heading west. He said they had two heavily loaded wagons with them and they travelled like a tortoise. He moved his body perfectly mimicking the creature's lumbering gait.

The old man was an elder of the Keekonyokie section with a face as lined as the Great Rift Valley and a body as spare as an old rawhide rope.

He said the cattle he tended were not his own, but belonged to an important white man who he described in detail.

'How does this man, Delamere, treat you and your family?' Ole Sadera asked.

'You know him?' the old man said, surprised.

'There can be only one as you describe him.' Ole Sadera felt it best to keep the matter of his blood brotherhood to himself.

The elder said he had been working on Delamere's ranch, Soysambu, for years. 'Some say he is a white Maasai, but that is just a joke. We don't care. He treats all of us Maasai very well.'

Ole Sadera studied the old man who seemed content to tend another man's cattle on land that he, his father and his father's father must have visited with their cattle many times over many, many years.

The herder told Ole Sadera he lived in an *enkang* with his three wives, and each month Delamere gave him a few rupees to pay the government's hut tax.

'What is to happen to you now?' Ole Sadera asked. 'The Purko and others in the north have been told we must leave Entorror.'

'What is that to us? Even the first time, when the whites told the Maasai they must leave the great valley, we stayed. Delamere allows us to graze a few cows of our own here. Many do not allow such favours. Soysambu is our reserve now.'

'How do you bear to be contained in such a small place?'

'You Purko live too far.' He threw both hands towards the horizon in a gesture to suggest that Entorror was too distant to comprehend. 'And you are troublemakers.'

It was a statement without rancour. The Keekonyokie had been aggressive neighbours of the Purko in the days when they shared the Great Rift Valley and their *moran* raided each other's cattle.

'You should forget those old ways,' the old man went on. 'The whites have so much land. Why fight them for it? Look at me, do you think I would have lived to this age if I had to fight you Purko? I have enough for myself and my family.'

Ole Sadera wished he could understand how the old man could find contentment sharing land under the condescending permission of its new owner, but he had a more pressing need.

Ploog would probably make camp in the forest beneath the looming form of the Mau Escarpment. It would be a fitting place to confront him for his crimes.

Moonlight on the knotted trunks of the acacia trees, now an eerie, luminous green. The Maasai warrior moves among them — a shadow lost in shadows.

A camp fire. Voices muffled in the smoke. The firelight sculpting stark masks from the dark faces surrounding the hearth.

A curlew's haunting whistle pierces the darkness, momentarily silencing them. Someone among them makes a joke and others laugh, but the silence soon returns. The *askaris* throw casual glances into the darkness pooling beyond the throw of the firelight.

The warrior finds the discomfort in their eyes pleasing. He fingers the blade of his *simi*.

Examining the men, he realises the two he wants are not among them. He circles the camp with soft footsteps.

Searching.

They are not there.

A sound comes to him from deeper among the acacia trees. It is familiar. It is the sound of whisky and bravado.

On silent feet the warrior leaves the encircled men and moves away.

The curlew's call bids him good luck in his hunt.

Ploog took a mouthful of whisky, belched loudly, and slipped his fingers under his shirt to give his belly a vigorous scratch. 'O'Rourke,' he said gruffly, looking down at the man sitting with his head in his hands. He gave him a nudge with the toe of his boot. The corporal mumbled and was still.

'O'Rourke!' he said again, this time giving his leg a kick.

O'Rourke came awake with a start, almost tumbling off his log. 'What!' he said, eyes wide, trying to focus on Ploog standing above him with his back against the fire.

'Whisky,' he said. 'More whisky.'

'Get it yourself,' O'Rourke muttered, and lowered his face into his hands again.

Ploog pushed him off the log with the heel of his boot. 'Get off your arse and go get another bottle from the wagon,' he snarled. '*Corporal.*'

O'Rourke rose, grumbling incomprehensibly. He gave Ploog a sideways glance as he struggled to pull on his boots, but kept his thoughts to himself.

'Lazy bastard!' Ploog threw after him as he shuffled off into the darkness towards the *askaris*' camp.

With O'Rourke's absence everything suddenly felt isolated and still. Ploog had chosen to have his tent erected at a short distance from his black soldiers. He knew it would be one of those nights when the *askaris* prattled on with superstitious nonsense, as generally followed a day when something odd had happened, which they construed to be an omen. If he hadn't sent someone back to challenge the man who had been following them for most of the afternoon, the matter would have gone unnoticed. But when the man had disappeared in the middle of the savannah, not once but three times, the whispers began to spread among the black *askaris*. He was a ghost, or the spirit of a soldier lost from his platoon. Some even thought it was Jesus Christ returning from the desert. They had many stories from their many lands, and Ploog knew they would continue well into the night.

The sound that had earlier surprised him returned. It was an odd whistle. Not an owl or any animal he could name. He shrugged, and kicked the ends of the wood into the fire. The flames reared, and a billowing cloud of sparks spiralled up into the dark foliage.

The warmth spread up from his boots to his groin, giving him a pleasing sensation. It brought on thoughts about when his next sexual adventure would present itself.

The assignment to move the Maasai through endless miles of wilderness had not been a welcome one for Ploog. He preferred a base camp in a town, and knew he would become testy without at least one woman a night. He fondly remembered Lourenço Marques, where he often had not one, but two and even three women in his bed. But he had found adequate relief among the whores of Naivasha and Nairobi. Between stints in the towns, the local women sufficed, some of whom came willingly to him, although he had begun to find the sex more satisfying if they weren't. The Maasai were particularly challenging. Such fighting spirit. He was becoming aroused by the thought that by tomorrow night he would again be able to take his pick among the lithesome native wenches.

Ploog drained the whisky, and threw the bottle into the night, cursing O'Rourke for his tardiness.

His amorous thoughts reminded him of his full bladder and he moved into the mottled pattern of silhouettes beyond the edge of the camp to relieve himself. The shadows seemed to shimmer as a broken cloud drifted across the face of the moon.

A crack from the fire made him swing around. A knotty piece of firewood sent another flurry of cinders swirling into the air. He scolded himself for his foolishness. The silence had begun to unsettle him.

He found a tree and unbuttoned his fly.

Another crack from the fire came from behind, and a hand — not his own — grasped his penis.

There was a searing, burning sensation, and he opened his mouth to scream, but it was stuffed with hot, bleeding flesh.

O'Rourke came stumbling through the bush, a bottle of whisky under one arm and another in his hand. He swore as the undergrowth pulled at his clothes and scratched his face. When he stopped to gather his bearings, all was silent. Even the low rumble of talk from the men's camp seemed to have disappeared. He put the thoughts of the Maasai stalking them across the Rift Valley from his mind.

A sound came from behind him, and he swung around to find nothing there. Even the light from the men's campfire was now out of sight. Ahead, there was the faintest pinpoint of light from Ploog's fire.

He hurried on, cursing his rotten luck to serve under a mongrel like Ploog in an operation to move a bunch of ignorant savages.

'Here you are . . . Lazy bum,' he said to the empty campfire. 'Ploog! Where are you? If you've gone to bed . . . Where are you?'

Silence. A bird call, lilting and sad. A strange sound for such an hour.

The fire had died and the tents were in deep shadow.

'Ploog? Are you in there?' he asked of the nearest tent.

A snap of a twig came from the darkness beyond the camp. 'Are you out there, Ploog? If you think this is some kind of joke . . .'

He placed the whisky by the fire and threw some sticks on the flames. He picked up a branch that was already alight and, lifting it above his head, peered into the darkness. He could see the soles of a pair of boots, toes down, in the bushes beyond the clearing.

'Drunken bum's dead to the world,' he muttered, walking towards them.

He kicked a boot. 'Ploog! I've got your bloody whisky. Not that you need it.'

The figure remained inert.

'Ploog?'

He tried to turn the body with his toe, but needed both hands to grab a shoulder and wrench it around.

Ploog's face turned to him — a bloody mess — wearing an expression of utter horror, eyes wide in a frozen stare.

'*Ahhh!*' O'Rourke staggered backwards from the body.

A figure came from the shadows — a flash of a blade. Before he could react he felt a gentle brush on his throat and heard a soft slicing sound. His hands came away from it bloodied. He tried to scream, but only a hissing, bubbling sound came from his slashed throat.

The shadow stood before him, grim-faced and solemn. It waited while O'Rourke's legs turned to jelly and his knees hit the soft earth of the jungle.

CHAPTER 48

'Wadley. Come in,' Edouard said, as his assistant's head appeared around the door. 'What do you make of this matter up on the Mau Escarpment? Are the Maasai mixed up in any of this grisly business?'

'Our people say it's most unlikely, Sir Percy. The Maasai don't usually mutilate their enemies — at least according to Briggs over at the King's African Rifles.'

'Really? One wonders how much the KAR know about these matters. They're such an uncivilised lot.'

'The KAR, sir?'

'No! Of course not, Wadley. I mean the bloody Maasai. Fornication, cattle thieving, violent insurrections. Wouldn't surprise me if they were into mutilation murders as well.'

'Quite so, Your Excellency. But in this case it appears we can assume that Ploog and O'Rourke were murdered by one or more of their own troops. I dare say they were a vicious pair, sure to have made enemies.'

'Hmm. Well, let's follow all the correct procedures and whatnot. We'll need an investigation. What about Coll?'

'On sick leave, sir. We got word from one of the Limuru settlers, Mrs Katherine Wallace. She says he's recuperating on her farm and will be unfit for duty for some time.'

'Wallace? The troublemaker with that Asian bunch.'

'It is indeed, Sir Percy.'

'Well, well, so that's the cosy little arrangement, is it?' Edouard fingered the cleft in his chin thoughtfully. 'We'll have to have words with Field Supervisor Coll when he reports for duty again, Wadley.'

'I should think so, Governor.'

'Meanwhile, get on to Briggs over in the KAR to assign one of his officer chaps to the *askaris*.'

'Yes, sir. And what orders shall I issue?'

'Orders? What do you mean, man?'

Wadley became flustered. 'I mean, are we going to allow the Maasai who have turned back to stay in Laikipia?'

'Good God, Wadley! What are you thinking? My orders are that those who have crossed the Mau are to be pushed along, and the others are to follow. And be bloody quick about it!'

Ole Sadera met Mantira at his camp, and then accompanied him to a place where they were able to speak in confidence.

'How has the journey been for you and your people?' Ole Sadera asked.

'We have lost three cows,' Mantira said grimly. 'But we were fortunate. Your friend, Swara, sent word back to us before we became caught on the escarpment. It could have been worse. Much worse.'

'Many others were not so lucky.'

'I have heard some names,' Mantira said. 'There was old Yeiyio and his second wife. And the woman who tended Saitoti's goats. And old Ntooto.' He was unsure how to convey the remainder of his bad news. 'And Nashilo,' he said simply.

Ole Sadera swallowed. 'She rests. Avenged.'

Mantira nodded. 'It is better we do not disturb the peace of the dead. And what is to happen now?' he asked.

'Swara says we can fight the government to stop them forcing us to move.'

'Fight?'

'He says fighting, but he means talking. He says the white man's law is clear. He and Dr Lewis have arranged for an elder of the whites, one who knows the British law, to speak for us.'

'How is it so?' Mantira said, pulling at his long ear lobe. 'Does not the British law work only for the British?'

'Swara says British law is for everyone. The man he has asked to help us knows its ways.'

'I cannot understand this. How can the British law tell the British governor to help the Maasai?'

'Swara says their law is powerful,' Ole Sadera said.

'But I have spoken to Delamere and Colchester. They have advised us not to resist the move.'

'Swara worries that they may mislead us.'

'That is impossible. We shared the brisket. We shared our blood. I have already spoken to them. Delamere has come here and spoken to the leaders. He has said the Maasai must move or there will be trouble. It is for the good. The British are strong and we are weak. We must be guided by our blood brothers' advice.'

Ole Sadera clenched his jaw. 'I know one thing — the governor has lied to us. Swara has seen what they offer us, and it is bad land. He says they have not built the water holes they promised, and where they have, there is no water. Disease is everywhere. Our cattle will die. It is not a good place for our people.'

'We must do as the governor says,' Mantira countered. 'The elders, the *laibon*, have said it must be so. The governor will honour his word.'

'We cannot trust him. Look how they treat us before we even arrive in Ngatet. They send *askaris* to harass us and beat us. Our cattle become starved and they die in hundreds.'

'The elders say no,' Mantira said defiantly.

'And what do you say, my friend?'

Mantira paused, uncomfortable under Ole Sadera's fierce gaze. 'I also say no. It is unwise to go against the whites.'

'This is our only chance, Mantira. Once we lose Entorror, once we are in Ngatet, we will never be able to reclaim our lost land. I will talk to the leaders — the *moran* as well as the elders.'

'They are defeated, Parsaloi. They have no stomach for the battle.'

'The elders never have the stomach for battle. They will always say we must talk, talk.'

'I also speak of the *moran*. They have no heart for a war. Not if the elders and the *laibon* say no.'

'I will speak to the warriors. They will follow me.'

Mantira shook his head. 'No, my friend, they will not. Whether it is with spear and shield, or with the books of law that your man would read for us — no one has the heart to stand with you. I have spoken to them. Delamere has spoken to them. They have seen many innocents die.'

'The warriors *will* listen to me. Why do you lie to me about this, Mantira?'

'I am your friend, and I do not lie.'

'My Il Tuati will support me. They will remember how I have led them to victory in the past. We will take the fight into the British court.'

'Savannah grass is only sweet before the dung sours it. The *moran* will not remember the past while the future is so dark. While the memories of these last days are fresh upon us, they will not want to see your face, Parsaloi. For now, you and your past victories are forgotten.'

'I will not be forgotten! They will remember how we have shared victory many times in the past. Against the Kikuyu, the Nandi; against anyone who wronged us. We will win, I tell you!'

'No, we will not win, for there will be no fight. All we Maasai can do is to hold what little we have. We will accept Ngatet. If we cannot have our northern homeland, we must be careful not to lose more.'

'Coward!' Ole Sadera said, leaping to his feet. 'I will not be beaten down by this injustice. If you will not join me, I shall find some way to fight, and fight alone if I must. We will not be driven from our land again!'

He had been torn by dark, unseen thorns, bruised by falls, stumbled into stones and, having finally mastered the night, endured the intense heat of the morning sun in the Great Rift Valley. Mantira had planted the seed of doubt, and it was that doubt that had stolen his courage. He was defeated before he began — afraid to test his age mates' support.

The night had been full of sinister sounds. A lion had stalked him for two miles, a hyena pack yipped and sniggered in his footsteps, and he had almost fallen over a hippo concealed in the moonless night on the banks of Lake Naivasha.

The morning was mercilessly hot, but Ole Sadera used the piercing sun on his back as a scourge to drive him onwards and away from Maasailand and the temptation to test Mantira's claim that his brother warriors would turn their back on him. He would rather fight the whites alone than risk losing his position of respect among his age set brothers.

The more he pressed ahead, trotting and stumbling and occasionally resting to revive himself, the lonelier he felt. Loneliness was an intense emotion for him — one he had fought all his life.

He passed the village of Limuru, ignoring the stares of the Kikuyu labouring in their food gardens and the taunts of the children.

He was barely able to lift his head as he turned onto the track to the Wallace farm through a forest of lengthening shadows. His mouth was filled with bitterness and regret. He tried to make spit, but only a froth of nothingness formed on his dry lips.

Katherine Wallace's farm came into view through the acacias. It was a welcome sight, and he was relieved to have made it.

But Katherine's farm was not home. He felt separated from Maasailand. Trapped between two camps, he was at home in neither.

Kira called from the veranda. 'Katherine, please come.'

Katherine went out, wiping her hands on her apron. Ole Sadera was coming down the road, head drooping and arms hanging loosely at his sides. 'Bring water,' she told Kira. 'And tell George,' she added.

They had not seen Ole Sadera since he had stormed from the house over a week ago. She was pleased that George had been given that time to recover, as he would otherwise have pressed on with the legal case if Ole Sadera agreed. During the last week there had been days when she imagined she could see George's strength and good health improving by the hour. His rasping gasps eased and the colour returned to his face. He told her he was on the mend and that it was all because of the loving care of a good woman. Katherine had shushed him good-naturedly and told him to stop his blathering. The fact was, she felt like a fraud for accepting his gratitude while experiencing such sublime happiness by the mere fact of his presence that she could scarcely keep the tears of joy from her eyes.

When she wasn't with George, she was preening herself. It was the only way she could describe her constant primping at her hair and pinching of her cheeks. She rescued a skirt from the cupboard that she had bought years before for social occasions and had hardly worn. She decided to wear it for him. George said it made her look younger.

She smiled a lot.

But there were times, too, when she became paralysed with the fear that he wouldn't get well, and it took all her determination and deception to hide it. She would hover over him in spite of herself, feeling like a useless block of wood.

On his bad days, Coll looked grey and frequently collapsed into paroxysms of racking coughs that he would try to smother in his handkerchief. These became spotted with bright red blood clots, which he hastily tried to conceal. On one such occasion, when he was gasping and his lips were blue, he asked her if she wouldn't mind leaving him alone until he felt better.

'George,' she said, patiently, 'I've missed years of your life because of your silly notions. I'll not lose another moment for any of that nonsense.'

Coll came out to the veranda as Ole Sadera reached the garden gate.

'Parsaloi, what in devil's name happened to you?' he demanded.

'It is nothing. I have come.'

'Here, sit, Parsaloi,' Katherine said, pushing a chair forward.

The Maasai leaned on it, but remained standing while he consumed a pint of water. Only then could he be encouraged to sit.

'Where have you been, my friend?' Coll asked.

He said he had come from the Laikipia Plateau and that he wanted to see the man Coll had suggested could speak for the Maasai.

'The lawyer? David Morrison.'

'As you said, I want to fight against what the governor has done.'

Coll became excited. 'You mean you will take the matter to court?'

'Yes. It must be done.'

'And you have the support of the Maasai? The elders?'

Ole Sadera hesitated. 'Will you help me speak to him?'

'Of course. He's in Mombasa. I'll take you to him.'

'No, George,' Katherine said. 'You can't possibly go to Mombasa in your condition.'

'But, Katherine, I must. Parsaloi can't go on his own. I'll be all right.'

As if to deny his argument, he started to cough. When he regained control he was sweating and gasping for air.

'George, I know what you're trying to do, and I think it's wonderful, but you can't go to Mombasa. It's madness.'

'But —'

'When you're well enough, and I can leave you alone for a few days, I'll go to Mombasa for you.'

'Please, Katherine. We have no time to spare. Morrison told Norman that to have any hope of stopping the move we must first get an injunction, then we have to go to the High Court. It doesn't take long to arrange it, but it has to be done immediately.' He took Katherine by the hand and squeezed it. 'This means so much to me, my love.'

At that point Katherine knew she was defeated, and could only hope to salvage what she could in an agreement that would spare George his health. She agreed to go to Mombasa to see the lawyer, making Coll swear to be a good patient and to send for the doctor immediately he felt any signs of distress. She gave firm instructions to Kira and Ole Sadera to keep Coll calm and at full rest.

George kissed her in appreciation and she smiled.

Later that night, when they retired to bed, he kissed her again and thanked her.

He fell asleep in her arms, exhausted and unsettled.

Katherine could feel his heart beat against her breast and hear his wheezing lungs struggle for air.

CHAPTER 49

Kira pushed open the bedroom door with her toe. The conversation between Coll and Ole Sadera paused and the teacup rattled on the tray as she walked to Coll's bed with it. She passed it to Coll without mishap and allowed herself a quiet sigh of relief. It had been days since Katherine had departed for Mombasa, and many meals served, yet she still could not remain poised with the *morani*'s dark eyes following her.

'Thank you, Kira,' Coll said. 'I was just now telling Parsaloi what an excellent student you are. Won't you read something for me to show him I'm speaking the truth?' He took a book from the bedside table and held it out for her.

Kira gulped and searched desperately for an excuse to be gone, but there was nothing that came to mind. With trepidation, she took the book and drew the chair as far from Ole Sadera as she could.

She sat and began to read, but the words in the first paragraph would not form and her pronunciation was ghastly. She swallowed and started again with a little more luck. After a few minutes her throat became dry again and she paused, now feeling resentment towards Coll for putting her into such an awkward situation.

'Perhaps you know some Maasai stories?' Ole Sadera asked.

She was grateful for the respite, but was still uncomfortable under his attention. 'No, I can't remember any,' she said in a small voice.

'Not even ones from your childhood?' he asked in Maa. 'Maybe a poem.'

His voice was reassuring; the lilting language somehow comforting.

'There was one about the woman who had beads and armlets to sell,' she said. The memory had suddenly popped into her mind. 'But I can't remember it.' Having let her thought escape, she immediately regretted it. She had no wish to encourage the conversation.

'I've heard that one,' he said, thinking for a moment. 'The young girls in the *enkang* would sing it. Is it a story about a beautiful young girl who is looking for a husband?'

She nodded. 'I . . . I think so.'

'Yes, and she had many beautiful ornaments to offer if she found the right *morani*.' He tapped his forehead then began to sing.

Come see my beads, come see my bangles
See how they shine, see how they spangle
How can you not take pity on them
With their eyes so bright and nowhere to lie?
Come take my beads, come take my bangles
And love them forever or else they shall die

She smiled in spite of herself. The *morani* had made a passable impression of a young girl singing the song.

'And how does she reply?' he asked. 'Do you remember?'

Kira hesitated, not yet ready to become involved.

He prompted her:

Woman I care not for such pretty treasures
I am a warrior and have no need of such pleasures
I am seeking a wife to keep and to marry
Or else I will go, nevermore to return
And wonder if I may have missed the one thing I yearn
In all of your village have you no more to offer?

'Can you remember the last verse?' he asked.

A vivid memory came suddenly to mind of sitting in a circle of young girls, laughing and singing the song. 'She accepted him,' she said, the excitement coming to her voice, and she recited the final stanza:

Then I can offer but one small suggestion
You can take all my beads, take all my baubles
And to ensure that you do not illtreat them
I will come too, to make my inspection
Of the house that you offer and what kind of pleasures
For I am too fond of my own special treasures

She stopped, aware of the meaning of her unguarded outburst.

The *morani* had a curious expression that quite made Kira flush with embarrassment. She mumbled an apology and retreated from the room.

Coll insisted he was strong enough for a walk, and although Ole Sadera felt otherwise, he agreed to accompany him.

After a few minutes, Coll began to lean heavily on his arm, and was gasping for breath by the time Ole Sadera had found a place to sit. He regretted agreeing to the walk. It was obvious to him that Coll was taking more time to recover after each downward spiral.

Coll began to talk about compiling a book of the poems and stories that Ole Sadera and Kira could remember. The *morani* said he could try to recall them for him, but that the younger head of Kira might be more productive.

'You seem quite fond of young Kira,' Coll said, his voice little more than a faltering whisper.

'Fond of her? I hardly know her,' Ole Sadera replied. But it was true that she was often in his thoughts. He wondered if Kira had the same laughter, and the same quick temper, as her half-sister. Could she make him feel as foolish at his mistakes as Nashilo had? Would she be mischievous and disobedient when he tried to insist she give him the respect due to every *morani*? These thoughts, these disturbing comparisons, were constantly in his mind.

'Mind you, I think she's terrified of you,' Coll said with a chuckle, which became a cough that left him gasping and blue in the face.

'Take soft breaths,' Ole Sadera told him, mimicking what he'd heard Katherine say numerous times.

'Yes, nurse,' Coll replied, stifling another cough. 'But you should get to know her better,' he went on. 'Kira, I mean. It will soon be time for you to marry.'

Kira haunted Ole Sadera, and he knew why. Her resemblance to Nashilo was both startling and unnerving. When he found himself thinking of her as he had Nashilo, of the warmth and firmness of her body, he felt guilty and depressed. He would sulk and berate himself.

He wished he could return to the savannah, to Entorror, for peace of mind and to regain some perspective on what was important, but he had no such option. His duty was to stay with Coll until Katherine's return. Perhaps during his visit to the lawyer in Mombasa — a mysterious and exotic place — he might be able to forget Kira and regain his senses.

Coll had recovered some composure.

'Come,' Ole Sadera said. 'It was foolish to bring you out here. You must return to bed.'

Coll coughed again, but stood with Ole Sadera's assistance. 'All right, I'll go,' he said. 'But don't you forget what I said about Kira. You should at least give it some thought.'

When the *morani* arrived at Katherine's farm, he liberated memories long cloistered in Kira's mind — memories that had lingered, barely perceptible and never analysed, of the time she was a child, before she was stolen away from her home. By his mere presence he reminded her of what it meant to be Maasai.

He became the catalyst to coalesce pieces of childhood memories from fragments gathered from overheard conversations between Katherine and George Coll. These recollections were of the Maasai as a proud people. Not in the narrow sense as was the case for many of the *moran* — a kind of swaggering conceit acquired through personal conquests — but a quiet assurance that to be Maasai was to be a member of the most fortunate of people.

The Maasai had retained their way of life despite the interference of the white invaders. The Maasai had not succumbed to the influence of any tribe — white or black — avoiding the threat to their heritage that change might bring. To lose their identity — and their faith in it — was a price too high to pay, regardless of the inducements that white civilisation offered.

According to Coll, when the Maasai ignored the temptations of white civilisation, the government tried to convince them to forego some of their more inconvenient habits, such as their total lack of interest in commerce. There was a chronic shortage of labour in East Africa and native muscle was the answer. Unless the Maasai became attracted to what they could purchase with rupees, as the other tribes were, they could not be induced into the workforce to earn the cash to acquire those things. When the Maasai continued to find no good reason to work for money, the government imposed hut taxes and poll taxes, to force them to acquire the rupees to pay them.

Kira had occasionally seen Maasai people during her visits to Nairobi, and had sometimes been tempted to make contact, but seeing her in Katherine's presence caused them to turn away. Perhaps they assumed she was one of the unfortunates who had sold her heritage for the material benefits of the white society.

Unlike Kira, Parsaloi knew exactly what it was to be Maasai. In his case, it was drawn from the tradition of all those who had gone before him — that long line of brave men who had fought for the Maasai way of life through the centuries; the millennia. A *morani*'s highest honour was to die protecting what was important for his people's survival. As she grew to know him better, Kira also became aware that behind that confidence in the rightness of Maasai culture as a whole was a strong sense of self-belief. She could sense that Parsaloi had no doubts about his role in life. He understood it, and took great pride in achieving it.

Coll said that Parsaloi's age set would probably be the last to know what it was to wage war against an enemy tribe. The British would see to that. Parsaloi and his age mates would be the last Maasai warriors. This made it all the more important to guard what remained of the old ways.

Seeing Parsaloi so confident of his role in life made her ache to return to her people, but she knew that making the transition from her present situation with Katherine would be difficult. She needed a guide to make that journey.

Parsaloi was a man who could not easily be ignored. She sensed the terrible determination in him. And he was a man to be admired. He had a reluctance to smile, but when he did, it illuminated his face. It appeared that, having escaped, his smile relished the freedom, playing in his eyes and softening his otherwise serious temperament. He was to be feared and admired, but she had no doubt that, should she decide to make the choice, he was the one she needed to guide her on her journey back to Maasailand.

Coll struggled up through heavy layers of sleep to find he was alone. Only moments before Parsaloi had been there, hovering over his bed, mouthing words that he couldn't hear. Kira had appeared at his side. She too seemed worried, and he'd tried to ask why, but the effort was too great and he had slipped back into a dreamless sleep.

The late afternoon sky was alight with bold swathes of red and orange. Dusk: a time for reflection. When camped on the savannah at such times, he often thought it a time for regret. It signalled a day burned to ash and discarded like all the other yesterdays, each followed by another night with the stars mocking his loneliness. But from his bed in Katherine's room, where the lingering resonance of her perfume reminded him of her, it splashed the walls with colour and lent the room a warmth it lacked when she was not there. Here was a dusk filled with hope; a departing, but with a promise of renewal. The night would bring another day to an end; and George another day closer to Katherine's return.

He tried to recall how long she'd been gone, but with a start he realised he'd lost track of time. He would ask Parsaloi to remind him when he came in. The Maasai was sure to tease him about it, but a man with so much time on his hands and so little to do while regaining his strength was apt to forget. He scolded himself for his idleness. He felt he should be out of bed, working on improving his strength. He'd spent so much time in bed in recent days that to lift an arm was an effort.

He vowed that tomorrow would mark a new start to his fitness program. He would begin with the walks that he and Parsaloi had recently ceased taking. Then he would drive the cart into town to meet the Thursday train, or whatever the next train from Mombasa might be, and give Katherine a surprise.

She was the joy of his life, and every day since they had been reunited he had thanked God for the blessed relief she brought to his loneliness. Before he met Katherine he had filled his days, the better to endure them. Now the very idea of life without her was inconceivable.

The light was fading faster than usual. He decided to go to the window to see the last of the day. He tried to lift his head from the pillow, but nothing remained of his strength. All he succeeded in doing was setting his heart racing.

He closed his eyes for a brief rest before making another attempt to see the sunset before it was gone.

The train from Mombasa rolled into Nairobi station amid the usual mêlée of porters, welcoming family and friends, touts and hawkers, and the idly curious natives from out of town. Katherine passed the soft leather bag she used as a suitcase out the window to a waiting porter, and jammed her handbag under her arm.

A moment later she was in the jostling, colourful crowd, forcing her way towards the platform exit and the array of waiting hire conveyances.

The distinctive Ali Khan, in his turban and knee-length gaiters, gathered her bag from the porter and assisted Katherine up into the seat of his open buggy. Ali knew most people within twenty miles of Nairobi, and could therefore distinguish between the lucrative upcountry fares and the small pickings from the townsfolk. When Katherine was settled, Ali touched the tip of his whip to first one, then the other mule, and they trotted off.

The same skills that enabled Ali Khan to spot a good fare equipped him with the best nose for news in Nairobi. There wasn't a scandal in the town or rumour worth repeating that he didn't know about. Nor was he too stingy to spread it about for free. As they rode along Government Road, past River Road and onto the road to Fort Hall, Katherine braced herself for the talkative driver's onslaught. She was impatient to get home to the farm and George, and wasn't interested in hearing any of his gossip. However, Ali remained unusually silent, and she thought he must have concerns of his own to ponder.

Having been alone for years, the brief time Katherine had shared with Coll had spoiled her for his company. She had been away from him for only seven days, but she ached to be in his arms again, to know that the enormous emptiness that had been her life since Bill died was now filled.

It wasn't until they reached the outskirts of the town at Limuru Road that Ali Khan broke his inordinately long silence, and that was merely to comment on the weather and to enquire how it had been in Mombasa. After that, he fell silent again, and remained so for the entire journey.

Katherine's trip to Mombasa had been a success. David Morrison — a much younger man than she had expected — had agreed to take the Maasai's case and said he'd been warned by Dr Lewis that the Maasai would pay his fees in cattle. The whole idea seemed to amuse him, and the case itself was consistent with his view that the natives should be free to work their land neither encumbered by the administration nor harassed by settlers who coveted it. He promised to commence work on the injunction immediately, warning her it would take time but was their only chance if they were to prevent the continuation of the resettlement. Meanwhile, he would work on their main case, which would require him to travel to Nairobi to meet Ole Sadera and gather witnesses and all the facts.

The dusty green acacia trees on the Limuru road hung hot and limp in the midday heat. Sunbirds twittered in the grass, and superb starlings and waxbills chattered and darted among the undergrowth. Ali Khan's silence seemed strained. Katherine put it from her mind. She was merely anxious to be home.

As they turned into the dirt track to the farm, where the soft dusk masked the clatter of cartwheels, she sensed something in the air that gave her an uneasy feeling. She couldn't be sure what it was — something subliminal. She strained all her senses, and just as she thought it was her imagination playing tricks on her, she heard an unusual sound. It came through the trees, wafting on the hot, still air. An animal sound, like nothing she'd heard before. It wafted and was gone, and then it was there again. It made the hair on the back of her neck stand up.

Ali drove the cart out of the forested entrance to the property and into the clearing leading to the farmhouse.

It appeared that the staff had gathered to meet her. But how did they know when she would be arriving?

The sound, now recognisable as a moan, a lament, droned across the clearing. It was Wanjira, and she suddenly knew what it was that had awakened her anxiety. The feeling had been there since joining the Limuru road, perhaps before that. When she climbed into Ali Khan's silent cart, she should have known something was wrong.

Now it was here, before her. Wanjira and the field staff standing outside the house, lined up along the veranda, Kira waiting at the bottom of the steps, Parsaloi coming from the house, down the steps, carrying a rolled blanket.

A body.

CHAPTER 50

After the ordeal of Coll's burial, the train journey promised a diversion to lift Ole Sadera's spirits. The train headed east and south across wide yellow grasslands, crossing the Athi River under the gaze of the brooding Endoinyo Narok. It clattered across the Kapiti Plains, home to his cousins, the Kaputiei Maasai, sending dense herds of wildebeest, kongoni and zebra galloping away through the dust and heat.

He had often seen the Uganda Railway locomotive from a distance, trailing long streamers of smoke on its snaking path to the crest of the Rift Valley escarpment, or huffing above the valley floor in a straight line from Elmenteita to Nakuru.

At Nairobi station, Katherine assured him that the train almost never came off the rails, but after a short climb out of Nairobi, the train gathered speed. Inside the cabin, where it was noisy, dusty, and a little unnerving, he wondered if Katherine had ever been on it when it travelled quite so fast and erratically.

When the initial excitement of the journey subsided, and the train settled into a steady rolling gait, the monotony allowed his mind to wander back to the day he lowered Coll's weightless body into the hole on the hill above the house. Katherine, red-eyed, her jaw set so tight that her voice was as brittle as dried maize husks, read from a black book while he and Kira stood at her side. The Kikuyu farm workers fidgeted and didn't know what to do with their hands. When Katherine closed the book, they shuffled away, undecided what to do next. With no indication from Katherine, they returned to their village.

After three hundred jolting, smoky miles, Ole Sadera had had enough of train travel. At the outset it had been an exciting adventure, but after a day and a half he just wanted it to end. Morrison had made the journey to Nairobi for their initial meeting, but said it was Ole Sadera's responsibility thereafter to meet with him in Mombasa, where the court case would ultimately be held. It was not a prospect that he faced with any enthusiasm.

He shared the tiny second-class compartment with an Indian family who had sneaked nervous glances at him for the entire first day's travel. Now they almost completely ignored him.

Outside the carriage was the Taru Desert — a wasteland of thornbush. No tree, rock or hill interrupted the monotonous, endless, completely flat, grey, desiccated scrub. In the cleared strip to each side of the train ran a narrow bald patch of red dirt, littered with the accumulated jetsam of thirteen years. Unlike the plains near Nairobi, there were few signs of any game. In the Taru, Ole Sadera suspected, survival would be even more difficult than in Ngatet.

He must have dozed off, for when he awoke the world had dramatically changed. The Indian children were chattering and he followed their pointing fingers out the carriage window to find a village where vibrantly dressed Swahili people moved among rows of food barrows piled high with pawpaws, sweet potatoes, coconuts and pineapples.

When his eyes ran ahead, the train tracks swept down a steep green hillside garlanded with banana trees, mangoes and palms. Beyond was a jungle of greenery, tumbling down, down, to where a trestle bridge spanned a flat stretch of water separating the island of Mombasa from the mainland.

On the far side of the island, an arc of white coral sand marked the boundary between the town, which seemed to huddle under the ramparts of an old stone fort, and the harbour, where a great many tall masts swayed in the ebb of the tide, and colourful sails flapped in the breeze.

But it was the immense expanse of incredibly blue water out even beyond the ships that astounded Ole Sadera. It filled the entire breadth of his vision, broken only by a long effervescent line of whitecaps that ran to the north and south further than he could see. Towards the east there was nothing to break the blue vastness until it joined the sky under a towering column of white clouds. It was impossible for him to comprehend the ocean or explain it in any terms he knew. It seemed to be a trick of the light — an illusion. A puzzle without solution.

Ole Sadera swallowed hard. He had known before he began that the battle to win Maasailand would be different from any he had fought. The whites and their courtroom had the advantage over him, but he had never shrunk from a contest. What did give him cause to reflect upon the wisdom of his decision to do battle alone was the theatre of war; a more exotic, treacherous, beautiful land he could not have imagined.

The train seemed to pause on the ridge; perhaps, like Ole Sadera, to reconsider the folly of taking the plunge down to Mombasa — a town caught in the very centre of that exotic world. But neither he nor the train had a choice. George Coll had fought hard to defend the Maasai's right to fair treatment and what remained of Maasailand. He had fought to the death, and if this was a cause to which a white man could offer his remaining days, it was a cause that Ole Sadera had to fight.

The train began its cautious descent.

David Morrison considered Ole Sadera the most unusual of the many odd clients he had represented in his ten years in British East Africa. In tropical Mombasa, far from the dry, grassy plains of his homeland, but still wearing his bright red *shuka* and long braided hair, the Maasai warrior looked like some exotic bird perched at the door of its cage, ready to fly away.

'It's good to see you again, Parsaloi,' he said, trying to get his client to feel at ease.

The Maasai nodded.

'How are you enjoying Mombasa?'

Another nod.

It wasn't encouraging. Morrison knew he would need an articulate plaintiff on the stand if he were to have a chance of winning the case.

He pressed on. 'I have some good news, Parsaloi. Our injunction has been granted.'

His client remained unmoved.

'That means the government must cease evicting the Maasai from the northern reserve, at least until we get our hearing in the High Court,' he added. 'Do you understand? The Maasai can stay in the northern reserve until the case comes before the court.'

Ole Sadera nodded. 'Yes, that is good.'

On their previous meeting in Nairobi, Morrison had been impressed by the Maasai's intelligence, but more particularly by his quick understanding of the basics of the British legal system. It surprised him that Ole Sadera was not more enthusiastic now. He knew about the injunction and its importance. Although the delay had been inordinately long, when the news finally arrived just a few days ago Morrison had been elated.

'Don't you understand, Parsaloi? The court has told the government it must stop moving the Maasai out of the northern reserve. It's wonderful news.'

'While we were waiting for this paper,' Ole Sadera said, 'the *askaris* never stopped pushing, pushing.'

'I know, I know. But now they must. We've won.'

'No.'

Exasperated now, Morrison said, 'Parsaloi, you don't understand. This is not our claim for redress and compensation; it's just like a restraining order while we prepare our case for the High Court next month. I tried everything. You wouldn't believe how hard I fought to get this injunction pushed through. I'd begun to think someone was pulling strings, but now all's well. You should be very pleased. We've had a win!'

'I am pleased because you have the paper, if that is what you wanted. But it is not a victory as you believe.'

Morrison sighed, beginning to think he'd misjudged Ole Sadera's capabilities.

'I went to the north as you asked me,' the Maasai continued.

'Yes. Good.'

'I travelled across the Laikipia Plateau for many days. There is no one there.'

'No one where? What do you mean?'

'I mean, there is no one in Entorror, Mr David. The *askaris* have already chased away the last of the Maasai. No one is in Entorror. No Purko. No Damat. No Keekonyokie. No Kaputiei. All the Maasai have gone. Gone to Ngatet.'

Katherine thought that Bill would understand. The quiet place under the old African olive tree was the right place to bury a friend as well as a husband, but the new grave under the tree needed a headstone, and for a long time she couldn't find the words to put on it. They had to be respectful, but not formal. They had to say something about George but balance what was written on the stone above Bill's grave.

She kneeled at her husband's gravestone, tracing her fingertip along the sharply chiselled letters.

Here lies William Alexander Wallace
24 October 1854 — 4 March 1903
Loving Husband of Katherine
Father of Billy
Taken by Lion

Taken by lion. It encapsulated Bill's life perfectly. Those who knew him would not doubt it, and those who didn't would suspect that beneath the cracked, bare earth lay the remains of an impulsive, reckless adventurer. And they'd be correct.

But George was not Bill. The succinct phrase that would epitomise his life took a long time to come.

He had been a coal worker, a student, a stock inspector and a game warden, and had not especially excelled at any of these roles.

He had despised the injustices committed by the government yet was a staunch supporter of Britain and its empire.

His passionate fight for fair treatment of the Maasai had consumed all the energy he'd had to spare. When it was gone, he withered.

Like George, she had no more energy for causes. She felt guilty about leaving the continuing fight to Ole Sadera, but she had nothing more to give. It was enough to lift her head from the pillow each morning to face another empty day. Even the effort to find a caption for the headstone took its toll. She had spent many long hours searching for the phrase, but eventually returned to her first choice, which had always been right for him.

She moved to the foot of George's grave. The newly turned red soil was still fresh and moist from a morning shower. She checked the new headstone against Bill's, now nine years old. They were of equal size, which pleased her. Her words, now chiselled into the granite, pleased her too:

Here lies George Alfred Coll
23 October 1875 — 14 December 1912
A man who cared

*   *   *

As a child in a tribe that considered his mother a foreigner and himself a freak, Ole Sadera learned how to conceal himself, either literally or metaphorically, so as to avoid the other boys' heartless jokes and treatment. Later, when his stepfather died, leaving him an orphan, he learned how to survive among strangers. But nothing had prepared him for the utter aloneness he felt in Mombasa.

The town seemed much larger than Nairobi, with strange houses of white stone huddled together along narrow alleys, but it was impossible to conceal himself in Mombasa. The elegant, finely dressed Swahili looked at him with curiosity, if not with suspicion and hostility. There was not another Maasai in the town, and the local tribes — the intensely dark, fine-featured Galla, the aloof Chonyi, and the nameless others — ignored him.

It was not only the strangeness of the place that caused him to feel cut off and alone. When Mantira claimed that Ole Sadera had lost the support and possibly even the respect of his age mates, he had felt a void open between him and his people. Now he needed to know if he had the support of his brothers before he could continue with the court case. It would require courage; not the courage needed to face a physical threat, but courage similar to that required to face the indefinable menace of the vast expanse of water beyond the breaking waves.

Despite his fear, Ole Sadera was drawn to the ocean by some morbid fascination. It held him spellbound, in the same manner as facing a lion during a hunt with nothing but a spear and *simi* for protection. Beautiful, powerful, deadly. Dangerously potent. It moved. It changed colour. Undulating, leaping, beginning, ending. At times it was a dazzling white that rivalled the billowing clouds. In other places it was the pale green of a dry-season dawn, but out towards the thundering breakers it was a deep blue-green — the colour of the sky before a storm.

The water lapped soft and warm at his feet, but beneath him the sand shifted and wriggled beneath his toes as if it were a living thing. The ocean washed this way and that like an endless flood, sucking the golden grains from beneath his soles, which sank deeper and deeper until he felt the sand would swallow him.

The pulsing surge of wavelets ran scudding to shore as if in fear of the roaring, breaking surf that burst and boomed on the reef beneath a halo of mist. Where the wavelets had been, the ripples made identical patterns in the wet dead sand. The very earth was shaped by the ocean's power.

Moving, changing, swirling.

He learned from others that the ocean ran as far as the eye could see, and even after it met the sky still it continued. He had been told that men in ships sailed across it for many days, even months, to arrive finally in England, or India, or even to islands — mere specks flung into the unimaginable vastness of water.

Ole Sadera knew with certainty that a man could surely lose himself out there, forgetting where he'd come from, where he had intended to go. There was nothing he could imagine to compare with it. The sea was a beautiful, exciting and deadly place.

Only once did he approach the water's edge at night — the ultimate test. At night the beast was even more threatening. His imagination played tricks with his eyes so that its depths revealed glimpses of unspeakable monsters beneath the innocuous wave tops dancing with phosphorescence. If he could wade into that black abyss, he could face any trial that lay ahead.

He edged into the dark mass, noting the reflections of the bobbing lights on the fishing dhows heading out to sea. The cool water crept up his thighs until he was standing waist-deep in it. His flesh tingled in anticipation of imminent attack, but the creatures respected his courage and spared him.

He felt hardened by the exercise. He could now face the court and face his brothers — in both cases to defend his claim that Entorror belonged to the Maasai.

CHAPTER 51

Ole Sadera left Mombasa with a feeling of relief, but with mixed emotions about calling on Katherine Wallace. The farm was a familiar landmark, but it held sad memories that came vividly back to mind when he emerged from the acacia thicket and saw the hill where the olive tree stood and where he had placed the body of George Coll.

He'd called his friend Swara because of the resemblance between the gazelle's soft call and Coll's repetitious cough. But only now did Ole Sadera realise there was another likeness, and perhaps the real reason the nickname had come to mind. Like the gazelle, George had lived under the constant threat of inglorious death. When felled by one of its many predators, the gazelle died not in a bloody and noble combat with a more powerful enemy, but pitifully, by suffocation, as the predator slowly crushed its windpipe. A life cannot flourish under such a threat, but, like the gazelle, George Coll lived his life as best he could until the stalking, ever-present predator took him.

And it wasn't until Coll's inert body lay in his arms like a dried leaf that Ole Sadera also realised how alike they had been. Neither of them had allowed many people to get close to them during their lives; both knew what it was to feel isolated and alone. George chose his isolation to conceal his illness. Ole Sadera had no choice. The ill omen surrounding his birth kept most at their distance.

He found Katherine hoeing the small maize patch beside the barn. The maize was almost ready for harvest. Even Ole Sadera knew it was not necessary to hoe it at that stage, but suspected that Katherine had need of the familiarity of routine.

Katherine was surprised to see him, and greeted him with polite constraint. Then she reached out a hand to touch his arm. 'I'm sorry, Parsaloi. I'm a little distracted with all this . . . this farm work. It's good to see you.'

He said yes, he was pleased to see her too, and they made a stumbling attempt at conversation, but between them was the strangeness of people who shared nothing but their grief. The silence grew, widening his discomfort. He felt Katherine was also desperately searching for words. He decided it was better to dispense with the polite formalities and get to the matter that had brought him there.

Katherine was taken aback. 'You want me to attend the court with you?' she gasped.

'If it is possible,' he said. Her reaction made him regret raising the matter. 'It would be good to have someone there who knows about the Maasai. Who knows what I should do.'

'But Mr Morrison . . . doesn't he tell you what you must say?'

How could he explain that it was not only the court that confused and worried him, but the entire world he had been removed to, where everything resounded with strangeness. Even the earth and water were unnervingly odd. In the coming weeks, he would have to face the courtroom too. He was secretly terrified of the impending ordeal.

'I thought you might want to be there. It is what George started. I think he would be there with me, if he were —'

'Parsaloi, I understand how you must feel. Down there in Mombasa alone. But I . . .' She looked around as if the farm might offer her an answer. 'I can't be there for you. I can't leave all . . . this.' She shook her head and looked distraught. 'No, that's not true,' she said. 'It's just that I can't be involved with all those . . . those other matters. I need to be alone. Just here on the farm for a while. I . . . I can't go back to fighting for other people, other causes. Not just now.'

He was immediately regretful of placing her in a difficult and embarrassing position because of his own weakness. To show he understood her feelings he gently touched her shoulder. It was lean, and as brittle as a bird's.

'It is nothing.' He was now anxious for it to end quickly. 'I go to Ngatet. I must meet with my age set brothers. I must tell them I will be speaking for the Maasai about our land, and what I say might cause trouble. I need their blessing before I can proceed.'

He had always believed that the eyes revealed what was in the heart. Katherine must have thought so too, for she forced him to turn away to avoid her probing gaze. A flicker of movement at the kitchen window coverings caught his eye. He turned quickly back to Katherine and asked how matters on the farm were.

She answered inattentively, saying they were good.

The discussion had made the atmosphere between them strained.

'So I must continue on my way,' he said. 'I have far to travel today.'

She nodded and said she understood.

There was nothing more to add, and he left her then, with the words of farewell more difficult between them than the greeting.

He marched out the home enclosure gate, ignoring the figure behind the window of the farmhouse.

During his journey to Limuru, he had dwelt on the matter of Kira, who was a cause of great discomfort to him. He still harboured the guilt caused by his attraction to her, and had determined to avoid speaking to her during his visit.

When he was safely away, about to enter the acacias, he looked back at Katherine. She was still standing at the edge of the crop, hoe in hand, staring into the maize.

Kira watched the exchange between Parsaloi and Katherine from the kitchen window. She hoped he would seek her out, but he trudged up the road without so much as a backward glance towards the house.

Kira was angry and hurt. She agonised over her decision for several minutes before dashing from the house.

She met Katherine on the pathway and they shared a wordless exchange. Katherine's resigned sadness softened and a smile came to her eyes, if not to her lips. 'Go after him if you must, Kira,' she said, nodding her encouragement.

The young Maasai woman hesitated. She had been very conscious of Katherine's emotional burden since George Coll died. She didn't want to leave her if she was at all distressed by it.

'And don't forget what I've told you, my dear,' Katherine continued. 'It is your life. You can decide to return to your own people, or stay.'

Kira had not forgotten. There hadn't been a day since Parsaloi told her about her family that she hadn't considered the possibility. Two things stood in her way. The first was her concern for Katherine. The other was her inability to go back to the Maasai alone. She was afraid of what she might find, and also that she might not be welcome. She wanted Parsaloi to take her back, but she didn't dare ask him.

Katherine took her hand and patted it. 'At least speak with Parsaloi. I think he needs someone to talk to. And if he asks you to go with him . . . Well, that's a decision only you can make.'

Kira kissed her on the cheek and dashed away, running up the path to the road, afraid she might already be too late to find him. When she reached the Limuru–Nairobi road, she could see no one in either direction.

Her heart was pounding in her chest so hard she could feel it in her ears. She bit her lip. Which way to go? She shifted her weight from one foot to the other, dancing about, unable to decide.

Parsaloi emerged from the bush to stand at the side of the road, where he planted his spear beside his foot and rested his weight on it.

His nonchalance maddened her. How could he play games in such a situation? She had a good mind to storm off. But she didn't.

'Why did you not come to the house?' she demanded.

'Does a *morani* take orders from a girl?'

'You could have at least said something after all this time.'

'There is nothing to be said.'

'Oh!' she spluttered, fighting to bring her anger and frustration under control. 'Where do you go now?' she asked more moderately.

'To Ngatet. I must speak with my Il Tuati and the others.'

'It is a long way.'

'Yes.'

'You have food with you?'

'Enough.'

'And water?'

'Yes.'

She searched her mind for something to say that would keep him there a little longer. Nothing came. 'Take me with you,' she said at last.

He was silent for so long she thought he was going to ignore the suggestion.

'No,' he said.

She had the absurd urge to fling herself at him; to strike him. She knew it was useless to argue, and remembered enough of Maasai behaviour to know the *moran* were unaccustomed to a woman disagreeing with them. To threaten their authority was an insult to their warrior status.

'When will you return?'

'When it is done. Maybe.'

'Maybe?' she said, trying not to let her anger rise again. She turned her back on him to show her disgust. When she turned back, he was gone.

Ole Sadera stood before the assembled Il Tuati warriors of the Purko Maasai, delaying the start to his address to let the anticipation and tension build.

This was the meeting he had threatened to have when he stormed off from his discussion with Mantira. He had been angry then, and shocked to hear Mantira say the Maasai would not support him in his fight — their fight — to regain their land. At the time, he had thought he could do what must be done alone, but now he knew otherwise. He needed to know that his people were behind him when he stood before the British court.

It was more than moral support. Morrison said it was very important that Ole Sadera found witnesses to bring before the judge; people who knew Maasai customs and could explain the Maasai's connection with their land.

And there was the matter of payment. Ole Sadera needed rupees that he didn't have, nor enough cows to sell to raise them.

On his long journey to Ngatet, he'd had the chance to reflect upon this moment; to plan carefully what he must say. He realised now that his people were afraid. Their world had been torn apart. Gone were the days when they could take their cattle to graze anywhere without fear or threat. They had seen their dominance crumble as the whites swept all ahead of them. In recent times, they had themselves been treated like cattle, pushed from one place to another. He knew that if they were to hold on to their land, the Maasai would have to stand united as they had in every battle. His Il Tuati still had fight in their blood. His task was to direct that energy towards a new way of doing battle. If the *moran* were convinced, the elders would not disagree.

He had chosen his time: dusk — a time the Maasai believed the spirits moved about in search of peace. It was a time people were careful of what they said. There was a saying that the spirits may be lost from sight but they are not deaf.

The warriors' long shadows fell at his feet as the red sun dropped towards the line of hills. Their faces were hidden in shadow, but Ole Sadera had chosen the position knowing it was more important for them to see his face than he theirs. He took a deep breath.

'Men of the Purko,' he began with a voice that carried to all. 'You know me. I am Parsaloi Ole Sadera. I am your brother. I come here to beg the help of the Il Tuati.

'We have fought our enemies in the past with spear and sword. Remember how we took the Loitai on the battlefield of Lailela Plains. They dared to test us, and we showed them the meaning of power. Do you remember the sweet taste of victory against the Kikuyu at the foot of Kinangop? Who could dare challenge the Il Tuati after such a victory?'

His age set brothers were warming to his words. Shouts of 'Yip! Yip!' came from a number of them.

'Today I come to ask you to again take to the field of battle, with me at your head.'

A ripple of excitement ran through the crowd like silk shimmering in the sun. More voices joined in the chorus of war cries.

'But this, my brothers, is a new battle. We have seen the coming of the British. They have changed our lives. Before that, we Maasai ruled our world. For the first time we have met an enemy who can match us on the battlefield. This does not mean we must surrender.'

A growl of agreement came from the Il Tuati.

'But it does mean we must change the way we make war. My battle plan will once again restore our pride; once again our warriors will dance in victory. Shall I tell you how?'

Their voices carried to the darkening hills.

'In every great army there is a weakness. That weakness, once found, will bring the army to its knees. I know the weakness of the enemy who will take our lands. The British can be defeated. Not by weapons, but by words.

'This time our weapons will not be the spear and *simi*. Our weapons will be the whites' own laws. The laws that are used to chase us from our land can be turned against them.

'Men of the Purko clan, we have always been first among the Maasai to take to the battlefield. But the new way of war does not mean we do not need courage. Men brave enough to stand before the enemy and defy them will win battles. This time we will fight our battle not on the savannah, but in courtrooms, in the very heart of the whites' *enkang*.

'Never mind that no blood will be spilt. Victory is ever sweet. Our words — your words — will cut the heart from those who would take our land.'

He paused, letting his message penetrate as he ran his eyes over the assembled warriors.

He raised his spear and shouted, 'Will you stand with me in this fight?'

A roar went up, sending the night birds into early flight.

CHAPTER 52

Cameron Moody quite enjoyed his infrequent visits to the Nairobi Club on the hill behind the governor's residence. As the editor of the protectorate's daily newspaper, he lacked the social status demanded for membership, which was usually reserved for senior public servants, leaders of the business community and members of the Legislative Council. For one reason or another, the settlers had chosen to take themselves off to the Norfolk. Moody suspected this quite suited the government club's membership who, as a result, were able to spend their leisure time untrammelled by the landed gentry with their petty grievances.

The large padded armchair creaked with the pleasing sound of fine leather as he took his seat in a quiet corner opposite the governor. The electric fan hummed overhead, and Moody was content to make small talk until the governor was ready to raise the matter he had called him there to discuss. As a newsman, he was not unfamiliar with the art of controlled leaks to the press. It would not be the first time a Nairobi Club member had used the confidential atmosphere of the club for an off-the-record chat.

They both fell silent as the waiter handed Moody his whisky and placed the governor's gin and tonic on the small table at his elbow.

After taking a sip of his gin, the governor said, 'When did we last have a drink and a chat, you and I, Cameron?'

'Year ago. Yes. November.'

'Hmm, how time flies.'

'Yes. Flies.'

Moody's clipped sentences were like newspaper headlines — short on prepositions and articles, definite or indefinite.

'Indeed. I thought it about time I bought you a drink, just to say I appreciate your good sense.'

'Hmm.'

'I don't believe we in government give enough recognition to civic-minded people such as yourself, Cameron. In matters of public interest, I mean. The thing that brought it to mind is that land case going on down in the High Court. You listed it in your Public Notices section.'

'Land case. Yes.'

'Some of these newspaper fellows would have made a meal of it. Good that you've kept it a bit quiet.'

'Quiet?'

'Yes. It wouldn't do to unsettle the settlers, so to speak. You know as well as I do that it would do no good at all to have a land claim come to the notice of farmers. Keeping it discreet will certainly go a long way. Well done.'

'Governor, not sure I —'

'Suppose it got out that the case had such repercussions? Imagine the sanctimonious outpourings from home. But there's no chance of the government losing this one. Can't afford to.'

'No chance?'

'Well, you never know. And imagine if it did. Where would land tenure be if everyone who had taken up leases lost them? It would be a disaster for the whole protectorate.' Edouard sipped his gin. 'And from what I've heard from the settlers — Delamere and his lot — they don't want to spread it about any more than you or I. Not a word of it. No need to panic anyone.'

'Not a word.'

'Just between you and me, the Maasai have a damn good case. I shouldn't be surprised if they turned the whole barrow over if they won. But they won't.'

'No.' Moody took a large gulp of whisky, trying to remain calm.

'Certainly don't want anyone getting too concerned about nothing,' Edouard said.

'No need to startle the horses.'

'Exactly, Cameron. I knew you understood the ramifications. It takes a really good newspaper man to know when to be discreet.'

Moody nodded. The tantalising front-page headlines danced before his eyes. It was flattering for the governor to think his small-town newspaper could rock the halls of power in faraway London, but it was obvious Edouard wasn't a newspaperman and didn't realise that the real story was not the court case, but the effect the outcome might have on the settlers. Many had fought hard for their excellent pastureland in the Laikipia Plateau. The Boer contingent had travelled halfway across Africa to stake their claims. They were a vitriolic bunch, and might even add a bit more colour to the story.

Moody decided to investigate the case further. A trip to Laikipia might add some human interest. He sipped his scotch and felt the familiar tingle of excitement as a huge story loomed in his mind.

If the Maasai actually did manage to win, all hell would break loose.

Cameron Moody left the Nairobi Club with a spring in his step. Sir Percy Edouard watched him go with barely concealed satisfaction. It had been almost too easy to plant the idea of the threat to land tenure in the editor's mind. From experience, he knew that Moody was an incorrigible gossip with no commitment to act responsibly in the public interest, although he always professed to do so.

He had no doubt the story would soon run in the *East African Standard*. The response from the settlers was predictable. There would be outrage and demands that the government do something. He would be sympathetic but say that the matters were *sub judice*.

The reaction would have an effect on every Maasai in the country, from the herders employed on white ranches to those attempting to make trade with or buy goods from the small stores around the reserves. With enough pressure, he felt the Maasai behind the case would be forced to return to their cattle.

He was now feeling better about the whole affair. If the press did not force the issue, the confidential information he had obtained from his attorney-general would.

The ceiling fans turned languidly above the Mombasa courtroom, but only a waft of hot air made it down to the sweltering occupants.

Ole Sadera shared a table with David Morrison, who sat behind a stack of papers and legal tomes. The court was about to hear Civil Case No 91 of 1912. The plaintiffs were Parsaloi Ole Sadera and seven others — all important age set representatives and elders whom Ole Sadera had convinced to join him in the challenge against the government. Their case was for the return of the northern reserve on the Laikipia Plateau, worth a million pounds. It also called for payment of five thousand pounds as damages for the failure to provide the road connecting the southern and northern reserves as promised in the 1904 agreement and compensation for the loss of stock as a result of the enforced move from the northern reserve — estimated at 97,910 cows and 298,829 sheep — at a cost of two hundred thousand pounds. The cost of depreciation to surviving stock was a further hundred thousand pounds.

When Morrison wanted to include the names of those who had lost their life on the Mau, Ole Sadera would not agree. He said it would not be proper to mention the dead in court. Morrison reluctantly agreed to remove the names of the deceased, but insisted the deaths remain a part of their case.

The defendants were the attorney-general of British East Africa and twenty others, including Seggi, the paramount chief, and the signatories to the 1911 agreement — none of whom were in attendance. It was ironic that Mantira was also a defendant although now in favour of the fight to recover their land.

Ole Sadera felt nervous and out of place. Morrison had persuaded him to wear underpants beneath his *shuka,* but had been unable to coax him into a shirt and jacket. The coarse woollen underpants itched and made him sweat. He tugged at them frequently, causing the judge, Mr Justice Hamilton — a hook-nosed man in a dusty, grey horsehair wig — to scowl down at him from his wood-panelled eyrie. It wasn't until late in the morning that Ole Sadera realised it was not he alone who displeased the judge — he seemed irritated by most things. He thought perhaps the judge also wore woollen underwear.

The morning session consisted of an endless listing of documents and statements.

Morrison made a spirited, but ultimately unsuccessful, attempt to have Maasai law applied in the case.

During the lunch adjournment, Morrison explained what had transpired that morning and what would now follow. He said he would outline their argument against the government and then begin to call in their witnesses and experts to support their case, which was that the 1911 agreement was void. This would restore most of their previous homeland, and was the best outcome they could expect.

The technicalities were lost on Ole Sadera, but he understood Morrison when he said that although the British had taken the Great Rift Valley from them in the 1904 agreement — land that had always been theirs — winning it back would be difficult. Their best hope was to make Entorror their battleground, in which case Ole Sadera felt the Maasai could feel vindicated.

Sir Percy Edouard unfolded the *East African Standard* and ran his eyes down the front page. The headline was two columns wide: COURT CASE UNSETTLES SETTLERS.

The story was typical newspaper sensationalism:

This reporter has learned through confidential sources that the court case now being heard in the High Court in Mombasa could destroy years of back-breaking toil expended by the hard-working people of the Laikipia Plateau and White Highlands.

It appears that the Maasai, encouraged by the Asian community and similar ungrateful recipients of the Empire's largesse, are about to tear up an agreement, freely given, to vacate land in the White Highlands.

The consequences of this dastardly act will be that the industrious white farmers will be thrown off their farms and cattle properties.

The story went on to report on mass meetings of Boer farmers in Eldoret and other farming communities elsewhere in the highlands. Temperatures, the article said, were running high, and there was talk of direct action.

The court report on page four was also helpful:

Proceedings in the High Court yesterday heard Sir Henry Mortimer for the defence demolish the poorly prepared case for the Maasai plaintiffs.

The expert witnesses called by Mr D J Morrison were described by Sir Henry as a rabble 'posing as civilised members of the protectorate who could be no more believed than a hornbill squawking in a coconut tree', which brought laughs from the gallery.

Case continuing.

Edouard smiled, then folded and closed the newspaper.

He had been careful to distance himself from the proceedings, but according to reports from his attorney-general, everything was going quite well. Morrison and his squawking hornbills had met their match.

In the crowded streets of Mombasa there were many strange faces, and skin of all colours and types: rough, mottled, scarred or burned red by the sun. Some had skin of pale brown, but many of the men working the ships on the wharf were blue-black, with swollen, purple lips and vivid markings on their face and body. There were those with skin almost as pale as that of the English supervisors. And foreigners with a yellow tint and eyelids half-closed and curled like a serval cat. Round or narrow, broad or square, the faces watched him pass as he watched them. Sometimes they exchanged comments in indecipherable languages.

The garments of the market-stall owners were the finest he'd ever seen. Bright *kikois* and white *dhotis* on the men; colourful printed *kangas* on their women.

Mombasa and its motley assortment of people were a never-ending source of fascination. It took Ole Sadera some time to realise that while he was studying them, they were equally curious about him.

His camp site on a muddy lane leading from La Perouse Road to nowhere in particular became a place of interest for small crowds of inquisitive spectators. After a week or so, only a handful of children appeared, staring bug-eyed as he cleaned the blades of his *simi* and spear, and watching him make his simple meals of maize and dried meat. But eventually his daily routine of cooking, eating and walking the two miles to Morrison's office became too predictable and even they abandoned him for more stimulating pastimes.

Thereafter, he remained in peace, except for the irregular appearance of a Swahili man who would follow him to and from Mombasa town. He never made eye contact, and initially Ole Sadera thought him simple-minded or somehow unable to quench his acute curiosity. After several days of the man's insistent attention, however, Ole Sadera became annoyed. But when he approached the Swahili man, he slipped away into the thick undergrowth of the pawpaw plantation on La Perouse Road.

This angered Ole Sadera, but his hunter's instinct advised caution. The Swahili showed skill in eluding him, which suggested that he was more than just a curiosity to the fellow. There was something more sinister in his presence. Ole Sadera felt like prey under the yellow eyes of a stalking predator.

CHAPTER 53

Ole Sadera was again on the front bench with Morrison as the court began to fill after lunch on the third day.

He had been in constant attendance throughout, and had tried to follow the proceedings with Morrison's help. Although he failed to understand the subtleties of much of the legal manoeuvring, he could read the body language and expressions of all involved and, through them, gauge the progress of their case. It was a contest of logic and persuasion — skills he had used all his adult life as an *olaiguenani*. He knew that his side was not doing well.

Ole Sadera admired Morrison for his tenacity and his optimism. He continued to rebound from setbacks even though his witnesses consistently failed to impress the court. He told Ole Sadera he had two big weapons yet to unleash. The first was his next witness, Ole Nchoko — a wily old leader of the Purko elders and a competent English-speaker. He was one of the seven other plaintiffs and had sworn an affidavit describing his personal losses. Ole Sadera had known the elder all his life. When he'd asked Ole Nchoko to stand with him in their fight, he'd known that the whites' court, with its wigs and pomp, would not intimidate the old man.

Morrison said his other key weapon would be Ole Sadera himself.

Unlike the Purko elder, Ole Sadera *did* feel intimidated by the court. He tried to fight it, but failed. There was nothing about the courtroom that was familiar or welcoming. The judge, defence lawyers, policemen and officials in wigs and gowns all appeared hostile and resentful of his presence.

He wasn't even able to overcome his discomfort outside the courtroom, where the people continued to stare at him and Mombasa enfolded him within its narrow laneways. Its high stone buildings pressed upon him, and their festoons of colourful woven awnings and trailing fabrics clutched at him as he passed. The town itself was on an island, surrounded by the threatening ocean. He sometimes walked to the bridge connecting the island to the mainland to reassure himself that his escape route was intact.

The court official called Ole Nchoko's name. The old man walked to the front of the court slightly stooped and with the aid of a stick. He wore an old pair of black trousers and a navy suit coat. He stood straight before the clerk as he administered the oath, then took his seat in the box.

Morrison was immediately on his feet, and strode confidently about the front of the court as he went through some preliminary questions. He established that Ole Nchoko was an elder of the Purko clan; a government-appointed chief; that he could speak Swahili as well as English, and had worked at times as a translator for the administration and others.

'Mr Ole Nchoko,' Morrison began, 'you are one of the plaintiffs in this case. Could you explain to the court the personal losses you suffered on your move from the northern reserve?'

'A quarter of my cattle die and half my sheep.'

'How did that happen?'

'The *askaris*. They make us hurry too much, and our cattle and sheep cannot find food and water. They grow very weak. The *askaris* they do not know why, they don't understand. Maybe they think it is diseases, or maybe they think they are too tired from too much walking, so they shoot it. Many of my cows, they die like this.'

'You say the *askaris* were to blame for many of your losses. Why didn't the government's supervisor do something about it? Why didn't he stop them?'

'Mr Coll, he was a good man. He very kind to us. He did everything for Maasai. But he is one man only. What can one man do when many men have guns?'

Morrison nodded. 'Indeed, Mr Ole Nchoko, what can any man do under such terrible circumstances? Can I now ask you to turn your mind to more general matters? You said in your affidavit that the southern reserve, Ngatet, was utterly unsuited to the northern Maasai's requirements. You listed five reasons. Can you explain these, please?'

'First there is no water in many places, so we cannot graze our cows there. And where there is water it is soon gone because there are few water holes and many cattle.

'And the sheep . . . the ground, everywhere, is not good for sheep.

'Next, there is the fell disease, which comes everywhere. Now it is in Entorror, which is a very bad thing, but before it was only in the south.

'Number four . . . There are many places where we cannot live because of tsetse fly and the sleeping sickness.

'And last, it is not our place. It is already the land for the southern Maasai.'

'What do you mean by that?'

'I mean, this land is already have too many people. Before, when the Maasai could have any land they want, the southern Maasai — the Loitai, some Damat, the Laitutok and others — they are in this place. They know it. They know it can have only few people and not good for too many cows, and they move around to follow rain and to follow grass.'

'Mr Ole Nchoko, I must ask, if this land is so utterly unsuitable, why did you move? Or more particularly, why did you agree to move?'

'Why did we agree?' The old man seemed to be asking himself the question for the first time. 'Did we agree? The government he come to us and say we must move. We say no, we do not want to move. We already agree to move once, when we go from Great Rift Valley. We ask, "Was that not enough land for you?" But they burned our *enkangs*. So we go.'

'But the Maasai *did* agree. You signed the agreement,' Morrison insisted.

'Some sign the agreement, yes. They say our paramount chief say we must sign and we must go. Now, I ask you, who is this paramount chief?'

He paused and the question hung in the courtroom. Morrison felt compelled to answer Ole Nchoko so that the interview could progress.

'It is the title given to the *laibon*,' he answered lamely.

'Yes, it is the *laibon*. He makes blessings of the cattle, and tells of the rain, and reading of omens. He is the *laibon*. Nobody is paramount chief of Maasai. Many stay in Entorror. Until the *askaris* come. Many *askaris* come with sticks to move the women and children, and they have guns in case the *moran* make trouble.'

'I understand what you're saying, Mr Ole Nchoko. You agreed to move but under duress.' Morrison glanced pointedly at the bench, nodding to the judge who sat impassively. 'Extreme duress,' he repeated for the benefit of the court reporter.

He referred to his notes. 'And returning to the matter of losses, do you know if any of the Maasai people died during the move?'

The old eyes glistened and Ole Nchoko took a deep breath before he answered. 'Yes,' he said. 'Many die. Many old people. Even the children.'

'And how did they die, Mr Ole Nchoko?'

'I do not know how they die, Mr Morrison. I can say some die in the Mara after we reach the southern reserve. But on journey to the south, I do not know. How does an old man die if he sleeps but never wakes? What kills a child in the highlands? Is it the cold? The wind? The rain? Can I say the mother killed the child because she could not feed it or could not keep it warm? Or do I say it was the foolishness of men who chase people onto the high places on Mau Escarpment? People who live long time in warm grass on savannah? I do not know why they die, but many, many die, it is true. Too many. I cannot count them.' He hung his head and slowly shook it. 'Even if government say I must know how many, I cannot count them. If I do not know their names, how can I know their number?' He smiled apologetically. 'I can tell you that seventy-nine die from the anthrax since we come to Ngatet. I know that number because district commissioner sends someone to count them. But on the Mau Escarpment? No one comes to count the dead, Mr Morrison. No one knows how many die up there.'

Silence hung in the almost tangible heat of the courtroom.

Ole Sadera's palms sweated, and his underwear clung to him and became entangled with his private parts as he made his way to the witness box to sit under the eagle-beak nose of the judge. His heart beat as if he were stalking a lion in long grass. His every sense became alert. He noticed for the first time the bent metal arm of the court stenographer's glasses, the loose tuft hanging from the judge's wig, and the click, click of the junior defence lawyer's pencil as he tapped it on his table.

David Morrison had tried to rehearse with him the questions he would ask and the answers he hoped Ole Sadera would give, but to no avail. The Maasai had no trouble answering, but when Morrison suggested he memorise the lines, using words like 'culture' and 'heritage' and 'tradition', Ole Sadera stumbled over them and he became confused and even more nervous.

In despair, Morrison told him to forget everything he'd memorised and to just answer from his heart. Ole Sadera now had difficulty remembering where his contrived answers ended and what had been in his heart to begin with.

Morrison went quickly through the preliminaries. Before Ole Sadera was able to compose himself, the lawyer was asking him questions about the Maasai and their way of life. As in the rehearsals, Morrison was particularly interested in why the Maasai were so attached to their land.

'It is our way,' Ole Sadera stammered, but was immediately dissatisfied with his reply. 'The Maasai way,' he added feebly.

Morrison nodded encouragingly. 'When you say the Maasai way, are you referring to your traditional way of life?'

'Yes.'

'And by your traditional way of life, are you referring to a tribal heritage, a tradition that goes back many generations, to when your people first arrived in the Great Rift Valley?'

Ole Sadera said he was, and managed to stumble through the remainder of Morrison's questions using single-syllable replies.

The defence counsel was offered the opportunity to question him.

Sir Henry Mortimer rose from his seat, gathered his black gown around himself and strutted to the front of the courtroom like a marabou stork picking his way amid the carrion. He approached the witness box wetting his lips, as if in anticipation of the feast he would have at Ole Sadera's expense.

'Mr Ole Sadera, I am having great difficulty keeping track of the meandering trail of fairy tales down which my learned colleague has been leading you. To begin with, what's all this about tradition and heritage? You Maasai have no written language, so what do those words really mean, I wonder. And as for you, I happen to know that you have had a very unfortunate life, haven't you, Mr Ole Sadera? You don't even have a tribe. You are not of the Purko tribe, as was suggested by Mr Morrison during his opening remarks, but one of the Laikipiak — a tribe that was wiped out by the Purko many years ago.'

Ole Sadera felt as if his very soul had been bared for all to see. Mortimer's use of the information in the hostile setting of the courtroom shook him to his core and emphasised his feeling of vulnerability.

'So how do you know what is tradition and what is nonsense?' Mortimer continued aggressively.

Ole Sadera was rattled. He stammered and glanced towards Morrison, who had paled and lost his reassuring smile.

'No tribe, and even if you had one, no history to relate. Where is your traditional culture then? How do you have knowledge of this preposterous claim that you have some . . .' Mortimer made a theatrical gesture with his arms, '. . . some mystical link to the land for all these years?'

'I . . . I can —'

'Precision, Mr Ole Sadera,' Mortimer said, interrupting. 'I would very much like you to be more precise about this so-called attachment to the land. In your own words, not those of Mr Morrison.'

'What is it you want to know?' Ole Sadera asked.

'Well,' Mortimer said, clasping his hands behind his back and strutting around the room, head down, as if deep in thought. 'In people who have a connection to their homeland, where their culture can develop over time and in the absence of invading cultures that might fracture that continuity, there is always a line of monarchs; its rulers. What evidence do you have of such a connection?'

'We have proverbs and songs to pass down the stories. And riddles meant to teach the children these things.'

'Riddles and songs,' Mortimer scoffed. 'My good fellow, the British Empire can trace its claim to England by a line of monarchs stretching back a thousand years from our present king, His Majesty King George V, to Alfred the Great who defended our land against the Vikings. That, my dear fellow, is heritage. I repeat, how can you, an illiterate orphan, know of history and heritage? The truth is you have no such knowledge. All your so-called history has been invented for you by Mr Morrison. Is that not correct, Mr Ole Sadera?'

'No. Mr Morrison knows nothing of Maasai history.'

'Quite likely, but it doesn't alter the fact that he has invented one for you and that you Maasai have absolutely no claim to the land you presently occupy. You are savages, wandering wherever the weather takes you, and following whatever brutal warlord presently powerful enough to grab control. I put it to you, Mr Ole Sadera, that your people are driven by the basest of instincts, and as for an intellectual connection to the land — utter balderdash. In fact, you have not the slightest notion of land tenure, and no concept of continuity let alone the refinements of primogeniture. In other words, you are nomadic wanderers with no knowledge of your previous rulers.'

Ole Sadera's blood was up. He no longer felt constrained by the formality of the courtroom. With great difficulty, he controlled his urge to leap the witness box railing and throttle

Mortimer for the sheer joy of removing his supercilious smirk. Instead, he took a deep breath.

'It is true; we move our cattle around as the new grasses come. Also to prevent overgrazing, which many whites fail to do. But we know where our land begins and ends. We know the boundaries of Maasailand.

'It is also true that we have no rulers like your English kings. We have no need for them. The Maasai choose people from their age sets. Each has a different task. The *moran* defend Maasailand. On the battlefield, they listen to age set leaders they have chosen for themselves. The warriors choose this man, the *olaiguenani*, because he is the best. He does not receive his honour because his father had it before him. He is chosen because he is special. Other leaders, chosen by elders, deal with things in the village. They make peace because people respect them because they are wise. They speak on ownership of cattle, and make arrangements for marriage, and set dates for naming children.

'We have no one ruler, that is true. We have no powerful king over all people as you have in England. But we have one important person who has his position through his father before him. He does not use power in battle or in village. He does not decide what must be done by anyone, but we believe he has special gift, and for that we listen to his advice. He is the *laibon*, and he guides Maasai people together. He see that rules through life are good. He make ceremonies to mark important times, like when a boy become a man and a warrior. He can sometime foresee disasters. For all these things we look to *laibon*, and he is the person we listen to about what you call heritage. He is connection with our land — Maasailand. We know all *laibons* that have ever lived. We know their names. We learn about them when we children, in riddles and rhymes you laugh about, and we know their names from now back to first man.'

He closed his eyes and began to recite with the rhythm and cadence of song. 'The *laibon* of all the Maasai is Seggi,' he chanted, 'who was the son of the *laibon* named Lenana, who was the son of the Great Laibon, Mbatiani. Mbatiani was the son of the *laibon* named Supeet, who was the son of the *laibon* named Kipepete, who was the son of the *laibon* named Parinyombi.'

Ole Sadera's resonant voice filled the stifling air trapped within the courtroom, continuing back through the generations to Ole Mweiya who came down from heaven and was found by Maasinta, the first Maasai.

There was a long moment of silence in the court.

Sir Henry Mortimer cleared his throat and fluffed among his papers before asking the judge for leave to approach the bench.

A whispered conversation took place.

The judge announced that the defence had brought an important matter to his attention and that there would be a short recess.

Everyone stood as the judge swept out of the courtroom, except Morrison, who sat open-mouthed, staring in awe at his client.

CHAPTER 54

Sir Percy Edouard, dressed in the simple clothes that a waterfront trader might wear while out to indulge some idle interest in court matters, sat in the back row of the near-deserted public seating section. He loosened the top button of his shirt and confirmed there was no one present who might recognise him.

He had arrived in time to join the court after an adjournment called by the defence team. His attorney-general had informed him of the tactic that had led to the adjournment and Edouard was there to experience the moment.

The judge rapped his gavel. 'The court recognises Sir Henry Mortimer for the defence.'

'Thank you, Your Lordship,' the wigged barrister said, rising from his chair. 'We have now heard testaments from so-called expert witnesses over the last four days, and it would appear there is no end to them. We were prepared to indulge the plaintiffs in the expectation there was something of substance in the offing, but alas, it appears we were mistaken. The point that we, for the defendants, made during the preliminary hearings of this case seems to have been lost on counsel for the plaintiffs. Our point, and one that Your Lordship will no doubt recall, was that this matter is not cognisable in this court. At the time we were persuaded to let the matter proceed in the hope that it might be proven to be so, but sadly it has not.

'It is our view, after receiving expert legal opinion from the colonial secretary and others, that whether or not the Maasai have rights to the land on the Laikipia Plateau is irrelevant. What needs to be determined is whether the agreements of 1904 and 1911 were contracts or, as we contend, treaties, in which case this court cannot hear the matter but must instead refer it to the Privy Council in Great Britain.'

Edouard smiled in satisfaction. His attorney-general's tactic had worked to perfection. There was no doubt that the High Court would have to concede its incompetence in the case. This would normally mean it would be reconvened in the Privy Council, but Edouard knew that the Maasai could not mount a challenge in London, or anywhere else.

Katherine drew the cart to a halt beneath a tree on the Limuru road. 'It's no good,' she said to Kira. 'I can't wait until we get home. I have to know.'

She opened the *East African Standard* to page four, spread it across her knees, and quickly scanned the story under the headline: MAASAI WIN EXTENDED RESERVE.

'What does it say?' Kira pleaded. 'Did we win?'

Katherine scanned the story to the end, looked at Kira, then went back to the beginning without uttering a word. The headline had conveyed a different impression to what she had gathered from the article. She read it again.

Kira implored her, 'Please read it to me, Katherine.'

'Oh, Kira, I'm afraid it's not good news.' But she took a breath and began to read it aloud, skipping over the author's comments on the various personalities and the legal technicalities involved until she reached the findings near the end of the piece.

'The Principal Judge of the High Court, Mr R W Hamilton, therefore concluded that the Maasai's case, whatever its dubious merits, could not be addressed by the High Court because the contested agreements of 1904 and 1911 were not contracts but treaties.'

'What does that mean?' Kira asked.

'Apparently it means that all that time and expense were for nothing. The judge says he can't make a decision on the land case because he can only make judgements on contracts, not treaties.'

'But at the top of the page it says the Maasai win.'

'A newspaperman's way of getting the settlers' attention, I'm afraid, Kira. He's referring to the larger reserve granted in the south. Nobody cares how much land the Maasai get down there, it's rubbish. The Laikipia Plateau is what they're interested in.'

'What will happen now?'

'It means that the case has to go to London before any decision can be made about the Maasai keeping the northern reserve.'

'Does that mean that Parsaloi has to go away?'

'If he wants to carry on the fight, yes.'

Kira turned her head quickly away, concealing her emotions.

'You care very much for Parsaloi, don't you, Kira?'

She was silent for some time before answering. 'I don't know what I feel, Katherine. Sometimes he makes me feel like a silly girl because I seem to do stupid things whenever he is watching. Other times he makes me so angry, I . . . I could beat him with a broom.' She paused, reflecting again on the question. 'All I know is that when I see him I get butterflies in my stomach, and now it scares me to know he might go away very far, for a very long time.'

'My, my,' Katherine said, putting her arm around the young woman's shoulders. 'It's worse than I thought.'

Governor Edouard sat back in his armchair and admired his surroundings. The Mombasa Club's dark wooden wainscoting and high moulded ceilings reminded him of some of the better clubs in London. It was certainly a cut above the best that Nairobi could offer, which he felt was fitting for the largest town and commercial hub of the protectorate.

Enjoying a celebratory drink with him was the government's counsel, Sir Henry Mortimer, and the attorney-general, Alan Warpole. Warpole had earned a reputation as a legal gutter-fighter after years doing battle with labour interests in maritime cases. He could match it with the best of the toughs on the wharves of Glasgow and London.

'Gentlemen,' Edouard said, raising his glass to them. 'Congratulations, and well done.'

They clinked glasses and allowed the waiters to light their cigars before Mortimer spoke. 'It was a good win, but let's not forget there could be an appeal.'

'Ah, that's where I have the advantage, Henry,' Edouard replied enigmatically. He didn't want to reveal his secret too soon.

'What do you mean, Percy? What have you heard?'

'I particularly enjoyed the final words of His Worship's judgement. Didn't you?' Edouard asked. '*Dismissed with costs. Splendid.*' He smiled and took a puff on his cigar.

'Surely the protectorate's not so short on cash that it matters?' Mortimer said.

'Not at all. But I happen to know that the Maasai are.'

'Really?'

'Indeed. That's why I was keen that you draw out proceedings for as long as possible. They are broke, gentlemen. You don't have to worry about an appeal. We won't hear from them again.'

'That's a relief,' Mortimer said.

'A relief! Why do you say that?'

'Frankly, Percy, I would have preferred to fight the case on its merits under contractual law. Mind you, the way things were going, we really had no choice but to use the treaty defence. The statements from the last two witnesses were telling. I was beginning to think we were done.'

'Well, regardless of all that, we won,' Edouard said with finality.

'Perhaps,' Mortimer countered.

'What do you mean, perhaps?'

'If they take it to the Privy Council I think we could be in trouble.'

Edouard sat forward in his chair. 'Good lord, Henry, what are you saying?'

'I'm saying that if the Maasai do take up the treaty issue, the Privy Council is an altogether different matter. For a start, they will look at precedents, and I happen to know of one that will interest them. It's a similar case of native title, called the Treaty of Waitangi. It was between the British Crown and the Maori chiefs on the North Island of New Zealand. The treaty gave the Maori the rights of British citizens and the right to ownership of their lands and other properties.'

Edouard sat back in his chair, ashen-faced. 'Good lord,' he said again.

The attorney-general waved it off with a dismissive hand. 'A lot of water to flow under the bridge before we get to that situation.'

'Actually, Alan,' Mortimer said, 'the Maasai are only one step away from the Privy Council if they choose to take it there. That step is the Court of Appeal here in Mombasa, where they will probably lose, but it won't affect their rights to go on to the Privy Council.'

Edouard swung around to his attorney-general. 'Are you aware of this, Alan?'

'Of course I am, but what is the chance that this illiterate rabble will take it that far?' Warpole ran a finger down the scar that traced a thin line from his ear to his chin. 'It will cost them a fortune. Or more importantly to them, it'll mean selling a large number of cows. Don't worry about it, Percy. I've had a man keeping an eye on things. That Maasai chap's like a duck out of water. He and his lot don't have the heart for a fight.'

'We *are* talking about the Maasai here,' Mortimer reminded him. 'The most ferocious tribe in this part of the world.'

'Irrelevant,' snapped Warpole. 'They'll not go any further with it. I'll guarantee it.'

'You'd better,' Edouard said with a cold smile. 'If the Maasai win this case, we're done for. I don't need to remind you what mistakes of this nature have meant for our predecessors.'

'Don't forget there are other ways to win an argument,' Warpole offered. 'There are people — let me call them *organisers* — who can assist in matters of this kind. A few rupees placed in certain hands can achieve wonders.'

Edouard fixed his attorney-general with an icy stare. 'I hope so, Alan, because should you fail me, you can forget your pension. All I could guarantee you would be a new posting too hideous to contemplate.'

A grey sky. The oppressive damp blanket of humidity. It was not a day to lift the spirits. A dismal drizzle pitted the flat uniformity of the sea, and a rivulet of rain ran down Ole Sadera's cheek to his chin, where it clung for a moment before dropping to his chest.

He was at the water's edge. Barely a ripple disturbed the sheet of silver that spread across the harbour. He had almost conquered his apprehension about that placid stretch of water between Fort Jesus and the lighthouse — benign in its tranquillity at the shore; so menacing where the harbour met the immensity of the ocean. Breakers rose there, relentless monuments of water that inexplicably lifted from the surrounding expanse to hurl themselves endlessly to a foamy death on the reef. He searched for a rhythm that would announce their arrival. Six heartbeats. Seven. Sometimes five. He felt within a hair's-breadth of understanding them, but each time he did, another anomaly appeared.

It was like his experiences with British justice. He felt always on the brink of understanding it, but never quite succeeded. When Frederick Jackson had found in his favour after the retribution raid at Kedong many years ago, it had seemed clear: the guilty would be exposed; the righteous vindicated. Now he was confused. He had returned to Morrison's office earlier that day to try again to understand how the men who had driven them from Entorror had won in the courtroom. Morrison again explained it in some detail, but Ole Sadera was at a loss. A technicality, Morrison had said. It meant nothing.

Ole Sadera turned to retrace his steps to the town, and his camp. As had become his routine, he scanned for the Swahili man who kept watching him at a distance. He thought he had seen him again as he left Morrison's office to walk to the beach. He had a large black umbrella, but had disappeared as Ole Sadera headed towards him.

Now there was a red umbrella, and a figure approaching him from the sea wall. As she drew nearer, he recognised Katherine Wallace.

'Hello, Parsaloi,' she said, holding out her hand.

'Missus Katherine. You are here.'

'I read about the case in the newspaper. I thought I would be coming to celebrate your success. I'm sorry it went wrong.'

'You have heard?'

'Yes, I've just come from Mr Morrison's office. He told me I might find you here.'

'Thank you for coming.'

'Kira is with me.'

He ran his eyes along the line of waterfront shops.

'She's in the guesthouse. She didn't want me to tell you she had come with me.' He made no comment, so she continued. 'I believe she's fond of you, Parsaloi. But she's afraid of you.'

Ole Sadera didn't want to think of the young woman with the tantalising and strangely familiar smile. He tried to keep control of his thoughts by turning to face the water.

'This is a strange place, Missus Katherine. Do you not feel it? There is something in the movement of the water . . .'

'Yes, the sea can be very calming,' she said.

It was not the description he had in mind, but it served to divert the conversation. He didn't want to discuss Kira with her, certainly not now that his mind was so full of other problems.

'What do you plan to do now?' she asked.

'We have lost.'

'Yes, but Mr Morrison thinks you will win on appeal.'

'He has told me the same, but I do not know what to do. I am defeated.'

'Oh, no, Parsaloi. You aren't defeated. This is just a setback. You have a good case. You must fight it.'

'Fight it,' he said, nodding. 'If only I could. But it is like fighting a . . . a . . . spirit. There is nothing there. I cannot defeat what I cannot see. I know nothing of these battles. I must go back to Maasailand.'

'What about the people back home? Didn't you say you had great difficulty convincing them to fight it in the first place? And now they have given you their support. You can't walk away.'

Ole Sadera, agitated, took a few paces away, then turned back to face her. 'Missus Katherine, I don't know what to do.

427

What do I know of British courts? While I am here, my people are starving in Ngatet. I feel I have been playing games while they are fighting to survive. I must go back.'

'The appeal,' she said. 'Just go on to the appeal. There are too many people relying on you. They have faith in you. George had faith in you. You have to go to appeal. If you are defeated there, then I agree, it's lost.'

'It is already lost. Mr Morrison has asked for his money, and I have no more to give.'

CHAPTER 55

The flash of red caught Ole Sadera's eye, and was immediately lost in the sea of white *dhotis* and many-patterned *kangas*. A moment later, it emerged again, the throng parting for the man in the red *shuka* as they might for a swaggering buffalo.

Mantira's wide white smile was revealed as soon as he spotted him, and only then did Ole Sadera realise the spectacle a Maasai made among the people of the coast. Even without a spear and shield, Mantira was a strange and formidable figure. He suddenly realised how isolated he felt without the companionship of at least one of his people. His eyes brimmed with grateful tears as he embraced his friend.

'You old elephant turd, I have found you . . .?'

'Look at you. As ugly as a warthog's bum. I could not believe my eyes when —'

'Have you not eaten for a month? Your gut is so thin —'

'When they saw you coming these Swahili jumped out of your path like they'd seen a crocodile.'

They broke into wild laughter, causing the locals to give them an even wider berth.

Instead of easing Ole Sadera's homesickness, Mantira's presence in Mombasa only worsened it. His appearance, wild and frightening as it was to the locals, brought back images of the savannah and friends and home; images he couldn't bear to recall while living alone in a strange place.

They found a shady mango tree behind the market overlooking the harbour, where they sat chatting for an hour. They relived their disagreements of the recent past when they had taken opposite sides in the argument over the fight to retain their land. Although neither would concede to being at fault, they talked until they had vented all their differences. Ole Sadera was glad they had cleared the air. He didn't want old animosities to spoil their reunion.

Ole Sadera then described the court case. He told Mantira of the arguments from both sides, and how, when it appeared they had proved their case, the judge agreed with the government that they had to start again in another court.

'Start again? What will happen now?' Mantira asked.

'Morrison says we must fight on.'

'And you?'

Ole Sadera looked out over the harbour to the white mist hanging above the reef.

'Tell me, how is it at home?'

Mantira described the chaotic situation. The northern newcomers had tried to find a niche in the already stretched resources in the south, leading to turmoil and, in some cases, bloodshed as tempers frayed. The age set leaders were finding it difficult to manage their warrior brothers. In the case of Ole Sadera's Il Tuati, there was total confusion and resistance to all attempts to pacify them.

'This is very bad. Without me, their *olaiguenani* . . .' Ole Sadera's voice trailed off in uncertainty.

Mantira shook his head. 'It is not so bad. We will talk to them. Ngatet is difficult, but we survive.'

'You have food? The cattle . . . are they well-fed?'

'This is not for you to worry about. You are here; we are there,' Mantira said dismissively.

'Morrison says the newspapers in Nairobi are saying bad things about us. Even here, people are reading about it. I have seen "Maasai" in the pages many times.'

Mantira's smile faded. 'To be truthful, many are saying we are troublemakers and greedy for land that is not ours. It is difficult to go to the markets without having an argument with the *dukawaller*, or getting bad words from the whites in the livestock market. People are angry. Several of our villages have been raided.'

'Raided? By who?'

'Kamba, Luo. Even the Kikuyu are becoming bold.'

'But we do not challenge their land.'

'No. It is not the Kamba or Luo we blame. Someone is causing them to make trouble with us.'

'But why?'

'The elders believe they want us to fight so the *askaris* can come and take the leaders away.'

'Ai, ai,' Ole Sadera said, shaking his head sadly. 'It is good that it is over. I will now come home.'

'What are you saying?'

'I am saying, we have tried and failed. Not every battle can be won.'

'Are you mad? Can you run home like a beaten cur?'

'It is not me who is beaten but our cause.'

'You must do what Morrison suggests. Now is not the time to retreat. These Kamba and Kikuyu,' he spat in the dirt beside him, 'they will think they have won.'

'Do you not have ears, dung beetle? I said we are finished.'

'Do you think I sat in that accursed train with the smoke in my face for two days so I could slap your back and tell you happy stories from home? No. First, I went with my brothers to Nairobi. We sold five hundred sheep and three hundred goats.' He broke into a broad smile. 'You should have seen the faces in Nairobi when we drove them through the town.'

'But why?'

'To get the rupees, you goat's udder.' He slid a hand into the fold in his *shuka* and pulled out a fat calfskin wad. Unfolding it, he revealed a stack of bank notes. 'For Morrison,' he said with a sweeping gesture. 'And to show others that the Maasai will not run when a fight is in the wind.'

When Ole Sadera told Morrison he agreed to go ahead with an appeal, Morrison said he could not allow him to continue to camp on the outskirts of town. He insisted his client move into the warehouse under his office.

'How do you like it?' Morrison said, pointing proudly at a furniture item with ornate turned columns and finely carved fretwork connecting the tops of the polished timber poles.

Ole Sadera studied it for some time. 'What is it?' he asked.

'Why, a bed of course.'

Ole Sadera studied it some more. He lifted the coverlet, prodded the horsehair mattress, and ran his fingertips along the lacquered headboard. 'What manner of bed is this?' he asked, not at all sure Morrison was not making fun of him.

'It used to belong to the Sultan of Zanzibar's chief eunuch. The chief eunuch was an important man in the sultan's palace.'

When Morrison explained the meaning of the word 'eunuch', Ole Sadera knew the lawyer was teasing him. But Morrison remained insistent that Ole Sadera should accept his offer.

'You can't be camping out there in the bush. It's just not done. People will think you're a little . . . well, odd.'

Having just learned the strange beliefs of the coast people, Ole Sadera accepted Morrison's use of the word 'odd' in connection with them. He agreed to move into the warehouse.

He returned to his camp site to retrieve the few small items he had left there. He sensed someone was following him, so he hid in the long grass beside the track off La Perouse Road. When he found it was the same Swahili who had been following him for weeks, he sprang on him, knocking him to the ground.

'Why do you follow me?' Ole Sadera demanded, his *simi* drawn and pointed at the Swahili's throat.

The man seemed not at all surprised by the ambush. He calmly told Ole Sadera he had some news for him, and that if he let him up, he could explain everything.

He was short and swarthy and had a long curved dagger protruding from under his shirt, which Ole Sadera took from him. He said his name was Ahmed and that a friend who cared for Ole Sadera's wellbeing had sent him.

'Who is this friend you speak of?'

'I am not permitted to mention his name,' the man said in a surprisingly soft voice. 'It is sufficient for you to know he is in a position to help you.'

Ole Sadera didn't like the man. He loathed his superior attitude. *It is sufficient for you to know* . . . He had built up an impression of the Swahili over the weeks the man had been harassing him by his uninvited presence. He despised his habit of sneaking about, always at a safe distance. He was like a jackal following a lion, forever out of reach but close enough to irritate and distract it. He had little time for a man with so little self-respect that he would hide himself in long grass to do the bidding of some nameless person. The unusual lapse that had allowed Ole Sadera to pounce on him seemed contrived. It was another reason to dislike him; why couldn't he simply have stepped up to him like a man to make his announcement?

'I need no help from you or people who will not be named.'

'There is no necessity for you to know. I must insist that you accept the simple conditions.' He had a slight lisp on the sibilants, reminding Ole Sadera of the hiss of a snake.

'I must accept nothing. Now get away from here. If I see you sneaking after me again, I will let you have a taste of my *simi* in your gut.'

Ahmed was silent for a moment, stroking his thick beard.

'There is no need for unpleasantness, my friend,' he said. 'I have a simple task to perform and when it is done, I will not bother you again. My employer asks that I inform you that you are living dangerously. He has assumed you are intent on pursuing the matter of the court case. This is not wise, he suggests. It is better for you to return to your home and forget what the white man, Morrison, tells you. You have no chance of succeeding.'

The mention of Morrison's name and the court case changed the complexion of the message. Here was someone who had access to matters Ole Sadera had thought were private. How could this man or his employer know so much? If they were able to know his every movement, how many were involved in watching him?

As if reading his mind, Ahmed said, 'Look around you, my friend. How many eyes are watching you? How many Maasai are here to help you, or give you guidance and advice? Even your Maasai friend will soon depart. Who will stand by you when the enemy comes? You cannot trust the *mzungu* — the white man.'

'Get away from me,' Ole Sadera growled, angry with himself for allowing the Swahili to creep into his mind.

Ahmed caught Ole Sadera's expression and backed away, raising his hands in a gesture of submission. He gave him one last sneering smile before turning his back and disappearing into the lush grass.

CHAPTER 56

Night had fallen over Mombasa by the time Ole Sadera left his old camp and made his way to Morrison's warehouse and his new bed. The usually bustling alleys were almost deserted and the heat, moist and oppressive, wrapped around him like a warm, wet blanket. The Arab shopkeepers went about the business of closing up against the night, working under paraffin lamps that sent eerie shadows scampering along the alleyways ahead of him and climbing the white coral-stone walls.

He was deep in thought. His inscrutable but persistent companion over recent weeks had unsettled him more than he cared to admit. At the warehouse door, he searched for the key Morrison had given him, but as he tried the latch, he found it unlocked. He swung it open and stepped inside, trying to remember where the lantern stood. As he stumbled around in the dark, he had the uneasy feeling there was someone or something in the warehouse with him. He felt at his belt for the reassuring presence of his *simi* and then immediately scolded himself — he was allowing the stalking Swahili to push his imagination too far.

He found the lantern and put a taper to it. The paraffin came slowly to life and as its weak light crept into all corners of the cavernous warehouse, strange shapes began to dance under its flickering flame. The eyes of some forgotten sultan stared at him from a portrait on the far wall.

A rat shot across the floor and disappeared between an ornate cupboard and a large porcelain-coated iron bathtub with filigreed scrollwork at each curved end. He followed it there, took his *simi* from its sheath and struck the bath. It rang like a bell and the rat scuttled past him and out through a hole in the skirting board.

He ran his gaze around the room one last time. When he was satisfied that all was as it should be, he shrugged off his *shuka* and threw it on the outlandish bed, debating whether he would sleep on it or take his chances with the rats. He pressed the padded mattress and decided to use it.

He sat on the bed, lifted the lantern's glass and extinguished the light. Before his eyes had become properly accustomed to the darkness, a shape moved between his position on the bed and the roof window that offered a glimpse of the star-studded sky. He scrambled for his *simi* and, as the door latch rattled, he lunged at the shape, throwing an arm around its torso and in the same motion bringing his *simi* up against its throat.

'Parsaloi! It's me!'

The shape was soft and as he loosened his grip around her, she turned into him.

'I could have killed you,' he said, breathing heavily as the adrenaline slowly subsided. She didn't move away from him, but remained pressed against his naked body.

'I . . . I became afraid you'd be angry when you found me here.'

'Why would I be angry?'

'Because I displease you.'

'You do not know what you are saying. You do not displease me. You . . .' He could feel her soft body against him and could think of nothing further to say. He wanted to be angered by her intrusion, but the only thought he had was of her yielding flesh against his. His member was rising hard against her, and he felt embarrassed by it. She could surely feel it too.

He struggled with the desire that stood in defiance of his guilt. This was Nashilo's half-sister, blood relative of the woman he had loved. But instead of drawing away from him, Nashilo-Kira's hands slipped up his chest to his shoulders and she clung to him. Feeling wretched, he tried to ease away from her enticing body, but he soon knew the battle was lost. He drew her to him and pressed his mouth against the soft firm flesh at the base of her neck to muffle the sound that escaped his lips.

'Parsaloi,' she whispered, and he lifted and carried her to the eunuch's bed.

Early morning was the time Ole Sadera made his forays to the waterfront. In the still air, before the sun's heat had time to stir it into motion, the sea was at its most benign. By taking such small steps, he planned to defeat his fear of it, but on that particular morning he had other issues to confront.

The night with Kira had disturbed him. He'd slept poorly, troubled by the strange sensation of a woman beside him, and by his conscience, for having given in to his weakness. The idea that it was Nashilo there with him tormented his dreams. At some point during the night he reached for her in the daze of sleep expecting to find her skin cold and damp, as it had been when he touched her on the Mau Escarpment. But it was warm. Kira moved under his hand and turned into his arms. He was momentarily lost between reality and imagination. Finally, he had fallen asleep again.

As the dawn made its presence known through the windows of the warehouse, he crept out of bed and walked barefoot to the waterfront.

Apart from the fishermen, there were few people about at that hour. He was therefore surprised to see an odd figure moving along the foreshore alley towards the warehouses. It was indistinct in the heat haze until it drew opposite him on the waterfront concourse.

'Mantira?' he called, unable to believe his eyes. He had bid his friend farewell the day before.

The figure stopped, and came towards him. 'Praise Enkai,' he said when he reached Ole Sadera. 'I thought I would have to spend another night in this bug-ridden town while I searched for you. Have you ever seen such cockroaches? I swear —'

'What is your news? You were leaving yesterday.'

'I did, and got as far as the rise on the other side of the bridge.' He pointed to the Rabai Hills overlooking Mombasa. 'Then that smoking heap of zebra shit refused to go any further.'

Ole Sadera was pleased to see him again. If he could muster the courage, he could talk to his friend about his situation with Kira. 'It is good that you are here. We have more time to —'

'No, they let the train come all the way down the hill again. Ai, ai! The screeching! You should have heard the noise from the wheels. The train is in the workshop for repairs. They say we will leave very soon.'

'Then why are you here?'

Mantira paused to collect his thoughts. 'Yesterday, on the hill.'

'Yes?'

'There is a Teita village, but not far from it is a Maasai camp.'

'Maasai! But I have never seen them in the town.'

'They are but few — some elders and women passing from the south, on the German side — with sheep for trade with the Teita. When we stopped and the railway people were knocking this and that to fix the stupid machine, I found them there. We talked. They asked why I was so far from home and I was telling them about you. The old man . . . he said he knew about you because someone came to ask for his help.'

'About me? Who was this person?'

'I don't know. The old man said he was a big Arab, with a rough voice, and with him was a Swahili man with a soft voice, or maybe he was another Arab. He wasn't sure.'

Ahmed's swarthy face and lilting voice came to mind. 'What did they want?'

'They offered the old man fifty rupees if he would take a message to a Maasai in the town. He said he would, but when they told him the message he was to deliver, he refused.'

'What was it?'

'He was to tell the Maasai he was in great danger and should go home. And on no account was he to board a ship.'

A cold hand clutched at Ole Sadera's heart. He nodded. 'Is that all?'

'No. There was another warning. About how easy it would be for a man to fall overboard on a long voyage to England.'

David Morrison once again stood at the front of the courtroom in Mombasa, this time to deliver his final address to the three judges of the Court of Appeal for Eastern Africa. After reviewing the findings of the lower court he moved on to refute them.

'Your Honours,' he said, 'the claim by my learned friend that my clients entered into a treaty rather than a contract is clearly wrong. Thirty years ago, when the Imperial British East Africa Company set up trading posts here, treaties were made with local tribes, but since then British East Africa has changed. The British Government has set up courts and those courts administer British laws. If a Maasai were to commit a murder or refuse to pay his taxes, he would be answerable to the courts as any other citizen would. If he were to take up arms against the government, he would be accused of treason, not of declaring war as between sovereign states. If the Maasai were members of a sovereign state, the chief of the Maasai would not be subject to the jurisdiction of the protectorate's courts as is presently the case.

'There is no difference between this protectorate and a crown colony where the citizens have both the privileges and liabilities of British subjects. The Maasai reserve is not a foreign country. If it were, a white squatter taking up residence on Maasai land could only be evicted by an Act of State, not by an administrative by-law, My Lords.'

He went on to cover several other technical matters before summing up.

'In conclusion, My Lords, what are we to say about the British Government's duty of care to those it would protect in its protectorate? Is it not its primary responsibility, indeed its very reason for existence, to protect the people it has come to enlighten? If it is true that the Maasai cannot sue for the return of their land wrongfully taken from them because of some supposed treaty, who is protecting whom? Is this not a case of the guardian robbing its ward?'

Morrison ran his eyes along the bench. Over his years in court, he felt he had developed the knack of reading the mood more often than not. If the judges' expressions were any indication of their present feeling, he would not be wagering a large sum on a favourable outcome.

As he returned to his seat with Ole Sadera, Katherine Wallace, sitting in the first row, gave him an encouraging smile.

Sir Henry Mortimer was invited to give his summary. With impressive oratory, Mortimer proceeded to repeat his arguments of the earlier trial.

'I agree with my learned colleague that if the Maasai were British subjects then there could be no treaty between them and His Majesty's government. But they are not. They are subject to the laws as laid down by their chiefs. The fact that in some instances the protectorate recognises contemporaneous jurisdictions between native laws and British laws does not imply they are British subjects. In fact, this is the distinguishing aspect of this case. The Maasai must be treated differently from British subjects because of their allegiance to their paramount chief.

'In so far as the treaty with the Maasai's paramount chief is concerned, it is the Crown's decision, and the Crown's alone, with whom it chooses to make a treaty. And whether or not the paramount chief coerced his subjects into signing the treaty, it is not for us to say. If it were, we might observe that coercion is often a factor in the making of a treaty.'

Mortimer droned on until the end of the afternoon, after which the judges adjourned to consider their opinion.

Morrison was drained. He had never fronted a more formidable foe than the combined strength of the government and its battery of lawyers under the leadership of the attorney-general of the protectorate and Sir Henry Mortimer.

He looked at his client, who wore the same unfathomable expression as he had from the first day of the first hearing.

Katherine Wallace was more transparent. She smiled reassuringly, but it flickered and was soon lost.

Her ability to read the mood of the court proved accurate. The judges soon returned and, in a quite short summary, demolished all hope that the judiciary of British East Africa would hear any argument that the Maasai be allowed to return to their northern lands.

The long journey to London, and the Privy Council, was their last hope for justice.

CHAPTER 57

The train puffed and spewed cinders and ash from its funnel, sending a grey pall wafting over the passengers awaiting the call to board.

Ole Sadera regretted the decision to escort Katherine and Kira to the station. Having exhausted all the available conversational topics, a silence fell and held sway for some time. It would have been easier to say his farewells at the warehouse. There was nothing further he could say to Kira that had not already been said. He had told her that his immediate task was to go to England, where the Privy Council would sit in judgement on the Maasai's land claim.

'You must be excited about your journey to England,' Katherine said, attempting to fill the silence.

'Yes,' he answered, avoiding Kira's glare. She would be indicating with her eyes what she had mercilessly repeated since he had told her, in a moment of weakness, about the threats made against him. She had begged him to abandon the trip to England.

Kira didn't understand duty and responsibility. He could not stay with her, nor could he take her to Maasailand as she'd asked.

To make matters worse, he knew Kira expected him to say something about the future — their future. Again, he could say nothing. If she were any normal young Maasai woman, it would be quite simple. In Maasailand, there could be no marriage until the next *eunoto* and his graduation as an elder. But Kira's situation was unique. It would be inconceivable that a young woman of her age would not have already been married. Because she had been raised outside the Maasai community, there were no rules governing their behaviour. Ole Sadera, felt lost. He wanted her, but there was no precedent to guide his decision. The question of marriage hung in the air like the cloud of ash billowing from the train's funnel. But he could focus on nothing beyond the ordeal of the sea voyage. After that, he and Kira could ponder their future.

The steam whistle gave a shrill blast.

'Well,' Katherine said, 'there's the warning call. We'd better be getting on board, my dear,' she said to Kira. Turning to Ole Sadera she added, 'I'm not at all sure about your decision to take the case to England, Parsaloi.'

Ole Sadera was stunned. 'But you said I should continue to fight.'

'The appeal, yes. But this is something quite different. From what I've heard and read in the newspapers, the Maasai are in great need of people like you. There are lives to be saved there — right now. I think the Maasai have a very strong reason to fight the government's decision, but I'm not so sure that now is the time to take it to the Privy Council. Lawyers are notorious for pursuing legal issues for the sake of it. Today it's the Maasai and their survival that is at stake.'

He had assumed Katherine believed it would dishonour George Coll's memory if he didn't fight the cause to the end. It did nothing to comfort him that she had reservations about taking the appeal to England.

'Having said all that,' she continued, 'I admire your courage. So if you go, may good luck go with you.'

Ole Sadera took her extended hand and thanked her for her help.

'You are a stubborn, stupid man,' Kira said when Katherine was out of earshot.

'I must do what must be done,' he answered haughtily.

'Why? You yourself have said the Maasai care more about keeping their cattle than selling them to send you to the courts. If there is no one in Maasailand who cares so much about winning, why should you? You should immediately go back to the southern reserve as Katherine suggests.'

Having made his decision, he dared not contemplate not taking the sea voyage. He decided to remain aloof, ignoring her arguments.

'Oh!' she said, realising his ploy. 'You are impossible!'

'Hmm . . . Stubborn, stupid and now impossible. I wonder who shared my bed last night.'

She was immediately contrite. 'Forgive me, Parsaloi. Because I have never felt this before, I don't know how to behave. Now that I know you, I want you always. I say harsh words because I have no other way to make you understand how much I want you with me.'

The whistle shrieked and the train jerked forward.

She took his hand in hers and placed it against her cheek. 'Hurry back to me, my love,' she said, and ran to the moving carriage.

He stood on the platform until the train was out of sight, knowing he should avoid such foolish sentimentality. He would need all his determination in the coming weeks to keep to his resolve to climb aboard a ship that would take him far away from home, and Kira.

Ole Sadera was in a deep sleep when the faint creaking of a floorboard disturbed him. He lay there in the half-world between sleep and consciousness, thinking at first that Kira had returned to him. He played with the thought in the languid moments it took him to realise that there were two separate noises coming from the black space of the warehouse. As he cleared his mind and concentrated deeply, he realised the sounds were close, and approaching from opposite sides of his bed.

He slid his hand across the mattress to find his *simi* and drew it carefully from its scabbard. He lay quietly, struggling to hear above the sound of his blood pounding in his ears. To move too soon against one would be to invite a counterattack from the other.

In the total silence, he was able to track the approaching sounds of bare feet and the almost indefinable rustle of soft cotton robes. He realised that he might be able to take advantage of a piece of good luck. The closer of the two would cross the line between where he lay and the skylight before the other reached the bed.

The silhouette appeared above him with an arm raised, ready to strike. Ole Sadera rolled to one side as the knife thudded into the bed where he'd been an instant before. The Maasai grabbed the knife arm, and his attacker grunted in surprise as Ole Sadera brought his *simi* up into the unprotected armpit. There was a scream of pain and the attacker flung himself from the bed with the *simi* still imbedded.

Immediately he released the first assailant and sprang to his feet, the second man, bigger than the first, moved in on him. Ole Sadera wasn't worried about his size advantage — as a child he'd always had to rely on timing and leverage to match the bigger boys — but the man was armed. He sensed the attacker carried his weapon in his right hand, so he circled him to that side, making it difficult for his long-bladed knife to reach its target in the darkness. After allowing him several unsuccessful swipes, Ole Sadera quickly moved in, seized the man's wrist and brought his arm down on his knee. He heard the satisfying crack as one of the forearm bones snapped. The man howled and dropped the knife to the floor, then made a dash through the door where his partner had already fled.

Ole Sadera slumped panting to the bed, his heart thumping in his chest and his anger on the rise. If the men had been sent to frighten him off, he was disgusted that they thought he would abandon his cause because of such childish tactics.

Behind the anger was a sense of relief. If all he had to fear was an ambush in the night, he felt confident he could survive until boarding the ship. But he knew it was a vain hope. The attack was not merely meant to frighten him. It was a serious attempt to kill him. The conspirators would try again, of that there was no doubt. He would need to take more care while he remained in Mombasa.

The warning of the old Maasai in the hills at Rabai came to mind. Ole Sadera could see a small sailing ship, miles from any sight of land, rolling in the powerful black waters on a moonless night. Somewhere on board was concealed an assassin awaiting his chance. A body, drugged and tied, was tossed overboard into the bottomless depths of the ocean. It sank quickly, never to be seen again.

He forced the vision from his mind, but was now bathed in the cold sweat of fear. He wiped his brow, and felt warmth on his chest. When he explored it with his fingertips he felt a jab of pain, and his hand came away wet and sticky with blood.

David Morrison eased the suit coat carefully over Ole Sadera's shoulders. 'There,' he said. 'I hope that didn't upset your dressing.'

'No, it is good.' Ole Sadera said. He had explained his injury by saying he'd hurt himself while shaping a spear with his *simi*. Morrison had fussed about it and insisted he attend his doctor, who had stitched and dressed the wound.

Morrison stood behind him as Ole Sadera appraised himself in the mirror — another reject from a royal palace.

'What do you think, Parsaloi?' he asked.

The image in the gilt-framed mirror wore an expression of incredulity. Behind it, Morrison beamed proudly.

The navy blue secondhand suit Morrison had given him was a little frayed around the coat cuffs, and the shirt had a collar that was tight and stiff. Ole Sadera had difficulty turning his head as the rough, starched material scratched against his throat.

'It is very tight,' he said at last.

'It's purely a matter of familiarisation. You'll get used to it. We all do. Now, what about the shoes?'

He tried to force his wide flat feet into the restrictive leather. He could only get them halfway in.

'Well . . .' Morrison said, running a finger down his jaw. 'Maybe we'll find a better pair over the next couple of days.'

Two days. The familiar hollowness in Ole Sadera's stomach returned. It did so whenever he thought of the sea journey. *Two days*. He was simultaneously relieved to have the waiting come to an end and alarmed at the prospect of the voyage.

The final days had flown by. Morrison had coached him — endlessly — on how to conduct himself in the Privy Council, and what to expect from the barrister he had retained to represent them.

But the coaching didn't end there. Because the limited finances did not allow Morrison to sail with him, there were the many details of how to conduct himself in London and even on board the ship. *Decorum*, Morrison would say, as if it explained everything. It was decorum that led to his insistence on the suit and the endless rules for all manner of otherwise simple activities. Even eating and drinking had their protocols. At the end of each day, Ole Sadera's head was full of what he truly believed to be useless information.

'I know it's a little, well . . . tight in parts,' Morrison said as Ole Sadera tugged at the crutch of the trousers. 'But why don't you wear it around here while I attend to some business matters?'

As Morrison closed the door to the warehouse behind him, Ole Sadera stared at himself in the mirror. He pulled one of his braids from under the coat collar and tried again to stretch some looseness into the starched neck of the shirt. It refused to give.

He did as Morrison suggested and wandered around the warehouse, taking occasional glimpses at himself in the mirrors. He tried to imagine how it would feel on board ship in such uncomfortable clothing, with the deck rolling under his feet and the wind blowing the foam from the wave tops.

It wasn't until he saw his *shuka* lying on the bed that the lunacy registered. He looked again at his European reflection. What had he become? Why was he in this strange town, dealing with matters he knew nothing about and being threatened by an invisible enemy? At home in Ngatet people needed him. In Nairobi there was a woman who wanted him. Why was he not with her?

He tore off the clinging suit coat, the suffocating shirt. He ripped off the trousers and threw the underwear into a corner.

After he had slipped on his red *shuka,* he reappraised himself in the gilt mirror before walking from the warehouse.

From the Rabai Hills, the Indian Ocean was a placid blue lake — a featureless expanse running from the luxuriant tropical coast to the sky. Ole Sadera had never doubted its beauty from a distance. It was only its nearness that caused him to distrust the massive rolling thunder of water that, once in its clutches, no man could defeat.

On the distant hillside, he could see the railway line, which followed the ridges before it shot like an arrow towards the Taru Desert. Beyond it, far away, was Nairobi. He could be there with Kira in two days. In a further two, they could be in Maasailand where he knew he was needed.

He suddenly felt an overwhelming weariness and he lowered himself to the hot red earth, propping his elbows on his knees and resting his chin in his hands. It was not the climb that had drained him, but his lingering indecision. Where did his duty lie? Should he take the battle with the English into their homeland, or return to his own and attend to more immediate matters that threatened the wellbeing of his people?

His age mates had chosen him to guide them in matters of importance but, surely, no other *olaiguenani* had ever faced such difficult choices. His inclination was to return to his home, but be was unsure that Kira and an escape from this unfamiliar world wasn't influencing that path.

It was his need to be in the company of his people that had sent him running and stumbling into the hills in the hope of finding the Maasai that Mantira had met on his interrupted journey home. He found the Teita village, but they informed him that the Maasai traders had gone.

He'd had no particular plan when he fled Mombasa other than to enjoy the companionship of a fellow Maa-speaker, and maybe discuss cattle and the grazing situation in their homeland, and whether the Germans were as difficult as the British to understand. It wasn't until he arrived and found them

448

gone that he realised he was actually running away from Mombasa. He wanted freedom from the overwhelming responsibility that awaited him there. Why couldn't someone else take the case for their land to the British court? Why couldn't he climb on the train and be what he wanted to be? Do what he wanted to do?

A faint whistle shifted his gaze from Mombasa far below, with its encircling ocean pounding ceaselessly upon the reef, to the railway, where a line of white smoke heralded the arrival of the Nairobi train.

EPILOGUE

Mombasa shimmered as the golden fireball came creeping from the Indian Ocean to commence another assault on the town. The sun shed its misty cloak as it rose slowly from the sea. Moisture quickly evaporated from the banana leaves and lush green foliage vying for space among the houses, and hovered in the airless morning.

Soon the sun was a blood-red beacon, bold and dominant, climbing into the white-hot sky with alarming haste. The rising air brushed the drab grey hills above the town, sucking ashore a faint breeze that warped and rippled the feathery curtain of vapour, fluttering the lateen sails of the fishing dhows gathered in the harbour.

Coral rock houses turned pink, and the cloaked shapes of early-risers moved slowly among long shadows.

The lighterman was preparing to push off towards the ship with important luggage for the passengers bound for Southampton via the Cape when he noticed a narrow figure, a man, emerge from among the houses. He was clothed not in the white of the *dhoti* but in red — obviously a stranger to these shores. He had a hesitant step, his long sinewy legs carrying him effortlessly but reluctantly along Vasco da Gama Street towards the jetty.

It wasn't clear if the stranger wanted to board the ship. It would be a voyage of weeks, but the red-robed man carried only a woven bag over one shoulder and a long gourd over the other.

A few paces short of the jetty, the man stopped to observe the Swahili lighterman and his assistants. Then his gaze turned to the SS *Quartermaine*, which loomed above the moored fishing vessels and the fussy lighters that moved about her like feeding tadpoles.

The lighterman shouted to the stranger; not as rudely as he might to a local, but in a tone that said that if the man wanted to take passage to the ship he needed to be smart about it.

The robed man glanced at him, but remained hesitant.

The lighterman could tell he had understood, but had perhaps thought better of travelling, or maybe, as many natives did, needed a moment to pray to all his small gods to keep him safe from the perils of the deep.

The stranger took a purposeful step forward, but then again paused. He turned to search the lane above the jetty, perhaps to find a friend or loved one there, but there was no one.

The Swahili lighterman called again, more urgently this time.

The black man moved slowly towards the barge, touching his feet to the sand and pebbled shore like a man feeling his way over hot coals. Once at the lighter, he tucked his woven bag under his arm and stepped briskly aboard, where he took his place at the handrail like a condemned man in the dock, staring back at the line of empty shop façades facing the water.

The lighterman barked orders to the men on shore, who pushed them off.

As the vessel came slowly about towards the *Quartermaine*, the robed man clung to the rail with one hand and turned to face the Indian Ocean. The waves crashed against the reef in a frothing white rage. He seemed to ponder them, then opened his palm and stared into it as if there was something of importance there.

Intrigued, the lighterman leaned over to take a look at what had captured the stranger's attention.

As he suspected, it was nothing — just two small stones.

AUTHOR'S NOTE

History is about who does what to whom. *The Last Maasai Warrior* is a novel based upon historical events, in which I have deliberately merged the *who* and *whom* characters to construct composite characters for the sake of the story. It is not that my characterisation is so wide of the mark that those familiar with history may find it confusing, but rather because they are so close to certain people and events. This is the dilemma of any author who tries to make a historical story entertaining. The dilemma for the reader (and especially one with a nose for history) is to know where the history ends and the fiction begins.

In spite of the many wrongs committed by the whites and their representatives in taking possession of Maasai land in what would become Kenya, there were many who were outraged by the behaviour of their countrymen. Readers of the history of that time will recognise in the characters of George Coll and Norman Lewis people such as Arthur Collyer, William McGregor Ross and Norman Leys, who were just a few of the many fair-minded people of that period who spoke up against the injustices. Even the main players in the alienation of Maasai land might be given the benefit of the doubt. As Elspeth Huxley writes in *White Man's Country*: 'Men like Sir Charles Eliot and Delamere worked for white settlement and for the foundation of a new British colony because they believed in it honestly as a proper ideal. Opinion cannot with justice condemn them for holding convictions which later events in Europe have shaken and perhaps destroyed.'

The characters Ole Sadera and Ole Mantira are based on the real life Maasai *moran* Parsaloi Ole Gilisho and Nkapilil Ole Masikonde who were two of the many Maasai people who fought vigorously to retain their land.

This leaves the category of what, that is, the facts of the situation. These are substantially historically correct. The Maasai were moved into reserves in 1904 and then were moved again from the northern reserve in 1911 causing considerable distress. Their court case was unsuccessful for the legal reasons given and no appeal to the Privy Council was mounted.

I used words like 'tribe', 'native', etc, and some more derogative words throughout the novel not to excuse them, but because they were part of everyday language in the period about which I was writing.

As in my earlier novel, *Tears of the Maasai*, I have made use of certain historical characters in Maasai history and taken many liberties in depicting the events of their lives to dramatise this story. No disrespect was intended to any person living or dead, nor was the telling of this story meant to harm the reputation of these important Maasai leaders.

It may be said that the Maasai failed, but the fight has not been lost. There are many Maasai today who maintain the rage. Their land claims may yet again be tested if Kenya, as is presently reported, agrees to investigate the issue of land reform.